THE WILL TO SUCCEED

This edition first published by Universe in 2020
an imprint of Unicorn Publishing Group

Unicorn Publishing Group
5 Newburgh Street
London W1F 7RG

www.unicornpublishing.org

A catalogue record for this book is available
from the British Library

5 4 3 2 1

ISBN 978-1-912690-68-8

Cover design by Pam Grant
Typeset by Vivian@Bookscribe

Printed and bound in Great Britain

THE WILL
to SUCCEED

Lady Anne Clifford's Battle for her Rights

A NOVEL BY

Christine Raafat

UNIVERSE

Contents

PART THREE

PART FOUR

Not Without Westmorland

For Christine Raafat

I rise early and go to the Standing,
the grass at my feet pearled with dew.
Gillyflowers scent the air
and small birds call in the trees

but this land is not my land

Knole shuffles its red-brick chimneys,
its casements and gables into a semblance
of order. Behind me the Wilderness
watches, deer hesitate in the bracken

these walls are not my walls

I open the Psalms and read
"I am like an owl in the desert."
I will copy the words into my book.
Once I dressed as a queen of Egypt

this place is not my place

a woman who put her fears to flight
and refused to yield.
Now I know what to answer:
I will defend my rights –

not without Westmorland

Author's Note

Lady Anne Clifford (1590–1676) was an English aristocrat and an early woman of letters. She kept accounts, books of record and diaries (often contemporaneously but sometimes retrospectively), for which I am entirely indebted to her. Many editions of her writings have been published and I am grateful in this respect for the work of D.J.H. Clifford, Vita Sackville-West, Jessica Malay and Katherine O. Acheson. I have also gleaned information about her life from many other sources; an invaluable one has been the biography, 'Lady Anne Clifford', by George C. Williamson (Second Edition 1967).

I have used Lady Anne's diaries extensively to write her story and have tried to interpret her character and experiences (as I see them) as closely as I can. Readers will understand that I have written a novel and therefore much of the detail of my writing has necessarily been the product of my imagination, including a few minor characters.

I have quoted a number of original letters and documents which are fundamental to the story; these are *italicised* in the text. In a few cases, where a letter is mentioned in the diary but the original text is not available, I have composed one to fit the bill; they are not italicised.

There are several words, commonplace during the seventeenth century, which may be unfamiliar to the 21st Century reader; I have explained them briefly in the **Glossary** on page 340.

If any event or personality has been misrepresented, or work used which has not been acknowledged, the error is entirely mine and I apologise unreservedly.

I hope the Lady Anne would not disagree with my take on her story.

Christine Raafat, Cumbria, 2019

ANNE CLIFFORD FAMILY TREE

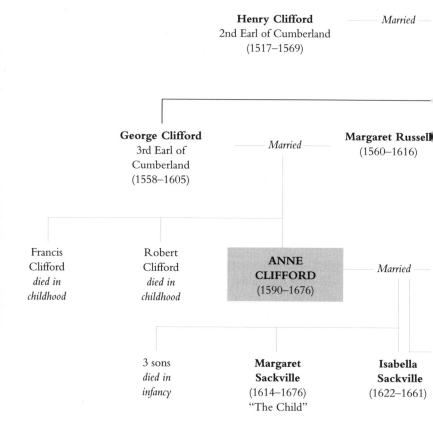

Henry Clifford
2nd Earl of Cumberland
(1517–1569)

——— *Married* ———

George Clifford
3rd Earl of
Cumberland
(1558–1605)

——— *Married* ———

Margaret Russell
(1560–1616)

Francis
Clifford
died in
childhood

Robert
Clifford
died in
childhood

**ANNE
CLIFFORD**
(1590–1676)

——— *Married* ———

3 sons
died in
infancy

**Margaret
Sackville**
(1614–1676)
"The Child"

**Isabella
Sackville**
(1622–1661)

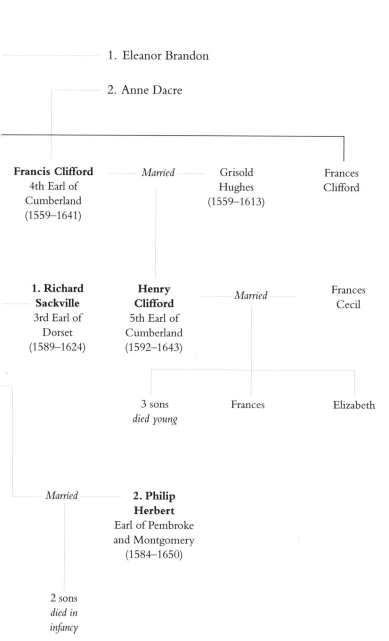

1. Eleanor Brandon

2. Anne Dacre

Francis Clifford
4th Earl of
Cumberland
(1559–1641)

— *Married* —

Grisold
Hughes
(1559–1613)

Frances
Clifford

**1. Richard
Sackville**
3rd Earl of
Dorset
(1589–1624)

**Henry
Clifford**
5th Earl of
Cumberland
(1592–1643)

— *Married* —

Frances
Cecil

3 sons
died young

Frances

Elizabeth

Married —

**2. Philip
Herbert**
Earl of Pembroke
and Montgomery
(1584–1650)

2 sons
*died in
infancy*

For Tony, with love and my thanks for everything.

Part One

CHAPTER ONE

1599

"PRAY, Lady Anne, do not run so far ahead! My old bones cannot keep up with you."

Anne skipped down the passageway, its stone floor and walls echoing her step and her trilling song. She enjoyed the feeling of the brocaded skirts of the best gown she wore for this occasion bouncing round her knees. Behind her, negotiating the uneven steps of the spiral staircase, hobbled Mrs Taylour, her governess since she was a small child. Anne was still small in stature; at nine years of age she knew she could be taken for a seven-year-old, but her behaviour and bearing were evidence of the gravity gained from those additional years. The only surviving child of George, 3rd Earl of Cumberland and his Countess, Lady Margaret Russell, Anne had dark eyes and a dimpled chin like her father, while her round face, full cheeks and the peak of brown hair on her high forehead reminded many people of her mother. She was confident and well-versed in the manners befitting a young noblewoman of her rank, but she was not a solemn or prim child; she was often merry and playful and could be mischievous.

Mrs Taylour reached level ground and realised that the passageway had fallen silent.

"Lady Anne! Lady Anne, where are you?"

The only reply came from the echo. Anne dived into an alcove further down the passage, where there was a bend so that she could not be seen from Mrs Taylour's direction. She held her breath, clutching her skirts to prevent them from rustling, and listened to her governess's approaching footsteps, ready to jump out for maximum effect.

"Lady Anne, you'll be the death of me!" Mrs Taylour gasped, her hand pressing against her chest and her sallow face softening with amused pride. Anne giggled with glee; she was in high spirits this May morning, on her way to meet her new tutor. She had heard much of Samuel Daniel, a well-known poet, so she was impatient to meet him and hear more about the literature she would be studying.

Lady Cumberland was waiting with Master Daniel in the small chamber which Anne and Mrs Taylour used as a schoolroom. A fire crackled in the grate and was reflected in the wooden panelling on the walls and the polished table where Anne and Mrs. Taylour studied. There were books on the table and on the shelves and more were piled up on the floor. A writing desk near the leaded window held Anne's inkwell, quills and a sheaf of paper. Anne examined the tall gentleman standing beside her mother; he was fashionably dressed, with a trim beard and, above a long, hooked nose, a pair of eyes so bright she felt they lit up the room. She liked him immediately and stepped forward, smiling, to curtsey to her mother and then to him.

"Good morning, my lady mother. Good morning, Master Daniel, I am Anne Clifford."

Samuel Daniel looked at her with curiosity; perhaps he had been wondering about his new pupil. She knew he was well-acquainted with her mother, and greatly respected her as a cultivated and intelligent woman of sound judgment, as did all who knew her. Was he wondering whether her daughter would be of a similar stamp? Anne determined not to disappoint him. He bowed low, with his right arm stretched out so that the white ostrich feathers of his doffed hat fluttered prettily behind him. He bowed also towards Mrs Taylour, who curtsied in turn. The introductions over, Lady Margaret indicated that they should all sit down.

"My daughter has loved the poetry of Geoffrey Chaucer since she was a very young child, Master Daniel. It was read to her before she could read herself, and I believe she continues to read the poems and tales now."

"That's admirable, my lady, I'm pleased to hear it. We shall certainly continue with that habit. Chaucer's tales are most instructive in the ways of the world," the poet said.

Anne, her face alight with interest, was delighted to hear this. "What else shall I learn?" she asked.

"We have many wonderful poets who write in the English language and are ornaments of it, as well as dispensing wisdom through its agency," Daniel said. "Men such as Spenser and Sidney have introduced a certain type of pastoral poetry to our language which is well suited to a lady of your lineage. I myself have written verses celebrating the Fair Rosamund, who was your ladyship's own ancestor, and other verses which my patron, her ladyship your mother, has generously allowed me to dedicate to her illustrious self." He stood to bow again in Lady Cumberland's direction.

A footman brought in refreshments of spiced wine and the knot biscuits that Anne had helped to make, and then they fell to talking about some of the philosophers Anne would study, even mentioning William Gilberd's exciting new work on magnets.

"I shall look forward to it, Master Daniel," Anne said, "And I should also like to become more familiar with the works of Virgil and Ovid who preceded them."

At this Lady Cumberland intervened, "There is every possibility of that, but only in translation, for I'm afraid my lord will not countenance the learning of foreign tongues."

Samuel Daniel nodded solemnly but made no comment.

❧

Anne saw little of her father during her childhood but grew close to her mother.

"Please tell me more about my lord father's voyages, lady mother," she said, while she was practising cross-stitch.

"My lord goes abroad on the Queen's business," her mother told her. "He sails to distant lands such as the West Indies and Madagascar, in search of treasure." Hearing this, Anne took down Ortelius's maps of the world and together they searched for these exotic places.

"They are a great distance away are they not, lady mother?"

14

she said. "Don't you think ships that sail the high seas are very romantic? I have seen them sometimes on the river Thames. They have very tall masts with flying pennants and look like a strange copse sprouting from the river! Pray tell me more about my father."

"Once, your lord father helped Sir Walter Raleigh when the Queen's Navy was fighting the Spanish Armada, and he brought news of their victory to Her Majesty. Queen Elizabeth holds him in such high esteem that she lends him ships with venerable names, such as 'Golden Lion' and 'Victory' to make his expeditions."

"My father must be a very special noble Lord!" Anne said.

"Indeed he is," Lady Margaret said, "And not just because of his sea-going adventures. During the year of your birth, the Queen chose him as her official Champion, to carry her favour at the jousts in the tilt-yards at Whitehall. Ask him to show you the Queen's favour – a glove that he wears pinned to his hat."

"Oh! What an honour! I will ask him," Anne said. "What a great man he must be."

During his next sojourn, after his daughter had exclaimed over the many jewels on the Queen's glove, the Earl took her hand and led her down a passage to a closet where she gazed, speechless, at a suit of sky-blue armour decorated with gold stars.

"And this," he said, "Is the armour I wear when I compete in the Queen's name."

❦

Another day, when heavy snow prevented a planned excursion on horseback, Anne and her mother sat near the fire with their embroidery. Anne begged for stories from the past and Lady Margaret began to recount the mysterious tale of one of Anne's ancestors.

"Henry de Clifford lived over a hundred years ago," the Countess began. "He became known as the 'Shepherd Lord', because he was raised by shepherds on the fells of Yorkshire and Cumberland to hide him from enemies who would have killed him in revenge for a murder committed by his father."

"I didn't know there was a murderer in the family!" Anne said.

"Henry was brought up as the shepherds' own child," Lady Margaret said, "He was not taught to read or write, in case his education should give him away. He spent all his life, until he was a man, tending the sheep and his great delight was to watch the course of the stars in the night sky from his shepherd's hut."

"What happened to him?" Anne asked.

"The story goes that when the wars swung the other way, Henry 'The Shepherd Lord' was presented to the new King. The Clifford honours and lands were restored to him and he was given a seat in parliament."

Anne clapped her hands. "What a wonderful ending!"

"Wait," Lady Margaret said, "That isn't the end! Henry married twice and had many children. When he was an old man one of his young grandsons asked him to read the family's fortune in the stars. He thought about it for a long time, and then he foretold that this grandson would have two sons, between whom and their descendants there would be mighty legal battles. He predicted that the male line of the family would end with those two sons or soon after them."

"Well," Anne said, "So it wasn't a good ending after all. But it hasn't come true."

"No," her mother murmured, "It's only a story".

Anne sometimes wrote letters to her father, but he rarely replied, although he had recently commented approvingly on her handwriting. His absence always left an empty feeling in her life and disappointment that he did not seem very interested in his only child, however hard she tried to impress him. He thinks me pretty and tells me so but would he have spent more time at home with us if my brothers, Lord Francis and Lord Robert had lived, she wondered. Is he disappointed that I am a girl? I try to show him that I am progressing in my learning and discourse, but I rarely have the chance of serious conversation with him.

Her mother sensed Anne's dissatisfaction, but misunderstood its cause.

"Don't worry, my dear," Lady Margaret said, "You are your father's sole heir. The ancient entail assures that."

"What is the entail, lady mother?" Anne asked.

"It's a legal term," her mother said, "Meaning that the lands and castles belonging to the Cliffords must be passed down only to their direct descendants. Each generation passes them to the next, whether that is sons or daughters."

❦

Even though he was often away, when the Earl came home from the seas he always made a fuss of Anne and sometimes brought her gifts. She was proud that he had a special version of her name, which only he used. Once, he summoned her to his chamber soon after he had arrived. She entered the room hopefully and inhaled its air of disuse, now overlaid with the scent of tobacco. A large wooden trunk occupied the corner near the window, its jumbled contents spilling on to the floor.

"Come, Nan, see what I have brought for my cleverest daughter!" he said as he pointed to a mysterious box covered by a heavy cloth.

"What is it, my lord father?" Anne asked as she approached.

"You must take off the cover and see what is beneath," he smiled, indicating that she should lift the cloth. Anne knelt beside the box, timidly lifted a corner of the cover and tried to peep under it. She could see only the box's wooden side above the darkness within. She pulled the cloth away and peered inside. There was something moving – no, many things moving – silvery segmented worms, wriggling and crawling over piles of leaves. She stared at them in fascination and then looked enquiringly at her father.

"Silkworms," he said.

"Oh! Are they for me?"

"Yes, indeed, but you must trouble to take care of them. They eat only mulberry leaves and must be kept neither too warm nor too cold. If you look after them well, they may one day spin some silk for you."

Anne was thrilled by this gift. She loved, and often played with, the cats and dogs which were always around the house but having sole responsibility for living creatures was a new experience and one that she took very seriously. The silkworms were a daily reminder of her father and a reassurance that he did think of her while he was away. Perhaps he missed her, as she missed him. She was not sure that he thought of her mother, however, and she sometimes saw a sad, far-away look on her mother's beautiful face when his name was mentioned.

CHAPTER TWO
1602–3

Anne was collecting mulberry leaves when her maid came to summon her to her mother's chamber.

"Anne, we shall visit your aunt at her country house, North Hall. Pray help Millie to prepare your things, for we shall travel tomorrow," said Lady Margaret.

"But why, why are we going away?" Anne protested. "Why can we not wait to see my lord father? I heard only yesterday that he will be home soon. Shall he join us at North Hall?"

"I thought you would be delighted about our visit. You always love to hear my sister talk of her times at Court, her duties as one of the Queen's favourite Ladies. And my other sister, Elizabeth, will also be there, with Frances," her mother said, tight-lipped as she dismissed her.

This was better news; Anne's cousin Frances, three years older than her, was someone she loved and looked up to. She went to prepare her silkworms for the journey, giving them plenty of mulberry leaves and wrapping their box in an old blanket to keep out the cold. If she couldn't stay to see her father, at least she could take her silkworms with her to make her feel a little closer to him. Millie would make sure the rest of her necessities were packed.

❦

Two days later, picking lavender in the gardens of North Hall with Frances, Anne found it hard to shake off the mood of disappointment.

"What troubles you, little coz? You are not your usual jaunty self; is something wrong?" Frances asked.

"Oh Frances," Anne turned a pinched face towards her, "I'm sorry! I am really very pleased to see you, it's just that… well… I wish we could have come a few days later, after my lord father had come home, that's all."

"Your father was expected home?" Frances asked.

"Yes. We heard his ship had docked and then we came away," Anne said.

"Did your lady mother give you any reason?" Frances said.

"No. She looked cross when I asked, so I didn't ask again," Anne replied. "I don't understand, Frances."

Frances stopped walking and stared silently at the ground for a while. Anne put down her bunch of lavender and began to twist her fingers in her apron and bite her lip.

"Frances?" Anne said.

"Yes, little coz," Frances said slowly, putting her arm round the twelve-year-old's slim shoulders. "I think I may be privy to a clue to this mystery, but I'm not sure that I should tell you."

"Please tell me, Frances, please. I can't bear not understanding things. It's easier to deal with bad news when you know the truth, but I'm constantly worrying about what is wrong and imagining all sorts of bad things because I don't know what it is. It can't be worse than the things I have already imagined. I pray you; tell me so that I may make sense of this distress!" Anne ran her fingers along the stalks beside the path, scattered shredded lavender flowers onto the ground and looked up into Frances's affectionate face.

"Very well," Frances said, sighing. Anne nodded to encourage her. "I will share with you what I know. I hope your lady mother will not be angry with me; she hasn't told you herself, so perhaps she doesn't want you to know, but I see how upset you are and I think you would feel better if you did."

"I won't tell," Anne said.

"Very well... I have heard it said," Frances took a deep breath and continued, "I have heard it said that your mother is angry with your father because he sometimes spends too much time with other ladies he likes, rather than her. That may be why she didn't want to see him and preferred to be here, in company with her sisters. What do you think?"

Tears brimmed in Anne's eyes. She gulped and tried to blink them away. She let go of her crumpled apron and threw her arms round Frances, burying her face in the folds of her cousin's satin cloak.

"I see," she said with a watery smile when she finally pulled away from the older girl's embrace, "Thank you, Frances. That makes more sense to me." She sighed and said,

"Would you like to see my silkworms?"

A few months later Anne was told that they would be going to visit Aunt Warwick again, this time at her town house in the city. Anne greeted this announcement with pleasure but was tersely told that it was a solemn matter and not an occasion for celebration. She worried that her aunt had perhaps been taken ill, but when they arrived at Bedford House Lady Warwick greeted them herself, as vigorous and warm as ever; Anne was her goddaughter, her namesake, and held a special place in her heart.

Shortly after their arrival, Anne was called to her mother's chamber. The curtains were closed and the candlelit room was dark and stuffy.

"Anne, pray come and sit down, for I have something of great import to tell you," Lady Margaret said. "It may be upsetting to you, as it is to me, but I hope you will take it bravely.

"The truth is that there is to be a change in our circumstances."

"I am attending your words, my lady," Anne said solemnly.

"The change is this; henceforth my lord your father and I shall no longer share a household. When he returns from expeditions in the future, we shall not see each other. I hope it will be possible for you to see him from time to time, but he will have to arrange this for you. In the meantime, you and I shall stay here for a while, where I hope you are content."

Anne stared at her mother in silence while her mind paddled like a swan's feet. Her first thought was that she must have done something terribly wrong to cause this calamity. Tears prickled her eyes and her hands went up to cover her face as if hiding her shame. Her distant hero was to become infinitely more remote and she could not think how she might have deserved this. When she looked up, her mother appeared so pale and sad that Anne jumped up and ran to her. Their arms went around each other and they both shook with the deep sobs that could no longer be contained.

When the wave of grief subsided, Anne pulled back and sat on a footstool at her mother's feet. She shivered. Realising that her most urgent question might never be answered if she didn't ask it now, she eventually looked up and said,

"Why, my lady?"

The Countess sighed and an expression of compassion replaced the distress on her face.

"My dear daughter, you mean the world to me and I would not hurt or distress you for anything if I could avoid it. I will answer your question; I think that at twelve you are old enough to understand and you must never believe that you are in any way to blame.

"The fact is that your father has decided to live with a 'lady of quality' in London. He prefers her company to mine and perhaps she is less inclined than I have been to comment on his profligate ways. Our marriage was not what either of us would have chosen, but my father saw it as desirable at the time and we made the best of it for a number of years. We even had some affection once but have grown apart and become intolerant of each other lately. I hope God will grant you grace to understand and to forgive us both, in His good time."

"Dearest mother, there is nothing for me to forgive. You are the best mother to me that I could ever imagine and I will never blame you for this, because I know that you have suffered greatly and without complaint. It is kind of you to say that I'm not to blame, but I can't help thinking that I might have done more to help. You are dearer to me than I can say and I shall be proud always to stand at your side." Anne felt her neck reddening and could not bring herself to mention her father.

The Countess continued, "I thank God that He has given

me such a loyal and loving daughter and I thank you, Anne, for bringing me happiness and joy even in the darkest of times.

"I'm afraid that we shall have to make sacrifices in the future and shall be more straitened than ever, since your father's recent expeditions have been unsuccessful. He is heavily in debt and we'll not be uppermost in his mind. My sisters have offered us generous help but I don't wish to depend entirely on them. I shall do all I can to keep Master Daniel engaged as your tutor, but it may be necessary to reduce the time he spends with you. I know that you'll understand the need for frugality and I fervently hope for both our sakes that your father's fortunes will soon improve."

Anne sat at her mother's feet and was silent for some time. She heard the rain beating against the window panes and the solemn and relentless tick of the clock. Heavy thoughts piled up in her mind like bricks, and then the silence was broken by a knock at the door. She left her mother to answer the maid's query, excused herself and went to make sure that there was a sufficient supply of mulberry leaves.

A few days later Anne, who had been very quiet since she learned of the separation, approached her mother with suppressed excitement. The Countess, busy preparing herbs for a remedial draught, looked at her with one eyebrow raised.

"My lady, my Aunt Warwick is to attend the Queen at Hampton Court tomorrow and she has said that with your permission I might accompany her," Anne said, trying to stop herself from jigging up and down. "May I go?"

Margaret placed a hand on her daughter's arm and said,

"It will be a diversion for you and one you deserve. I am pleased that your aunt has suggested it; of all the Ladies of the Privy Chamber, you know, she is the closest to the Queen and you will begin to learn the workings of the court. Go, child, with my blessing and enjoy it, but remember all you have been taught about good manners."

"Oh, thank you, lady mother! Shall I wear my brown brocade gown with the lace cuffs? I feel very grown up in that."

When the coach was ready at the door and Lady Warwick descended the stairs in Court dress, Anne could not take her eyes off her and said, "Oh, my lady aunt, you look magnificent! I can't help admiring your gown; everything seems to sparkle."

Lady Warwick was wearing a black velvet bodice encrusted with pearls and strings of pearls hung round her neck. Her stiffened ruff and lace cuffs were decorated with gold thread and her black silk skirts stood out from her pinched waist to cover her ample hips. She was helped into the coach by two sturdy footmen and settled herself before she spoke.

"I thank you, Anne. But you know, sometimes carrying the weight of all these clothes is almost too much to bear." The coach lurched into the crowded street as she continued, "Under these wide skirts is a heavy farthingale, strapped round me with tapes so tight that I feel like a trussed goose. It is impossible to move faster than a sleep-walker!"

"I think the result is surely worth the effort," Anne said. "You look very grand indeed!"

"You will see many courtiers and visitors in rich clothes at court," said Aunt Warwick. "And you will find that there are strict rules about who is allowed to wear what. For instance, only the highest ranks can wear silk, velvet, cloth of gold or the colour purple, so if you see these you will know that the wearer is someone of great importance."

"Thank you for telling me that, Aunt Warwick," Anne said, noting that her aunt's apparel included both silk and velvet. "I can see that I have much to learn about these matters before I can become part of that glittering world."

It was a short ride from the house near the Strand to the river, where the Countess of Bedford's shallop waited at a busy landing stage beside the Fleet Bridge. This magnificent barge with its colourful canopy, rowed by a crew of eight liveried men, was one of the speediest and most luxurious vessels on the Thames.

Anne watched smaller and slower craft scuttle out of the way of the notable Bedford boat, but it rocked alarmingly when other vessels passed nearby and made Anne feel rather queasy. As she settled into the lavish cushions she noticed that familiar buildings alongside the Thames looked different from this angle. There was Somerset House gliding past on the right and Whitehall Palace, then the Houses of Parliament and behind that the square towers of Westminster Abbey. Lambeth Palace rose from the marshes on the southern bank, its red brick façade complementing the green of the walnut tree close by. Soon they were clear of the city; there was less traffic trying to cross the river under their bows and trees and meadows replaced buildings on its banks.

After three hours Anne was relieved to disembark at the palace. Hampton Court was a seemingly endless labyrinth of passageways and opulent rooms, everything becoming more luxurious as they made their way through the commotion to approach Queen Elizabeth's apartments. Anne held close to Aunt Warwick, afraid of losing her way in the throng. But it was clear, from the way the crowds parted to let them through, that Aunt Warwick was recognised by everyone as a person of very high rank indeed. The nearer they came to the Queen, Anne noticed, the higher the rank of the people who crowded there and the more sharply orders were given and obeyed.

"We are now very close to the Queen's audience chamber," said Aunt Warwick at last, leading her into a small, less crowded side-room with seats lining the walls and some small tables. "You may remain here and you will find young pages and attendants of noble birth who will be happy to pass the time playing cards and other games when they are not engaged in errands for their lords and ladies. I will send my attendant to check that all is well with you and shall come to see you when I can."

"I shall be very happy here, my lady aunt. I like nothing better than making new friends and observing the people around me," Anne said.

She was greeted boisterously from time to time by many of her contemporaries there, including Richard and Edward Sackville, waiting on their grandfather, the Earl of Dorset; Alethea Talbot, daughter of the Earl of Shrewsbury; and Elizabeth Manners, niece of the Earl of Rutland. Gradually she relaxed and began to enjoy the spirited atmosphere among these young people, all vying for recognition and benevolence from the most influential of the courtiers around them. Anne's relationship to the Countess of Warwick, she found, was a trump card with many of them. With Richard Sackville, a young man of her own age, she found a common interest in literature and they shared thoughts about the philosophers and poets they had read.

"Do you know Chaucer?" Anne asked him.

"Of course, and I enjoy his tales of pilgrimage on the way to Canterbury. I think he writes of serious ideas in a way which makes them seem interesting and often amusing. I love the Miller's Tale – it tells of a student at Oxford University, where I myself shall attend, and makes me laugh a lot."

"I have not read that tale," Anne said, "But I find his writing vividly descriptive and his characters most entertaining."

"The Miller's Tale may not be suitable reading for a young lady such as yourself," cut in Edward Sackville, who had been standing behind his brother while they talked. Anne looked at him, wondering what he meant by this, but Richard dug his elbow into Edward's ribs and they moved away, pretending to fight. Anne felt sure Edward had deliberately distracted Richard's attention away from her.

❧

Sometimes Anne could admire the Queen from afar when she glimpsed her passing by, but she knew she was most unlikely to meet her. One day, after they had returned to Bedford House from attending the Queen at Greenwich Palace, Aunt Warwick was talking to Lady Margaret about friends of hers who were also Ladies of the Privy Chamber. Anne was reading her Book of Psalms, but she looked up when Aunt Warwick mentioned her name.

"The Queen noticed Anne at Court today," Aunt Warwick was saying. "She asked who she was and then complimented me on her bearing and behaviour. That created a stir amongst the Ladies!"

Anne looked down at her book again to hide the joy and pride that coloured her face.

The next time Aunt Warwick was with the Queen, Anne stayed in an antechamber, as usual, to play backgammon with one of the pages who attended the Queen's Chamberlain. It was a busy morning and the room was full of young courtiers. Suddenly their attention was seized by a quickening, a stir in the atmosphere as people flickered into life, jumped to attention and began to scramble.

A resounding voice announced, "Her Majesty the Queen!"

Anne and her companion leapt to their feet and everyone fell silent, bowing and curtseying as the white-faced monarch appeared in the doorway, her skirts filling the space as she haughtily surveyed the chamber. Aunt Warwick materialised at Anne's side as the Queen stepped down into the room and came towards her.

"I have noticed you here before, child. You are Cumberland's daughter, are you not?" the Queen said. Anne straightened up from her well-practised curtsy and replied,

"Yes, Your Grace. You do me great honour." She curtsied again. As she looked up into the Queen's face, she noticed that the whitened skin was much more pock-marked and wrinkled than her portraits showed, some of her teeth were missing and the rest were blackened.

"I have told your aunt that she should be very proud of you," Elizabeth said in a loud voice as she turned and stalked slowly out of the room.

A hubbub broke out around Anne. People who had never paid her much attention in the past surrounded her, questioning her and declaring their surprise at the fortune of this child in being singled out by the sovereign who had never given many of them a second glance. Most of them seemed admiring, but a few, including young Edward Sackville, were clearly envious and Anne was relieved when they lost interest and drifted away.

Anne and her mother were reading Samuel Daniel's poetry in the luxurious drawing chamber at Bedford House, when a maid came to say that Lady Warwick wished them to attend her in her chamber.

"Come in, come in," Aunt Warwick said with more animation than usual. "Sit down, Margaret. Anne, sit here."

"What is it, sister? What's happened?" Margaret asked.

"I have some news for you both and I have no doubt that you will be as excited as I am when you have heard it!" Aunt Warwick said. Anne and Margaret looked at each other.

"Pray tell us then, don't keep us..." Margaret said, but was interrupted by her sister.

"I am trying to tell you, but you must let me speak!" Aunt Warwick said. They were silent. Aunt Warwick took a deep breath.

"Some of the ladies and I were playing 'One and Thirty' today when the Queen walked in and we all stood as quickly as we could. You will never believe what she said!"

"Oh!" Anne and Margaret groaned together.

"Wait!" Aunt Warwick said, "I'm coming to the point! The Queen's words were, 'I am thinking of making some new appointments to the Privy Chamber. Some of you ladies are nearly as old as me! I have resolved that when she reaches the age of fourteen, the Lady Anne Clifford shall become a Lady of the Bedchamber, in the footsteps of her aunt.' There! What do you think of that?"

Anne and Margaret gasped. Margaret spoke first.

"That is wonderful news, sister. We are honoured."

"I can hardly believe it!" Anne said. "I can't wait for my birthday next January. I shall be so proud to serve our glorious Queen. No-one could ask for more!"

Not long afterwards, Aunt Warwick brought very worrying news on her return from court.

"The Queen is sickening," she said. "I don't know what ails her, but I fear she may be mortally ill. She is nearly seventy years old and her physicians said today that she must not be moved from Greenwich. I fear the worst. We must prepare ourselves."

Anne would not give up her dreams yet. She prayed night and day for her sovereign's recovery, but only a few days later Aunt Warwick returned home early with a very sad face.

"Her Grace died during the night," she told them tearfully. "I was with her at the last. It was a peaceful end, like the last few years of her great reign. God rest her soul."

Anne cried bitterly. Margaret tried to comfort her, but she was inconsolable for many hours. Not only had she lost her beloved sovereign, but her ambition to become, like her aunt, one of the great Queen's most intimate and publicly recognised ladies, had been dashed.

The whole country mourned 'Gloriana', who had reigned for 45 years of relative peace and prosperity in the land. Without an immediate heir, the dying Queen had proposed her distant cousin, James, King of Scotland as her successor. Anne went out into Cheapside with Frances and their ladies; they mingled with the crowds and heard the proclamation of the new King's accession.

"Frances, I am still troubled by the Queen's death," Anne said. "But I can't help being excited by the feeling of change and renewal in the air!" Frances agreed.

Plans were laid for a funeral worthy of Good Queen Bess: Aunt Warwick and Lady Margaret were to take their turns as watchers around the body of the Queen until the funeral.

"I was favoured by the Queen! I loved her dearly and I wish with all my heart to pay my respects," Anne said, clenching her fists and pumping her arms to emphasise her words. "In a few months' time I would have become a Lady of the Bedchamber. Please, please my lady mother, arrange for me to take a turn or two as well."

Margaret frowned.

"No, Anne, it will not be possible; you are too young to undertake such a task. You had as yet no official position at court and it would not be fitting. Your aunt agrees with me and I am certain that your father would say the same."

Recognising the finality of her mother's words, and knowing better than to argue, Anne tried to swallow her frustration. It grew even stronger when she was also told that she was too small to walk in the funeral procession through the streets; she was permitted only to stand in the church to hear the service. But I shall content myself with bidding farewell to my dearly beloved sovereign in that way and welcoming the new era, she told herself.

CHAPTER THREE
1603

"I have lost the position at court that I have held for the greater part of my life, as well as my beloved sovereign and friend," Aunt Warwick told Anne and Margaret. "I have no more interest or purpose in life." They could find no way of comforting her. The Queen's death was a tragedy for her; she collapsed and withdrew to North Hall to mourn, feeling far from well.

Lady Margaret decided that she and Anne would travel to her ancestral home, Chenies in Buckinghamshire, where they were joined by Cousin Frances.

"There is to be a Royal Progress from Edinburgh to Windsor," Frances told Anne. "It will be like a great river of people meandering south. I have heard that there will be so many people accompanying the King and the Queen that they will often have to travel separately! Few of the great houses where they will stay are large enough to accommodate them both, along with their trains of servants and supporters. Your father will be with the King."

"And we shall go north to meet the Queen's train," Margaret announced. "We must pay our respects to Her Majesty and travel part of the way with her, as is expected of the wife and daughter of one of the foremost noblemen of England."

"That is exciting! Do you know what she is like?" Anne asked.

"She is a princess of Denmark and Norway," Margaret said. "I believe she is a cultured and educated person."

"How old is she?" Anne asked.

"I think she is about thirty years old," Frances said. "Eight years younger than the King. They have a son, Henry, who is about nine and a second son, Charles."

"You know so much!" Anne said.

When they reached Althorp they found chaos such as they had never seen before. Queen Anne's people had been unable to organize the crowds and it was clear that there was no chance of their being presented to Her Majesty before it was time to leave again.

"There's a rumour," Frances told Anne as the procession slowly wound its way along the narrow lanes of Northamptonshire, "That we are heading for Grafton. My mother told me."

"Grafton! But that is my lord father's place! Are the King and Queen to be entertained there? Pray, lady mother, tell me more about it!" Anne said, almost rocking the coach in her excitement.

"I regret my dear that I know no more than you do," Lady Margaret said, "I believe there is to be a banquet, but I shall not be the hostess for the royal visitors. Frances's mother, my sister Elizabeth, is helping your father and by now the preparations for such a magnificent occasion must be well under way. I am no longer regarded as the mistress of your father's house, even for this day. But of course we shall attend the banquet." The Countess spoke as of a commonplace, but Anne flushed with emotion.

"Well I shall not go!" Anne declared, her voice rising as her anger with her father came to the surface. "Father is still your wedded lord, is he not? It does him no credit to spurn and humiliate you in this way. The fault is his in this falling-out between you, yet he punishes you as if you are the one who is in the wrong. No, I shall not attend his royal carousal!"

"I have never heard you criticise your father like this before," Lady Margaret said, her raised eyebrows giving away how taken aback she was by this outburst. "And I am not sure that it is seemly, although I sympathise with your angry feelings and am touched that you take my part.

"But let us consider this invitation further. What would result from a refusal?"

"I think my father might be angry and from that he might learn how angry I am with him!" Anne said with considerable heat, turning to face her mother who remained unruffled.

"Why would he be angry, do you think?" Margaret asked.

Anne hesitated and frowned.

"I don't know! Perhaps he does want me to be there, but he pays little enough attention to me at any other time, so I find it hard to believe that is the reason."

"Imagine yourself in his shoes," Lady Margaret said reasonably. "You have invited your only child to the very grandest of occasions, attended by the King and Queen, and she refuses to accept. What would you feel?"

Anne struggled with her own feelings of anger and neglect, glancing at Frances, who gave her a nod of encouragement. Anne then tried to imagine what her father's emotions might be in this situation and sat back.

"I suppose he might feel slighted?" she ventured, more calmly.

Lady Margaret continued, "And is it possible that anyone else might seem to have been slighted on this occasion, if we refuse to attend?"

Anne's face and neck flushed darker as she thought about it and she took in a sharp breath. She well understood the juggling that would go on throughout the court with all the courtiers and great families vying for influence and position with the new King and Queen. This banquet was her father's bid for recognition and, however furious she was with him, she knew it would be unforgiveable to jeopardize that. Her head drooped and swung slowly from side to side as she bit her finger and stared at the floor, gradually recognising the possible consequences of her impetuous reaction.

"Oh! Do you mean the King and Queen? I should not wish that at all! I am sorry, my lady. I was angry because I saw that my father had slighted you and I wished to pay him back. I still feel he deserves that, but now I see that I'd allowed the feelings of my heart to carry away my reason. I must swallow the bitter potion and learn the lesson that . . . that . . ." her voice trailed away as she fought back tears, uncertain what she was really trying to say.

"That a hasty decision, made on the crest of a wave of emotion, is often one that will plunge you unthinking into a trough of trouble!" her mother finished off with satisfaction, indicating that the point had been made and the conversation was over.

Now thirteen, Anne was allowed to appoint two young women to attend her. The first was to be her companion and lady-in-waiting; Lady Elizabeth Wharton was the daughter of a baron, chosen because she was a northerner who shared Anne's interest in literature and was an accomplished needlewoman. Fair-haired, taller than Anne and a year and a half older, she nevertheless deferred to her in the characteristic way of a shy, quiet, but by no means subservient, attendant. By taking this post she would learn more about the running of a noble household and take part in many social occasions. It was a chance to improve her marriage prospects.

The second young woman, chosen to be Anne's maid, was Mary Whitcroft, a plump 17-year-old gentlewoman whose father was a member of Lord Cumberland's retinue. She had become an authority on fashionable dress, although her rank did not permit her to wear court dress herself, and she was sometimes outspoken in her criticisms of the attire of others, however grand. There was also Millie, a young maidservant whom Anne shared with her mother.

Anne approached the banquet with jumbled fears and excitements. As she prepared for it in the chamber allotted to her and her ladies, they chattered about her dilemmas.

"I am excited!" Anne said. "I love to be part of a great throng at a grand occasion such as this, but I am also angry that my father is humiliating my mother by excluding her from the arrangements. I don't know what to think!"

"Is your lady mother angry about it?" Mary asked.

"I don't think so," Anne said. "Millie, do you think my mother is angry?"

"No, my lady," Millie said, tying on Anne's bum-roll for the latest French farthingale. "My Lady Margaret has never mentioned it in my hearing."

"Well then, you have nothing to worry about, Anne," Elizabeth said. "If your lady mother is not annoyed, why should you be? Mayhap she's pleased that she doesn't have to do all the work or take responsibility for the arrangements and the feast!" They all laughed as they admired the gold thread embroidery on the fine fabric and the delicate lace edging to the low-cut bodice which showed off Anne's newly-developing breasts.

"How will my father treat me, though?" Anne said, as another thought occurred to her. "Will he acknowledge me before all these important people?"

"Of course he will, you may be sure of it," Elizabeth said. "You are his only child, his heir, the most precious thing in his life! And once we have finished dressing you in your new gown and adorning you with finery, his pride in you will be doubled!"

Mary exclaimed over the new shorter skirt which left Anne's small feet and fashionable shoes on view and said, "I will thread gold wires through your hair so that it will catch the light. And if you wear the pearl necklace and drop earrings that he brought home for you from his voyages, your lord father will be so delighted with you that there will be no question of him ignoring you."

When their work was finished they turned her round to look at her reflection in the mirror and she was startled to see an alluring young woman of whom any man might be proud.

They were right; the Earl, beaming, took her aside.

"Nan! You are beautiful! I had not noticed that you are no longer a child; how lucky I am to have such a daughter to grace my house and to present to my new Sovereign! I am proud that you are growing up to be a jewel of the House of Clifford."

"Thank you, my lord father. I am proud to be your daughter and to be part of this grand occasion in your house." Anne said, a little stiffly. She knew this was not the time to mention how angry she was with her father for his treatment of her mother, but it made her reticent.

"Please stay close to me for the reception and the banquet so that I may present you to their Majesties," the Earl said.

"It will be a great honour to do so, my lord Father. I will try to be a credit to you and our ancient name. The house looks beautiful and I'm sure their Majesties will be impressed by your hospitality."

☙❧

Anne was struck first by the paleness of the Queen's skin and her very fair hair. The Queen inclined her head, smiled kindly and said, in an accent that mingled Danish and Scottish so that Anne found it hard to understand,

"My namesake! What a pretty child you have, Lord Cumberland."

Anne curtseyed deeply but could not take her eyes off the jewels that sparkled round the Queen's neck and in her hair. She felt only slightly affronted at being called a child; at thirteen she was still less than five feet tall and was used to being taken for a girl of ten or eleven. Through the banquet she remained at her father's side, close to the royal party, where she could observe the King and Queen.

During the dancing that followed several friends gathered round her, including her cousin Frances, now sixteen.

"Frances! I am so pleased to find you! I have had a thrilling time being with my father and in company with the King and Queen, but I believe I need to come down to earth now! You are always such a steadying presence." She embraced Frances and the heat of her burning face was soothed by the older girl's cool cheek.

"And you look beautiful today, Frances," Anne continued, stepping back, "I admire the rich colour of your gown, your lace trims and the way you have held your hair back with a wire. I must try that!"

They were joined by a number of their friends and there was great admiration among the curious young women for the Queen's pale colouring.

"Have you ever seen a more beautiful complexion?" Frances said.

"I know she is much younger than the Old Queen," Alethea said, "But her skin looks a lot more natural to me."

"Her paleness does not seem to be achieved through the application of lead, like the Old Queen's," Elizabeth concluded and they all nodded in agreement.

"The Queen's Danish accent makes it difficult to understand her at first," Anne told them. "But you get used to it after a time and then you can make out her meaning. And the King's Scottish accent is almost as hard to grasp!"

Frances, more experienced in grand occasions than Anne, was in a teasing mood and made several comments about the young men who frequently looked in Anne's direction. There was one whom Anne did not recognise, whose insolent and challenging stare was too disturbing for her to ignore. She looked away from him immediately and turned to Frances.

"Who is the young man with fair curls, a pointy chin and a very high forehead, Frances? He is wearing a fine red doublet and huge glittering rosettes on his shoes. I don't remember ever seeing him before; I would not have forgotten such a girlish face. There he goes now, cutting a caper again!"

Frances scrunched up her eyes to see the person Anne was describing.

"I think he could be one of whom I have heard tell, named Robert Carr. He is a close friend of Sir Thomas Overbury and it is said that he will stop at nothing to gain the King's notice and favour. He has come from Scotland with the King and is the younger son of a knight from the Scottish borders. Does he please you, coz?" Frances asked, but Anne frowned,

"No, coz, he does not please me," she replied sharply. "I find his glances quite troubling; they make me feel very uncomfortable. Let us go into the far hall; I do not wish to join the dancing whilst he is part of it." She hurried forward and Frances was almost left behind in the crush.

"Well, that is the first time I have ever known you to be displeased by the attentions of a young blade!" Frances exclaimed as she caught up. They moved into the second room of dancers and Anne relaxed and began to smile again. The young men were still attentive, but she was altogether happier in the company of acquaintances from her days at Queen Elizabeth's court.

"My Lady Anne Clifford!" Richard Sackville exclaimed.

He made an exaggerated bow and she curtsied low, suppressing a laugh at his mock formality as he grasped her hand and led her to join the stately Pavane. He was easily the most fashionably dressed young man in the room, resplendent in one of the very latest D-shaped standing collars with stiffened lace tiles decorating its edge and so many tiny buttons down the front of his waistcoat that she could not have counted them even if he had stood still for two minutes.

"I think we can look forward to good times in the new court, don't you?"

"How so, my Lord Buckhurst?" Anne replied, using his title in return.

"I hear from my brother Edward that the new Queen loves entertainments and masques and will seek to involve the young people of the court in many such agreeable occupations. Will you not be pleased by such a prospect?"

"Oh yes, that is good news indeed! I shall look forward to becoming one of the Queen's ladies if that is truly the case," she replied, her pleasure showing on her glowing, candle-lit face and in her sparkling eyes.

"Is it certain then that you will be in attendance on the Queen?" he asked.

"My lady mother and my aunt believe so," Anne said

"Good, then we shall see each other frequently at court."

"Will you have a position there?" Anne asked.

"My grandfather hopes that I may become a companion to Prince Henry when my time at Oxford is done. I should find that very agreeable – not least because it would give me more opportunities to see you! The prince is a most appealing boy and my grandfather is practically rebuilding his house at Sevenoaks in order to entertain the King and Queen there. It will be huge and very grand! There is even a Wilderness!" He was boasting, she thought,

"Fit for a King then!" Anne said.

"Of course; fit for a King – and a Queen called Anne!" He twinkled at her; she thought he winked but she wasn't sure, and she suddenly felt flustered. She was rescued by the ritual of the dance, as its sequence led her away from him for a time. One of the people she now encountered was Edward, that very brother whom he had just mentioned; they were close in age and in other ways, being inseparable and reputedly even sharing a mistress. Edward seized her hand quite roughly and yanked her towards him so that he could hiss into her ear during the pass,

"Trull, I've been watching you with my brother – leave him alone!"

Shocked, Anne could make no sense of what she had heard. Perhaps she had misheard, or maybe it was meant as some strange joke; she didn't know Edward as well as she knew Richard, so it was hard to be sure. She shook her head to rid her mind of those words, kept on dancing and realised that she was about to rejoin Richard. She collected herself and considered what to say when she returned to his side on the next turn of the dance.

"And I hear tell that Philip Herbert has already been made a gentleman of the Privy Chamber!" she said, as if there had been no interruption in their conversation.

"Yes indeed, he is in high favour with the King – mainly for good looks and prowess in hunting and hawking it seems!" Richard said. "The King's taste inclines that way. I hear he is encouraging him to marry Susan De Vere. I believe Prince Henry prefers more literary pursuits, as do you and I, which I shall happily follow with him."

"But you yourself often enjoy other kinds of sport, do you not?" Anne said.

"Well! What can you mean, my Lady Anne?" Richard said in laughing outrage. "Are you not as prim and proper as you look, then?" Anne blushed in confusion but hoped that he hadn't noticed in the flickering light of the many beeswax candles which her father had extravagantly dispersed throughout the house.

"I meant only – I've heard that you gamble on the cock-fights sometimes," she replied. Their smiling eyes met, they both laughed and her embarrassment was banished. The touch of their hands lingered for a happy moment longer than the dance required. Looking round the room she caught Frances's eye and received a nod of encouragement.

Later she would repeatedly go over every word and gesture of this conversation in her mind, teasing out all its meaning and any secret messages it may have held and wanting to re-experience the new thrill she had enjoyed that evening, dancing with Richard Sackville. She found that if she forced herself to banish the thought of him for a few minutes, she would feel a tingle again the next time he invaded her mind. She dismissed the memory of Edward's words, putting them down to drunkenness.

Anne felt the relief of a burden lifting from her. She no longer had to worry about how her father would behave towards her; he could not have done more to make her feel welcome and had been proud to show her off to his royal guests. She had escaped the attentions of the disturbing Mr Carr. And her mother, keeping in the background on this occasion, was looking benignly on her in a way which made her feel cherished and approved. The hall was warm, the rosemary and lavender on the rush-strewn floor embraced the dancers with perfume as they were trodden underfoot, and the music raised her spirits. Her step lightened as the musicians struck up a lively Galliard and the dancers became animated. As her skirts swirled about her with the swing of her hips, she realised that she was happier than she had been for a long time and was surprised that this had come about in her father's house and on this occasion, which had previously appeared so daunting. Richard returned her radiant smile.

CHAPTER FOUR
1603–4

Anne cherished her memories of the Grafton banquet. They warmed the dull days of her return to London and a much quieter life. She missed the glamour of the Old Queen's court, the company of the friends she had made there and, most of all, the vivid presence of Aunt Warwick. So she was pleased, a short while later, when her mother said,

"I've decided, Anne, that we shall pay a visit to my dear sister of Warwick, to bring her some comfort and physic. She has been very melancholy and ill since the death of the Old Queen and I hope that after a few weeks of our care she may be well enough to travel with us to rejoin Queen Anne's train. And I think it will be beneficial for you to have a change of surroundings; you've been lacklustre recently, which I can only put down to your age. When girls pass thirteen, I've noticed, their mood often becomes changeable."

Anne was pleased to hear that they were also to be accompanied by her Aunt Bath and Cousin Frances. Of course she looked forward to seeing Aunt Warwick, but this time her anticipation was troubled by the knowledge that her favourite aunt was unwell and she wondered anxiously what they would find when they arrived at North Hall.

The grooms saddled the horses before first light and the party gathered to mount and make a start as soon as the sun was up because the winter days were short. There was hoar frost decorating the bare hedgerows and Anne was well wrapped up in furs with her new Spanish leather gloves and a hooded cape. As soon as she had mounted her favourite bay mare, Ginny, she was impatient to start and positioned herself to ride out of the courtyard behind Simon Meverell, her mother's head Gentleman of Horse; with his superior knowledge of the roads he was appointed to lead the way. Wisps of his thin grey hair were escaping from his cap and his prominent nose was reddened by the cold. Anne glanced back, looking for Frances. A head taller than Anne, she was wearing a most becoming bottle green riding habit and a fur hat, but she was not yet mounted when Anne waved to her, called a cheerful greeting and rode on through the archway.

The morning promised well; the sun was now gilding the tree-tops from which the rooks rose in an irritable cackling cloud. The ground crunched under the horses' hooves and the berries of holly and hawthorn gave a warm glow to the hedges lining the way, their darkness set off by the frost and the virginal snowdrops at their foot. Mr Meverell bade her a polite 'Good morning, my lady' and Anne held Ginny to a steady walk beside his grey. They skirted Clerkenwell Green and struck north along the road towards Highbury.

"Now, my lady, I feel we are really on our way," Meverell said, relaxing into his saddle as he looked over his shoulder to make sure that the rest of the party were on their tail. Anne felt excited by a sense of adventure and grinned at him.

"Yes, it is good to be free of four walls and feel the air and the sun on one's face," she said. "I sometimes tire of the winter when I cannot go forth. How long do you think we shall be on the road?"

Ginny shied suddenly at something moving in the under-growth and Anne hoped that Meverell was impressed by her horsemanship as she held tight and brought Ginny back under control. She wasn't the daughter of the Old Queen's Champion for nothing! She stroked Ginny's neck and the mare shook her head, whinnied and calmed.

"There will be about four hours riding time needed, milady, but we'll stop for an hour to water and rest the horses when we reach Wood Green. We should make North Hall by one or two of the clock, all being well, while there is still plenty of light."

"This journey puts me in mind of the Canterbury Tales of Geoffrey Chaucer," Anne said. "Have you read them, sir? I find them most entertaining and often pick them up if I am in need of cheer."

Meverell nodded but seemed hesitant to make any comment, so Anne continued to chatter about her favourites among the stories. Eventually he joined in and they were both surprised that time and distance seemed to have shrunk when they reached the resting place where they were to break their journey.

"Anne, why did you not wait for me?" Cousin Frances had caught up at last and Anne was delighted to see her but puzzled that her anxious face was not as joyous as her own.

"Coz, it is a great pleasure to see you, but pray. . . is something wrong?" Anne spoke with a vague feeling of misgiving which she tried to ignore.

Frances led Anne a little way off from the groups of riders and said quietly,

"Anne, of course I'm very glad to see you. Please pardon me for saying this, but I think it was mistaken of you to ride ahead all the way here, alone with a gentleman. I believe you may have angered your lady mother and it will not go well with you."

Anne's hand went up to her mouth and her eyes widened as she realised the truth of her cousin's words.

"Oh . . . but . . . Frances . . . We were only talking of the pleasures of the journey and the similarities between this journey and the one undertaken by the pilgrims going to Canterbury. I meant no harm and certainly no displeasure to my lady mother! What can I do?" Anne looked round anxiously and saw that her mother had stepped down from her coach and was surrounded by a circle of ladies of the household.

"I don't think much can be done now," Frances said, following the younger girl's glance. "You'll have to wait until we arrive at North Hall to see what your mother's judgement is. Meanwhile, will you ride with me the rest of the way?"

"Of course. Thank you, Frances," Anne said.

"Did you see the gown that Alethea Talbot wore at Grafton?" Frances said, to distract Anne.

"Yes," Anne said. "I liked the colours, but Mary pointed out that it wasn't the shorter length that is fashionable now."

"I don't think everything that is fashionable is necessarily pleasing to the eye," Frances said. "Look at the 'lovelocks' that some of the young men are sporting now!"

"Oh, yes!" Anne said, "That long strand of hair worn over the shoulder! That is a good example of a bad fashion, Frances!"

The rest of the journey passed by without Anne brooding too much about her misdemeanour and its possible consequences, but when the fine tower and chimneys of North Hall came into view, her heart began to beat uncomfortably hard. Her worry about her aunt was now challenging her equal dread of what her mother would say and she felt reluctant to dismount when they reached the courtyard. She stroked Ginny's warm neck before handing her over to a groom and slowly followed Frances into the house. Aunt Warwick was not in the hall to greet them and Anne's heart sank further. She stood disconsolately looking about her at the bustle of arrival and the servants rushing to and fro with baggage and furnishings. That was where Millie found her and curtseyed,

"My lady, I have received a message from your lady mother's gentlewoman, asking you to go to Countess Margaret's chamber before I send your things to your quarters," Millie said. "I am to accompany you there."

Anne followed the familiar swaying skirts of her maid up the broad staircase and along a richly decorated passageway to a dark, carved door upon which Millie gave a loud rap. Anne, startled, wished she had been gentler, but there was no response from inside and Millie cautiously opened the door. No-one had yet arrived in the spacious room that had been allotted to the Countess of Cumberland, so the two young women could only wait, awkwardly avoiding the subject which brought them there and was uppermost in their minds. Millie stationed herself near the door, while Anne went over to the window and miserably gazed, without seeing, at the gardens below.

The door opened to admit two footmen carrying boxes of Lady Margaret's property, followed by two of her waiting ladies who curtseyed to Anne and proceeded to unpack the boxes into a chest at the foot of the great curtained bed. Anne was hoping they would leave before her mother came into the room, but just then Lady Margaret swept in and they all curtseyed. The Countess acknowledged the waiting ladies and dismissed them, to Anne's relief, before she turned to Anne with a very stern look. Anne curtseyed again, eyes downcast, and did not speak.

"I suppose you know why I have summoned you here, Anne? "

"Yes, and I am truly very sorry, my lady mother. I beg you will find it in your heart to forgive me."

"Your behaviour this morning was unseemly and unworthy," her mother said. "I did not expect to see my daughter make herself the subject of adverse comment and criticism and I cannot let this go unpunished. I thought you had learned the lessons of good conduct that have always been gently offered to you in the past, but a stronger reminder is clearly needed. Tonight you will sleep alone in one of the tower rooms. After we have dined, Millie will take you there and return the key to me."

Anne gasped and took two steps towards her mother, clasping her hands tightly together in entreaty.

"Oh no, please no, my lady mother! I've never slept in a room alone, even in a familiar chamber. I shall be so afr . . ." She was cut off by Lady Margaret's gesture and words of dismissal.

"You will thus have time to think about what you did and learn better."

Anne was shaking as she left her mother's chamber, shocked as never before that her gentle mother should inflict such harsh punishment on her; if this was what growing up was like, perhaps she would rather remain a child. She parted from Millie, who went to see to Anne's belongings, and wandered downstairs in search of Frances, but she had no idea where Frances's room might be. In spite of the bustling servants, the huge house seemed grey and subdued, having nothing of the usual warmth and welcome with which Aunt Warwick's presence had always imbued it on previous visits. This was turning into a most miserable event, she thought, and began to wish she had not come. The earlier sunshine had turned into a cold, dim drabness. She remembered a happy summer-time with Frances and other friends in the gardens of North Hall some years ago and decided to go outside to see whether her mood would be lifted there. But the winter sun had left the parterre and the garden was desolate. It did nothing to raise her spirits and she turned back to the house.

Just as she did so she heard a window flung open. She looked up as she heard Frances call her name and saw her beckon. Delighted, she would have run into the house to join her cousin but remembered just in time that she was no longer a child and must behave decorously. She found Frances in the west passageway and allowed herself to be led into the chamber where Frances's maid was unpacking. Frances took one look at Anne's face and dismissed her maid.

"Anne, what is happening? Have you spoken with your lady mother? I expected that we would be sharing this chamber, but your baggage has not been brought in and you look distraught."

Anne threw herself into Frances's arms and the pent-up tears flowed down her cheeks and made dark patches on Frances's silk bodice.

"My mother is punishing me for my indiscretion this morning and I'm to sleep alone tonight – in a locked room in the tower! I'm so afraid, Frances, I cannot bear the thought of it!"

"Oh, my poor coz! I feared as much but hoped it might not be so. We must think of a way to give you courage and make the night pass quickly. Come; pray help me put these things away before we're called to dinner."

They busied themselves with Frances's gowns, petticoats, shifts, stockings, bodices and shoes and Anne began to feel better, but it took some time for the desolation she had felt to leave her and she dreaded the forthcoming night.

"Be sure to keep your Prayer Book with you," Frances said. "Your mother cannot deny you that. And I promise to try to find a key and come to you once the house is quiet." Anne wondered how long that would leave her alone and afraid, but she was comforted, nevertheless, by her cousin's kindness and promise of help.

❧

When the rattle of Lady Margaret unlocking the tower chamber roused them just after dawn the next morning, Anne and Frances both leapt anxiously from the bed. Frances hastened to explain,

"I acted only out of pity, my lady, and in the conviction that my cousin Anne was truly repentant and had learned her lesson well. I did not mean to go against your ladyship's commands."

In their fluster neither of them noticed that the Countess did not appear either surprised or angry to find Frances there, but said simply,

"I am pleased to hear it, Frances. I hope that I shall never again have cause to be so severe." Anne jumped to her cousin's defence and said,

"My lady, I did not intend to be disobedient. I enjoyed the ride and Mr Meverell's company and discourse. I didn't think that I was doing wrong, but Frances corrected me and explained and I realised that you would be displeased. I hope you will forgive me."

"And I hope that you realise that you are no longer a child, but a young lady, and with that comes responsibility," said Lady Margaret. "It is not enough to _be_ virtuous, you must always be _seen_ to be virtuous, and your behaviour from now on must reflect that. If you will accept this, then you have my forgiveness and you may move into Frances's chamber today."

When she left the room, the two young women hugged each other in relief.

"It was almost as though she knew you'd be here!" said Anne, but Frances just held her close.

❧

Later that day Lady Margaret took Anne to visit Aunt Warwick in her chamber. Anne entered tentatively and was shocked by her aunt's appearance. All the authority and command that had been so characteristic of her personality seemed to have seeped from her and she looked shrunken, weak and helpless. But it was reassuring to see her tired, lined face transform into the familiar warm smile when she saw Anne enter the room behind her mother. Anne was hesitant to embrace her aunt, who looked so fragile wrapped in her layers of fur, but ran to her side and held her cold hand to warm it between her palms. Aunt Warwick spoke quietly, with some visible effort,

"Welcome to North Hall once more, dear child. I thank God for his mercy in granting me this great pleasure."

"And I am so pleased to see you, dear Aunt Warwick. Can I do anything for you?"

"Indeed, the days are long and dreary. Any time you can find to be with me would cheer the hours and give me solace."

When she saw that the bond of affection between her sister and her daughter was as strong as ever, Margaret slipped from the room.

"Would you like me to read to you?" Anne asked, indicating the books piled on the side table.

"It would be more than a pleasure; it would bring a breath of renewal when I thought never to feel that again, with the springtime so slow in coming." Aunt Warwick sighed and closed her eyes for a moment as though even the feeble winter light tired them.

"Then I shall come to you every morning and read from whatever books you wish, and together we'll welcome the lengthening of the days! My lady mother hopes that you'll be well enough to accompany us to join the Queen in a few weeks' time, so we'll have something to work for."

"Your mother has been very generous in bringing me potions and medicines to help me, but I fear my recovery may not be as rapid as she hopes," Lady Warwick said. They both fell silent, thinking about the shadowy implication beneath this statement, until a log in the grate shifted noisily and roused them. Lady

Warwick suffered a fit of coughing and was unable to speak until it had subsided. When she had recovered her breath she asked slowly,

"Is there any news from court? Didn't I hear that you may become a lady-in-waiting to the Queen?"

"Yes, it has been spoken of, but nothing is settled. I do wish I could have been a lady- in-waiting to the Old Queen, as you were, dear Aunt," Anne smiled, but Lady Warwick frowned at her and wagged an admonishing, misshapen finger.

"You well know that that would have happened had the Queen lived on. But surely, my dear, this appointment would bring you as much pleasure as mine did all those years ago?"

"I intend no disrespect to Her Majesty at all," Anne said, "And I hope to be forgiven for saying this, but I don't feel it would be as prestigious, because Queen Anne is the queen consort, whereas Queen Elizabeth was the monarch and none in the land was higher than her.

"And everyone is saying that standards at the court have slipped since the Old Queen's death," she continued. "We noticed that ourselves when we sat for a while in the rooms of Sir Thomas Erskine at Tibbalds." Aunt Warwick looked shocked and puzzled;

"Sir Thomas is Captain of the Guard; surely there's no decrease in the protection afforded to the King and Queen?"

"No, I don't think there is," Anne said. "But there was an increase in something else, much less welcome!" She suppressed a giggle.

"You speak in riddles, Anne; pray tell me what you mean," her aunt said.

"I mean that we all came away from there with lice! I don't think that would ever have happened at the old court, would it?"

"No indeed!" said Lady Warwick. "I am surprised and not a little dismayed at what you tell me. But times do change, my dear, and we must make the most of what we have. Take pride in it if you are asked to attend the Queen, for it is the highest honour available to a young noblewoman at court nowadays and at fourteen you are exactly the right age for more exposure to society."

Anne could see that their discussion had cheered her aunt, who had joined in with some animation, but it had also tired her and it was time to leave her to rest.

"I shall return on the morrow to read to you," she said as she bent to kiss the soft grey cheek and her aunt squeezed her hand in gratitude.

⁂

But the Countess of Warwick was not destined to join the new Queen's train, nor did she ever again leave North Hall. In spite of the profusion of care and love which her sister and niece lavished upon her, she died a short time later on a dark day in February. They were not alone in mourning her, for she had been one of the most influential people at the court of Elizabeth and Anne had been right in thinking that there was a world of difference between a waiting lady to a monarch and that to a consort.

Aunt Warwick was buried in the family vault of the chapel at Chenies, her ancestral home, and her funeral was attended by the representatives of every great family in England. Anne was comforted by Cousin Frances, who held her frozen hand through the funeral service and spoke consolingly about the Holy Spirit and the inevitability of death.

"Hold tight to your loving memories of our dear Aunt Warwick, Coz, for in that way she will live on in us," Frances said. "Remember that our souls will be linked with hers for eternity. She had a wonderful life, but there is no life that does not end in death. So we were blessed by her presence for all of our lives and now we mourn; that's better than if she had never lived, is it not?"

Anne would always recall her cousin's words, which comforted her in this bereavement and in subsequent ones. She missed Aunt Warwick's warm presence for many years, prayed for her soul, and often recalled their conversations at North Hall, drawing consolation from the knowledge that she had been a comfort to her aunt during the final fading weeks of her life on earth.

Anne attended Queen Anne's court regularly and took part in the entertainments and activities there, but it didn't have the glitter of Elizabeth's train. She was pleased and honoured to be chosen to play in several of the masques the Queen loved so much, and the Queen always acknowledged her and was often kind. With her many friends from the highest noble families, Anne enjoyed the companionship and privileges of court life and was privy to news and gossip. Richard Sackville became a companion to Prince Henry, so she saw him from time to time and looked out for him often. His brother Edward was less in evidence; he was rumoured to have gone abroad after some trouble. Philip Herbert married Susan De Vere with the encouragement of a handsome dowry from the King and the promise of the Earldom of Montgomery for Herbert in the near future. Robert Carr had succeeded in becoming King James's favourite, making him vainer and more annoying than ever. Anne avoided him when she could but was aware that their names were sometimes linked by the gossips. She didn't think Aunt Warwick would have been any more disappointed than she was by her lack of promotion; to be a lady-in-waiting to this Queen was to be like a minnow compared to the Countess of Warwick, who had been a Triton in the Old Queen's court.

CHAPTER FIVE
1605

Anne was happy with her situation at the court of Queen Anne. At fifteen her face remained round and her brown hair still reached below her knees when she was standing, but her reflection in the mirror showed her that, although she remained tiny, not yet grown to five feet tall, the shape of her body had changed. She gazed with pleasure at a form which was now clearly becoming that of a woman and she loved to dress in a way that showed off her new curves. She enjoyed the company of the fashionable young women around the Queen's court such as Alethea Talbot and Susan De Vere, and, as Richard Sackville had forecast at Grafton nearly two years ago, Queen Anne was always planning the next entertainment and kept them very busy.

Anne had to fend off once again the attentions of the loathsome Robert Carr.

"Come, Lady Anne, let us play Barley Break in the garden on this warm spring day," Carr suggested, in that voice that set her teeth on edge, grabbing for her hand.

"What is this Barley Break you speak of?" Anne asked.

"I can't believe you don't know Barley Break!" he squealed, attempting to put his arm around her waist. "It is the best of games for lively couples like us; we just need two other pairs to join us, then we all chase each other, just like the birds do in Spring!"

Anne dodged out of his way, but he continued to make embarrassing suggestions interspersed with high-pitched laughter, braying like a delirious mule. She blushed, feeling certain that everyone was staring at them, making more of his behaviour than she would like. When she continued to refuse, he pouted like a spoilt child before walking away with a rude gesture and another whinny. She took a deep breath and wiped her palms on her skirts, later complaining to a sympathetic Elizabeth about his unwanted attention.

"I have heard some gossip," Elizabeth said.

"Oh! What are they saying?" Anne asked.

"Just that he clearly has his sights set on you," Elizabeth said. Anne grimaced.

❦

As well as her court attendances, Anne enjoyed the time she spent with her mother and the many educated people who were drawn to Lady Margaret by her broad knowledge and interests and her appreciation of their creative talents. During the summer the King and Queen were to visit Scotland and court activity would cease. Lady Margaret made plans;

"I'm touched that my dear brother William has, in his great kindness, offered to lend us his manor house at Cookham, Anne. He thinks we are both in need of some time away from London, in a country place where we'll find peace and rest; I believe it has beautiful gardens. I intend to inform our friends so that we may gather around us a group with whom we can read and converse."

Anne beamed with pleasure at the prospect of spending time in the country with congenial female company.

"That sounds idyllic! I thank my uncle for his generosity and thoughtfulness and I'll go and choose some books to take with us." Court life was wonderful, but keeping up with the fashions, the events and the gossip and being constantly on public display, to be scrutinised and criticised, took a toll on her emotions and her zest for life. This would be a welcome time of private recreation.

While she was sorting through books and considering what to take to Cookham, Anne came across a sheet of paper on which someone had written, crossed out, written over, crossed out and inserted words in a haphazard way. She could barely make any sense of it. Clutching the sheet, she hurried back to the chamber where she had left her mother and asked Lady Margaret what it was.

The Countess scrutinised it and declared it to be in Aemilia Lanyer's handwriting.

"I believe it is the rough outline of a poem which Aemilia was writing the last time she was here," Lady Margaret said. "She indicated that it was to be dedicated to me. Look, here at the top, I can just make out some words that look like 'Right Honourable and Excellent Lady' – I think that is how she planned to address me. And there is a passage here," she said, pointing, "which I find particularly difficult to decipher, but part of it goes '. . . the world . . . receive no blemish, nor . . . (something), by my unworthy hand writing . . .'! How amusing that we should so struggle to read that!" They laughed. "We shall be certain to ask her about it if she joins us at Cookham."

"So she will be with us?" Anne asked.

"I hope so; she is certainly one of the people I am inviting."

"I do hope she'll come; I find her such an interesting person. There are very few female poets and I can think of none but her who has published her work," Anne said.

❦

Travelling west from the city, the beginning of the journey into the country took them close to the north bank of the great bustling river Thames, crowded with trading craft of all shapes and sizes, then away from it until they approached Windsor and could see the silhouette of the castle's towers and battlements against the sky. Here the river reappeared in a different guise, smooth and calm with its traffic of swans and sails, like small and large flecks of pale paper on the blue surface. Anne breathed the clear air with pleasure and anticipation, and when they reached Cookham and saw the warm brick mansion, surrounded by its green mantle of trees and gardens, she recognised Arcadia and knew she would be happy here.

Aemilia came to Cookham shortly after they themselves arrived, bringing a fair copy of the poem dedicated to Lady Cumberland. It seemed to Anne to ramble at length, but she liked the passage which went '. . . *the mirror of your most worthy mind, which may remain in the world many years longer than your Honour, or my self can live, to be a light to those that come after . . .'*. Her mother's mind was something Anne was beginning to appreciate and she was comforted by the idea that it would continue to illuminate her life, even when her mother was no longer there.

❧

On a warm still morning which heralded a hot day, Anne, Margaret and Aemilia, dressed in comfortable loose linen clothing, were sitting in the shade of a gnarled apple tree in the rose garden, inhaling the perfume of the flowers. They were discussing the portrayal of women in the Bible.

"I wish to turn these images around," Aemilia said, "Depict good women, such as you, and show that they would be able to get just as close to Jesus Christ as men. Look at Eve! Was it her fault that she gave in to the serpent?"

"What do you mean?" Anne asked her.

"I mean that she, like other women of her time and since, was always compelled to follow men, to be guided and guarded by them and to obey them. How then was she to resist the serpent when it told her to eat the apple?"

Margaret protested,

"Eve had been told by God that she should not eat the apple."

But Aemilia was in full flow,

"If men are to set themselves up as of a superior nature to women, then men must protect women from dangers such as beguiling serpents. But what did Adam do?"

Anne was puzzled and frowned with concentration.

"I think I see what you mean," nodded Lady Margaret slowly, thinking, "Adam let her eat the apple when he ought to have stopped her. And then he ate some himself."

"Exactly!" Aemilia declared, emphasising her words by pressing the flat of her hand on the table. "You have my meaning precisely, dear lady! If Adam was so much stronger than Eve, he should have shown her how to stand up to the serpent and he himself should have resisted. Why is the fall of man always blamed on woman? Adam was, at the very least, partly to blame!"

Anne had been listening intently and her eyes were shining as she joined in,

"I've always thought that women's ways would be more to Jesus's liking than would men's," she said. "I think the Bible teaches us that Jesus stood for love and humility, not the angry and violent ways of men. Why should women submit to men's judgement when their own is usually so much better?"

"You will go far, Lady Anne," Aemilia said. "I can see that your mind is as sharp as your lady mother's and that you have the spirit to go with it."

Anne felt proud at this praise from one whom she admired, but only a tiny smile escaped on to her face as she concentrated on the argument that continued to pass back and forth.

Later, Lady Margaret suggested an afternoon ride through the shade of the woods;

"We could follow the path towards the river and return by the winding lane," she said.

‿◦‿

On their return, Lady Margaret was informed that a servant had arrived from her husband and was waiting to speak to her. Anne and Aemilia went to stroll in the gardens while Margaret received the messenger. Anne was uneasy and wondered what message the servant had brought; her parents were not in the habit of communicating with each other very often, so it might be something important and she wondered if it could be something to do with her. She heard Aemilia say that her family crest showed a silkworm moth and a mulberry tree, which excited her memories of the silkworms she had kept as a child, but she was distracted and wasn't really concentrating on what Aemilia was saying. She pulled some rose petals from their flowers and inhaled their calming scent from her palm. She tried to look as though she was listening and to nod in the right places; Aemilia didn't seem to require any more response than that and just kept on talking.

Anne was not surprised when Millie appeared, bobbed a curtsey and said,

"Lady Margaret requests your ladyship be good enough to join her in the Long Gallery, Lady Anne."

Anne excused herself from Aemilia's company and hurried up the stairs to the panelled gallery, where many large windows flooded the ancestral portraits and glowing furnishings with summer light. She found her mother looking very thoughtful, but not upset or angry. Lady Margaret motioned for her to sit down and addressed her gently.

"Anne, I have heard from your father that he wishes you to come to him at Grafton Regis. You are to return with his Steward, Mr Machell, who brought the message, and your departure cannot be delayed beyond tomorrow or at latest the day after. I fear you may be disappointed by this news, as I am, but there is no remedy for it."

"I am indeed disappointed, my lady mother," Anne said. "I am very happy here and had looked forward to staying another month or more. How long does my father intend that I should remain with him at Grafton? Perhaps it'll be possible for me to return to Cookham after I've done my lord's bidding?"

"I don't know how long you are to stay there, that will be a decision your father will make when his business with you is done," Margaret said.

"Do you know what business that is, my lady?"

"I believe he wishes to discuss the question of your marriage, but I know no more than that."

"My marriage! Surely my father will discuss that matter with you rather than me if he has proposals to consider?" Anne felt blood pumping into her head. What had put this subject into her father's mind? Who had made an approach to him that he needed to discuss with her?

"I hope that I'll be privy to any firm plans he has," her mother responded, "But he and I resolved many years ago that a marriage agreement for you would never be sealed without your approval, so I think that may be why he wishes to seek your views before mine. We both desire to spare you the suffering that arose from my father's decision that we should marry."

"I'm grateful that you have thought of me in this, but I wish I could just stay here and continue with our innocent pursuits as we'd planned. I don't feel inclined to consider my marriage instead." Anne's lip began to tremble and she turned away from her mother, blinking back tears and biting the side of her finger.

"Pray, Anne, don't upset yourself. You may be certain that your father has only your best interests at heart and won't insist upon anything that isn't to your liking."

Anne went to take her leave of Aemilia, feeling sad and disappointed. The journey would take two days, she calculated, therefore it made sense to leave as soon as possible in the hope of returning after a few days to pick up the threads of their fascinating conversations. She hurried to instruct Mary, who would accompany her to her father's house.

During the journey she calmed her nerves with the memory of her mother's reassuring words and as the coach approached Grafton her mood began to lift. She became aware that she was looking forward to seeing her father again and felt pleased that he was paying attention to her. He was always affectionate and generous when she was with him, although she found his lack of these attributes in respect of her mother very galling and had to work hard at barring her critical thoughts from bursting out in accusations which she would later regret. After the death of the lady with whom he'd lived when he left her mother, she had wondered whether they might be reconciled, but this hadn't happened. She had realised then that the trust that had been broken could never be repaired and she understood that, although Lady Margaret had forgiven the hurt and humiliation done to her in the past, she could never expose herself to the possibility of any future repetition of it.

The Earl of Cumberland came out eagerly to greet Anne as soon as the coach drew up in front of the old mansion, but he descended the stone steps slowly and cautiously, grasping the balustrade. Although he was beaming, she was shocked that he had aged so much in the months since they had last met and looked thin, stooped and grey. She wondered, as she stepped down from the coach, whether he'd been ill.

"Nan, welcome back to Grafton!" he said. "It's a great pleasure to see you and I hope your journey has been agreeable."

"Thank you for your welcome, my lord. I am pleased to see you and I'm grateful to you for sending your coach to fetch me. The journey was pleasant and without incident and in these long summer days we made good progress."

Anne and her gentlewoman were to occupy the chamber which she remembered from the time of the royal banquet as the best in the house, the one that the King had occupied. It had leaded windows looking on to the gardens, meadows and woods beyond; she saw with a pang that it was not as beautiful as Cookham, but it was gratifying to be treated as an adult and an honoured guest in her father's house. She wondered when he would speak of that adult business that had brought her here, and what he would say.

Her father had planned diversions for her and suggested that they spend a few days enjoying the amenities of Northamptonshire before discussing more serious matters. Anne thought of the uncertainty about her future which might spoil the days she would spend with him and was anxious to return to Cookham as soon as possible.

"My lord, I am most grateful for the care you have taken to plan my entertainment," she said. "But in the few days we are to spend together I think I should prefer to discuss the serious matter first. Then I would be released from any doubts about that and be free to enjoy your company subsequently." The Earl laughed and hastened to reassure her,

"My dear Nan, I'm not planning to send you away again as soon as you have arrived! No, I wish you to stay here for the rest of this month of August so that we shall have the pleasure of each other's company for a few more weeks. I shall thus make better acquaintance with my beloved daughter before she becomes a woman and is removed from me by an eager husband. It will be a delightful time together, don't you agree?"

Anne made every effort to hide her initial dismay and managed a sincere smile in reply to her father's kindly enquiry.

"I didn't realise that my visit was to be such a long one, my lord. It will be a privilege to come to know you better after being long deprived of your company." As she was saying this Anne realised that he might take it as criticism of his desertion and she hurried on to try to make amends, "But I must beg you again to consider discussing the future with me soon, for I cannot but believe that it will weigh on my mind 'til 'tis done."

"Very well, I can see that you feel you'll have no peace otherwise," the Earl said. Then there was silence.

"What is your wish, my lord?" Anne asked, trembling with fear of what the reply might be.

The Earl stood with his back to her and stared out of the window for a long time, apparently mulling over ideas which she wished she could read through the back of his head. She fidgeted and gazed round the great hall, seeing it as at had been for the lavish banquet with which her father had welcomed the new king and queen. She remembered the anger she had felt on her mother's behalf and the dreadful ill-feeling at that time between her separated parents, and she gave silent thanks that things were, if not repaired, at least a little easier between them now. She drifted into recollection of her first brush with Robert Carr, and then her conversation that night with Richard Sackville, wrapped in the warmth and gaiety of the celebrations, and she gave a startled jump back to the present when her father turned and cleared his throat to speak. She looked up, trying to read his expression, but his face was obscured by the light from the window behind him and she could see only the silhouette of his head.

"My greatest wish, Nan, is for your happiness and well-being," her father said. "I desire to see you safely embarked on life with a man whom you can respect and love. When your mother and I married we'd known each other for years and were friends. But I know now that a man and a woman can find something beyond friendship and that is my wish for you. My Lady Margaret and I had no wish to marry and although we made the best of it for a while, we spent much time apart and grew less and less close over the years until, by whatever cause, no good feeling toward each other remained.

"That is why I ask for your thoughts on the matter before I make any suggestion."

Anne was taken aback by the kindliness of his tone and the personal revelation of his words; she recognised the truth of what he'd said, but her father had never before spoken to her in this vein. She tried to take in this new experience and bring order to her confused thoughts. Was this the way adults talked? Was her father treating her as an adult? Was she being initiated into a strange new world now that she was of marriageable age? He took her silence for modesty and encouraged her to speak,

"You're growing up, Nan. Remind me how old you are."

"I'm fifteen and a half this month past."

"Don't tell me there is no young man at court who has made a favourable impression on you," her father said, smiling. "I have observed you dancing in the masques and taking part in games and pastimes and have no doubt at all that there have been young men in abundance paying attention to you! Pray, what are your thoughts? Am I right?"

Anne swallowed hard and took a deep breath.

"My lord, I hardly know what to say," she said. "Thoughts of marriage have not been occupying my mind, but you are correct in thinking that I have enjoyed the company of a number of young men . . . and some I've liked better than others."

"Tell me your preference."

"Well, I do know that there has been talk that I might be matched with the King's favourite, Robert Carr, but . . ." her voice tailed off and her troubled gaze dropped. The dust on the floor showed up in a shaft of sunlight. Her father looked at her with a puzzled frown,

"Do you favour him?" he asked. "I hear tell that the King may soon bestow a title on him, so . . . a suitable match for the daughter of the Earl of Cumberland, perhaps?"

"Oh, no, my lord! No! Pray pardon me, for I see that I've misled you!" Anne said. "I did not mean to indicate any liking for Carr; quite the opposite! I wished only to dissuade you from any such suggestion, for I cannot see that marriage to him would be satisfactory in any way." She stopped, agitated, but fearing to say too much in case her father was about to propose this match.

When she looked up, twisting her fingers together, Cumberland was smiling down at her. He took the chair opposite and relaxed, leaning against its tapestry-upholstered back and stretching his legs out in front of him.

"I'm relieved to hear it!" he said. "For a moment I feared that your judgement was less sound than I had taken it to be, but I'm reassured that your drift is not in that direction."

"Oh no, my lord. Robert Carr seems to me a very coarse and ill-educated person, determined to establish himself in the King's favour at whatever cost. I cannot imagine having an interesting conversation with him on any subject under the sun."

"Then we're agreed – you shall not be betrothed to Carr. Set your mind at rest. But tell me, who does your favour fall upon, my dear?"

Anne was overwhelmed by the relief that his words brought and hardly heard the question until her father repeated it.

"I . . . I . . . Please pardon me my lord, but I blush to mention the name of one whom I hold in high regard . . ."

"Then I shall spare your blushes and name Richard Sackville, Lord Buckhurst! Is it he?" Her glowing face gave him his answer, though he knew he was almost certainly right, from observing them dancing at Grafton and from whispers he had recently heard at court.

She laughed in embarrassment.

"How did you know?"

"Think of it as a lucky wager!" he said.

"I do indeed like Lord Buckhurst, we are friends," Anne said, "But we haven't spoken of any personal matter between us and I've told no-one of my feelings until now."

"Very well, I shall speak to his grandfather, the Earl of Dorset: he is the Lord High Treasurer and I know him of old."

"Oh no, not yet!" Anne burst out. "Pray forgive me, my lord father, but there's one important reason that I must beg you to delay, and that's to show due respect towards my dear lady mother. She must be consulted first, before any further steps are taken. She's always been my closest friend and support in all things and I would not upset her for anything. I hope she'll have no objection to the match, but I must know her opinion before any decision is made."

Anne watched his face as a succession of thoughts flitted across it. It was clear to her that this response pleased him less than her previous ones, but he sighed and assented, giving her credit for loyalty to her mother and courage in standing up for it. Anne wondered whether there would be a long delay before her parents communicated with each other.

"Would it please you, my lord, if I should mention this matter to my lady mother?"

"Indeed it would, for then she would be assured, as am I, that the suggestion meets with your approval."

"Then I'll write her a letter to inform her that we have discussed it, but I shall not be able to give a firm reply until I've spoken with her again," Anne said. "And whatever happens, I do have your word that any approach from Robert Carr will be rebuffed, don't I, my lord father?" He nodded, smiling broadly.

❦

Anne was satisfied by the outcome of her audience with her father and decided to make the most of a few more weeks of his company; wasn't this what she had always craved? She missed her mother and was still sad that her stay at Cookham had been cut short, but she wrote frequent letters and sent greetings to Aemilia and other friends who would be keeping company with Lady Margaret, and received warm, news-laden replies. The weeks went by slowly but pleasurably enough, and she wondered whether Richard Sackville thought of her as often as she missed him. She dared not give way to hope with the matter so far from settled. She was in no rush to be married; she looked forward to returning to court and enjoying the company of her friends there, the bustle and the gossip, but Richard was constantly on her mind.

At the end of August, her father rode with her to Greenwich, where they parted on the best of terms. He was to return to Whitehall and Anne was to rejoin her mother at Sutton in Kent, where they would make final preparations for the resumption of court activities.

Anne did not long delay speaking with her mother about the discussion she had had with her father. Although she was apprehensive and awkward to begin with, Lady Margaret made it easy for her by her gentle manner.

"Pray tell me, my dear, what thoughts your father had on the matter?"

"My lord father was gentle and considerate, as you'd told me he would be, but he frightened me at first with talk of Robert Carr! I had meant to rule him out at the beginning, but my father mistook my mention of his name and spoke as if he might be considering him." Anne looked horrified at the thought and Lady Margaret soothed her;

"My dear, you know that I would never have countenanced that match."

"Yes. I didn't think of it at the time, but you are right – and it turned out that my father would not either, he was merely sounding me out."

"How did Richard Sackville's name arise?"

Anne admitted that her father had guessed where her preference lay. She was happy to talk about Richard Sackville and was pleased that her mother was listening with a slight smile of approval.

Lady Margaret had no objection to the proposed marriage of her daughter to the heir to the Earls of Dorset, particularly in view of Anne's obvious leaning towards the young man, and she and Anne both wrote letters to Lord Cumberland to confirm her approval. During the following days Anne imagined her father talking to Lord Dorset and waited impatiently for his reply, hugging her dreams to her heart.

CHAPTER SIX
Autumn 1605

By late September the King and Queen had returned from
Scotland and it was time for the court to reassemble. Doublets
and gowns had been ordered for the new season and everyone
felt refreshed, with that energy that comes after a break, full of
anticipation for the forthcoming merry-go-round. Anne would
attend the marriage of her friend Lady Susan De Vere, daughter of
the Earl of Oxford, to Philip Herbert, he of hunting and hawking
fame, younger son of the Earl of Pembroke. Philip was still in high
favour with King James, who had provided a large dowry for the
bride and would play a prominent role in the lavish ceremony to
be attended by the whole court. Philip was then created First Earl
of Montgomery by the King.

Anne revelled in the company of her friends, greeting them all
warmly – with one awkward exception.

"Greetings, my lady!" Richard Sackville bowed. His open smile
was friendly. The thump of Anne's heartbeat distracted her and she
struggled with the thoughts that filled her mind.

"Oh, Richard, you took me by surprise! I... I... yes, greetings,
indeed, greetings...," she stammered. Did he know? Had her father
spoken to his grandfather?

"Have you enjoyed the summer recess?" Richard asked.

Anne grasped this lifeline, relieved to be able to respond to his
question, but blushing despite herself.

"I did, I thank you. I spent a most pleasant time with my mother
at Cookham and then with my father at Grafton."

The memory of her conversation with her father brought even
stronger colour to her cheeks and she looked down and fumbled
with her cuffs, suddenly intensely interested in the complicated
pattern of their lace. Surely, if he knew of a conversation between

her father and his grandfather, this would be the time for him to mention it?

"I too enjoyed the country life, hunting and hawking in Kent and Sussex," Richard said, without concern. "It was good to spend time with friends, but I am pleased to be back at court and to see others again," he smiled at her.

Embarrassed by her own awkwardness and certain that he had noticed it, Anne brought the conversation to an end on a pretext and scurried away. It was a situation which she was unable to discuss with anyone, for if it became public knowledge that an approach had been made but nothing came of it, she would be humiliated in the eyes of the world. She could glean no clues from Richard's behaviour; he was his usual friendly, slightly teasing self, but she felt confused about how to respond to him and wished she knew what was happening. She kept her distance, as always, from his brother.

Amid all this mixed joy and tension, an unexpected trouble arose. Lady Margaret spoke to her after a hurried breakfast.

"Anne, I've had news of your father today, but not of the kind we were hoping for. Machell has informed me that his lordship is sick and has asked for me; he has been brought to lodge at the Duchy House near the Savoy Hospital, where he can be more easily looked after. I'll prepare some remedies for him and go to him tomorrow."

"I am dismayed to hear that, my lady mother. Pray take my best wishes to my lord father and give him every assurance of my love and affection. I do hope he will recover soon and I'm certain your physic will restore him."

Anne rushed away to answer the Queen's summons to Richmond. It was a busy day for the Queen and the ladies of her court, who were to attend an archery tournament, and Anne would remain at Richmond for several days. She was too busy to think of anything else during her time there, but as she returned to Clerkenwell almost a week later, she remembered with a jolt that her father had been sick when she left. She had received no further news; perhaps that was good news and he had by now recovered.

When she arrived at Clerkenwell House she sought out her mother but was told that Lady Margaret had gone to visit her husband again, as she had done every day since Anne's departure. Everyone she spoke to expressed the opinion that his Lordship was extremely sick and that Lady Margaret's remedies did not seem to be working this time.

Anne practised her lute all afternoon and had nearly learned Dowland's new 'Melancholy Galliard', at least to her own satisfaction. It suited her mood. When her mother entered the room, Anne looked up from her music and smiled. At fifteen she was still tiny and the large instrument on her lap made her look even smaller. She was a pretty girl, but the only way she could hold the lute, with her arms stretched to encompass it, was ungainly and awkward. As with all her studies, she was determined and conscientious and Margaret gave silent thanks for a daughter who gave her so much reason to be proud. Anne laid her lute down and rose to kiss her mother's cheek.

"You look tired, my lady mother. Where have you been?"

"I've been to see your father and I need to speak with you about what he told me, Anne," her mother replied, sitting down wearily.

"How is his sickness today? Were you able to help him with your remedy?"

Margaret shook her head and sighed.

"It is a great sadness to me that in spite of a lifetime spent studying the distillation and extraction of herbs and minerals for medicinal use, and the many people whom I've been able to help with my potions, it seems that on this occasion my lord is too far gone to benefit from the draughts I've prepared for him." Margaret sighed again, looked hard at Anne and continued.

"He is very sick indeed, Anne. He asked to be kindly remembered to you and sends you a message of his love. He has written a most affectionate and repentant letter to me, assuring me of his love and begging my pardon for any wrong he ever did me. He commends his brother to me and begs me to think well of him, and lastly he commands me to take great care of you."

Anne caught the glint of tears in her mother's eyes.

"May I visit him? We found much to talk about when I stayed with him at Grafton in the summer." She was thinking of the discussions they had had regarding her possible marriage arrangements, when she had refused to reach any final agreement without consulting her mother. Perhaps this was what her mother was alluding to; her stomach gave a little skip of excitement. But the Countess's face was solemn, her brow heavy.

"Yes, I think you should see him soon. But I wish to tell you now about his will." Anne looked at her expectantly while Margaret hesitated.

"Your father has made provision for me," Margaret said. "I am to have the use of the Westmorland estates as my jointure for my lifetime. And you, my dear, will receive fifteen thousand pounds as your portion." Anne nodded and waited for her mother to continue. "The titles will go to your Uncle, of course . . . as will the estates in Craven and, eventually, my jointure lands in Westmorland."

It took a few moments for Anne to grasp the implication of this. Having been brought up in this noble family and being familiar with the royal court, she knew that, as a woman, she could not inherit the earldom. But the estates were a separate matter and she had always understood that the Clifford lands in the north of England would be hers.

"What do you mean?"

"I am telling you that your father has bequeathed all of his estates to his brother Francis and the Clifford heirs in the male line. He thinks that he is doing the best thing for you, because he's very heavily in debt and it is his view that by leaving them the lands they'll be better placed to sort things out and pay those debts. He also has some mythical belief that his brother's line will end, so that the estates will eventually revert to you in a better state than they are now. But I truly cannot think there is any reason to share his confidence in that idea, especially if it is based on the myth of the Shepherd Lord's prophecy, as I suspect it is."

Anne was silent. She was trying to understand what had happened and why her mother was so calmly giving her this information, overturning her world, or at least her position in it. At the same time she was shocked that the talk of wills made her father's death sound like an imminent reality. She traced the outline of the pattern on her damask skirt with her forefinger. Eventually she said,

"I am relieved to hear that provision is to be made for you, my lady. Things had been so difficult between you and my lord father that I sometimes feared it might not be so. But as for the other...I can hardly grasp it... Do you agree with him, my lady? Please can you explain it to me?"

"No, Anne, I do not agree," Lady Margaret said. "I believe that this will is illegal and has no standing, other than as a sick man's invention. It won't stand up to legal scrutiny, I'm certain. Have no fear, the Clifford estates are rightfully yours as your father's sole heir. I'll look into the records and prove that this is so, and then we'll contest it in the courts of law. You shall have your inheritance."

Margaret spoke with calm authority, then reached out and patted Anne's arm as she stood to leave. Anne hurried across the room to open the door for her and returned slowly to sit on the window seat. The news was disturbing in two ways; her father was mortally sick and likely to die, which was bad enough. But she also had to take in that he had bequeathed all the lands in the north, her lands, to her uncle. Fifteen thousand pounds was a huge portion, one that would ensure her an excellent marriage. But it did not provide the security that being a great landowner in her own right would bring, and the lands would not be hers to bequeath in turn to her heirs. Her father had never paid the estates much attention; perhaps they were just bleak hills with flocks of sheep, but there was something special in the idea that they had been passed down through the Clifford line, father to child, for centuries – and she wanted to be a link in that chain, not the reason for it to break.

❧

As she entered her father's dimly lit chamber, Anne was reminded of her last visit to Aunt Warwick at North Hall and was shocked by his grey, sunken face, straggling beard and thin unkempt hair. She shrank from approaching the great oak tester-bed with its rich hangings and pile of furs, although she had intended until this moment to embrace her father. She curtseyed and mumbled a greeting, taking her cue from Lady Margaret, but he gave no sign that he was even aware of their presence. She gazed round the oppressive room, at the tapestries on the walls and the dark oak chests and silver candlesticks, which reflected the flicker of the logs burning in the grate under the ornate carved over-mantel. The air was stale and she found it hard to breathe. Lady Margaret sat down and Anne took up her place at the opposite side of the bed. She fixed her eyes on her mother's face and avoided looking at her father again.

They sat silently for a while, hearing only Lord George's rasping breath, the ticking clock, the shifting of logs in the grate and the muffled sounds of vendors and rumbling wheels down in the street, and then Lady Margaret began to read aloud in a very gentle voice. She read of God and his holy angels. She read of Satan's devouring teeth. She read of the angels' defence of the soul and its ascent into the kingdom of heaven. Anne felt herself drift into a tranquil sanctuary as her breathing slowed to the rhythm of her mother's phrases. She was able to look impassively at the still form of her father, so small on the great bed, and found that the earlier horror had left her. The peace emanating from Lady Margaret had enveloped him as well as their daughter and Anne felt closer to both her parents than she had ever done before. She took her father's cold, bony hand in hers and thought she felt a tiny feeble movement in response. She had no idea how much time might have passed while they sat there together, but by now the light was fading.

"God's will be done," Lady Margaret said, as she closed the book.

"Amen," they said together.

Part Two

CHAPTER SEVEN
1606–7

Her father's death changed everything.

Anne was grateful now for the time she had spent with him at Grafton and the memories she held. It was cruel, she thought, that her father was taken from her just when they had become close, but she gave thanks for his love and prayed for his soul. There were other times when she wept, and times when she felt angry. Her uncle, the new Earl of Cumberland and his Countess, took over the titles and all the Clifford estates and property in Craven and Yorkshire. Anne's mother became the Dowager Countess, with the right to occupy and benefit from her jointure, the Westmorland estates, for her lifetime. There was a year's mourning for Anne's father and she wondered whether the black mourning clothes suited her as much as they suited her mother, thinking that they made her own skin look sallow, but Cousin Frances reassured her that they made her look grown up and elegant.

Anne was aware of Lady Margaret's sadness for what had once been, but they both kept busy with practical matters as they had always done. Mother and daughter hastened to ensure that Lady Margaret became Anne's guardian until she reached the age of twenty-one, to thwart the many noble families who would wish to snap up a young ward of court with a large dowry in order to marry her to one of their sons.

On the thirtieth of January, Anne's birthday, there was frost on the ground and they had been reminiscing, by the fire in Margaret's chamber, about the sunny days they had spent at Cookham.

"Now that you are seventeen," Margaret said more seriously, "we need to think carefully about your future. We must pursue the question of your father's will and your inheritance; I have taken advice from my brother about whom to consult on this matter. He suggested I seek the assistance of a Mr Kniveton in establishing your rights to claim the Clifford lands. He is one of the foremost authorities in the country on such questions of inheritance and family history and he is a knowledgeable and industrious gentleman who is willing to help us by searching the archives. He'll examine all the legal documents concerning the Clifford family and their property, going back about three hundred years, in order to put the strongest case before the court of ward. Such a labour will take many months, of course.

"I have a suggestion to make, and it concerns both my jointure and your claim: I'm minded that you and I should visit those lands in the north, the Westmorland estates. There must be many documents there relating to the history of the Cliffords, which will help with our case if we can find them. And I wish to see what repairs are needed at Brougham and Appleby castles before I take up my dower residence there."

Anne nodded.

"You've never been in the north since you were an infant," Lady Margaret went on, "And you have never been to the county of Westmorland, or Brougham in that county, where your father was born and where I shall live in the future. I want you to see those lands of which we often speak. Equally importantly, I believe we both need to show ourselves to the people there, that they may know those to whom their allegiance – and rents – are now due. It's over a year since your father's death; what do you think?"

"That sounds like a great adventure!" Anne declared. "Perhaps I have the love of travel from my father; I've often wondered what the north is like when I've heard stories of it. Yes, I do surely wish to see those lands . . . then perhaps, having seen them, I shall no longer want them!" They both laughed.

"The journey will take a week or more," Margaret said, "and we'll be away for several months, so there are many preparations to be made. We'll set out for Appleby in July. I'll search in the archives there for any documents relevant to your claim that will contribute to Mr. Kniveton's work. And we'll make ourselves known in the area."

❦

Afterwards, Anne admitted to herself that she was less enthusiastic about the visit than she had pretended to her mother and wasn't entirely jesting when she had said that she might no longer want the lands once she had seen them. A week's travel away; that was a very long journey and every day she would be going further from Richard Sackville, increasing the distance between them.

What would they find when they got there, she wondered. The idea of the lands that formed her inheritance and connected her directly with all her forebears was both exciting and romantic, but the place might turn out to be bleak and dreary. Who had ever heard of Appleby and Brougham? And her mother had said they would be away for months, so who could know what might happen during that time; she might return to find Richard married to someone else. Her anxiety rose as she thought about it; the question of her marriage had been put aside during the period of mourning, but that was over now.

Although she was preoccupied with this, Anne was hesitant to raise the matter with her mother and only found enough courage to ask her question about a month later, as they were climbing the stairs at Austin Friars so that she spoke to her mother's back.

"I have been wondering whether my lord father (God rest his soul) had spoken to Lord Dorset before he fell ill. Do you know whether that had happened?"

They reached the drawing chamber and sat down facing each other before Lady Margaret replied,

"I don't believe there can have been any discussion, Anne. I feel certain that your father would have told me of anything that had happened and he did not mention it. And I have heard nothing from Lord Dorset. Has Lord Buckhurst given you any sign?"

76

The mention of Richard gave Anne the familiar delicious lurch of excitement in the pit of her stomach, but she answered her mother evenly,

"No, he hasn't, neither by word nor deed."

"Then I believe my surmise to be right and no discussion has taken place," Margaret said. Anne must have looked crestfallen, for her mother continued, "I am sorry if you are disappointed, but of course we can approach the matter again, now that I am officially your guardian."

"I am in no great hurry; I asked because, being uncertain about whether there had been an approach, I felt a little awkward in Lord Buckhurst's company. I am reassured if you think that he does not know of the idea, then I can behave more naturally with him."

"I'm pleased that you mentioned it, Anne," her mother said. "I have been considering how to proceed with the question of your inheritance on the one hand, and the possibility of your marriage on the other.

"I think," Margaret continued after a thoughtful pause, "That it might be better to move forward on the inheritance matter before we make any decisions concerning your marriage, as the one may affect the other. Whilst we remain here, we have the advantage of our position at court, which may be of assistance for both the claim and your marriage. I don't wish to move to my jointure house in Westmorland until your affairs are more settled."

"I am content with your reasoning and I agree that establishing my claim is more urgent than my marriage," Anne said. But she made this dutiful response whilst being aware of feelings of both disappointment and anxiety, which rose to the surface like flotsam on a wave. She cast a worried glance towards her mother.

"Would you like me to ask your Uncle of Bedford to ascertain whether an understanding can be reached with the Earl of Dorset, so that the idea of a betrothal may be broached for the future? Lord Buckhurst is a young man with whom many may wish to make an alliance, is he not?" Lady Margaret smiled encouragingly.

"Oh, you have heard my thoughts!" Anne's serious black eyes were bright and her cheeks pink with relief, in spite of her effort to appear nonchalant. "I should have more peace if I knew that there was some accord of that kind. Pray do ask, my lady."

❦

Before they set out, Lady Margaret came into Anne's chamber one evening while she and Millie were sorting linen for the journey.

"Millie, could you leave us for a moment, please?" Margaret said and continued when the maid had gone, "Anne, your uncle made an enquiry of the Earl of Dorset regarding a marriage between you and his grandson, but the Earl wishes to discuss it first with his son Robert, Lord Buckhurst's father, who is presently out of town. He promises to have a more detailed response ready for us when we return from the north. I hope this sets your mind at rest."

It's all I'm going to get for now, Anne thought. She sighed with disappointment and resignation as she closed the lid of her chest. They hadn't even set off yet; the return from the north was many months away. She felt powerless and sad.

❦

Anne stepped down from the stuffy coach in which she and her mother had been travelling for several endless days. She had resented every clop of the horses' hooves that took her further from London, from her life of entitlement at the royal courts and her friends there, and from Richard Sackville. She wondered where he was, who he was talking to, whether his brother was speaking evil against her, who he was flirting with, whether he thought of her and, most of all, when she would see him again. She missed both his teasing and his seriousness. Would the promised discussion with his father happen or would it be forgotten amongst all his grandfather's important affairs of state?

Her spirit sank further as they traversed featureless moors and passed through tumbledown villages where dirty children stared open-mouthed at the splendour of the coach-and-six. Were the Westmorland estates going to be like this? During the early days of the journey they had stayed with friends and relations in comfortable houses, but further north they sometimes had to put up in inns along the way and Anne was inclined to grumble.

"I am hungry, tired and stiff from being jolted in the coach all day; may I not expect a better welcome than this, my lady mother? There isn't even a fire in the grate!" But Lady Cumberland's expression was stern and unsympathetic as she said,

"Indeed we must appreciate the comforts we enjoy, but we must also pay heed to the very many people throughout the land who never know anything but harsh conditions, Anne."

"But I am not enjoying any comfort," Anne protested, shivering.

"The people I am talking about," her mother said, frowning, "Walk rather than riding in a coach, from necessity not choice. They are cold and wet from lack of good clothing and shelter, they eat poor food all their lives yet they still need to work the land and toil for others in order to feed themselves and their children. We have a fortunate destiny and shall not complain of our lot."

Anne was chastened and ashamed.

As they made their way north the landscapes, hamlets and towns they passed through changed in character and gradually Anne found herself becoming drawn to take more interest. Colours muted, brick gave way to stone, accents broadened and lush pastures were replaced by steep valleys with alternating dark forests and bare rocky outcrops. Stagnant village ponds had been homes to ducks, but were now, she saw, replaced by clear streams that loitered and bustled while darting swifts and martins drank from them. The air freshened and hesitant breezes became an insistent wind, bending trees to its will.

After many days they stopped at the summit of a long steep pull to rest the horses. They were amid a vast expanse of flat grey limestone blocks, which made Anne think of a giant's cobbled yard; they stretched across the bare plateau as far as she could see. The place might have seemed desolate, even in sunshine like this, without the bubbling call of the curlews' welcome.

Anne got out of the coach to gaze across the broad green valley below, its opposite side bordered by a wall of bare hills fading into the distance to west and east. To the south-west bigger mountains were outlined beyond the hills. She shielded her eyes and looked down into the valley where she could see scattered settlements: red stone homesteads with grey slate roofs sheltered by stands of trees; reed-thatched stalls and cultivated plots amongst fields and open commons where dotted sheep and cattle grazed. Anne was astonished and awed by this peaceful scene and by the distance she could see in every direction. It was like nowhere else she had ever been and it felt like the top of the world.

"What is this place?" she asked.

"Before you is the Eden Valley, in the county of Westmorland, where sit my jointure lands," her mother said.

"It is indeed a garden paradise!" Anne said, without taking her eyes off the scene.

The coach then made its slow way down the hill until the tower of a castle came into view above the trees.

"This is Appleby," said Lady Margaret, instructing the coach driver to continue past the castle gates and take the lower road, circling through the centre of the small town so that Anne could see the Church and the ancient black and white Moot Hall. People stopped to stare as the tired horses slowed to heave their load back up the steep hill towards the castle, finally skirting the high walls to enter by the great gates on its western flank.

They stopped in front of an archway, bright like a lantern with the sunlight shining out from the courtyard beyond. The journey was over and they had reached Appleby Castle which, until now, had been nothing but a name to Anne. She alighted quickly, took a deep breath and looked about; the air was sharp and clean and she felt it clear her head in seconds. She was suddenly elated; it was worth all the discomforts of the journey to feel this thrill in the land of her forefathers.

From the right she was shadowed by the square bulk of a tall and ancient stone keep, with a small turret on each of its corners from which coloured pennants were fluttering. To her left was the broad wall of a house with many tall windows, though she could see no door on this side. The coach moved tentatively forward, blocking the archway's beam, so she turned away to take in the view from this high point. Beyond the trees green hills led her eyes to bluish more distant hills, rolling and basking in the sun like sleeping animals. One had a semi-circular bite missing; another giant's work, thought Anne.

A roaring sound from below enticed her to step forward and peer over the edge of a precipice. She gasped at the bird's eye view of the clear, tumbling river Eden below her as it swung in a great looping embrace around the prominence on which the castle stood, its banks overhung by oaks and sycamores, with flashes of sapphire water reflecting the sky.

Anne gazed, listened and breathed her fill, then turned to enter the courtyard. She was impatient to discover more but wished that Richard was here to share her joy; she imagined he would respond as she did to this magical place and she wondered whether they would ever come here together. From the archway she turned left and crossed the courtyard to a flight of broad stone steps, thanking the footman stationed at the top, who bowed and held open the studded oak doors for her. She stood on the threshold looking round the hall, allowing her eyes to grow accustomed to the darker interior, and then taking in the panelling and the carved stone fireplace. She was pleased to see glowing logs in the grate as she inhaled the smell of beeswax and lavender, wood smoke, old stone and fresh linen. It smells exactly as it should, she thought.

She stepped up to the large windows in the opposite wall, which gave onto a view of the trees, river and fells that she had seen from the top of the steep rock face outside. Looking down from the open casement she could see that this side of the house rose up like a cliff from the rocky precipice above the river, commanding the eastern prospect and providing a magnificent defence against attack. Now, to her right, she could also see a ford and a mill taking water from the river to slake its thirsty wooden wheel. She stood still, filling her memory with every detail of this landscape; blue hills, green trees, dark red stone buildings and clear rushing water.

"Beg pardon, my lady," Millie's voice cut into her reverie, "But I'm come to tell you that your chamber is prepared and I would show it to you if you please."

❧

By dusk, which falls late in the evening during the northern summer, Anne had explored some of the castle and had greeted, and been greeted by, many of the guards, footmen, cooks, maids, grooms, joiners, stonemasons, wheelwrights and gardeners who kept it running. She fell asleep contentedly, leaving the casement open a chink, in spite of Millie's protests, so that the last sound she heard before she slept was the rushing river far below and the wind rustling the leaves of the trees that clung to the precipice. When she woke she knew instantly where she was and smiled before opening her eyes, stretching luxuriously.

"This is more beautiful than anywhere I have ever been," she told herself. "It feels like home."

❧

Lady Margaret lost no time in locating the castle's muniments room and, along with her Secretary, threw herself into the task of sorting, reading and making notes on all the jumbled documents she found there. One day she emerged, dusty and crowned with cobwebs, and declared to Anne that she had found evidence concerning the belief Lord Cumberland had expressed on his death-bed regarding the Clifford inheritance.

"Anne, you remember the myth of the 'Shepherd Lord' that you so loved when you were a child? I've come upon writings telling that tale! Perhaps there is more truth in it than we believed. Henry de Clifford was indeed hidden from danger as a child and brought up by a family of shepherds in Cumberland, not knowing his true birth. What the documents show me is that his grandson was Henry, the second Earl, who was your father's father, and his two sons must therefore mean your father and Earl Francis. Your father must have remembered this tale from his family and believed that the prophecy would come true."

"Yes, it does sound like the same story," Anne agreed, putting aside her Psalter. "Perhaps that is why my father made that statement on his deathbed and believed that the male heirs would end. He made provision for me to inherit in that event, did he not?"

Lady Margaret nodded,

"Indeed, those were the terms of his will. However, I don't think we can leave your inheritance to chance in the hope that the foretelling will come about! I'll continue with the searches – there are mountains of papers to sift through – and find the ones that are important to our case. I shall be able to show them to Mr Kniveton, who will be able to use them to prove the case with facts in the courts."

"But that would also be in accord with the prophecy, would it not dear lady mother, for was there not mention of 'great suits at law'?"

Lady Margaret responded only, "Oh, dear!" and they both laughed.

❧

Sometimes Anne would assist her mother with this work, but the beauty of the place constantly called out to her and when she felt in need of a break, she would wander off with Mary to explore further.

"Wur'sta gaan? Doos'ta ken these paats, m'laady?" a groom enquired, when she requested horses for herself and her gentlewoman. The dialect was like a foreign language and she asked the groom to repeat what he had said. As he did so it began to sound familiar, resembling the speech of her father and uncle, particularly when they were addressing each other, and she found that she could make sense of it. She would soon be fluent in Westmorlandish, she smiled to herself, but for her bemused companion it might take longer. She reassured the groom that they would not go out of sight of the castle on its prominence, but he insisted on accompanying them, for their safety, and his local knowledge proved useful in their explorations. Each excursion into the surrounding area brought new treasures to Anne's mind and she delighted in the gentle pace and the harmony of nature and people. It reminded her of the Bible quotes she had pinned to her bed-hangings since she was a girl, especially Psalm 104:

"Man goeth forth unto his work and to his labour until the evening. O Lord, how manifold are thy works! In wisdom hast thou made them all; the earth is full of thy riches."

The weeks at Appleby passed swiftly and much was gained by Lady Margaret's searches and by the contacts they made with local people. It was clear that the estates had been neglected in Earl George's time; methods had become slack and the landlord was known to neither tenants nor officers. Often rents had gone unpaid, and some of the tenant farmers were surly about a new landlord who would soon be living amongst them and possibly curtailing their freedoms. Anne noticed how her mother addressed them all, even the most churlish ones, with firm respect, and how many of them responded politely to her soothing approach. They're not used to being treated with humanity, she reflected.

CHAPTER EIGHT
1607-8

As autumn advanced and the days shortened, Lady Margaret decided that her searches at Appleby Castle had yielded sufficient evidence in favour of Anne's claim to allow them to move on to Brougham. Anne was sad to leave Appleby, where she had felt such a sense of belonging, but looked forward to exploring another part of Westmorland and of the valley called Eden.

Brougham stood on the side of the River Eamont, a tributary of the Eden, which flowed placidly between grassy banks, so different from the hustling Eden at Appleby. They were shown the room above the gatehouse where Anne's father had been born; Margaret decided to take this as her own chamber for the duration of their visit. The red sandstone castle seemed at once more ancient and homelier than Appleby. Anne had no difficulty in imagining her mother settling here for her dowager years in tranquil contemplation of the river and the hills, or riding through the surrounding forests, which were singing now with autumnal colour harmonies. When Anne discovered the tiny oratory high in the south east corner of the gatehouse, she was so charmed that she rose at first light every morning to pray there and to see the sun rise.

❦

Christmas was a jolly time at Brougham. The household, delighted to have Lady Margaret and Lady Anne in residence, celebrated with the traditional twelve days of merriment and feasting. A troupe of jugglers gave performances in the great court until they became too drunk to catch their props and had a near-accident involving knives. Bonfires were lit and sheep and cattle roasted on the spit, with roast swan as the centrepiece of the Twelfth Night feast.

There was further celebration three weeks later, for Anne's

eighteenth birthday. The sons and daughters of local nobility and gentlefolk were invited to share the occasion. Once the guest-list had been completed, Anne sat near the window watching some children daring each other to slide on the ice at the edge of the river. She laughed as the tallest boy, who had been urging the smaller ones to try, slipped and tumbled with his legs in the air, then tried to look nonchalant as he struggled to stand up again. She sent Millie to take some roast chestnuts down to them, recalling an occasion at Hampton Court in the time of the Old Queen when she had enjoyed gathering round a brazier with friends after a game of curling and munching the hot nuts. Frances was there, she remembered, and Richard was amusing them by tossing nuts into the air and catching them in his open mouth. She smiled at the memory and wished they could both have come to her celebration tomorrow. London seemed very far away.

She shone like a lantern attracting moths, with all the young people gathering round her and admiring her gold-embroidered sleeves, her pale skin and her courtly dancing. She was not accustomed to being at the centre of attention; at court she was one of many beautiful young women who were all dressed in the latest fashions and costly jewellery. But here, where she was the daughter of the most powerful land-owning family, she was the one holding court and being treated like royalty. It was a heady feeling and she wished Richard could have seen her success in these Clifford lands. None could have guessed that her heart was aching.

❦

"The best gift I received on my birthday was the snow that fell overnight, so that I woke to a scene of white magic!" she declared to her Howard relations when the Clifford ladies visited them at Naworth Castle in Cumberland about a month later. Anne and Lady Margaret were by this time on their way back to London but had chosen to travel north first, in order to see the Howards and admire the splendid new residence that they had created within their castle. The journey was much discussed and Anne observed,

"I think it very strange that this is the first time I was ever in the county of Cumberland, for my parents were the Earl and Countess of Cumberland, as were my grandparents and great-grandparents before them!"

"Yes indeed and the links between our families also go back to those times," ventured nineteen-year-old Francis Howard, speaking fast and nervously. "We have, I believe, a common ancestor in our great-grandfather, William Lord Dacres, who is buried in Carlisle Cathedral. I hope our county is not a disappointment to you, Lady Anne?"

"No, indeed not, Cousin Francis. I think it a very beautiful county, perhaps second only to Westmorland," Anne said, "But I admit to having spent a very little time, a few days only, in Cumberland, compared with many weeks in my beloved Westmorland."

Francis Howard spluttered and Lady Margaret gave Anne her "Apologise now" look, but Anne was unabashed, laying her hand reassuringly on the young man's arm.

"I mean only to say that Westmorland has stolen my heart so completely that nowhere can compare with it, Coz, . . . not that there is any criticism whatsoever to be made of Cumberland, which is also beautiful, as I have observed on our journey here."

"Westmorland is the land of your inheritance, so it is little wonder that you see it in that way," interjected Francis's father, Lord William, and they continued to discuss the claim, the entail and the research that Lady Margaret had undertaken. Lord Howard remembered some papers that might be useful and took her off to his well-stocked library to search for them. Anne and Francis strolled in the cliff-top garden looking down to the river below, reminiscent of Appleby but, she concluded privately, nowhere as fine.

❦

The journey south was slow after the winter snows and rains; the roads were mired and the landscape of the high moors was bleak, windswept, dark and desolate. Lady Margaret told Anne and the servants that she intended to break their journey at Skipton Castle, Anne's birthplace, for a few days of rest for themselves and for the horses to recuperate their strength. She wished to make some preliminary searches in the muniments room there as well, feeling confident that there would be much of relevance to Anne's claim in the Cliffords' Skipton archives. Beyond that, she said, she hoped the journey would become less arduous for everyone as they made their way back to London.

They clattered up Skipton's main street, with its market and shops, towards the Castle. Then the church came into sight on their left, the site of Earl George's tomb, but Anne hardly had time to think about this before the massive watchtower was looming over them, flanked by its stolid companion drum towers. The portcullis was closed. The postilion sounded his horn and shouted for attention, then stepped down to hammer on the iron bars. There was no response. He banged and shouted again,

"In the name of the Lady Margaret, Dowager Countess of Cumberland, and the Lady Anne Clifford, open up!"

A groom joined him and they continued beating and shouting until a guard slowly appeared, stretched, scratched his groin, and then sauntered towards the grill. Anne and Lady Margaret were astounded at this reception. The postilion repeated;

"Wake up, you guffin! Open up this 'cullis and give my ladies entry!"

The guard stood with feet apart and stared insolently through the bars. He hawked and spat on the ground, hands on hips, but made no move to order the portcullis raised. He was joined by a second slovenly keeper, who swore at the postilion and made a rude gesture. At this, Lady Margaret and Anne began to feel very nervous and reached for each other's hands, at a loss to understand this extraordinary behaviour.

"By these hilts!" the groom said, returning the gesture, 'Twill be the worse for you when your Lord hears of your treatment of his kinswomen."

"Rot on, sire! Our orders to exclude these women come

straight from Lord Francis, who denies them entry for that they take suit against him. Away with you!" and he turned his back and walked away.

There was nothing to be done. After a hurried consultation with the coachman, Lady Margaret directed him to turn around and take the road to Beamsley. She would show her daughter the almshouses she had begun building for poor women of the parish. Then they would surely be able to take shelter nearby for a few days with Mr Clapham, an old friend who had helped with their foundation. She sent a servant to ride ahead to his manor house and warn Mr Clapham of their approach.

"Welcome dear ladies, welcome indeed!" Mr Clapham beamed, "This is a great honour and an even greater pleasure! I am delighted to see you both, come in, come in!" He stepped back, opening his arms wide in greeting. They followed his portly form into a warm and comfortable drawing room.

"Pray be seated Lady Margaret, Lady Anne. You must be cold and tired. Sit here beside the fire while I set the servants to preparing food for you. I'll return with some mulled wine in a moment." He went off, chuckling "Well, well, well!"

Later, after they had eaten, were warm and had recovered from their ordeal, he said,

"Forgive me, Lady Margaret, but your messenger told me when he arrived that you'd been unable to gain entry to Skipton Castle. Of course I'm delighted to have this opportunity to entertain you and I sincerely hope you will remain with me for many days, but may I ask how you were prevented from lodging there? Wasn't that very same castle your birthplace, Lady Anne?"

"Yes," replied Anne, "I was born there, but, as I left it when I was but a few weeks old and had never returned, I was very much looking forward to seeing it for – almost – the first time!"

Lady Margaret nodded.

"I had many times promised my daughter that we would visit

that noble place," she said, "Especially since my deceased lord, her father, lies buried in the church hard by. This time I had the added ambition of searching the castle's Clifford archives for evidence of the history of the inheritance, to support our claim that Lord George's will was illegal and that the entail applies."

"I see," nodded Mr Clapham, "And what transpired when you reached the castle gates?"

Lady Margaret explained what had happened and Anne expanded on some of the details.

"In the end there was no alternative but to leave," Margaret concluded.

"Surely he had no authority to be rude to you, or to refuse to welcome you to the castle?" asked Mr Clapham.

"He indicated that he was acting on the orders of Earl Francis," Lady Margaret said. "And that our legal challenge to the will was the reason for their refusal. My searches were to be barred. So, there was nothing we could do and my first thought was to come and seek refuge with you, dear Mr Clapham. But I am sorry that we were not able to give you more notice of our arrival."

"Pray think no more of that, dear ladies. I'm shocked that you have been treated thus, and by your kinsman! It is unforgivable. I repeat that you are welcome to stay here for as long as you wish. It will be my greatest pleasure and honour to offer you all the hospitality at my disposal."

They spent a few days with Mr Clapham, although he would have had them stay longer, but London was still many days' journey away and the time was approaching when Lady Margaret's lawyer and Mr Kniveton must present the first petition of Anne's inheritance claim to the Court of Ward.

CHAPTER NINE
1608–9

After their return to London, Margaret and Anne visited the Howards again, at Norfolk House, their London residence. As soon as the coach drew into the courtyard Anne recognised the Dorset arms on a shiny blue coach standing nearby. Her heart began to beat so loudly that she half expected her mother to hear it.

When they entered the drawing chamber, Richard Sackville hurried towards them.

"All hail, Lady Margaret, Lady Anne! Welcome back," Richard said. He bowed ceremoniously and kissed Margaret's hand, then turned to Anne. "You have been many months away. What thought you of those northern lands when you finally saw them?"

"Oh, they are beautiful!" Anne said, surprised and pleased that he remembered where she had been, blushing despite herself. "You have never seen such clear rivers or bluer mountains. I am certain you would have been as impressed as I was, Lord Buckhurst! Westmorland is a place like no other and the valley of the River Eden is a veritable Paradise! I loved it at first sight!" Her words came pouring out, as though he had snipped the corner off a sack full of seeds. Resisting this deluge, Richard glanced round the room and abruptly changed the subject.

"I believe we are both related to the Howards! My mother is a member of that great family; Lord William Howard is my uncle. I am told that you also have Howard relations – is that so?"

"Yes, my mother and I visited Lord William at Naworth when we were in the north. I learned there that my great grandfather was William, Lord Dacre; his daughter Elizabeth became the wife of an earlier Lord William Howard, and his daughter Anne was my father's mother," Anne said.

"So, the Cliffords and the Howards have been connected for

generations. I believe there are so many Howards all over the country, everyone must be related through them!" Then he cupped her elbow and drew her away from the group.

"It sounds as though you were reluctant to come back," he said quietly, "But I am happy that you did. And it seems there may be an even closer connection between our families soon, for I believe there have been diplomatic approaches made between your family and mine."

"Be assured, I returned willingly. I hope the negotiations have been to your liking?" Anne said.

"I believe we shall see eye to eye in this, as in most other things," Richard said, searching her face. "Seeing you again gives me renewed confidence that the treaty will be a victory for both sides. Are you of a similar mind?"

"Oh, yes," Anne said, smiling with relief. Richard took her hand and kissed it and they returned to rejoin the company.

Anne was relieved that the understanding had finally been acknowledged, but she had spent so long thinking only of Richard and worrying about whether the match would ever come about, that she had given no thought at all to other possible suitors. Over the next days she realised the enormity of the decision; she began to doubt herself and wonder whether she had made a wise choice.

Eighteen now, she was the focus of interest for more than one young courtier and she knew that the final decision could not be far away. There was the King's odious favourite, Robert Carr, whom she had discounted but who still made passes at her whenever he could. Only the other day he had pointed at her on her way to the Queen's court and declared to his companion that she was his destiny. She shuddered. There was also young William Cavendish, another northerner and wealthy heir to the Earl of Devonshire; he had grown up at Chatsworth and was a youth who enjoyed all the pleasures of aristocratic life. His name had sometimes been mentioned in the same breath as hers, but they rarely saw each other and had little in common. And then there was Richard; but was her feeling for him a good basis on which to choose a husband? The responsibility for making the decision weighed heavily and she was not confident that she was wise enough, or experienced enough, to make the best choice.

Nevertheless, her thoughts often converged on Richard Sackville and hearing his name spoken sparked a frisson through her body that was far from unpleasant. He would be taking part in all the Christmas celebrations and would certainly be the best-dressed of all the young men vying for attention at Court, even though his family was still in mourning for his grandfather; Thomas, the Lord High Treasurer, had died suddenly at a meeting in the King's council chamber earlier in the year, making Richard's father the second Earl of Dorset.

Anne met her friend Alethea Talbot, who had been married for two years now, in a dressing room within the sprawling Palace of Whitehall. They were trying to have a conversation, the way young women do, but there was so much buzz and bustle that they were finding it hard to hear one another. Such noisy excitement was natural when a bevy of young noblewomen, and their maids, had assembled for the first time to begin rehearsing a masque for the Christmas celebrations at the Court of King James and Queen Anne. The Queen loved masqueing, as Richard had remarked at Grafton nearly four years ago, and this year she had engaged Ben Jonson as writer and Inigo Jones as designer of the scenery and costumes for the '*Masque of Beauty*'.

"I hope Master Jones won't make me look like the front of a palace!" Alethea shrieked at the top of her voice. Anne giggled and added, "Nor the back of a church!" She wished it was quieter and that they could have a more private conversation. She was longing to ask Alethea about married life.

"Alethea, there is something I'd like to talk to you about. Would you be able to stay behind for a short time when the rehearsal is over?"

"Of course. It has been long since we have chattered as we used to do," her friend replied.

They found an alcove and huddled together conspiratorially. Alethea raised an enquiring eyebrow and Anne, after a slight hesitation, declared,

"I fear that I am being very indecisive about an important matter and I need your advice."

Alethea nodded. "You speak of marriage?" she said. Anne laughed with relief at her friend's perceptiveness.

"It is not so strange that I should understand your problem!" Alethea said. "Every unmarried girl over fifteen has the same worry and the whole Court is talking about you — eighteen and still a maid! They link your name with every young man who glances in your direction. Why, only this morning I overheard Lady Roos declare that she knew, for a certain fact, that your betrothal to Robert Carr was about to be announced and she had seen the two of you giving each other secret glances over dinner at Lady Knolys's the other day. So what are you undecided about?"

"My parents' marriage was not decided by them; my mother's father was guardian to my father and decided that they should be married. It was not what either of them wanted and it ended in the disaster of their separation. This creates two problems for me! The first is that I wish to avoid entering into a marriage which might turn out to be as disagreeable as theirs. And the second is that, because of their experience, my mother insists that I must approve any match before it goes ahead. But, Alethea, I don't feel competent to make such a decision! My mother has so much more experience and wisdom than I do in these things; surely she would be a better judge than me about who is a suitable husband?"

"So is the rumour true, Anne? Are you to be betrothed to Robert Carr?" Alethea asked.

"Oh, no!" Anne said. "I have no inclination whatsoever in that particular direction, believe me, Alethea! My mother and I have both ruled him out. But please tell me about married life and what to look for in a husband, for I feel sorely lacking in the wisdom needed to make the decision."

Alethea hesitated. Anne could see that she was weighing up what to say and how to begin, so urged her on,

"Dear Alethea, please don't hold back, I need your knowledge and wifely wisdom!"

"Very well, I shall try to give you the kind of advice that might have been helpful to me. I am lucky that my lord, Thomas, and I are well matched, but it might not have been so. We hardly knew each other before we were wed, but my parents chose well for me. I can see that you feel the burden of the responsibility you must bear for the decision." She drew a deep breath and thought for a moment, her face serious.

"The first thing I would say," she continued, "Is that friendship between you and your lord, and an interest in the same kind of things, is important, so that you can share those parts of your life together, not just the nights. Thomas and I love to study classical times and have an interest in the sculptures to be found in ancient places like Rome, so we are brought together by such discourse and travel. And in doing this I feel I am almost my lord's equal, for my knowledge is equal to his and my opinion can sometimes sway him, as his does me."

"Dear Alethea, I think that must be excellent advice! It helps me to see more clearly which direction I should take," Anne said, thinking of the interest both she and Richard Sackville had in literature and philosophy.

"There are also many other things that make a difference, I think," Alethea said, smiling at her friend. "Your wifely duties must be performed, but if you can come to delight in them your burden will be so much lighter. If you thrill to your lord's touch, if you can imagine without repulsion his eyes and hands all over your body, then producing an heir for his great family becomes a pleasure to you and a source of happiness for you both in wedlock.

"Beside these two things there are others, but perhaps of lesser significance. If you have respect for each other's friends and family there is great comfort in their society – and shared gossip can be very diverting! I believe that it is also of great benefit if you can develop sides of yourself that are beyond the influence of your lord, such that the time you spend away from him is as pleasant to you as time in his company. I find the hours or days when my lord is not with me can seem interminable unless I can immerse myself in my own interests." She hesitated, then said, "If you can achieve all this, you will have a perfect marriage!"

"I am so grateful for your advice, Alethea!" Anne said, her doubts dispelled. "How can I thank you enough? I shall bear in mind all that you have told me and hope to make this decision with greater ease and confidence because of it. I shall not look for a perfect marriage, but hope to achieve one that is…well… more good than bad."

"Don't forget that, although she is not making the final decision for you, your mother would never allow an unwise match," Alethea added as an afterthought, "And good luck!"

Anne gave no more thought to William Cavendish or Robert Carr.

The '*Masque of Beauty*' was so lavish that it took a long time to prepare and was not performed until 14th January, rather than during the twelve days of Christmas. But it was a success. The scenes and machinery created special effects on the stage; the magnificent representation of an island floating on calm water at night, with the moon arriving there in a silver chariot drawn by virgins, brought a gasp from the audience. There were beautiful costumes, graceful dances and melodious songs and Anne threw herself into her part with all her energy and enthusiasm, loving her exotic green and silver costume and thrilled to be with her friends at the centre of a court event in which the Queen herself took part.

There were two performances, attended by Anne's mother, her Cousin Frances and almost everyone else she knew, but she still missed Aunt Warwick and wished she was among the crowd. The King was there for the first presentation, but it wasn't the King's eyes that she could feel on her; even with her back turned she was aware that Robert Carr's gaze followed her like a hound at the chase, never leaving her for a moment. He was seated close to the King, as usual. Not far from them she saw Richard Sackville and young Prince Henry, both wearing square lace collars with starched petals and blue satin doublets with tight sleeves, the most fashionable and luxurious clothes of the moment with many jewels and ornaments about them. She wrenched herself back to the masque just in time to begin the next dance, but her heart continued to beat like a herald's drum for as long as she remained on the stage.

A few months later Anne was involved in another masque, the '*Masque of Queens*', in which she was chosen to play Queen Berenice of Egypt. Inigo Jones explained her part to her while he was fitting her costume:

"Berenice was famous for the beauty of her hair, Lady Anne, and thus you came immediately to mind when I considered this part, because you also are known for your luxuriant hair. But we can't show your hair, because Berenice's hair was sacrificed as an offering to the gods," he said, as he placed a pointed dome like a helmet, with a large feathered plume, on her head. "Therefore, I have designed this extravagant head-dress to conceal your hair."

The dress to accompany the headdress was a complicated affair of skirts, sleeves and a cloak secured with a large jewelled clasp on one shoulder. The bodice was a transparent film of gossamer silk which reached from neck to waist but concealed nothing. Mr Jones expressed himself very satisfied with the result. Anne's breasts, just past her nineteenth birthday, were now those of a grown woman and she had no hesitation in consenting, along with some of her other unmarried friends, to this costume arrangement for the masque.

The day after the second performance of the '*Masque of Queens*', Lady Margaret took the unusual step of coming into her daughter's chamber. Anne was surprised and wondered what had brought her there, but Lady Margaret seemed in no hurry to explain. She spent some time reading and admiring the notes and quotations which Anne had, since childhood, been in the habit of pinning all over the hangings of her bed so that she was reminded of them every day. Many of them she already knew by heart and would be able to quote for the rest of her life.

"I see you are fond of the Holy Scriptures as well as of poetry," Lady Margaret said approvingly, reading aloud: "'*I lift up mine eyes unto the hills, whence cometh my strength*'. That will be my case shortly, when I take up my jointure residence in Westmorland! And what's this, 'Preserve Your Loyalty, Defend Your Rights', where does this originate?"

"I don't know," Anne said, shaking her head. "But I thought it so well-expressed that I've adopted it as my motto!"

Lady Margaret smiled and sat down.

"Perhaps now is a good time to defend your rights," she said, finally coming to the point. "I have received a message from the King's favourite, Robert Carr. He believes he will soon be given an earldom by the King and he wishes to marry you. When we have spoken of him in the past you have expressed no liking for him, but he is most pressing about it, so I came to seek your view. Tell me if you have had a change of heart, for it is your right to decide yea or nay."

"My view has not changed, dear lady mother. Robert Carr has no place in my heart and I have no wish to marry him."

"That settles the matter then. I shall send back a message immediately and we'll not speak further of it." To Anne's relief, Robert Carr was thus dismissed as her suitor.

The very next day Lady Margaret requested Anne to come to her chamber. When she entered the stately room with its tall arched windows, her mother was smiling and wasted no time in declaring,

"It seems to be the season for marriage proposals! I have just heard from Lord Buckhurst, who informs me that his father is mortally ill. He wishes his marriage to you to be sealed immediately as there is a danger that, at nineteen, he will be made a ward of court if his father dies whilst he is yet unmarried. What do you say?"

"I shall think myself fortunate to become his wife," Anne said breathlessly after a brief pause, adding silently ". . . at last!" and feeling relief and excitement flood in waves through her body.

"Very well, we shall proceed today if that is your wish and you're certain of it. I'll send for Lord Buckhurst. The marriage will be irregular because no banns have been read, but you can seek absolution later from the Bishop's Court and have it recognised by the Church."

Responding to Anne's anxious look Margaret added,

"We can't wait for banns, my dear, but we can take some comfort from the fact that my chamber here was formerly the chapel of the Augustine Friars. We shall trust that God will look kindly upon your vows and bless your marriage." She patted Anne's hand.

"Yes . . . yes . . ." Anne stammered, her mind whirling with this sudden realisation of the dreams she had cherished for years. She felt as though nothing could penetrate the tumult in her mind. There was only just time to change into her rich court dress and have her long hair coiled up and decorated with pearls and gold wires by her ladies before Richard arrived. He was very finely dressed and came into the chamber looking confident and every inch the courtier with embroidered silk hose, large shoe rosettes, lace cuffs and collar and a fashionable black ear-string. She was glad that she had made as much effort as she could on this day. He removed his swirling cloak and gloves, handed them to the footman and bowed low to her mother and to her, saying

"I wish you a very good day, my ladies, and I hope that my haste hasn't caused you inconvenience or discomfiture. My sincerity cannot be doubted, I trust, for our families have spoken of this alliance for some time, and the hour is come to seal it."

Lady Margaret welcomed him and added, "We're glad to conclude this union of our families today, Lord Buckhurst, and pray that the Earl of Dorset will make a speedy return to good health."

"May God hear your prayer, my lady."

He smiled sideways at Anne, suddenly looking shyer than she had ever seen him before, taking her trembling hand to place a small gold ring on her finger while they made their vows.

By the end of the day Anne Clifford, who had awoken thinking that this was a day like any other, had become Lady Buckhurst, wife of Richard Sackville, Lord Buckhurst. There was little by way of celebration, because of the suddenness of the decision and the precarious health of Richard's father. And this title was hers for barely forty-eight hours; on the death of Richard's father two days later they became the Third Earl and Countess of Dorset. Anne remained at her mother's house for a while after the marriage and the funeral of the Second Earl.

Richard inherited vast estates in Kent and Sussex and, once his mother had moved to her dower house, Anne became the mistress of Dorset House on Fleet Street in London and Knole House in Kent, one of the greatest country houses in the land. This was the mansion that had once belonged to Henry VIII, which Richard's grandfather, Thomas Sackville, the First Earl, had extended and aggrandized with the intention of hosting the King and Queen. He had even ensured that the joiners and carpenters left witch-marks on the joists beneath the floorboards, to reassure the superstitious King that witches would be prevented from coming down the chimneys. The royal visit had never happened though, because of the sudden death of Earl Thomas.

Anne often thought about Alethea's advice and felt herself lucky indeed to have married her friend. They had many interests in common and it was a relief to be able to spend time together in public and in private, doing what they enjoyed, without being subjected to prattling gossip and teasing voices. When they attended Court and visited friends, their pride in each other was evident and the looks and touches they exchanged revealed more than they realised about their increasing intimacy. This gave rise to some envious comments about the surprisingly harmonious outcome of such a hasty union. One diarist made a remark along the lines of "marry in haste, repent at leisure", which they both found very amusing; Anne's thoughts turned to the three years of agonized waiting that, for her, had preceded the hurried nuptials.

❦

She thrilled to Richard's touch more and more. She contemplated Alethea's words when he was absent, imagining his hands exploring every crevice, mound and peak of her body and re-experiencing her body's response to his touch. When she and Richard visited Alethea and Thomas, Alethea took her to see their basement collection of ancient sculptures. The sensuous semi-naked forms affected Anne in a way which would not have been possible before her marriage and prompted her to divulge more to Alethea while they were alone together than she would normally have done.

"Dear Alethea, I am constantly grateful to you for sharing with me your thoughts concerning marriage. I have found them so true and so reassuring, especially in dispelling any apprehensions I may have had about whether our intimacies were something to endure or to enjoy!"

Alethea laughed,

"I am truly delighted that you understood my meaning so well, and that it helped you in that way, dear friend. I find I must entirely believe that this woman's body I have been given is not simply a vessel to be filled and emptied, but a fine instrument to be played by my lord for the pleasure of us both!"

"I thank you for your wisdom. I cannot say more!" Anne said in a fit of giggles.

There was only one flaw in her joy at this time; the presence of her brother-in-law, Edward Sackville. He was a year younger than her husband and carried none of Richard's responsibilities. Proximity to him revived the memory of his threatening words at Grafton years ago. His behaviour towards her now, as his new sister-in-law, was no more welcoming; he made constant efforts to monopolise Richard's company and entice him away from her to go gambling and carousing. He was a hot-headed young man who was frequently in trouble and she often found his behaviour reprehensible. After killing a Scottish nobleman in a duel in the Netherlands he had to avoid the King (who was trying to stamp out duelling among his courtiers) and spend months abroad to evade prison. Edward sometimes looked at her in a way she found difficult to interpret, and in Richard's presence he had a teasing manner towards her which was deliberately annoying. Richard nevertheless sang his praises and excused his excesses, asking her to be patient with him so soon after the deaths of their grandfather and their father. Anne still had doubts, which she did her best to conceal, only privately concluding that Edward Sackville would certainly have dissuaded Richard from this marriage had it not been for the haste with which it was concluded.

❦

At the end of the year there was sorrow, as Lady Margaret prepared to leave London to take up her jointure in Westmorland.

"Dear lady mother, why must you go so far away?" Anne asked. "You could remain at Austin Friars, or Sutton, or Chenies, and visit your lands in the north from time to time. Would you not prefer to be close to us and other members of your family?"

"I can't remain here, Anne, whilst my tenants toil to pay their rents to me," Lady Margaret said. "You saw during our journey how neglected some of the lands and buildings are and how resentful of their absent lords the people have become. I must go and live among them, help them to repair the neglect of my lord's time and earn their respect and their dues. We'll write to each other and exchange news constantly and make visits when we can, be assured. And now you have a young husband on whom to depend, instead of this old woman!"

"I hope your words will prove true," Anne said. "I shall be so impatient to see you, even the minute you depart. I cannot imagine life without your constant presence and your wisdom, which I have always valued and depended upon. Pray return soon my lady."

They held each other close for a long time before Anne could bear to let her mother climb into the coach with Millie. Her eyes filled with tears as she watched it draw slowly away as if reluctant to go.

CHAPTER TEN
1610-11

The next few months were a time of immense happiness for Anne and, she believed, for Richard too. They spent time at court and in the company of friends, shared ideas about literature and philosophy and enjoyed entertainments as they had always done. Whilst Richard gambled extravagantly on cock-fighting and tilting competitions with Prince Henry and the King, Anne played cards and gossiped with Susan, Alethea and other young wives around the Queen. Away from the throng she and Richard grew close in ways which had not been possible before, delighting in learning how to give each other pleasure; Richard led the way in this, but Anne, mindful of Alethea's advice, followed eagerly and with diminishing restraint.

Plans were being laid for the investiture of Henry as Prince of Wales. Anne's old tutor, Samuel Daniel, was commissioned to write a masque which he titled 'Tethys' Festival' and Anne was cast as a River Nymph representing the River Aire, which flowed past the place of her birth – that same Skipton Castle from which she and her mother had been barred by her uncle, Francis Clifford. She was thrilled to be performing once more in the Queen's masque, and this time took great pleasure in the eyes that followed her; the eyes of Richard Sackville.

❧

Anne and Richard were often drawn to the company of writers and students, and Anne praised Richard for his support of both scholars and soldiers. They met a poet, Anthony Stafford, who was beginning to be known for his unusual devotional works. They engaged in several conversations with him, which reminded Anne of the discussions between herself, her mother and Aemilia Lanyer at Cookham. Stafford was disdainful of women, but Anne, bolstered by Dorset's supportive presence, challenged him on this and put up a mettlesome defence of her sex.

"Are you not persuaded, Lady Anne, that the Bible must lead us to conclude that woman is a weak vessel, one easily misled by Satan's wiles?" Stafford asked.

"Indeed I am not, Master Stafford, for are there not many examples in the Bible of, on the one hand, strong and virtuous women and equally, on the other, weak men who are led astray?" Anne spoke calmly, her face serious.

"That is an interesting approach, Lady Anne. Can you put forward examples to support your contention?" Stafford said, while Richard tossed Anne an encouraging nod.

"Yes, I can," Anne said, "I think of Hannah, who gave up her cherished son to God's service, and I suggest Esther also, who risked her husband's wrath to save her people from slaughter. Surely these cannot be called 'weak vessels'?"

Stafford removed his cap, scratched his head with the long middle finger of his left hand and replaced the soft hat at a crooked angle.

"Very well," he said, "But where are the weak men with whom you wish to add weight to your argument?"

"Oh, there are some, Master Stafford, even though the Bible was written by men and therefore we may expect bias!" Anne responded. "I cite David, who was one of the bravest warriors but nevertheless succumbed to a moment of weakness and temptation which cost his soul dear. Also Solomon; he was tempted by riches and wealth to think himself greater than the Lord God. Even Peter, who was chastised by Paul for hypocrisy towards the gentiles, could be seen as one misled by vanity."

"I see that you are not persuaded to my view that woman is a weak vessel, Lady Anne, and you yourself show me, by your arguments and your skill in debating them, that you are a lustrous example of a woman who is far from weak. But I still cling to my thesis that man is better able to resist temptation than is woman."

"Master Stafford, how can you have it both ways?" Anne

declared, leaning forward to confront him directly, "If man is strong and steadfast in the face of evil, how can you explain the actions of men such as Adam and Samson, who gave in so cravenly to women when they ought to have been protecting their 'weaker' sisters from temptation?"

Stafford's face registered surprise and bewilderment. He looked to Richard for a sign of support, but Richard was delighted by his wife's mastery of this argument and his enchanted gaze was fixed on her animated face. Stafford stood, bowed deeply and said,

"My lady, I am astonished! You make me re-assess my opinion of your sex and I honour you as I have never before honoured woman."

They enjoyed several such lively discussions with Stafford. A later one centred on his increasing veneration of the Virgin Mary, whom they agreed was the Mother of God and free of sin. But when he began to speak of her as one who could intercede with God on man's behalf, as though she was herself a divine being rather than human, they felt his views were becoming too extreme and then the friendship cooled.

Richard and Anne were talking, over a breakfast of onions with honey and buttered eggs, about the similarities and differences in their education. Anne mentioned her father's embargo on foreign languages as being a handicap placed on her that did not apply to her husband.

"No, you are right, I have not suffered that obstacle," said Richard. "Quite the opposite; my grandmother has asked me to spend time in some of the countries nearest to our shores, to become more familiar with their languages and customs. And Edward is always admonishing me that I should go to France; he loves all things French."

Anne thought little of these remarks, despite the inclusion of her brother-in-law's name. It didn't cross her mind that Richard would consider forsaking her company for foreign parts so soon after their marriage. However, the subject came up again later.

"My grandmother has said that when I travel to the Low Countries and France she will give me introductions to some of the great houses of her acquaintance there," was Richard's casual statement. It brought the subject into stark relief.

Anne froze, then turned to look at him and responded with a sense of panic;

"What do you mean, my lord? What is this ambition, of which I know nothing?"

"Of course you know about it!" Richard said. "I told you that I had made promise to my lady grandmother that I would travel to complete my education."

"Have you not forgotten something?" Anne said.

"What have I forgotten? What do you mean?" Richard said.

"It seems that you have forgotten that you are now married," Anne said, "And that I, your wife, might have something to say about you going afar for your 'education'! Do I count for nothing beside your grandmother?"

"Pray, my lady, do not take on so!" Richard said. "This is a promise I made to my grandmother before we were wed and she has said that she still wishes to hold me to it, so I cannot refuse."

"And when do you intend to undertake this journey?" Anne asked. "How long will you be away?"

"I shall leave next spring when the weather is clement for sailing." Richard said. "I suppose the tour will take about a year."

Anne was shaken, but there was no point in any further argument; the plan was laid and it was clear that any objection would be brushed aside.

Richard was attentive and affectionate as usual during the coming weeks and she persuaded herself that he had no choice and meant no harm to her. He even said once or twice that he didn't want to leave her and would stay if he could, but his anticipation increased as the time approached and he couldn't hide his excitement.

She resolved to wish him well and see him off with a buss and a smile when the time came.

Before the time of Richard's departure, another shocking event of an entirely different nature befell her. A messenger arrived from Anthony Stafford, bringing a copy of his latest book, the second volume of 'Stafford's Niobe', which he had dedicated to her. Partly irritated and partly flattered, she sat down to read the dedication and flick through the book. She sent for Christopher Marsh, her steward and secretary.

"Mr Marsh, I beg you read this and tell me your thoughts without delay," she said as she pushed the book across the table towards him. Marsh had never seen his young mistress so tight-lipped and lost no time in fulfilling her request. He returned within the day, flinging the book down on to the table and asking permission to speak his mind.

"My lady, you asked for my thoughts on that which is written here and I would share them with you. I fear that the author of this work has over-stepped propriety in the dedication to your ladyship. But I hesitate to say more until I hear your reason for requesting my comments."

"Thank you, Mr Marsh." Anne said. "You have confirmed my own impression that the dedication could be perceived as improper, even scandalous, being so overwrought and unseemly in its exaggeration. '. . . *incomparable qualities of mind and body*' indeed! I have never seen such a paean of glorification applied to the likes of me and it does not sit well with me. I am not the Old Queen, to be praised to the rafters for political advantage! If this is widely published there is no knowing what gossip will make of it and I cannot have my reputation so besmirched.

"I'm concerned also about the ideas expressed in the book, though I have not had time to study it closely and have but glanced briefly at one or two pages. Is it fitting that my name be linked with the content of this book? My lord and I were once close with Stafford, but we had reservations about the direction of his thinking the last time we spoke with him and we have not kept company with him since. Pray, what can be done?" Anne's dark eyes spoke eloquently of dismay and apprehension.

"Leave it to me, my lady," Marsh said. "I certainly agree that the dedication must not stand. I did not find the content of the book, as far as I could ascertain it, to be as unacceptable as you suggest, but I will speak to those responsible and make it clear that this grovelling flattery is not to survive in any form or with any link to your name. If the dedication and your name are removed, with your permission, then the content is of no further consequence to you. Be assured, I shall move with all speed and you shall not be embarrassed or seen as complicit."

"Thank you, Mr Marsh. I am most grateful for your calm judgment."

She showed the offending tract to Richard later and told him of the steps she had taken to deal with it, hoping that he would recognise that she was innocent of any action likely to provoke it.

"Dear heart, my anger is all for Stafford," Richard said. "He has repaid our friendship and support like a snake in the grass and you are deserving of no criticism whatsoever. I am proud of the way you have dealt with the matter so speedily, and you can be assured that Marsh will pursue it to such great effect that no-one else will ever read that fawning, unctuous dedication."

Two anxious days later, Anne received an abject snivel of apology from Stafford, pleading that he had desired only to repay the kindness and friendship he had been so fortunate to receive from her and Lord Dorset, and to recognise her pre-eminence as an exemplar of her sex, an outstanding female sage... etc, etc. He promised to ensure that no further copies would bear the dedication and that it would be removed from the few copies already printed.

Anne showed the letter to Dorset and to Marsh and then threw it into the back of the fire, relieved that that was the end of the matter.

❧

Happy as she was to have had Richard's support in the Stafford affair, Anne was struggling inwardly with the looming prospect of his travels abroad. She recognised sadness in her mind because she was not with child, as she had thought she would be by now; if she had been, she thought, he surely would not have left her? She would not attend court without her husband, so would remain alone at Knole, where she felt isolated and powerless. As the day of his departure approached, she recalled Alethea's advice and tried to think of interests of her own and ways to occupy the days, weeks, months that stretched ahead.

She was, in name at least, mistress of Knole, and yet she had little involvement in the running of the house or the supervision of the servants. There were few chances to exercise those skills of good housekeeping instilled by her mother throughout her childhood, and she realised that Richard's absence might give her that opportunity. She mentioned this ambition to him one afternoon while dinner was being served, thinking that she could have improved the meal with some ideas of her own, but Richard dismissed her suggestion impatiently;

"Oh no, there is no need or place for you to interfere in matters of housekeeping or kitchen work. Edward Legge, my Steward, has been in charge of running this house for years and he knows exactly how it all works and what is to be done. Pray leave him to it – I would not have his nose put out of joint by your meddling!"

The size and grandeur of Knole overwhelmed her, but Anne had to admit that the great house ran smoothly under the proficient eye of the stewards and dozens of other servants, whose roles were all prescribed and well-practised and none of whom felt any need of direction from a young and inexperienced Countess. Her beloved mother was now far away in the north and her friends were in London and not to be prised away from the Court. Alethea was busy with her two little boys and her art-collector husband, who sometimes took her with him on his travels to classical sites. That thought aroused in Anne an unwelcome pang of envy.

Anne kept her vow of seeing Richard off with a smile and a kiss, but after his departure she cried sad and lonely tears. Although surrounded by a hundred people, and rarely out of sight of curious eyes, at twenty years old she had never felt so utterly alone and abandoned. Books were, as always, a solace and she read and had some of the servants read to her, but a year seemed an endless time stretching ahead into infinity. She looked forward to visits from friends and relations, but they seemed like momentary glimpses of a faraway world now denied to her. She started some intricate embroidery, rode in the enormous park, wrote longing letters to her mother and walked with her ladies in the gardens and the 'Wilderness' surrounding the house.

She found a spot in the garden which she called The Standing, where she could sit and contemplate the turrets, chimneys and windows of the huge house. Knole was now her home, though it sometimes felt like a prison, and she reflected bitterly that 'home' was meaningless if the bricks and mortar did not hold those whom we love. There was some comfort to be found in The Standing; a soothing peace that came over her when she breathed deeply of the fresh air and the scents of moss-covered walls and woodland humus. She took to carrying her prayer book up there and reading to a background of birdsong and rustling leaves. Sometimes she had the company of a bright-eyed, friendly robin and often a dunnock took up his position on the topmost twig of the apple tree behind her and warbled so loudly that she laughingly accused him of trying to deafen her. The place restored her equilibrium.

Occasional days were brightened by a visit from one of the ladies of the local gentry or a conversation with the vicar. The arrival of a letter from Lady Margaret, with news of her successes and frustrations as the landlord of the Westmorland estates, was eagerly seized on. It aroused memories of the mountains of the north, the crisp air and beautiful rivers and waterfalls she had seen around Appleby and Brougham; she longed to return there as much as she pined for her mother's company. These reminders brought tears again, so she turned her mind to the different longing she felt for Richard; that hurt, too, but in a way that was somehow more bearable. A letter from Richard was a rare highlight, with news of his travels and assurances of his affection, but it made her desire worse. So the time dragged by and the boredom ground along and the loneliness ate into her loving heart until she thought she could never feel happy again.

CHAPTER ELEVEN
1612–14

She was woken by his hands caressing her thighs. It was a dream she had been enjoying and she resisted relinquishing sleep, until she turned to snuggle forward and met the hardness of his body. Her eyes popped open to be greeted by his smile in the dawn light.

"Oh!" was all she said before his lips closed over hers with greedy urgency and she was rolled on to her back, responding with her entire body to his movements and touch.

"Welcome home, my lord!" were the breathless words she whispered as he entered her.

"I can feel you have missed me," was his reply.

It was a while before either of them spoke again.

"It's as though I have been raised from the dead!" Anne said later that day, her eyes gleaming, when he asked for news of events during his absence. "Apart from the welcome arrival of spring, nothing has happened in all these months; you cannot imagine how dull and lonely I have been without you. I have nothing else to tell you, so you must relate your travels and bring some excitement into my life at last."

"Have I not brought enough excitement to you for one morning?" Richard laughed as he touched her hand.

She now had time to inspect him closely; had he changed or simply become unfamiliar? His body had felt the same and they had taken up where they'd left off a year ago, but his face seemed somehow altered. It had the same dark, pointed beard, but the moustache was different; the ends were longer and they pointed upwards slightly, which implied a smile on his lips and suggested that she should smile in return. She had no difficulty in doing so today. She thought she detected some ageing and darkening of his skin, but his twinkling eyes were the same and she found them as irresistible as ever. His high forehead had perhaps become a little higher; could he have lost some hair?

One thing that had changed was his dress; he was as immaculate as his reputation had always considered him, but the clothes he was wearing were of a different fashion. She noticed that his hat had a taller crown than she remembered, and his lace collar was a bit like an unstarched ruff. The colours he was wearing were darker and duller than previously; he was not quite the popinjay he had been. Gradually, as she examined him, his features fell back into their accustomed form and she couldn't remember how she had ever seen him as different.

Richard had most recently been in the Low Countries and had returned home from Antwerp, the memories of which were freshest in his mind.

"I saw some wonderful paintings by an artist called Pieter Paul Rubens. He has spent time in Italy and his representations of classical scenes, on huge panels, are wonderfully executed. There's one in the City Hall in Antwerp, where the truce was negotiated between the Dutch Republic and Spain, and it is truly impressive. I'm certain it must have influenced the delegates!"

"Did you meet the artist?"

"No, I didn't, but I did manage to visit his studio with my friend Mathis, who has known him for a long time. Rubens was born in Antwerp. Mathis persuaded the City Fathers to recall him from Italy to paint this picture and they allowed him to build a new house when he came back to the city. The Cathedral has a series of his magnificent paintings of The Cross. There were others in the studio, too, equally beautiful, and many exquisite drawings. PPR is a wonderful artist; I hope he will come to London to decorate some of our great buildings and I shall certainly commend him to Prince Henry."

"You spoke of a truce between Spain and the Dutch Republic. Was it agreed and has it made a difference?" Anne asked.

"Oh, yes. It was agreed before I left these shores – indeed, it was one of the reasons for going when I did, because the truce ended the Dutch revolt against Spain and the war which had gone on for over 40 years, and at last made it safe to go there. Antwerp hopes to gain many benefits from peace and I felt an optimism and energy in people there."

"Tell me more about your travels, I find it most absorbing. What about France?"

"In France I stayed in chateaux, 'castles', but mostly they were more like our grand houses than the old-fashioned and dilapidated buildings we call castles. They belong to wealthy noble families and are often luxurious, so I was comfortable there."

"What did you eat? Is the food abroad different from ours?" Anne asked.

"Not very different, but I ate some things I liked very much and other things I could not have swallowed, had my hosts not been present!" Richard grimaced and Anne's face contorted sympathetically.

"There was good hunting," Richard continued, "When I visited the de Pavee family, acquaintances of my grandmother at Villevieille, we ate some excellent venison we had killed. In France they prefer sauces with meat, rather than making it into pies as we do. And the wines we drank from their own vineyards were far superior to the sour stuff we often have here; there was no need to mull it."

"Did you talk with philosophers?"

"I did meet some, especially in France where they take that kind of education and discourse very seriously indeed," Richard said. "There were even a few women who joined in the philosophical discussions in the area around the University of Paris; I think you would have enjoyed it, but you might have been disappointed that there was little discussion about the position of women. A lot of talk was about the relative merits of Catholicism and Protestantism, where I thought French ideas differed somewhat from our own. The French nation is steadfastly Catholic."

"Thank you, my lord, for sharing some of your impressions

with me. You bring the foreign lands to life with your enthusiasm and I can almost imagine that I was there myself!"

$\backsim$

The loving atmosphere continued for several weeks and Anne's mood rose day by day. She had thought that she would never be happy again, but she was proved wrong and she sparkled like a crystal in the sun.

The only real news she had to offer him concerned the progress of the researches and claims undertaken by Mr Kniveton and Lady Margaret.

"My lady mother has begun proceedings against my father's will, that I might reclaim my inheritance," she told him, as they strolled together through the lapis haze of bluebells in the Wilderness. She was astonished to see a cloud flit across his face as she glanced up at him.

"I wonder that you still pursue this," he said, frowning. "Your uncle is content to take on your father's debts; I cannot see why you would wish to change that when there is no gain for you." He withdrew his arm from her shoulders.

This response was so unexpected that Anne was silenced for a few moments as his words sank in. She stopped and turned to face him.

"But... but... my lord, we speak of my inheritance, the lands which are rightly mine, my position as my noble father's sole heir. Why should I not pursue my rights under the law?"

They each repeated their point of view several times before shaking their heads in disbelief that the other could not see the sense of their argument. They dropped the subject for now, but Anne was left wondering in astonishment where Richard's ideas had come from; she had fully expected that her husband would be pleased to hear of the progress Lady Margaret had made and would be supportive of her cause. She teased out all the possibilities in her mind until her suspicions eventually centred on Edward, who, she concluded, must have been with Richard for at least part of his time abroad.

Later in the year, other events caused sadness and grief to them both. In August Anne heard of the death of her cousin Frances Bourchier, who had often been her companion and comforter. Frances died from a burning fever whilst staying in Lady Margaret's house at Sutton in Kent.

"Frances was my rock, my example, the person I looked up to more than any other except my dear mother," Anne wailed to Richard. "I cannot believe that she has been taken from me when she was but twenty-five years old. Her loss will be so hard to bear. I shall raise a memorial to her in the church at Chenies where she is to be buried."

Richard soon had his own grief to contend with. In November, the death was announced of his friend Henry, the eighteen-year-old Prince of Wales and heir to the throne. The country was thrown into deep mourning for this remarkable young prince who had promised so much, with his talents and beliefs that were a perfect fit for the requirements of a King of England. He was an excellent scholar, man of arms and patron of the arts, as well as a fervent Protestant.

Rumours swarmed that his sudden death could have been brought about by design (poison was often mentioned), but many did not believe that anyone could have wished him ill. Richard was in despair, by turns angry and sorrowful. He blamed himself for the loss of his constant companion, believing that there must have been something he could have done to prevent this dreadful outcome and cursing himself for having spent so much time abroad.

"I saw him only a few times since my return. I could have been with him all those months and maybe could have saved him from this fate had I been here!" Richard declared repeatedly. One day he failed to come to dinner and no-one could say where he was. An instinct took Anne into the Chapel where, slipping quietly through the door at the back, she found him kneeling before the altar, praying vehemently for the soul of his prince and for forgiveness for himself and his sins. This was so unusual that she felt concerned for him and waited silently until he sensed her presence and turned towards her. He looked utterly ravaged, his eyes red from weeping and his hair and clothes most uncharacteristically awry. Her heart went out to him and she hurried forward, her hands outstretched. He took and kissed them and they held each other in a close embrace for many minutes until his sobs subsided.

"I thank you for coming to me Anne, and for giving me what comfort you can," he said.

"I would I could give you more, my dear lord, for it grieves my heart to see you in such distress."

"No matter, you are here. I've never before experienced the absence of hope and I shall not forget that you held out your hands to me when I felt myself cast out from the world." He kissed her lightly on her neck and they walked hand in hand from the Chapel and down the broad stone steps into the east wing. She felt warm satisfaction pervade her being at having been able to comfort him in his grief.

Gradually Richard recovered enough to tell her that he wished to take a leading part in planning the celebrations of the marriage of Henry's sister, Princess Elizabeth, for which the court would come out of mourning. Henry and Elizabeth had been very close, and, as Richard knew, Henry had approved of his sister's betrothal to the Elector Palatine.

"In this way I can commemorate my dear friend and also restore my name to people's lips at court, for I have ever been linked with the Prince; without him I fear I may struggle to keep my name high in the ranks of so many courtiers," Richard said. "I shall devise skilful games, tilts and races to be held at the celebrations and shall order the most luxurious clothes anyone could imagine for both of us. You and I shall be the causerie of the court once more!"

❦

Anne was relieved that her husband had regained his enthusiasm for life and she encouraged his involvement in the festivities, knowing that it would pull him out of his gloom, but she found the costs frightening and wondered how they would ever pay for all this. Nevertheless, she enjoyed being at court again, wearing fine clothes and joining in the celebrations with the many friends whom she had not seen for a year or more, including the bride, Princess Elizabeth, who greeted her warmly with a kiss. She was sufficiently distracted to prevent her worrying too much about her lord's expenditure, or her dread of resuming the arguments and that dull life at Knole.

A scandal concerning Anne's one-time suitor, Robert Carr, and Richard's cousin, Frances Howard, occupied everyone at court for some time. Frances had been married at the age of 13 to the equally juvenile Earl of Essex, who had then gone abroad for two years. Anne had some sympathy for Frances in this situation, but not with what happened next. During her husband's absence Frances fell in love with Carr, so rejected Essex on his return and demanded a divorce, citing non-consummation of the marriage due to his impotence. Essex disputed this. The stakes were raised when Carr, the King's favourite, was created Earl of Somerset. Such manna to the gossips resulted in frenzied tattle.

"Have you heard? In order to prove she is a virgin, she is to be examined by a committee!"

"Yes, but I also heard that she has requested to be veiled during the examination – 'for modesty'!!"

"Modesty? Pah! I never heard that word applied to the Countess of Essex before."

"Wait though... if she is to be veiled during the examination, how are the committee to know that they have examined the right woman?"

"Oh!"

"I also heard that the Earl of Essex has defended his manhood, displaying it in all its glory to his friends!"

"And it has been said that he insists he can perform very well with other women but fails with his wife because she scolds and abuses him so."

"Well, whatever the truth of all this, it seems the lady would stop at nothing to marry Carr, and to my mind Essex is well rid of her."

Overhearing such talk, Anne kept her thoughts to herself, but wondered at Frances's choice of husband and remembered her own panic when she had thought a marriage to Carr might be under consideration. Could his closeness to the King have made him more attractive to Frances, she wondered.

Eventually the way was cleared for the marriage, which was another great social event calling for magnificent dress and extravagant celebrations. How would Frances cope with sharing her new spouse with the King? Anne shuddered, but wished her kinswoman luck.

❧

Before Christmas, Anne had exciting news for Richard and Lady Margaret; a child would be born in the summer. It was early in her pregnancy, but Richard was attentive and kind and Lady Margaret promised to come south as soon as she could. To Anne it seemed that since Richard's return, blessings were being heaped upon her. She no longer felt lonely or dispirited walking in the gardens alone. She took up her favourite seat at the Standing and told her friend the robin about the child in her belly and her hopes for a son who would give joy to the lives of herself and Richard and bring them even closer than they were at present. Apprehension sometimes mingled with her happiness, but she pushed away thoughts of the dangers of childbirth, trusting in God for a safe delivery. She sewed small garments for the baby, wondered at the swelling of her belly and the miracle of the creation of a new life. She wished she could talk to her mother; writing letters wasn't the same.

Her contentment was marred by the appointment to Richard's household of a new attendant, Matthew Caldicott; the son of a gentleman from the shires, he became Richard's secretary and confidant and very rapidly gained the title of "My lord's favourite". He was tall, slim and elegant and, Anne thought, bore himself confidently, like a nobleman, although she knew he was no such thing. Richard and he were of a similar age and quickly became inseparable. They caroused together, hunted together and gambled together, all at Richard's expense, for Caldicott certainly had no money of his own. Richard's frequent references to Matthew annoyed Anne and she kept hearing what Matthew did, what Matthew said or what Matthew thought.

"My lord, do you not have thoughts of your own, that you must constantly be quoting Mr Caldicott?" she sniped one day.

"I have thoughts, my lady, but not such as would be pleasing to you, perhaps!" Richard said.

As Anne had predicted, the expense of the extravagant celebrations at court had left Richard very short of money. She tried to encourage him to be a little less prodigal; but Richard now dismissed her mood as the consequence of pregnancy and took little notice of her opinions, continuing to delight in Caldicott's company and being increasingly influenced by him. At last he had someone he could confide in and be sure of a sympathetic hearing, especially about his money worries. He was besotted. Anne saw them with their heads together and wondered what they were discussing, but they didn't share their ideas with her, which increased her uneasiness about Caldicott's presence.

Eventually Richard was ready to put the plan to Anne. He bounced into her chamber after she had retired, made an exaggeratedly low bow, kissed her hand and declared, with a flourish,

"My lady, I have excellent news from your uncle of Cumberland!"

Anne laughed and was intrigued, eagerly assuming this must mean progress on her claim.

"Pray tell me my lord," she smiled.

"Lord Francis has agreed that he will make a substantial payment to us in exchange for the renunciation of your claim to those northern lands. It is the perfect solution to all our problems! Are you not delighted, my sweet?"

Anne's face fell and she hesitated, sensing that more hands than his were at work here and that she would be pitting herself against them all if she spoke her mind. Images of several faces flashed through her mind, but she dismissed those of Edward Sackville and Matthew Caldicott for now and concentrated on the one before her, searching deep into her husband's eyes without defiance,

"No, my lord, I am not delighted. I have no wish to renounce my claim," she said evenly.

"What? What are you saying? Is this not the best solution, one that will do away with arguments and the need for any further suits at law?"

"I do not wish to renounce my claim," Anne repeated with a slight frown.

"I don't believe the evidence of my ears! Can you seriously oppose this wonderful scheme? Matthew and I have worked so hard to bring this about, in the belief that it would be as appealing to you as it is to me. It releases us from much of the debt I have incurred at court, and it releases you from any further legal arguments about your inheritance. Is it not a blessed relief for us both?"

"I don't know why you assumed that it would please me, Richard. I have no wish to renounce my inheritance, even to gain the advantages of which you speak." Her face was stony-serious and she shook her head.

"Hah! Your time of confinement is close," Richard said. "I do not wish to pursue this discussion to the possible detriment of our child. There will come a better time for this conversation and I am certain you will turn around to my point of view when you are able to consider it more dispassionately. It makes so much sense and you are, above all, a rational being; it is one of the things I love about you! I bid you good night and hope to find you well-rested on the morrow."

She tried to protest. He kissed her and left.

CHAPTER TWELVE
1614-15

Before the birth was imminent, Anne and Richard travelled up to London and installed their household comfortably at Dorset House, where Anne's ladies ensured that all was organised in readiness for when the midwife would be needed. Later, Lady Margaret travelled to London to attend the birth and stayed in her old quarters at Austin Friars. Of course she had made the long journey from Brougham in order to assist at the birth of her first grandchild, she told Anne, but she also wanted to continue her researches into the legal precedents and arguments concerning her husband's will and the entail on the Clifford inheritance. Many documents in the Tower of London were relevant; she must seize this opportunity to forward Anne's claim and she lost no time in repairing there.

"Whether you are delivered of a boy or a girl," Margaret told her daughter, "my searches will be of benefit to you and your heirs."

Anne shared Richard's latest ideas with her mother, who supported and encouraged her to continue with the argument and to use all her persuasive powers to oppose his suggested arrangement.

"I feel certain," Margaret said, "That our case against your father's will is iron-clad and that your lord will see the sense of our position once the lands come into your possession. Selling the 'family silver' is never a good way to guard against future times of need."

During the heat of the afternoon when Anne's waters had broken and her labour started, she sent a messenger to the Tower to alert her mother. The messenger returned, breathless, and Anne heard him speak to her attendant in the next room,

"Pray tell my lady . . . I went with all speed, but . . ," he gasped, "When I reached the Tower . . . I found the gates already closed against all comers! None was to be allowed in or out, and it is my belief . . . that my Lady of Cumberland missed the signal to leave, is still there – and so must remain there until the morrow."

Anne groaned; she really needed her mother's steadying presence now to help her through this pain, but a few minutes later, when the pang subsided, she smiled at the thought that Lady Margaret was so engrossed in her searches that she had not heard the call to leave the Tower before the gates were locked. How typical of her dear mother!

It was a long night for Anne, her attendant ladies and the midwife, who calmed her with soothing cups of spiced wine when she panicked and urged her on to greater efforts with a fortifying drink of warm milk with camomile and egg yolk when she flagged. They rubbed ointment on her belly to speed up delivery and they spoke of the redemptive power of the pain as part of Eve's and everywoman's penance. Anne heard some of what they said, but it seemed to be happening somewhere remote and distant and she was too possessed by her labour to pay attention.

Late the next day, Anne smiled at her mother's embarrassment and fury at having missed the birth of her first grandchild, forgave her and proudly presented her with her namesake, Lady Margaret Sackville. Richard came to see her, too, and sat beside the bed holding Anne's hand and gazing into the crib.

"My child, my child, my child," he repeated in a whisper, as if trying to conjure the essence of those strange words.

Richard was delighted with his daughter and brought her gewgaws and trinkets every day. He was proud, too, of his wife, to whom he presented a diamond ring, and together they celebrated and thanked God for their child's birth. They planned her christening to be held in the chapel at Great Dorset House before Lady Cumberland's return to the north, so that she could stand as godmother to the baby. They teased the Countess about taking care not to miss the ceremony. They took to calling little Margaret 'The Child', to distinguish her from her grandmother, and the name stuck.

When the time came for Lady Margaret to leave London, Anne promised to make a return visit to her.

"It has been a wonderful thing for me to have you with me at this time," she said. "I shall miss you greatly and shall not be content until I see you again, dearest mother. Next year, God willing, I shall make the journey to Westmorland as soon as the winter snows and rains have passed."

"You must write to me regularly of the child's progress and your own health, for I shall be wishing I was here to see it for myself," Margaret said. "I pray that all our efforts will be successful in bringing the inheritance business to a conclusion and that we shall be together again soon. Go well in God's presence and may His blessings be upon you all. Farewell." Anne clasped The Child in her arms, looked after the coach as it receded, and wept.

There were further celebrations of The Child's birth when they returned to Knole and everyone sought a glimpse of her and admired her sweet countenance. The return was softened for Anne by the welcome they received from servants, tenants and friends, but she was still plagued by fits of weeping. Richard was kind and gentle, but dropped occasional remarks concerning the agreement with Lord Cumberland, to remind her that the matter was still unresolved. She was uneasily conscious of the background presence of Matthew Caldicott, but thankfully saw and heard little of him.

When Richard returned to London, Anne took little Lady Margaret and her wet-nurse to another of Richard's properties, Bolebroke Castle in the north Sussex Weald. There they could enjoy a more intimate setting with fewer servants and yet could return to Knole very quickly should the need arise. 'The Child's' first smiles and first teeth were all cause for great rejoicing, and each sneeze or snuffle struck fear into her mother's heart.

Running like a noisy underground stream was Anne's constant awareness that at any moment her husband could start up the inheritance argument again and that she must maintain her guard in order to resist him. When he had spent time in Edward's company she was especially vigilant, but she also began to suspect Matthew of advising Richard to oppose her. She frequently wrote to her mother of these things and of the Court gossip, beseeching her to write back quickly to bolster her resolve. On the tenth of November she wrote: '*My Lord is still earnest to press me to the finishing of this matter with my uncle of Cumberland, but by the power of God I will continue resolute and constant.*'

Anne had always looked forward to seeing Richard, but now began to dread his visits as he pressed harder and harder for her agreement to accept the money offered by her Clifford uncle and cousin. She clung to the hope that he might change his mind, at the same time fearing that he never would. She despaired at the slow progress of her mother's case as it worked its way through the labyrinthine circuits of the courts, and the legal arguments which never seemed to reach any conclusion. She clutched at rumours that her uncle was losing his wits and she admired and loved her husband for his kindness and love for their daughter. But he was becoming insistent, even threatening, over the matter of her inheritance, and that of her three-month-old child, and she put all the strength she had into standing firm against his entreaties and threats.

"You are my wife and you *will* obey me in all things!" Richard's narrow face flushed as he rose to his full height and stood over her, his feet apart and his hands on his hips, an image of power that reminded Anne of the Holbein portrait of Henry VIII she'd seen on a mural in Whitehall Palace.

For a moment she gazed at the wrinkles in the fashionable embroidered hose around his shapely ankles, and then looked up to meet his glare. Her black eyes glittered and her heart was beating so hard she wondered whether he could hear it, but she took a deep breath to steady herself and when she spoke her words were clear, gentle and conciliatory.

"You are my dear lord, for whom I have the greatest affection, love and loyalty. I will obey you in all things – excepting only this one. In the matter of my inheritance I have no discretion or freedom, because the law is on my side and I have promised my mother that I shall never surrender my rights to the lands in Westmorland."

"It's a poor wife who will not help her lord!" Richard said. "You think more of your mother, shut away on the cold northern moors, than of your husband and child who are here at your side. I *demand* that you accept this offer from Lord Cumberland!"

He stomped back and forth in front of her, his fashionable heels making the floorboards tremble. Anne remained silent, twisting the silk cord of her gown between her fingers, and gazed through the lattice window at the deer grazing in the park.

"For Christ Jesus's sake, Anne, it is full ten years since your father died and left his lands to his brother; you and your mother must accept it now. I warn you that if you will not do as I ask I shall be very reluctant to keep company with you." He was getting into his stride and his footsteps were marking time to emphasise his words as he moved away from her. He seemed to be implying that she must choose between her marriage and her inheritance.

She watched his retreating back, still unable, despite herself, to stop admiring the contrasting colours of his silk doublet and slashed sleeves, the curves of his slim legs and his proud bearing. She forced herself to look away into the fire and was entranced by the flickering flames and the red glowing cavern at the centre of the logs. For a moment she almost managed not to hear what he was saying as he continued;

"Everyone at court urges you to agree, even the *King*; he is asking when the claim will be settled. And your Uncle Cumberland and his son are offering such generous terms, it is madness to refuse. They may withdraw at any time and we shall never have such a chance again." He turned and approached her, bending low to look into her face, and his voice dropped, coaxing and wheedling.

"Please, my sweet, please do as I ask and agree to the composition so that we can live together in contentment as we used to do." His mouth smiled, his lips shining red from the middle of his dark beard, but his eyes were neither loving nor friendly.

Anne looked up at him, her face a mixture of compassion and determination. She, too, wished they could return to the joy of former days and she longed to reach out and hold his dear face between her hands, but this disagreement ran too deep for superficial gestures and she must stay strong. Would he really leave her? She couldn't be sure, but she knew for certain that he wouldn't come to her tonight. When she began to speak her voice matched his, patiently explaining as if to one who did not understand,

"I cannot, my lord. My father's will is unlawful; he had no right to leave his estates to anyone but me, his only surviving child. The lands have been entailed to the Cliffords, parent and child, son or daughter, since the time of King Edward the Second and are by rights mine, not my uncle's, nor my cousin Clifford's. *I* am my father's heir. They know that I am right in this, that is why they are offering such a fortune for my agreement, but I will not be bought." Taking a deep breath and gripping the cord more tightly, she swallowed and continued in a louder, firmer voice,

"Hear me and believe me, Richard; I will not be bought! My lady mother has had the entail researched and the line of inheritance through the family traced so that there is no doubt about it. My father was mistaken, though I can only think that he believed he was doing it for my good, because I was young and a woman. But I am as strong in this as any man and I will not surrender."

In contrast to the words and the voice in which she spoke them, she could feel herself wavering. She longed to see her mother, but Richard had denied her even that by refusing to allow her to travel to the north until the question of the settlement was resolved.

"You are impossible!" Richard exploded, turning his back on her. "You cannot be reasoned with." He began to walk away but stopped for one last sally and turned to face her, the stiffened petals of his lace-edged collar trembling like aspen leaves.

"Do you give no thought to the costs of running our houses and servants, the expense of my responsibilities at court? The income from the estates is spent before I receive it. Most of my inheritance from my father is gone, as is your portion, yet you would deny me the fortune that is offered if you will but renounce your claim to those far off, barren moors in the north! We have no use for them nor need of them. There is no point in you holding out for them; what will you do with them if you get them? Don't be such a mule, Anne! There will be enough to keep us in a bed of down for ever, if you will just agree . . . and I will be the best husband to you that you could possibly wish for! In all other things but this we are so much in accord."

Only a scream would emerge if she were to open her mouth to speak now; his reckless extravagance and gambling debts were the principal reasons for his lack of funds and she was close to flinging bitter accusations at him about his profligacy, in this and other ways. Was her obstinacy driving him away, into the arms of others? There were women in London, such as Elizabeth Broughton and Martha Penistone, whose names she knew had sometimes been linked with his. And there was his relationship with Matthew Caldicott. She longed for him to stop spending so much time and money at court and live a quieter life with her and their baby daughter. The arguments they kept having reminded her of her parents' quarrels before their separation.

She was frightened, but it would do her cause no good at all to light the fuse of her anger and allow all the resentment to explode in his face. Every time the disagreement ended the same way, but to her great joy they had always been able to make up after each quarrel. Her fear was that there would come a time when he would no longer return to her with his customary affection and passion, so she swallowed hard, wiped her red eyes and said quietly,

"My dear lord, do you not see that we would not be 'in a bed of down for ever', as you put it, because this money would follow the rest in a few short years and we should be left with nothing?"

"No, wife, no, no, *no!*" His anger was returning and his colour rose again as he began to shout, gesticulating with his hands and arms. "I am in debt *now* and some of my creditors are pressing very hard for settlement. They are insistent, some of them quite threatening. If I cannot pay them very soon, or at least show them that I will be in a position to pay in the future, I shall be forced to leave the country and live abroad as an insolvent exile. You will never see me again – and it will all be *your fault!*"

"I am sorry, my lord, there is nothing I can do," Anne said.

"Is that your last word?"

"It is, you know that. It always has been, and it always will be."

There was gossip aplenty at court to provide welcome diversions, but to Anne's dismay things between her and Richard were not improving. Sometimes in Lady Cumberland's letters she was critical of Richard, but Anne leapt to his defence in her replies;

'…in everything I will commend him, saving in this business of my land, wherein I think some evil spirit works, for in this he is as violent as is possible, so as I must either do it next term, or else break friendship and love with him. God look upon me and deliver me . . .'

Two months later she wrote even more passionately;

'…whatsoever you may think of my Lord, I have found him, do find him, and think I shall find him, the best, and most worthy man that ever breathed, therefore, if it be possible, I beseech you, have a better opinion of him, if you knew all I do, I am sure you would believe this that I write…'

Sometimes she felt unable to disclose the injustices she received at his hand, because Lady Margaret was so bitter against him that Anne could not bear to damn him further in her eyes. She begged Richard to allow her to visit her mother in the north once the Child reached her first birthday, but he would not hear of it.

"Your presence is required here until this business is settled. You cannot disappear into the wilds of the north when we need to come to an agreement and sign the papers to allow the composition to be completed. The lawyers argue on and on but there must be an end in sight, the dispute must be settled. When that is done, you will be free to visit your mother in Westmorland."

"I take it ill, my lord, that you prevent me from visiting my dear lady mother. She has been unwell and cannot travel, yet you refuse to permit me to go to her."

"I give good reason why you should not go at this time. Why does your good sense desert you when we talk of this matter? In all other ways you are kind and rational and the best wife I can imagine, but in this one thing . . ." and his voice tailed off as he walked away, shaking both fists in the air. "Aagh!" was his last word.

Anne watched him go with a mixture of sadness, relief and fear. She was determined to continue with her claim and knew that she would always have her mother's constant support and help in this, but she was beginning to believe that her husband was equally strong in his determination that she should give it up. She knew that several powerful and influential supporters were ranged with him and against her; these included her own kinsfolk, her Clifford uncle and cousin, as well as her husband's intimates, his brother Edward and his 'favourite' Matthew Caldicott. But it seemed also that the Court was split by this dispute and that there were numerous other noblemen who took his side. She had little support from anyone save her mother and one or two members of her mother's family such as Lord William Russell, and sometimes she even doubted him. She began to distrust everyone around her and perceived glances and looks, even between her servants, that she would not have noticed previously.

Richard went up to London after the New Year festivities in order to attend a hearing in the Court of Common Pleas with Lord Cumberland and his son. He took Caldicott with him of course but left his wife and The Child at Knole. Richard and the Cumberlands all agreed to be bound by the Court's decision, thus gaining the approval of the judges, whereas Anne declined to be a party to the suit or to accept that the judgment would be binding. Her mood fluctuated according to whether she received affectionate letters or bad news from London and she often wandered in the Wilderness thinking, 'I am like one of these blades of grass bending back and forth, up and down with the wind!'

CHAPTER THIRTEEN
February 1616

Anne finally joined Richard at Dorset House on Fleet Street in February, to attend a wedding, and he seized the opportunity to speak to her about her claim. His expression was serious as he stood squarely before her, resplendent in black velvet and cloth-of-silver, with his arms folded across his chest in a posture which made her think he was unlikely to listen to anything she said.

"We must settle this matter of the Clifford estates," he began, in a loud voice which she assumed was directed more at Caldicott at the other end of the room, than at her, a yard in front of him. "Don't imagine that you can bury your head in the sand and ignore the Court of Common Pleas. A decision will soon be made, whether you like it or not, and you must at least agree to abide by the decision of the Court."

"My lord, I have no wish to fall out with you, but equally I do not wish to be involved in any way in these proceedings, or to agree to the outcome, because I am very clear in my mind that I will not renounce my claim to the Clifford lands." Anne spoke calmly and with more authority than she felt. "There is the case brought by my lady mother which concerns my legal right to the lands which my uncle holds. That is not yet decided and there can be no agreement concerning those lands until that question is settled; the primary dispute is whether those lands are rightfully mine or my uncle's."

She was satisfied that she had been able to express herself with clarity, although her heart was thumping. Her hands had become clammy and she rubbed them on her skirt, forgetting that she was wearing court dress until the metallic thread of the embroidered brocade scratched her palms.

Richard's face registered irritation, impatience, anger and

disbelief in quick succession. He wagged his finger as though speaking to a naughty child and glared at her with steely eyes;

"Well, the Court may have a different idea of right and wrong. If they award the money offered to me by Cumberland in return for your relinquishment of any claim you may have to those lands, I shall require your signature on the documents immediately. And I must warn you now that if you do not agree to this arrangement, you will no longer be able to count me as your husband."

Shocked, she could hardly recognise this cold, hard man as her husband anyway, she thought, as she watched him and Caldicott exchange smirking glances and leave the chamber together.

A few days after this altercation, Anne received a visit from two of her friends, Lady Grantham and Mrs Newton. She welcomed them into the luxuriously furnished Drawing Chamber and sent for The Child, who delighted them with her lisping speech and golden curls. Her bobbing curtsy earned such applause from them that she hid behind her mother's skirts and could not be coaxed out again, so her nurse took her away. When they asked her age, Anne proudly declared that Margaret was now one year, seven months and fourteen days old.

The main purpose of the ladies' visit then became clear.

"We must warn you, dear lady, that we have heard that you are to receive a visit from the Archbishop of Canterbury very soon," Lady Grantham said.

"Warn me? How alarming; what do you mean, Barbara? What do I have to fear from the Archbishop?" Anne said, passing glasses of mulled wine.

"We hope you will think carefully about your response to him," Alice Newton said earnestly. "He was chaplain to your husband's family in years gone by and will have only the best interests of the family in mind."

"Everyone at court believes that the best thing for you would be to accede to the agreement that your husband and uncle are putting before the Court of Common Pleas," Lady Grantham urged.

Anne understood from this that her business had become the stuff of gossip and conjecture by all and sundry. She suspected Matthew Caldicott and Edward Sackville of spreading word of her quarrels with Richard, but she explained patiently to the ladies why she was unable to agree to the arrangement and eventually silenced all their arguments before they left, deflated and shaking their heads.

Exhausted as she was by this encounter, she then received another visitor; her cousin Francis Russell, her mother's nephew, was one whom she expected would support their case. But Francis was angry about her stubborn refusal and urged her to consider her position and admit that she had been wrong in order to save her marriage. It was a bad-tempered meeting.

Battered by all this unexpected opposition, Anne called on her friend Lady Wotton and together they visited Westminster Abbey. She found herself standing in front of the magnificent new tomb of Mary Queen of Scots, lately erected by order of her only son, the King. Anne was awed, not by the glowing white marble of the effigy, or the gilded canopy on its pillars of black and white marble, but by the story of this unhappiest of queens. What despair must she have felt, spending twenty years imprisoned and then hearing that she was to die by the axe on the order of her cousin Elizabeth, the Queen of England? Another cousin who did not support a kinswoman, Anne reflected.

"Are you all right, Anne?" asked Mary Wotton, wondering at the length of time Anne had stood there and the faraway expression on her pale face.

"Yes, thank you," Anne sighed. "I am recalling that my husband's illustrious grandfather, Thomas Sackville, was the person chosen by the Old Queen to take the news to the Queen of Scots that she was condemned to death. Back at Knole we have a set of old wooden carvings depicting Christ's Passion, given to Thomas by this queen in gratitude for the delicacy with which he imparted that message. I was trying to imagine how a woman could act thus at such a time. Do you not think it denotes extraordinary courage, generosity and piety?"

"The story certainly is a moving one," Mary replied, "and it is said that she faced execution with the same grace and courage, even smiling as she approached the block and placing herself under the axe without movement or sound of protest. She must have felt herself free of sin and able to welcome death as an end to all her troubles."

Anne fleetingly wondered whether she would welcome death if it came to end her own troubles but shook her head to banish such thoughts. Her problems seemed diminished beside those of the Scottish Queen.

She took the arm of her friend and they spoke of their young daughters; Mary had two girls, either side of The Child in age.

"I wanted to name my second daughter Anne, in honour of you, dear friend," Mary said. "But my husband was set on naming her for his lady mother, so she became Hester!"

❦

By the time Anne reached home darkness was falling and she was shuddering uncontrollably. She was grateful for the diversion that the visit to the Abbey had provided, when, on her return, Richard told her that the following day would see a meeting of a great company of noblemen at Dorset House.

"They all, none excepted, wish to see you consent to and sign the award made by the four judges at the Court of Common Pleas," he said emphatically.

Anne, huddling close to the fire, made no reply.

❦

After a sleepless night during which she developed a heavy cold, Anne found herself trembling as she entered the long gallery with all its Sackville family portraits. She was faced by a gathering which included Richard, the imposing figure of the Archbishop of Canterbury, her brother-in-law Edward Sackville, her cousin Francis Russell, Lord William Howard and many other important men, all gathered to press her into agreeing to their argument. She greeted each one civilly, clutching a handkerchief and fervently wishing her nose was not bright red and running. Then Archbishop Abbot took her aside and guided her into the small library in order to speak privately.

"My child, I'm sorry to see that you are unwell and will pray for your rapid recovery. I come in the hope that together we can reach some understanding to bring these disputes to an end.

"The judges have awarded the composition, as you know; your husband is to receive a great portion from your uncle in return for your surrender of your claim to the Clifford lands in Westmorland. Your husband and your uncle and cousin have accepted the judges' decision. Your signature is the final assent needed to complete the legal process. Are you not persuaded that this is a fair and just settlement which, when thus signed and sealed, will resolve the arguments between you all?"

Anne sneezed and shook her head.

"I cannot accept the award, my lord Archbishop," she croaked.

They talked for a long time, with the Archbishop more and more forceful in his contention, but with Anne managing to hold to her points without becoming flustered.

"My lord Archbishop, I do not have the power to make this decision. I am bound both by the law, which says that my father's will was illegal, and by my mother's part, for these lands were left to her as her jointure and she lives there still, believing in my right by entail to inherit them from my father after her death. She has spent years searching all the documents and confirming my rights as sole heir to my noble father. By any count my uncle should never have taken them. Pray do not ask me to defy both the law and my lady mother, for I can do neither."

"The law exists to serve us, not to enslave us, Lady Dorset," the Archbishop said. "You would be well served in this case to follow God's law and your marriage vows and to make peace with your husband. Do you realise how grave is the danger you are in? You have set yourself in opposition to your lord and that is against God's will. If you persist in this sin you must suffer the consequences and it will not go well with you in this world or the next. Think carefully, my child; think of your duty and of how much sacrifice it is worth making for so small a return. Hold to the sanctity of your marriage, for without it you are lost."

Anne was astounded that the Archbishop should speak to her in this way, and very frightened by what he was saying about her marriage. He was calling her a sinner! She struggled for words with so many dark thoughts swirling round in her mind. She gazed at the book-filled shelves surrounding her and sought inspiration from the brown leather bindings and gold lettering. She took a deep breath and stood as tall as her diminutive stature would allow, looking up into the stern face of the most important representative of the Church after the King.

"My lord Archbishop, I hold my love of God and my marriage as the two most sacred elements of my life and would never seek to gainsay either. I love my lord dearly and have no wish to part from him. I seek constantly to please him, but in this single matter we find that we are unable to accommodate each other. Thus I cannot accept that it is I alone who must bear responsibility for the falling out, when my lord is as obstinate in his way as am I in mine. Please forgive my contradiction, my lord; I must aver that I have every due respect for you."

Her eyes fell and there was silence in the room. She became aware for the first time of the low rumbling of many men talking in the adjacent gallery and remembered that they were all waiting for her and the Archbishop.

The Archbishop grunted and scratched his grizzled beard, making a rustling sound that reminded Anne of mice in the wainscot, though she suppressed the thought and the smile which threatened. He removed his cap to run his fingers through his hair and then replaced it. He cleared his throat before meeting her eyes again.

"May I ask, my child, what drives you to continue with this suit when so many are ranged against you?" he said in due course. Anne noticed the softening of his tone and was relieved that he had not lost his temper with her as Richard would have done by now; they had been closeted together for well over an hour. She suddenly remembered Lady Wotton's words of yesterday and thought carefully before replying quietly,

"My lord, the sole reason that I continue is that I believe I am right and they are wrong."

"And nothing your Archbishop has said has shaken that conviction!" he said, with a snort that was almost a laugh.

"I believe that I have the support of both God and the Law, my lord."

"So you will not put your hand to the agreement?"

"I cannot, and I will do nothing until my lady mother and I have conferred together."

And so, after an hour and a half, they rejoined the company in the gallery. Every man, it seemed, must have his say and they all used flattery and threats in equal measure, putting intolerable pressure on her to yield. Her head was pounding, her cheeks burning. Sometimes many spoke at the same time and such a cacophony engulfed her that she could hardly hear what any one was saying.

"...a lady of such outstanding...", "...so stubborn...", "...someone who commands the respect of...", "...your lord and your marriage...", "...think of your child...", "...known for good judgment and...", "...benighted lands in the...", "...as the Bible says...", "...even the King wishes...", "...may live to regret...", "...no sense in..." it went.

Anne held tight in her spinning mind to the belief that she was right, and kept to the last point she had made to the Archbishop as the men and their voices swirled around her;

"I can and will do nothing until I have conferred with my lady mother," she repeated several times.

In the hope that Lady Margaret might be less obdurate than her daughter (and thus proving that he didn't know his aunt very well), Francis Russell finally proposed that Lady Anne be given leave to visit her mother.

"As long as they will return answer by March 22nd, whether they will agree to the business or not," William Howard suggested.

This met with a general nodding of heads and grunts of relief that something, however small, had finally been agreed upon. The only person who did not seem satisfied with the morning's work was Richard, who looked thunderous but said nothing. The Archbishop brought the meeting to a close by reciting the *Nunc Dimittis* and all knelt for his blessing. Anne and Richard were the last to leave, by doors at opposite ends of the gallery. Anne was exhausted and ill, but jubilant that she had stood up to all their flattery and threats and had finally won the opportunity to visit her mother in Westmorland. She had not expected to come through this meeting so well, having believed that she must either agree to the composition or lose Richard.

⚬⚬⚬

She found energy from her miraculous escape and dispatched servants immediately with a triumphant letter to her mother telling of her coming, and messages to several friends in London with news of her journey. She was finally able to retire to her chamber and nurse her cold with her mother's warm honey, cinnamon and lemon remedy. She reviewed the events of the day with satisfaction but knew full well that this would be only a temporary respite. She had a month's grace before the answer was due and she would remain with her dear mother in Westmorland for as long as possible and make the most of it.

There was further good news when Richard told her he would travel with her part of the way. Then there was the bustle of organisation for a journey she had thought she would never be able to make.

When the final preparations were in place and the great assemblage of horses, coaches, carts and riders was about to set off, Anne's hopes of spending some time with her husband were dashed. She learned that they were to travel in separate coaches; she would have Judith and Lady Willoughby for company, while Richard and Caldicott would travel together. It was the starkest reminder of the chasm between her and Richard and the contrast between their lives.

On the morning of the fourth day of the journey, Richard told her he would accompany her only as far as Lichfield, where he and his company would turn back, leaving her with ten attendants, led by Rivers, and thirteen horses. He had been distant and reticent throughout the journey, but she had kept hoping that the next day would bring some kind word or loving gesture. None came, and when he left her, with a formal farewell, to continue the journey alone she felt more aware than ever before of the gulf that separated them. Her heart weighed heavy as his coach bore him and Caldicott away and it was only the thought of her loving mother waiting for her at Brougham that prevented her from turning back to plead for his affection.

The second day of the route from Lichfield to Manchester took them over difficult moorland terrain.

"My lady," Rivers approached her at first light, his handsome face furrowed with anxiety, "I fear we have a long and dangerous journey before us this day. The Inn-keeper warns me that the descent of some of the hills will be impossible for the four horses drawing the coach; the way is often steep and rutted and will be slippery with the rains. Parts of the road may have been washed away and even the covered carts may fare badly."

"Then we shall take the horses out of the shafts and walk them down the steepest hills, Rivers," Anne said. "My ladies and I will also walk down and thus lighten the coach so that the men can lift and direct it as needs be. If the horses struggle with the covered carts we can do the same with them."

"You have put my mind at rest, my lady, and I thank you."

The moors were windswept and boggy, bare of trees and dark with dormant heather plants, gorse, clumps of reeds and squat bilberry shrubs under lowering cloud. The work of getting the coach down the steep hills was hard and slow and was accomplished with much shouting and some swearing, but Anne urged them all on and praised their efforts, paying no heed to her dirty wet feet and sodden skirts. The winter rains had swept away the road in places on the hills and some of the hollows on the tops still had frozen snow in them. A ragged man told them he was gleaning for coal to warm his hut, where he was caring for an early lamb that had lost its mother. He directed them away from a crag where landslips had made the way impassable and was thanked with a silver coin.

They saw no-one else for miles, until valleys began to open up towards the west and scattered habitations and a few bare winter trees appeared. They had to cross a river by a makeshift narrow bridge where Rivers's horse slipped and fell into the fast-flowing rocky stream. Horse and rider were soaked but miraculously unhurt, although time was lost in the struggle to haul the rider back onto the bank and recapture and calm the frightened horse. Darkness fell early but they travelled for sixteen hours that day and, after suffering many mishaps, arrived gratefully at Manchester at about ten o'clock at night.

❦

The final days of the journey to Brougham were less alarming and they made good time, arriving to an uncharacteristically emotional welcome from Lady Margaret. Anne was shocked to see the changes two years had wrought on her mother's beautiful face, but ran to her arms and held her close, putting that enquiry off until later.

Lady Margaret dried her tears and smiled for this daughter

whom she had missed more than words could say. She took her hand and led her into the Great Chamber where a feast had been prepared to greet her, great logs were burning brightly in the fireplace, candles were lit in the sconces around the walls and two musicians struck up as they entered. Millie was standing beside the table, beaming with pleasure at seeing her young mistress again. This is a wonderful welcome, everything I have longed for, Anne thought, as she sank down on to a velvet-cushioned chair and relaxed in the warmth and music, with a cup of mulled wine and her mother beside her at last.

CHAPTER FOURTEEN
March 1616

Anne slept well that night for the first time in months. Something to do with feeling safe, she thought as she woke, but the longing for Richard and The Child surged back and threatened to overwhelm her. She forced herself to leave her bed and hurried to pray in the tiny oratory in the corner of the keep. Prayer calmed her and restored the joy of being close to her mother, but she remembered the shock of her mother's changed appearance; the dread she had pushed out of mind yesterday would have to be faced today. She prayed fervently for her mother and determined to talk with Lady Margaret about her health at the earliest opportunity.

Lady Margaret rose late and it was not until they were preparing to take an afternoon coach-ride into Whinfell Forest that Anne had any opportunity to refer to her worries. As soon as Lady Margaret had been handed into the coach and settled herself comfortably among the cushions, Anne drew a deep breath and gently took her hand.

"Tell me, dear lady mother, how it is with you."

"The Lord blesses me with fair health, my dear, but I cannot deny that the years seem to be catching up with me. I'm not full of energy as once I was."

"I pray God that the years are all that ails you," Anne said. "I devoutly hope that there is no other trouble, no agues or distresses, to add to the burdens of your mind and body. You are the dearest treasure of my life."

Lady Margaret looked into her daughter's anxious face and squeezed her hand.

"I daily thank you and the Lord God for your love, my daughter, and I promise you that there is little I can tell of but a niggling sometimes in my side, which comes and goes like the flickering of shadow and sunshine through trees. My herbal remedies are sufficient to deal with that."

As she spoke, Lady Margaret turned away from her daughter and looked out of the coach window at the sunshine dappling the leaves and branches of the forest. Anne couldn't see her face or tell from her voice whether her mother's lightness of tone hid deeper concerns, but she remained anxious about the changes she could see in her mother's features. She fell silent, swaying with the lurching of the coach, until she decided that further questions at this point would be fruitless and changed the subject;

"I think of my lord and your little god-daughter and wonder how they fare," she said. Lady Margaret welcomed the change of topic.

"I too hope that your daughter fares well; I am sure that by now she is a beautiful child. But I find I have only reproaches for your husband when I think of the way he treats you. Surely he should be supporting and aiding you in your claims, not threatening and bullying you to give up that to which you are entitled? I believe you tolerate too much from him that is reprehensible."

Anne bristled at the criticism of her husband and was irritated that her attempt to change the subject had landed her in another difficult spot.

"What would you have me do?" she said, tightening her grip on the strap, "I have held to my rights in law and have stood up to all he has done to persuade or coerce me to do otherwise, as we agreed I should." She realised that she had spoken more brusquely than she had intended and immediately regretted it. "But I apologise for speaking sharply to you, dear mother, I had not intended any rebuke."

"It is not *your* behaviour which causes me concern, Anne; I have no criticism of you. It is your husband, with his spendthrift ways and lack of support for you, who makes me angry," Lady Margaret said.

"I agree that his spending is part of the cause," Anne said. "In order to maintain his position close to the King he lives very extravagantly and has to gamble huge sums to match the King's wagers. But you do not see the sweet and kind man he is at other times, nor the loving father he is to our daughter. If you did, I know that you would be less harsh in your judgment of him. I do not wish to part company with him, lady mother, so I don't oppose him any more than is necessary to defend my rights. In all other ways, I assure you, we remain good friends."

"You have great loyalty to him, which I must admire, but I do wish he was more of a friend to you in the matter of your inheritance," Lady Margaret said.

"So do I! But he looks at this matter from a different stance and he can no more see my point of view than I can see his," Anne said. "So, we remain friends when we can and we fall out when this subject is raised. It has been thus for years and I cannot foresee how it will end." Anne's mind conjured an unbidden image of Matthew Caldicot and Edward Sackville, their heads bent together with Richard, and a feeling of loathing crept over her which she could never share with her mother.

"Well, let *us* not fall out over it!" Lady Margaret declared. "I believe we see eye to eye on the matter, don't we, and it will soon be time to send word back to London. What do you think that reply should be?"

"Oh, we must refuse the settlement, of course," Anne replied quickly, relieved by the change of subject. "I haven't even shown you the papers that they wish us to sign, but the business has not changed. The judges' award requires me to agree to renounce my claim to the Clifford estates in return for a large sum of money to be paid to my lord by my uncle of Cumberland and his son."

"And you do not wish to agree to this composition?"

"You know that I do not. I never shall," Anne said.

"Good," Lady Margaret concluded.

❧

As the time drew closer for their answer to be sent, Lord William Howard, accompanied by his son and another cousin, came to

Brougham with the gift of a dappled grey mare for Anne. She was pleased with the horse, but her answer when Lord Howard broached the question was the same.

"My lord, we have no other answer but a direct denial to the Judges' Award," Anne told him when they had repaired to her mother's chamber. William Howard turned angrily to Margaret Clifford.

"You have not persuaded your stubborn daughter to agree to this generous settlement! I thought we could depend upon your good sense and level judgment to see that the most satisfactory way of dealing with this matter would be to accept the Judges' Award!"

"We do not see it so, my lord," Lady Margaret replied softly.

"But it is a generous settlement and greatly in your daughter's favour."

"I pray you; do not presume to tell me what is in my daughter's interest, Lord William. Lady Anne wishes to retain her rights to the estate which was entailed to her several hundred years ago. The law is clear and she will not surrender those rights," Margaret said.

"You are as stubborn as each other! No wonder my nephew is driven distracted by you. Now I see that he does not exaggerate!" Howard said.

Anne glanced at her mother and saw that her usual calm demeanour was giving way to an angry flush. She was beginning to feel afraid that things would run out of hand when the door opened and Sir Timothy Whittington was announced. He was a kind and jovial knight whom Lady Margaret had come to know well and respected, and Anne breathed a sigh of relief. He bowed to all the company and Lady Margaret called for refreshments. When spiced ale and oatcakes were served the tension in the chamber dropped perceptibly and Sir Timothy engaged Lord Howard in an animated discussion of the best points of hunting hounds. The day was saved and the answer was sent off to London with Sir Timothy without further comment or quarrelling. Sir Timothy called from his saddle that he would look forward to seeing Anne return to London with her retinue after Easter.

On Easter Sunday two weeks later, Anne and Margaret took Holy Communion in the Chapel at Brougham, listened to a long sermon from the priest and spent much of the rest of the day in Lady Margaret's chamber, sewing and discussing the Resurrection and its meaning for their present-day lives. Anne, able to concentrate on her embroidery at last, felt relief that the answer to the Judges' Award had finally been dispatched and she looked forward to enjoying the remainder of her stay and making the most of this precious time with her mother. The misgivings about her mother's health remained, and Lady Margaret herself made it clear that she too would like the visit prolonged. It was a time for the closeness and quiet companionship that they had both longed for whilst apart.

The following morning a great clamour of men and horses passing through the gatehouse signalled the arrival of Richard Sackville's cousin, Charles Howard, and his companion John Dudley. They were shown into Lady Margaret's peaceful chamber, still wearing their mud-spattered riding clothes. Anne and her mother put down their embroidery and rose to greet the visitors.

Howard and Dudley bowed to both ladies and Howard handed each of them a letter. He stepped back, his eyes on them, clearly expecting them to break the seals and read the contents there and then. Margaret and Anne exchanged glances as they recognized the seal of Richard Sackville. Anne broke the seal on her letter and read a brief message. She recognised Caldicot's hand, but the signature was undoubtedly Richard's:

'to Anne, Countess of Dorset.
Madam, Your refusal of the Judges' Award is received. I desire that my Coach, Horses and Servants be immediately returned to me. I do not wish you to accompany them. You will remain where you are.
R. Sackville, Earl of Dorset'

Anne's eyes passed over the words and then passed over them

again. She tried to grasp their meaning. She blanched. Alarmed, Lady Margaret tore open her letter and gasped. She spoke to the men standing awkwardly before her.

"Pray go down to the great hall where my servants will see to your needs. My daughter and I will join you there presently."

As Howard and Dudley clattered down the spiral staircase and peace returned to the chamber, Anne and Margaret sank back into their seats. Anne covered her pale face with her hands.

"I have feared and dreaded this day for so long, mother. What am I to do?" She bit her lower lip and stretched out her hand to take her mother's letter, as if she believed its message might be different from her own, but dropped both on to the floor after glancing at it. There was silence in the chamber until Lady Margaret burst out,

"What does he mean by this? What drives him to send such a message? He is everything I thought him and worse! This cannot be, you must forbid them to leave."

"At the moment I am too shocked to think," Anne said. "I will do nothing until my head clears enough to decide on the best course of action."

Lady Margaret shook her head but saw the sense of her daughter's words and sent Millie to fetch them both some spiced wine.

For an hour or more they tried to look at all the complexities of the situation. First Anne proposed that she should do as her husband demanded and send the servants, coach and horses back to him.

"But that is just what he wants! You cannot cravenly give in to him when he is being so unreasonable," Lady Margaret objected.

"Should I then refuse to return his servants and property to him? I fear he will simply become more angry and unreasonable – and who knows what he might not do then," Anne said, sensing that there was nothing to be gained by blindly opposing her husband's demands without good reason.

"I don't understand why you excuse him all the time, when all he does is stand against you," Lady Margaret argued.

"I don't excuse him, but I do try to forgive him and not let the poison from the arguments about this business of my inheritance spread throughout our marriage," Anne said, realising as she said it that this was what she had been doing for years without being aware of it. Parting from Richard was unthinkable, and yet here she was, apparently on the brink of just that, and now quarrelling also with her mother, who had always been her greatest support and help.

"Please help me to think clearly about what I should do now, dear lady mother," she said in a low, flat voice.

"I will do all I can," her mother said. "You make me realise that it is your wishes, not mine, that are important here. He is truly a lucky man to have a wife such as you."

Anne took a deep breath to calm herself and spoke slowly: "Let us look at what routes are open to me. I can do as he says – send his men and horses back to him. Or I can refuse to let them go. If I send them back, I can either return with them, or do as he says and remain here. I do not want to anger him further by refusing to obey his orders, so the first question is answered; I shall send them back."

"Very well, you are determined on that," her mother said. "Then you must decide whether to go with them or stay here."

"Yes, that is the most difficult question and I have not found an answer to it. If I return against his wishes I may anger him further, but if I remain here with you, as he demands and as I had hoped to do, I may be perceived as having deserted him and I don't know when I may see him or the Child again. At least if I am there I may be able to talk with him." She sighed heavily, realising the hopelessness of her position and seeing no way forward.

Lady Margaret was thoughtful. Suddenly she rose and moved slowly and stiffly across the chamber. She grasped the door handle and turned to Anne,

"You are right; talking can sometimes sort things out. I'll go and talk to the messengers who brought these letters."

"Wait, I must come too."

They descended the spiral staircase and found Cousin Howard and Mr Dudley in the great hall of the castle, partaking of bread, cheese and ale, and surrounded by the servants who had accompanied Anne to the north four weeks ago. There was a buzz of excitement in the air and they had clearly been discussing Lord Dorset's demands. Lady Margaret walked towards Howard, stood straight and addressed him directly.

"You will not make any move until my daughter has reached a decision," she said.

Howard looked up at her with a blank expression and slowly rose from his seat at the table. He stared down at Lady Margaret for a moment, emboldened by his mission, then said,

"Is that so, my Lady? Well, I already have my orders from Lord Dorset and I'll carry them out as he commanded. We'll be leaving shortly with Lord Dorset's coach, horses and servants. Lady Dorset is not required to make any decision; she is to remain here."

Anne's mind suddenly cleared and she broke in;

"Wait! You will leave, as you say Sir Charles, but before going you must all sign to say that you go without me by my Lord's direction and contrary to my will. Steward; pray draw up a paper to show that." Anne saw a look of relief on her mother's face but was anxious not to allow time for the men to leave without signing and added, "Do not tarry."

The steward hurried from the room and returned a short while later with a large sheet of vellum. Anne glanced at the top of the page where he had written, beneath the date of 1st April 1616:

'A Memoranda that I, Anne, Countess of Dorset, sole daughter and heir to George, late Earl of Cumberland, doth take witness of all these gentlemen present, that I both desire and offer myself to go up to London with my men and horses, but they, having received a contrary commandment from my Lord, my husband, will by no means consent nor permit me to go with them. Now my desire is that all the world may know that this stay of mine proceeds only

from my husband's command, contrary to my consent or agreement,
whereof I have gotten these names underwritten to testify the same.'

Most of the sheet remained blank for the signatures of all those present. Anne nodded to the steward, who read the words aloud before placing it on the table, with a quill and a pot of ink, for her to sign. Lady Margaret signed it next with her usual flourish, then each man signed his name in turn, some rapidly, some laboriously and some with a simple cross. Lastly, Judith and Willoughby signed. Howard drummed his fingers on the table and Dudley tapped his foot on the floor, but finally the steward sanded the ink and presented the paper to Anne with a bow. Willoughby and Judith bade a tearful farewell to their mistress as they and the men all took their leave. There was a great clangour and shouting as they passed through the gatehouse. Suddenly the castle fell silent.

"I believe you have done the best thing and the signed disclaimer was an inspiration, my dear," Lady Margaret said. Anne sighed, sinking on to the refectory bench.

"I had to do something," she said, "But who will take any note of such a document? Sometimes I long for all these arguments to be over with and I almost think it would be worth giving in, just to be rid of them. I imagine that I would be at peace then, but I know I would not because I should bitterly regret losing my inheritance." Tears filled her dark eyes.

"For the moment anyway," Lady Margaret reassured her, "You have given your Lord no further cause for anger, and without surrendering your rights. That is a comfort."

"I am still uncertain about my decision to send my folks away without me, even with the memorandum signed by all the witnesses," Anne said. "I think now I should have gone with them, even though it was against my Lord's wishes. Perhaps I could send a messenger after them and ask them to wait for me."

"I am disappointed that you are not settled with your decision," Margaret said, "But if that is your wish then by all means send one of my men on the swiftest horse."

Anne dithered. She had always known her own mind and had never before experienced this paralysing indecision, but it was impossible to read Richard's intention at this distance and she was frightened by the coldness of his letter and his decree that she should not return to him. She did not want to desert her ailing mother. Equally, she longed to feel the loving embrace of her husband and child. How could she choose between them? How could she predict the outcome of either course of action? She left Lady Margaret in the great hall and wandered through the gatehouse towards the river bank, her thoughts swirling like the eddies in the water. She paced up and down the goose-cropped turf, but her mind would not settle and eventually she returned to instruct a messenger to follow the servants and ask them to stop and wait for her. She wished him well and watched him set off at a gallop in the tracks of the coach and horses.

The messenger returned after nightfall to report that he had ridden as fast and as far as he dared but had been unable to catch up with the Dorset train. In despair, Anne and Margaret retired to the Countess's chamber and spent the night talking in circles. By dawn Anne had distilled the argument;

"If I fail to return I could be believed to have deserted my lord, even though it was at his request. That would be seen as unpardonable."

"I agree that such an outcome would be undesirable," Lady Margaret said.

"I shall return to London," Anne said.

Messengers were dispatched to catch up with the travellers and request them to wait for Lady Anne. She would be accompanied by two of her mother's officers on the hard ride towards the summit of the Pennines, where she hoped to find the coach and servants with whom she would proceed to London. Anne and Margaret both cried bitterly at this parting, their hearts heavy with foreboding and grief that they might never meet again. They set off together in Lady Margaret's coach, but had travelled barely half a mile when Lady Margaret indicated that she would return to the old red sandstone castle.

They clung to each other for long minutes in the privacy of the coach. After many kisses and much well-wishing on both their parts, Anne reminded herself of her mission to reach her servants and coach as soon as possible. She tore herself away to mount behind Hodgson, her mother's most trusted officer, for the dash to the summit of Stainmore. That, she thought, looking back at her mother's crumpled face, is the hardest thing I have ever had to do, and she fought to hold to her resolve, with tears streaming down her face.

Hearing the urgent sound of galloping horses, curious heads popped out of doorways along the way to wonder at the strange sight of two fine horses ridden hard in a southerly direction by two liveried manservants and a weeping noblewoman. They stopped in Brough to water the horses and heard that the Dorset party had been there overnight but had left at first light; they were hours ahead. The ride over Stainmore was steep and bleak, with few trees or habitations, but they knew that two horses, even with one of them carrying two riders, could make better time than a coach. Finally, the road levelled then began to drop and trees appeared round small clusters of buildings. They learned that their quarry were only a few miles ahead, and at Rokeby they caught up with them at the inn. They met with a mixed reception; Howard and Dudley were displeased that the Earl of Dorset's orders had been defied, but the servants, particularly Judith and Willoughby, were delighted to see Anne.

CHAPTER FIFTEEN
April 1616

The eighth day of travel brought them to the village of Ware, within a day's journey of London. A messenger was sent ahead to announce that they would reach town on the morrow and to break the news that Anne was with the party.

Anne had been happy to have Judith and Willoughby in attendance on her again and had allowed herself to be distracted by their cheerful chatter during the journey. The further south they travelled the more the spring foliage and flowers added to the optimistic mood, but for Anne sorrowful thoughts of her dear, sick mother often occupied her mind. Now, as they approached Tottenham, she began to be afflicted by other feelings of dread and foreboding as well. What kind of reception would she receive? Would her banishment by her husband continue, now that she was here? Would he take it further and end their marriage, as he had threatened? Would other people know about his insistence that she remain in the north? Would friends take sides?

She shook herself and resolved to face up to whatever was in store for her. She had chosen her way and had no regrets. She heard loud greetings as the coach slowed and stopped. Her heart was beating hard and her hands felt damp in spite of the chill in the coach, then the door opened and she saw that her husband's coach, men and horses had come out from the city to meet them and escort them to Dorset House. She looked in vain for Richard; he was not with them. She felt both disappointment and relief at his absence, but it was reassuring that he had publicly acknowledged her arrival; perhaps his anger had subsided a little. At least she was not publicly disgraced.

They made their way through the narrow streets chock-full of people, vehicles and animals, to Dorset House, but Richard was not present there either, so the following day they continued to Knole. When the outstretched stone frontage and octagonal brick chimneystacks came into sight, Anne instructed the coachman to stop before the gatehouse so that she could enter on foot. As soon as the great wooden doors were opened, she was rewarded by the sight of her daughter, waiting with the nurse in the shelter of the archway. She ran towards them and scooped up The Child into her arms, smothering her with kisses, exclaiming at how much she had grown and admiring her embroidered linen bonnet with its pretty flowers. The two-year-old, shy at first, then squealed with delight and wrapped her arms round her mother's neck, bringing tears to Anne's eyes. She hugged The Child close, blinked hard and looked around the Green Court; a line of household servants had come out to greet her, but there was still no sign of her husband.

Taking The Child by the hand and acknowledging the servants, she crossed the wide courtyard and passed through the Inner Wicket into the smaller Stone Court, with its delicate Doric colonnade, then entered the Great Hall from beneath the carved oak screen. She gazed around; everything was familiar yet seemed different in scale from how she remembered it. It felt very strange and dreamlike to be walking here again. After the weeks she had spent at Brougham's ancient unadorned stone castle, she felt she had returned to a different world in this grand house which was such a luxurious modern palace, a memorial to Richard's grandfather and his unfulfilled ambition to entertain the King and Queen.

They mounted the painted staircase with its large Sackville griffons on the newel posts and entered the Drawing Chamber. The Child ran happily towards a beagle pup that she kept as a pet, trilling "Mama here, Mama here, Mama here" like a little bird. Anne picked up a soft ball to roll it across the floor and laughed as it was chased by both The Child and the dog. The Nurse gathered up toys and child to return to the nursery, but Margaret wriggled free and ran back to her mother for one last hug and kiss, then the young beagle padded out behind them on over-sized paws.

Richard entered the room quietly, without any of his accustomed swagger. Anne longed to greet him, touch him, tell him how much she had missed him, feel his arms around her, but his indifferent expression discouraged any show of affection.

"You're back," he stated flatly.

Not knowing what to say, Anne was silent. The tension became so uncomfortable that she eventually said,

"Yes my lord, we've been nine days on the road." She tried to gauge his mood, half expecting a harangue about her disobedience, but none came and he remained silent, not even looking at her. His coldness was worse than anger and she clasped her hands behind her back so that he would not see how much they trembled.

Eventually he said,

"We shall speak tomorrow," turned on his heel and walked out.

Anne sank on to the nearest chair and slumped there, unable to rouse herself to go to her chamber. She really ought to change out of her heavy, stained travelling clothes, she told herself. Her ladies would be unpacking her chest and might need some supervision. But she would leave it to them. She needed to think.

It was clear that Richard was displeased, probably with both her rejection of the Judges' Award and with her return from the north against his instructions. She had thought that being here would be an advantage because she would be able to talk with him, touch him, cajole him, and he had, after all, said that they would talk tomorrow. But now that she was here and had seen him, she wondered what she had thought she could say to him that would persuade him to accept her back? Now she feared that there was little she could do that might soften the stoniness of his heart. She had nothing to offer him but her love and that, it seemed, was no longer of any value to him without her surrender of her inheritance. His reception of her today had destroyed any possibility that she might have imagined of winning him over through the old attraction; he had been impervious, repelled and repelling. She had no tools or weapons with which to attack that wall of cold indifference.

Anne slept little that night and knew that she looked haggard when Richard came to speak to her in the morning. He was still cold and brusque, his face set, as he demanded that she return to him the papers from the court that she and her mother had been asked to sign and seal.

"I am afraid that is not possible, my lord, for I have left them at Brougham with my lady mother," Anne said. And that was all the talk they had.

The following day Richard, his cousin Thomas Glenham, and Matthew Caldicott went to London. Anne expected to be sent for shortly afterwards, but no word came and she whiled away four days as best she could until a letter came from Richard. She felt a thrill when she recognised his seal and hastily broke the letter open, but there was no affectionate greeting.

'Madam,
It is my Duty to inform you that I am asking you now, for the last Time, to tell me whether or not you will agree to sign the Award of the Judges in the Matter of your Inheritance. If you will not, my Patience will be exhausted; I shall not repeat this Request and things will not go well with you.'
The letter was signed formally, 'Richard, Earl of Dorset.'

Anne was upset by the tone, as much as the content, of the letter, but had no doubt as to what her reply should be. As ever, she decided to give herself time to reflect before sending her response, but that did not alter her resolve. The next morning she wrote back:

'My Lord,
My answer to your Demand is that I will not set my Hand and Seal to the Award of the Judges, nor will I stand to it, whatsoever misery it may cost me. I commend you to God and remain your affectionate and devoted Wife, Anne Dorset.'

Ten long days dragged by. April was coming to an end and the sun rose early and set late. The Wilderness was full of bluebells, the lawns were green as emeralds and the birds were busy feeding nestlings. Fruit trees were dressed in their finest pink and white gossamer and a thrush took up a perch at the top of the tallest pear tree in the orchard and sang incessantly of his territorial pride. To Anne it felt as though the world was carrying on without her, ignorant of the pain in her heart and the hiatus in her life, the suspension of all activity. She neglected her appearance, failed to dress her hair and wore the same unfashionable clothes every day. She played half-heartedly with the Child and her beagle, chatted distractedly with her women and rode in the park without seeing the families of deer and rabbits which grazed there. Her mind was full of dark churning anxieties that roamed around her husband, her mother and the business of the lands, without ever settling. Each morning she rose early and took her prayer book up to the Standing. After reciting the Lord's Prayer she asked for help again and again, speaking to God as to a loyal and trusted friend.

"Hear this prayer, almighty God, from your most faithful servant. Be merciful unto me in these troubles; help me as You have always done. Grant me Your grace and let Your divine light shine upon me and those I hold dear. Bless my mother, my lord and my child I pray and hold us all in Your merciful hand. Amen."

May Day dawned bright and warm, but the morning brought no news from Richard. In the afternoon, just as Anne and her ladies were preparing to sit down to dinner, Rivers arrived from London and requested a private audience:

"I hope I find you well, my lady" he said with a deep bow. She was glad to see his dependable face once more, but today it was coloured with concern. He seemed hesitant to deliver the message he brought and she began to feel afraid.

"Yes, Rivers, I thank you, I am in good health by the grace of

159

God. Are you come directly from London? Do you bring word for me?"

"Yes, but I fear that I bring no good tidings," said this most loyal servant. "My lord sends you word, my lady, that you are no longer to live at either Knole or Bolebroke, by his command."

Anne gasped and paled. There was silence and Rivers looked away, unable to bear the stricken look on his mistress's colourless face and in her dark-encircled eyes. Eventually she said,

"I need to speak with my lord. What does this banishment mean, Rivers? What is his intention? Where must I go? When shall I see him?"

"I regret, my lady, that I have no answers to any of your questions. My lord simply sent me to tell you that you are no longer to . . ." Anne held up her hand to stay his words and said,

"I heard your message, Rivers, and I understood that I am not to live here or at Bolebroke, but I do not comprehend what this means regarding my ties to my lord, or what will happen in the future."

"Forgive me, my lady; I do not know either. Pray permit me to withdraw." She waved him away and Rivers bowed again as he left the room.

Anne sat down with her head low and her hands covering her face. When her housekeeper, Mrs Stewkley, entered the room to attend her mistress, she didn't see her at first until a stifled sob drew her attention to the small hunched figure in the winged chair in shadow near the fireplace. She hurried to Anne's side and put an arm around her shaking shoulders.

"My lady, what ails you? What can I fetch for you? Are you sick?" Stewkley said.

Anne struggled to get control of her voice and her trembling lips.

"No, not sick, but sick at heart, dear Stewkley."

Mrs Stewkley knew her mistress too well to press her further; she waited for her to be ready to say more. Anne eventually drew a deep breath and sighed, drawing herself up straight.

"Rivers has brought a message from my Lord; he commands that I shall live neither at Knole nor at Bolebroke. I know no more than you do beyond those stark words."

"Oh, my lady, that is indeed a strange and troubling message. What shall you do?"

"I don't know, but I think I must try to speak with my lord. I am afraid of annoying him further and making a bad case worse, so I must think carefully and prepare thoroughly to make my pleas. Pray bring me paper and ink and I will begin to pen some thoughts."

Mrs Stewkley returned with spiced mulled wine as well as the writing materials. Anne, fortified, began to feel better — action, especially writing, was always her best means of dealing with difficult matters. She settled to her task as Stewkley quietly closed the door.

CHAPTER SIXTEEN
Early May 1616

The next day Anne was still trying to decide how best to approach Richard when Judith came rushing into the chamber in a great flurry. She brought herself up sharp when she saw her mistress, but Anne could see the flustered concern on her face and felt a weight drop in her own belly. What now?

"What is it, Judith? It is unlike you to be so discomposed. What has happened?"

"Oh, my lady, forgive me! The servants are all talking about it and Mr Legge has said it's true, so it must be, but still I can't hardly believe it. Please tell me that they're mistaken!"

"Judith, dear Judith, pray calm yourself. Is Mr Legge come down from London? And what is it that you, and all the servants, are talking about? What has so upset you?"

Judith's eyes widened in horror and her mouth fell open as she realised that Anne had not heard the news.

"Oh, my lady! Oh, no! I could not stand to be the bearer of such bad news to you! I thought Mr Legge must have told you first, but I see now how mistaken I was."

"I haven't seen Mr Legge today. He has brought me no message from my Lord. Tell me now what you've heard," Anne commanded.

Anne watched Judith as she gulped and smoothed down her skirts and apron, twisted her chapped hands together, collected her wits and tried to find some kind words with which she could impart the talk from everyone's lips. Judith's eyes darted round the room as if searching for an escape, but finally she blurted out:

"Please forgive me, my lady, but Mr Legge has told one of the servants that his Lordship will come down and see your Ladyship once more, which will be the last time that you will see him again unless you put your hand to the award."

"Is that the sum of it?"

"Yes my lady, that is all."

"Very well, you may leave me. I thank you for giving me warning, Judith; I would not be kept in ignorance."

As soon as Judith had closed the door, Anne leapt from her chair and paced around the room. She silently pummelled the red velvet cushion on the chair near the fireside. How dare Legge, her husband's Steward and chief officer, give such news to the servants before informing her? He must have a very low opinion of her, influenced no doubt by the likes of Caldicott and Edward, her brother-in-law. Her agitation was overwhelming and she must clear her mind so that she could reason with Richard and avert this catastrophe. She had long dreaded and expected it, but now found herself, in reality, totally unprepared for it. At least there would be one further meeting with Richard; she must hold on to that thought and muster all her armaments. She went to the window and saw that gentle spring rain was falling softly like tears on the sunlit lawns, with a rainbow arcing over the park; perhaps it was a ray of hope, but it faded away a moment later. She took a deep breath and sighed.

Exhausted by her efforts and worries, she went early to bed, drawing the bed curtains to keep out the evening light and sinking gratefully into the warm embrace of the feather mattress and pillows. Thoughts of Richard invaded her mind: Richard happy and affectionate, Richard playful, Richard at court, dressed in his finery and gambling on cockfights and card games, Richard spoiling The Child, Richard considerate, Richard dancing and flirting, Richard her lover, Richard arguing about her inheritance, Richard and Matthew together, companionable and close, sharing secret looks, Richard aloof and haughty, Richard arrogant, Richard with Martha Penistone, Richard angry and vindictive, Richard plotting with Edward, Richard excluding her from his life... Richard, Richard. Images of his face, his eyes, his hands, the sound of his voice and the taste of his kisses assailed her. She ached for his presence.

Sleep was impossible. At first light she rose and prayed, as always remembering her mother in her prayers and asking God to protect her as well as The Child, Richard and herself. She begged for strength to face what the day would bring and resolved to deal staunchly with each set-back.

She didn't have to wait long to put her resolution to the test. Peter Baskett, Richard's Gentleman of the Horse, arrived from London.

"Greetings, my lady."

"Welcome, Baskett. You must have left London at first light to arrive here so early. Is your mission one of urgency?"

"Not so much urgent as important, my lady. I bring you this letter from my Lord."

Her hands shook as she broke the seal and the paper danced in front of her eyes so that she had to put it down on the table in order to be able to read it. She read it twice, dismissed Baskett and sat down heavily on the nearest chair.

'To Anne, Countess of Dorset.

Madam, It is my wish and intention that my Daughter, Lady Margaret Sackville, shall be brought to me at Great Dorset House in London. She is to depart from Knole tomorrow in company of her Nurse and two maids. Pray do not delay her Departure. I remain your assured attendant, Richard Sackville, Earl of Dorset.'

Tears sprang to her eyes; this was an unforeseen woe. She had never imagined that Richard would use The Child as an instrument of punishment against her. How could he do such a thing? He would never have dreamed up such a scheme himself . . . where had this idea come from? Dark thoughts of Caldicott crowded her mind, immediately followed by similar suspicions of Edward Sackville, her other enemy. She would not let little Margaret go, it was unthinkable. And they would not break her with their evil plotting.

She remembered her resolution to stand loyal to her principles, but then also thought of the promised meeting with Richard. If she refused to let The Child go to him, would she not be creating another source of argument between them? Could she risk making him even more angry with her? And what about The Child; she would surely suffer by becoming a weapon in their battle. Little Margaret loved them both, as indeed they both loved her; her trusting nature must not be destroyed by any involvement in the bad feeling between them.

Anne suddenly craved the happy laughter of The Child and sent to the nursery for her to be brought down. She dried her own eyes and the sight of the little girl running towards her, her burnished curls bouncing and glowing in the sunlight, brought a joyful smile of welcome to her face as she held out her arms to draw her daughter close.

"Come, my Lady Margaret, shall we gather bluebells in the Wilderness?" she suggested, and was tugged by the hand in answer. The Child soon had an armful of bluebells and ran off to show them to her nurse. Watching her go, Anne knew that she would be able to send her to London the next day with a sincere and warm blessing and a clear knowledge that it was the best thing for them both.

Later she sent for Edward Legge, greeting him with more calmness than she felt.

"Good day Mr. Legge, I trust you are in good health and that you know that his Lordship has asked that Lady Margaret be sent to him in London tomorrow?" She indicated that he should be seated.

"I thank you and yes, my lady, Baskett brought me news this morning. I trust you are content for her to go?" He hovered near the chair, uneasy in front of her.

"I have decided that she shall go," Anne said. "Though, at first, I was far from happy with the notion. Her nurse, Mrs Bathurst, shall go with her and her two maids, and no doubt she'll be accompanied by yourself and others of the servants as you deem necessary. I know that she'll be in good hands and well cared for, though it is grievous to me that she is thus to be removed from me." She sighed and Legge shifted uncomfortably on his chair.

"I believe his Lordship is dismayed," he said, "that you still stand against him and against the Judges' Award, my lady. Forgive me if I speak without warrant, but I believe he is close to despair in the matter and intends to speak with your Ladyship but once more. He is running out of time and patience."

"I know this, Mr Legge, and I thank you for telling me the truth on this occasion," Anne said, seizing the nettle. "I was distressed to be told by the servants that I was no longer to live at Knole; I would have valued receiving such news from you, before the servants were informed."

Legge stood up again looking agitated.

"I am sorely grieved that you learned it in that manner, Lady Anne. You should have heard that message from me, I agree, and the fault is clearly mine. The servant I confided in was sworn to keep silence until I had had the opportunity to speak to you, but I must have been overheard and the news was known to all and sundry before I could speak to your Ladyship. I humbly beseech your forgiveness."

"I will grant that, Mr Legge, and pray do not look so downcast."

Here, Anne was overcome by the sorrow that had been hanging over her for days and she bit her lip as tears prickled her eyes. Legge cleared his throat and thanked her and she continued.

"What am I to do, Mr Legge? I have no stomach for this fight, any more than has my lord. It has gone on and on and is wearing me out; I've said everything I have to say more times than I can number, but my Lord and I can reach no understanding on the matter. My Lord has the power to punish me in divers ways for my stance, but the only power which is in my hands is to keep saying 'No'. There is nought else to be done and I would that it were finished."

Legge nodded respectfully but made no further comment.

The following morning Anne made a supreme effort to appear cheerful as she prepared The Child for her departure as light-heartedly as possible.

"Why me go to Lonnon an' not you, lady mother?" Margaret wanted to know.

"My Lord your father wishes to see you, sweet heart, but I must remain here. I'm sure you will have a merry time in London and see many friends. Nurse Bathurst and Jane and Penny shall go with you and I promise that you and I shall see each other again soon."

"I wan' you come too," Margaret said sulkily, glowering from under lowered brows, but Anne hugged her close and kissed her neck, which always made her giggle. She wriggled away and climbed into the horse litter that had been prepared for her, waving as the party moved off.

Anne turned disconsolately back to the house, wondering how long it would be before she could keep that promise. There was still no word from Richard about when she might see him again and he would be occupied with The Child now, so it probably wouldn't be soon. She sighed heavily and sent a footman to ask Mrs Stewkley to bring her some refreshment.

As she squared her shoulders and walked more purposefully through the labyrinthine corridors, her mind turned to her dear mother and she determined to send a letter to her without delay. She would tell her of The Child's departure and her own sadness and isolation, as well as asking after the Countess's health. If only she could go north again! Richard would never consider another visit so soon after her disobedient return a few weeks ago, intent as he was on punishing her for her opposition to his demands. Everyone she cared deeply about was now far away and there was little comfort to be found in this place, where her Lord's servants surrounded her and often seemed to know more about how he was minded than she did.

Thoughts of her own situation were banished the following day when she received letters from several of her mother's servants and acquaintances in the north. They reported that Lady Margaret was extremely ill and they thought her in some danger of death. Anne busied herself, preparing a basket of cordials and conserves to be sent and writing letters to her and replies to her well-wishers. Rivers would be sent to London that day to arrange their onward dispatch to Westmorland.

When that was done she ate a light dinner, having little appetite for food when her mind was full of the news of her mother's dire sickness. She retired early to her chamber, longing to be alone with her thoughts, but was disturbed by a commotion outside and then by loud knocking at her door. She heard Judith remonstrate,

"You can't enter, my lady has retired!" and a man's voice responded;

"I am sent by my lord with orders to give this letter only into my lady's hand."

Anne called out for them to enter and took the letter which the messenger proffered, before sending him to the kitchens for some supper. She broke the seal under Judith's watchful eye. The letter was brief and gave only one clear message. It dropped from her hand and she looked up into Judith's enquiring eyes.

"My lord informs me that he has determined that The Child shall live at Horsley and not come hither anymore."

"Is Horsley far away, my lady?"

"It is where my lord's sister lives; I believe it is in the county of Surrey." Anne's voice was flat. How many more tortures could they invent to inflict on her?

"Oh, my lady, how can that be? I never heard of such a thing. Poor little Lady Margaret – she'll be lost without you."

"She has her nurse and her maids with her, Judith; I think she won't miss me too much. But it's harder for me!"

"You are very pale, my lady, let me bring you some ale or spiced wine. You have suffered a great shock."

Anne's only reply was a slight shake of her head. Alone again, she allowed herself to feel anger at Richard for the way he had tricked her into allowing The Child to be taken from her. Who was behind this piece of treachery? She pondered her plight and tried to think how she might respond to this latest blow. Gradually her thoughts calmed and as she lay down she began to see, like a chink of light in the darkness, a new possibility. She fell asleep, exhausted by the day's pile of troubles.

At first light she sat, pen in hand, composing one of the most important letters of her life. After some crossings-out and a false start, she wrote:

'My Lord, I do earnestly beseech you that I might go, not to the little House that you have appointed for me, but to Horsley and sojourn with my Child. I have done your Bidding in sending her to you and I humbly beg your Favour in this one thing. Meantime, I await your visit and hope to see you that we may discuss the Matters that divide us. I remain your devoted and loving Wife, Anne Dorset.'

She wrote affectionately also to her sister-in-law, Lady Beauchamp at Horsley, asking that she might come to be with her Child and calling on God to bless the household. A weight lifted from her as she closed the letters with her own Dorset seal and sent them with a footman to be delivered in all haste.

Her spirits lifted again when Rivers came from London with the news that he had heard from her north-country kinsman, Lord William Howard, that her mother was not in such danger as they had feared. The relief was like a river in spate washing her off her feet, but she ended the day with a headache that caused her to excuse herself and go to lie down. The heap of worries returned to remind her not to trust good news. Ten days had brought the breakdown of her marriage, the removal of her child and messages that her beloved mother was near to death; one good day would surely not reverse her fortunes.

The following day, Sunday, Anne attended the service in the

Knole Chapel where the new Rector of Sevenoaks, the Reverend Dr John Donne, preached a sermon on a verse from Psalm 102: *"He will regard the prayer of the destitute, and not despise their prayer."* The sermon was interesting and Anne took comfort from it; at least she was not destitute and she could afford to give alms. She would invite the Rector to sup with her one day soon.

For now, energised by the sermon, she sent for Legge.

"You wished to speak with me, my lady?"

"Thank you for attending me, Mr Legge," Anne said. "I respect your position as my lord's steward and therefore his most senior officer and I well know that you are held in high esteem for your loyal service. I believe that in some ways we are in similar places in relation to my lord, yet sometimes it feels as though we are in opposition to each other. I would not have it so.

"I want to put my view of the argument to you, to place before you some of my own thoughts. I do not wish to do this in order to dispute my lord's views, but to complement them.

"I hope you will agree that in all things, other than the argument over my birthright, I have been the most faithful and devoted wife that my lord could have wished for."

Legge nodded and she was encouraged to continue.

"I have been true to him in all things and have always obeyed and respected him. I have done his bidding and sought to please him, even when I was not bid, and have always supported him throughout the days of our marriage. Is it not so, Mr Legge?"

"That is so, my lady. I believe you speak truth, for I have not heard my lord make any complaint against you except in this one matter."

"I would remind you of this, Mr Legge, for I well understand that, as his faithful servant, you wish to take my lord's part when he and I are in dispute about this business. But it is also true, is it not, that at all other times my lord and I are close and of one heart and mind?"

"Indeed my lady, it is, and I have heard my Lord express his admiration and affection for you at those times. If I may venture to say so, I believe that is what makes this business so tragic for you both."

Anne was satisfied that she had improved Legge's opinion of her and that he might be more considerate and sympathetic towards her in the future.

❧

She looked up Psalm 102 in the great family bible in the Chapel and was transfixed when she found that several of the other verses applied strongly to her own situation. She recited the familiar opening verse: *"Hear my prayer, O Lord, and let my cry come unto thee. Hide not thy face from me in the day when I am in trouble; incline thine ear unto me: in the day when I call answer me speedily."*

Reading on, she almost jumped when she read: *"I am like a pelican of the wilderness: I am like an owl of the desert. I watch, and am as a sparrow alone upon the house top. Mine enemies reproach me all the day; and they that are mad against me are sworn against me."* Nothing could be closer to her own feelings at this moment; Dr Donne had led her towards words of comfort. She glanced down the page and saw that the next psalm began: *"Bless the Lord, O my soul: and all that is within me bless his holy name."* As she read this again, out loud, she felt understood, consoled and no longer alone. She looked up at the Queen of Scots' carvings of Christ's passion and once more was reminded that her situation could be worse, much worse.

❧

Shortly before dinner, Judith came to tell her that Matthew Caldicott had arrived from London and requested to speak with her. Anne received this message with a grimace but agreed to see him. When he was shown in Caldicott bowed low and greeted her respectfully. Anne responded coolly. She felt no warmth towards this usurper, one of those enemies who were sworn against her and whom she could never trust.

"My lady, I hope I find you well."

He bowed again with an exaggerated flourish. The man was

171

dressed like a courtier in all the latest finery, with large rosettes of black ribbon and silver lace decorating his shoes, a jewel hanging from one ear and sleeves with heavy gold embroidery slashed to show voluminous silk shirt sleeves underneath. She knew for certain that it had all been paid for by her husband and that, if she allowed her inheritance to be sold, it too would go on similar extravagances. If he brought a message from Richard she would hear him out, but would have no discussion with him. She inclined her head slightly, her dark eyes coolly holding his gaze but giving no encouragement.

"I am well, I thank you Matthew. Pray tell me what message you bring from my lord."

"My lord has sent me to you with this token of his esteem and proof that my message comes directly from him."

He held out his open palm to her, on which she saw that he offered a small gold ring, one which she instantly recognised. Richard often wore it; the marriage ring of his grandparents, Lord Treasurer Thomas Sackville and Lady Cicely. This token did indeed give authenticity to Caldicott's mission. Anne took the ring and looked up into his boyish features.

"My lord greets you," Caldicott said, "and bade me tell you that he will come here next week to speak with you. He also informs you that the Lady Margaret is not yet gone down to Horsley and will not immediately go there."

Anne nodded and removed her own wedding ring, replacing it with the one that Matthew had brought. She proffered her ring and said:

"Take this to my lord as token of my love and tell him I await his coming. Thank him for his message and news of The Child, and I bid him and you God-speed. I thank you for attending me."

She inclined her head and turned away as Caldicott bowed stiffly and left.

She sighed as the door closed behind him, wishing that Richard had sent a messenger with whom she might have felt a greater affinity. But she had to acknowledge to herself that Matthew, whatever she thought of him, was Richard's closest confidant and therefore the one her husband would see as the best person he could send to her. Richard would never understand the anger and jealousy she felt about his closeness to this man, or about the way that Matthew had wheedled his way into her lord's affections and so often turned him against her. She felt keenly her own lack of someone close in whom she could confide; I am truly like 'an owl of the desert', she thought, and went to write her diary.

CHAPTER SEVENTEEN
Mid-May 1616

There was little to occupy Anne in the days she spent waiting for Richard to come down from London. She neglected her dress again and brooded on the problems she faced. Her trusted servant, Christopher Marsh, approached her while she was wandering aimlessly in the Wilderness. She was leaning over the wall, watching a herd of dappled deer grazing quietly in the shade of the trees.

"My lady," Marsh said after the usual greetings. "May I speak openly of these matters concerning your disputes? I wish to speak only out of regard for you, as I see that you are worn down by the business."

Anne turned to contemplate this reassuring figure in his quiet brown clothes, so different from the flamboyant dress of the courtiers and nobility. He was deferent and retiring in manner, though an educated man who frequently read to her from the philosophers and wrote down her comments and memoranda. His face was long with a prominent chin and his light brown hair typically hung down over his brow in a floppy forelock. She valued his opinion.

"Pray continue, Mr Marsh. I am indeed exhausted, but you are a true friend and I would hear your thoughts."

"My lady, it distresses me to see you so brought down by the arguments and so unhappy," Marsh said. "Would it not be wise to draw the matter to a close?"

"I would willingly do that, Mr Marsh, if only I could find a way to finish it, but I have thought about it night and day for many months, years even, and can see no solution that would meet the case," Anne said. "If you can suggest a path that I could follow to bring it to a conclusion, please show me the way. As you have perceived, I have a sorrowful and heavy heart and would, above all, be reconciled with my lord."

"It is painful to me to see you in such anguish, my lady. I would have it otherwise and would offer counsel to bring you peace."

"Marsh, I know and believe that you have my interests at heart and that you are loyal and sincere in what you say. But I am impatient to hear your solution and would bid you – pray, stop beating about the bush and give me your counsel!"

The flash of irritation, albeit accompanied by a smile, spurred him to speak with a degree less diplomacy than was his custom with her.

"I can see only one way of solving this problem, my lady, but it is one which I fear you find difficult to contemplate. I ask myself which is worse for you: to continue to suffer as you have already done for many months, or to consider accepting the Judges' Award, which would settle the question for good?"

She began to protest, but he continued with uncharacteristic assertion,

"I myself cannot bear to see you brought down so low by worry and troubles and I cannot imagine how you can support it. Pray at least consider what I have said, dear lady."

Anne could hardly believe that Marsh, who had always stood by her and been her faithful attendant in every way, had now joined the pack pressing her to forsake her rights and principles. She looked at him, aghast. His eyes were serious and concerned, full of sincerity.

"No, Mr Marsh, this will not do!" She shook her head. "You are asking me to give up my birthright; to abandon all the work my dear lady mother has done to make the case clear; and instead to cave in to my lord, my uncle and my cousin after all this struggle. I cannot do it! And I can't forsake my beloved mother now, when she is mortally ill. It could be a death blow to her. I know that you speak out of loyalty and affection for me, and I thank you for that and for all your faithful service which I value beyond measure, but I hope to make you comprehend that I must fight this battle to its end, not simply for myself but for my family, past and future."

"Aye, my lady," Marsh said. "I wish it were not so, but I see that in your mind there is no other way. You are brave and certain in your spirit and that must be what sustains you against the rest of the world – for I believe most folks would have you consent – and most folks in your situation would have done so before now.

"And yet could you not consider that there may be some arrangement which would satisfy his lordship without forcing you to relinquish your claim altogether? Some way of giving your Lord hope that, under certain circumstances, he might achieve the outcome he desires?"

"Mr. Marsh, I know that I am seen as stubborn and wrong-headed in this matter," Anne said, "But I have to believe that truth and right will triumph in the end. The law is on my side, whatever the judges have said, and the Clifford entail stands to benefit me and my heirs. God has always looked after me and I believe He will stay with me, so I shall hold on. Time will tell who is to be proved right in the end. I sincerely thank you for your honest opinion and I shall keep in mind all you have said."

"I see you are not to be moved, my lady," Marsh said as he bowed and edged away, "But I thank you for hearing me out and as always I wish you every good fortune and a beneficial outcome from this business, whatever your decision. I shall always remain your devoted servant."

Anne watched him take the path towards the house, then leaned against the wall and clutched her head in her hands. Was there anyone left in this world except her dear mother who could see the case as she saw it? A few of her female friends had occasionally made supportive comments and applauded her courage, but even they often implied that she was letting down her husband and should comply with his wishes. Now even loyal Christopher Marsh had joined their group. The rest of the world, from Edward Sackville and Matthew Caldicott to the Archbishop of Canterbury, condemned her as a stubborn, wayward and perverse woman, deserving of no sympathy.

❧

Anne was in the Long Gallery, contemplating the portraits of famous figures placed there years ago by Richard's grandmother Margaret Howard, when another visitor was brought to speak to her. Mr Graverner, Richard's gentleman usher, was second only to Edward Legge in the hierarchy of those who served the Earl. He was in high spirits, having come down from London where, he reported to Anne, Richard and several of his friends had won a great sum in a cock-fighting match.

"Then," he added, "there followed some kind of fracas between their side and their opponents, with unkind words exchanged, but no greater harm done."

She heard from him stories of great times in London, with Richard and his associates attending plays, horse races, cocking matches and bowling alleys, sometimes in the company of the King. The more money Richard lost to the King, the higher he rose in his favour.

The longer Graverner went on speaking of the merriment at court and the central and popular part that Richard played in it all, the more clearly Anne saw the contrast with her own life. She remembered with a sharp pang the times she had shared with her husband at court and the closeness they had enjoyed then. There was no news of The Child and she wondered whether Richard even remembered that he had taken her away, or had forgotten her in the whirl of his exciting life. She cried herself to sleep that night and woke while it was still dark, to worry about what troubles the next day might bring and then to rise and pray.

❦

The arrival at midday of her mother's footman, Thomas Petty, answered the question. He brought letters from Westmorland, written by various friends and attendants of her mother's, but flicking through them she found nothing in her mother's hand and her heart sank. The letters were distressing; Lady Margaret was very sick, they told her, and so overwhelmed by pain that she was unable to write herself. They sent messages from her, bidding

Anne to stay strong and remain at her lord's side. Nothing would be gained by disobeying his orders, they wrote.

The outlook was thought by all to be gloomy and they feared she would not recover from such a state. Thomas Petty was openly upset about his mistress's ill health, but he knew that Richard had forbidden Anne to travel and he avoided pressing her to go north again. It was the clearest indication Anne had yet received that the time might be close when her dear mother, her one true supporter and friend, would be taken from her.

Nothing could be worse than this and she took her prayer book out to The Standing in the dusk to pray more earnestly than ever before. Her God was truly now her only helper and she gazed at the flickering lights in some of the windows of the house below her and saw in them the fragility of life and the guttering of the best and strongest spirit she had ever known.

❦

The following day was no better. Instead of an answer to her prayers she received a brief and brutal letter:

Esteemed Madam, I write to warn you that unless you yield to your Lord's desire in the business afoot, and unless you yield immediately, you will be undone forever and there will be no going back. There is to be no further delay, the matter must be settled. I remain, Madam, your obedient servant, Matthew Caldicott.

Anne was angered by this interloper's meddling in business that she regarded as private between Richard and herself, even though she knew that the whole world gossiped about it. Caldicott had no scruples, nor even any shame about addressing her in this way and at this time. He must be very certain of my Lord's regard, she thought bitterly. She would not reply; she threw the letter into the back of the fire and watched it turn black and then curl its sinuous ash around the logs in the grate. She wished she could as easily rid herself of its author.

❦

The next morning she dressed in the drab taffeta gown and mustard-coloured waistcoat which had become her usual habit during these long days when nothing happened and she saw no-one. But this day brought a surprise, even though it was something she had spent several weeks waiting for.

A great clattering, much scuttling of servants and the sound of men's voices heralded the arrival from London of Richard, accompanied by his cousin, Cecily Neville, and the inevitable Caldicott. They were all arrayed in the latest fashions and offered a dazzling sight as they descended from the coach, the men handing Lady Cecily down, one at each side, their silks, satins and jewels glowing in the sunlight with all the iridescence of an ostentation of peacocks. No wonder the servants are rushing about in a frenzy, Anne thought, as she welcomed the travellers and led Cecily through the Great Hall and up the staircase. Morning light streamed through the mullioned windows on to the magnificent carved and painted Sackville leopards rearing on top of the newel posts, reminding Anne of the power of this family in which she felt such an outsider.

It was vexing to have to entertain Cecily when she wanted to run and embrace Richard, but perhaps one of his reasons for bringing his cousin was to keep some distance between himself and Anne, even after a month apart. She made as good a fist as she could of chatting to Cecily, who was not particularly receptive and had surely noticed that her mind was elsewhere and her heart was not in it. Cecily's disdainful looks also told Anne that her dowdy attire had been noted. Richard took her to one side, but his words were not the ones she had hoped for.

"It is not the first time I have come here to find you undressed," he said. "But it is the first time you have embarrassed me before a member of my family. I am most displeased. I wish you to remember that, in my absence from Knole, you are my representative here and must always be attired in the dress appropriate to your position and title." He slept in a separate chamber that night.

After supper the following evening, Cecily declared she would retire for the night and swept out in a swish of silk. As soon as the door had closed behind her, Richard broached the subject of the Award and an argument erupted.

"You are so stubborn and obstinate! Pray listen to reason for once and let me explain to you the advantages of the award which the judges have made," he said. "It will benefit you as well as me and is the best we can possibly hope for. Let us take it while we may, before it is lost to us."

"I would prefer to discuss this matter with you alone, my lord. I cannot pay full attention to you with the distracting presence of Matthew," Anne said.

"No, I wish Matthew to stay. I see no reason why he should distract you; you are simply trying to avoid the discussion, as usual. You are playing for time as you always do and I will not tolerate any further delay! The Judges' Award must be accepted. If you will just say 'yes', all will be resolved, then we can celebrate and retire for the night."

"I am mortified that you find my presence upsetting, Lady Anne, but the matter really is as simple as my lord says it is," Caldicott said, smooth as oil.

"This is intolerable!" Anne said. "I will not discuss the matter any further with both of you here. I shall never give my agreement to the judges' arrangement, so there is nothing simple about it, nor anything to discuss. Goodnight!"

❧

Tempers had cooled by morning and Richard lent Caldicott one of his best horses and sent him to join a deer-hunting party in the park. Anne dressed carefully in her favourite green damask dress embroidered with gold and a fashionable ruff, lace cuffs and transparent apron. A pearl hung from her left ear by a black cord.

Anne and Richard talked first of other matters, and Anne learned that The Child had now gone to Horsley, where she was with her aunts, Richard's two sisters, and their husbands. Her three servants had accompanied her there and she was well. Anne was comforted to have news of her and thanked Richard for his reassurance.

She had decided what she wanted to say to her husband and now took a deep breath.

"My lord, I have waited many weary weeks to speak with you about this business and I would not have you believe that I have any wish whatsoever to delay; the truth is quite the opposite."

"Very well, I am here now, so let us look at all the possibilities," Richard said. "We must come to some conclusion. You will not accept the Judges' Award, that is clear, but I have been looking for some other way that we could come to an agreement which would suit us both and end the arguments."

Anne, surprised, was reminded of Mr Marsh's words and wondered whether she could see his hand in Richard's change of tone. What was it he had said? 'Perhaps there is some arrangement you could make which would satisfy his Lordship without you having to relinquish your claim altogether?' Was there a glimpse of hope here?

"It would be my dearest wish and greatest pleasure to consider any suggestion to which we could both agree," Anne said. "What do you have in mind, my lord?"

"I'll be frank with you. You know already of my need for means to settle the most pressing of my debts."

She nodded and he continued,

"Most of my property is pledged in some way to my creditors, except that which is required to provide the income for our household's needs. I have no hope of being able to meet my future obligations without reducing our income, unless I can show that I have some credible new hope of prospects and advancements."

"I understand that, my lord."

"Good. Then you will also comprehend that I am casting about for the means of demonstrating such prospects. I think there may be a way of doing so, if you will agree."

"Pray tell me what that is, as long as it does not require me to withdraw my claim to the lands in Westmorland."

"It does involve the lands in Westmorland, but not the renouncement of your claim. My proposal is that your lady mother should make her jointure over to me, for which I would return to her an annual rent. This would meet my requirements for additional income but avoid the need for the withdrawal of your claim. What do you say?"

Anne slowly turned her gaze to look at Richard, trying to work out the meaning of his words. She repeated them in her mind and understood them. There seemed to be no trick, no way of misunderstanding them or of re-interpreting them. He wanted her mother to assign her jointure over to him, in return for an annual rent. That would not require Anne's renouncement or signature. On Margaret's death the jointure lands would, as Anne and Margaret believed, become Anne's under the entail. Any dispute then would be between herself and Richard on the one hand, and Francis and Henry Clifford on the other. If Richard was satisfied that the arrangement would meet his needs, and if her mother was willing to agree to it, perhaps this was the answer to her prayers. Her eyes searched his face and found only hope and sincerity there.

"I must have a little time to consider, my lord, but I see no immediate objection, except that my dear mother is most grievously ill at the present and I would not have her troubled at this time."

"You must decide before I leave for London later today. I need to know your mind and have your assurance that you will write letters to your lady mother straight away."

"How would you have me send the letters, my lord?"

"Send them with Marsh but have him bring them to me in London on the way north, that I may see them."

"You will have them in two days' time; I will send for Marsh and have them composed without delay. And I thank you a hundredfold for devising this way out of our difficulty."

They were stiff and guarded with each other after the months of hostility, but the nearest thing to a smile that they had exchanged in all that time passed fleetingly between them now, and he touched her arm as he left the room. It was like the first signs of a thaw after a long hard winter. It would take longer for them to be able to relax into warmth with each other, but what a relief it was to have reached this point – and there had been no more talk of her leaving Knole.

CHAPTER EIGHTEEN
Late May 1616

With the letters dispatched to her mother and the relief that came with the cautious lessening of tension between her and Richard, Anne suddenly found she could give her attention to other matters. She encouraged friends to visit her at Knole and caught up on some of the latest news.

Lady Selby visited from nearby Ightham Mote. She told Anne that there was much talk again about Robert Carr, now Lord Somerset, and his Lady, about whose divorce from the Earl of Essex there had been so much gossip in the past.

"My dear Dorothea, I am all agog!" said Anne. "Pray what is being said now?"

"Well now they have both been arrested, charged with murder!" Lady Selby said. Anne gasped.

"Who are they said to have murdered?"

"Sir Thomas Overbury," Dorothea continued, "The gentleman poet who befriended Lord Somerset on his first arrival at court as simple Robert Carr. Overbury was opposed to the affair between Carr and your kinswoman from the beginning. Later, he wrote and published a long poem which many took to be a warning to Carr that she might be fit for a mistress, but not suitable as a wife."

"Yes, I remember that," Anne said. "Wasn't it called 'A Wife'? It was much talked of when I was at court for the marriage of the Princess Elizabeth."

Dorothea explained that Lady Essex and Carr had been enraged by Overbury's poem, particularly her ladyship, because it threatened to destroy all her schemes. Once married to Carr, the King's favourite, she got the King on her side and contrived to have Sir Thomas imprisoned on false accusations. After a few months in the Tower, Sir Thomas died and there had been rumours ever since that she had brought about his death because he knew too much about her; the story went that she had had him slowly poisoned by bribing the warder and an apothecary who supplied arsenic and mercury. This talk could not be suppressed and in the end the King had to act; Lady Somerset was arrested and confessed her guilt. She was sent to the Tower, along with her husband – who protested his innocence of any intrigue.

"They are condemned to death – but no-one believes that the King will ever countenance their execution," Dorothea concluded.

"Well, we shall see," Anne said with a frown, recalling her own brush with Robert Carr. "King James has been very fond of Lord Somerset for a long, long time – but on the other hand, the King always wishes to show that he is a wise judge."

"You are right; it must be a dilemma for the King!" Dorothea said.

"I have clearly missed much by being absent from court for so long," Anne said.

"You surely have, dear friend," Lady Selby said. "And I must tell you that I have lately heard some folks say that you have done well in standing firm against the judgment of your affairs made in the court of appeal."

"This is indeed a new tune, for I've had the entire world against me until now!" Anne said.

"Yes, that's true, but I think some people are beginning to see that your lord is unreasonable in treating you so ill and they are persuaded that your cause is a fair one."

"I'm so grateful to you for that news, dear Dorothea – you cannot believe how much it lightens my heart – and also for the gossip with which you have entertained me!"

❦

The happy interlude was short-lived, for the next day Anne welcomed Kendal, one of her mother's servants, and begged him for news.

"I bring you the worst possible news, my lady," Kendal said.

"I have ridden very hard to carry word to you that the Dowager Countess died five days ago at Brougham, between the hours of six and nine at night. The pains had been insupportable for many days and her cries were piteous. So, for those in her household, the end seemed a blessed relief for her and all who cared for her. I am wretched to bear such tidings to you, my lady." He handed her a rolled and sealed parchment, saying, "I bring you this, to be given into your hand only."

"This is the heaviest of news for me, Kendal, but I thank you for making such haste. This must be my lady mother's will." She took the scroll and broke the seal but could not read the document through her tears and set it to one side, believing that it probably held no surprises for her.

When the weary Kendal had departed, Anne gave way to grief. She could not be comforted for many hours and Judith was in despair as to how to soothe her mistress. She refused all food and drink, sobbing and wailing repeatedly,

"Why? Why? Why must I bear this most lamentable cross? Has even dear God now deserted me? At twenty-six years old, I am alone in the world!"

Eventually, exhausted, she slept while Judith kept watch outside her chamber to ensure that she was not disturbed.

❦

Anne shed more tears the next day over her mother's will. It contained so much of her sweet nature and her generous concern for her relatives, friends, servants, tenants and the poor, that Anne could hear her voice in the phrases expressing her wishes. Especially poignant to her was the reference to '*my dear and noble sole daughter and heire*'.

There was one request which Anne found very unsettling, in which Lady Margaret specified that her body should be buried in the place where her brother had already been interred. This, Anne knew, was at Alnwick in Northumberland, a very long way from any of Margaret's lands and far from her late husband's tomb at

Skipton. It was a double blow, for not only was her mother's body to be taken far away, but in her distraught state Anne also took this to be a sign that she would be dispossessed of her inheritance; her mother must have foreseen that the land would be seized by the Cliffords and was therefore not a fit place for her interment.

When Anne started weeping again Judith feared the worst, but a short while later she recovered sufficiently to instruct a servant to take her mother's will to Richard, who was at Lewes for a great meeting and entertainment of sporting noblemen. Then the Bishop of St David's came to comfort her and later she was able to send to Ightham Mote for Dorothea's husband, Sir William Selby, who hurried to her side.

"Lady Dorset, may I offer you my deepest condolences in your grievous bereavement. Your dear mother was known to all as the epitome of grace, goodness and learning. Her loss will be felt by the whole world, but by none as keenly as yourself. I know that she has been your strongest support for many years and you will miss her desperately. If I can be of help to you I would offer my services with pleasure at any time."

"Thank you indeed, Sir William," Anne said. "I am indebted to you for your understanding, which is a comfort to me. And there is one matter on which I would value your advice at this time."

"Be assured, Lady Dorset, that I am entirely at your disposal," Sir William said with sincerity.

"My lady mother has appointed that her body should be buried close to that of her brother, Lord Francis Russell," Anne said. "This I know to be at Alnwick in Northumberland, which I believe to be close to the place of your birth and where you still have many connections and kin. I would regard it as a great favour and aid if you could advise me on the best way of conveying my dear mother's remains to that place, from Brougham in Westmorland, and how to arrange for the building of a little chapel there."

"I can certainly do that, my dear Lady Anne, and will be honoured to do so," Sir William said. He hesitated and then continued, "Please forgive the question, but I am puzzled as to why you wish your lady mother to be interred so far from your own lands and forebears."

"Oh, Sir William, I most certainly do not! It is only by reason of my mother's will that I am forced to consider this at all," Anne said. "I had thought she would be buried with my father at Skipton Church, close by the castle where she bore me, but this is not her expressed wish, perhaps because that place is under the control of my uncle and cousin, who have been our enemies since my father's death." She was close to tears again and bit her lip.

Sir William nodded and looked away.

"Then your request is easily met," he said. "I shall send orders for a carriage and horses draped in black to be sent to Brougham to convey the corpse to Alnwick. And in a few days' time I'll bring you the information you need concerning the chapel you wish to build. Pray rest easily, Lady Anne, in the knowledge that everything that needs to be done will be done for you and for the Dowager Countess. It is a great honour to me to be able to serve you and you may depend upon me."

"I cannot fully express my gratitude to you, Sir William; your assistance is beyond value," Anne said. "You have set my mind at rest when I could never have managed these arrangements from so far away, whilst drowning in this great ocean of misery."

The following day Richard sent word that he would come to her tomorrow on his way back to London from Lewes. This was a comfort to her, but even more welcome was a letter from a retainer of the Dowager Countess's in the north, informing her that a further codicil to Lady Margaret's will had been found in which she stated that she should be buried wherever her daughter thought fit. Anne felt a load lift from her with this news, like a dark thunder-cloud being blown away. She sent word immediately to Sir William that she would not need Lady Margaret's body transported to Northumberland after all and received a kind and understanding reply.

Richard arrived very early the next morning. She felt him register her red eyes and strained countenance as she welcomed him warmly, though their greetings were stilted, as though they had lost the habit of friendship.

"It is a pleasure to see you, my lord. I trust you are well and have enjoyed the sport and company at Lewes."

"Aye, well enough. You have sorrowful news my lady, and much to grieve you, on which I would condole with you," Richard said, kissing her hand.

"Thank you, my lord. I heard yesterday, to the comfort of my soul, that my lady mother had expressed a further wish that I might bury her where I see fit."

"That is some consolation to you in truth, Anne, and I am glad of it," Richard said. "You must write to Westmorland concerning this and giving instructions for the treatment of the body until you can go to bury her.

"Now I need to sleep, for I am dog weary," he continued, "And must then go to London where I shall seek advice on securing the jointure lands to our advantage. I am determined that we shall take possession, though it will not be easy and will surely be opposed by your uncle and his son. At least I believe they will stay their hand as long as Lady Margaret's corpse remains at Brougham."

Anne was surprised by the sudden change that had come about in Richard's attitude and it took her a few moments to realise that this most dreadful of all events had had the unforeseen result of bringing her husband on to her side, in opposition to her Clifford relatives. The arguments with him were over!

"I thank you my lord," she said. "I shall instruct Rivers to write the letters while you sleep. I shall request that the body be wrapped in lead until they hear from me and I'll inform them that you desire to take possession."

Before Richard left for London later that afternoon, Anne had a request to make;

"My lord, I shall need to order mourning clothes and would

come up to London soon for that purpose."

"Then come in four- or five-days' time, when I shall have taken counsel about what is to be done." It was almost shocking to her to find their conversation so harmonious.

Amid her preparations for going to London, Anne was surprised to learn that both Marsh and Rivers had come down to Knole and were anxious to speak with her. It was unusual for them both to undertake the same task and she thought there must be something of great moment afoot. Their message, however, was a simple one. After offering their deepest sympathy, Marsh said:

"My lady, we come from Lord Dorset to inform you that he has spoken with Sir William Howard and with learned counsel and has written to Lady Margaret's servants and tenants in Westmorland, telling them to keep possession of her jointure for him and you."

Rivers added, "And his lordship looks forward to your arrival in London."

"I thank you both," Anne said. "This is unexpected news. I had thought that my uncle of Cumberland would have quietly taken over upon my mother's death. I am most grateful to my Lord for his swift action and to you both for bringing me news of it. Pray convey to him my thanks and tell him that I shall join him in London tomorrow, God willing."

After their departure Anne thought about the message, the fact that it had been sent at all, and the change of circumstances that had begun to ripple through her life. It was a novelty that Richard was now defending her right to the lands. She thanked God for His mercy and prayed fervently for her mother's soul.

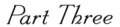

Part Three

Chapter Nineteen
Early June 1616

The heavy silence during the coach journey to London the next day was broken by a young maid taken into the household to help Judith in place of Millie (who was recently married).

"Are you not excited to be going up to London Town, my lady?" Faith asked.

Judith shushed her, but Anne looked at her beaming rosy face and spoke kindly;

"I'm sure it seems very thrilling to you, Faith, but I've known it all my life. I was brought to London as a babe-in-arms and have had many very good times there. I might be more delighted now, were it not for the loss of my dear mother; I'm afraid that shadow darkens everything at present."

Faith started to speak again and Judith aimed a kick at her ankle to silence her but missed.

"Oh! I am very, very sorry, my lady," Faith said, reddening. "I meant no harm but was carried away by my own excitement. I do beg pardon. I cannot imagine what it must be to lose your mother, for mine was lost at my birth so I have never known what it is like to have a mother."

"I am sorry to hear that, Faith. Pray then, who raised you?" Anne asked.

Judith frowned at Faith, but she had piqued her mistress's interest and there was no quietening her.

"I was raised by my grand dam and my aunt. They were an old woman and a young one, for my mother was the eldest of my granddame's seven children and my aunt was the youngest, so as she was nearer in age to myself than to her sister, my mother."

"And your father, child?" Anne asked.

"Oh, my father was a sailor, my lady, and I hardly saw him. He

192

came from his ship once to see me when I was about four or five years old and I thought him a stranger and ran from him," Faith replied.

"Well, that is a strange thing, Faith, for my father also was a sailor and I saw but little of him when I was a child. That is how my mother and I became so close. Without a mother, the absence of your father must have been distressing for you."

"Truth to tell, having known no different I didn't really notice. I was a good child, the youngest in the house, and my grandma and my aunt were kindness and company enough for me."

"Then you have been very lucky," Anne said.

"Oh, yes, my lady, and I know it well. And because they raised me to be clean and neat and to sew, wash and mend, I am doubly lucky because now I have been taken into your Ladyship's service, which I count the greatest boon that could have befallen me."

"You have earned your place here, Faith, and I believe you are of great help to Judith, is she not, Judith?" Anne said, turning to the older woman.

Judith looked relieved to be drawn into the conversation and took the opportunity to say what had been in her mind.

"Aye, my lady, she is that. But she does have a habit of chattering too much!"

"Well her chatter this morning has made the journey less wearisome for me and has taken my mind off my woes, so I'm grateful!" Anne said, watching their faces as Judith gave the maid a wry look and the girl grinned in delight.

"But don't take advantage of Judith's good nature, Faith," Anne added, to Judith's clear satisfaction. "If you do as she tells you and learn from her, she will fashion you into a commendable lady's maid."

❧

"Welcome to Great Dorset House, my lady," Richard bowed and kissed her hand as she alighted from the coach. It wasn't an overwhelmingly affectionate welcome, but it was an improvement on anything she had received from him during the past half-year, even seen through a veil of grief.

"I thank you for that, and for your swift action in securing the possession of my lady mother's jointure lands," Anne said, as he led her into the drawing chamber.

"That had to be done," Richard said, frowning. "The delay you have caused by your refusal of the agreement with your Clifford kin means that they may now simply take over the lands, which (by your father's will) revert to them following your mother's death. If they succeed in that endeavour they will have no reason to offer us anything. All will be lost.

"I have written as your representative," he went on, "and have acquired a command from the Privy Council that Appleby Castle, already entered by force by Lord Cumberland's men, shall be restored to the possession of our people, as it was at your lady's decease. Rivers has set off to Westmorland this morning to deliver the papers and report on what he finds the situation to be.

"In the meantime," Richard's voice became more forceful, "I wish you to make an agreement with me that your rights to the lands in Westmorland shall be passed to me and The Child."

Anne was taken aback by the suddenness of this demand and the tone in which it was delivered. She sat down. Clearly, the atmosphere had not improved as much as she had imagined and she needed to think nimbly about this new challenge.

"Why, Richard?" she asked. "What advantage would that bring?"

"It would simplify matters," Richard said impatiently. "It would simplify matters and I could pursue them in my own name, avoiding delay."

"I don't see that it would benefit us at all," Anne said. "It is clear in law that the lands are mine, through the entail. Were they to be transferred to you, their ownership would become more complicated and the case would be obfuscated, would it not?"

"You are as stubborn as ever!" Richard tutted.

"I am not willing to agree to your proposal, my lord. They are my lands and I wish them pursued in my name," Anne said.

Richard protested and left, but in the evening he returned to Dorset House with Lord William Howard.

"Lady Anne, what a pleasure to see you in London," began Lord William, smiling broadly and extending his hand as Anne rose from the chair where she had been reading the tracts that her mother had spoken aloud at her father's deathbed nearly eleven years ago.

"We have not had your company in many months," Lord William said, then remembered the circumstances and his face and voice suddenly became mournful. "I offer my deepest condolences and hope I find you in good health?"

"I thank you for your concern, Cousin William. I am well. Pray be seated."

They exchanged further remarks as a servant brought in a supper tray and they settled down with crystal glasses of ruby wine.

"Richard has been telling me of your reluctance to allow him to take on the rights to your mother's jointure lands, Anne," William said, crossing his legs and looking into her eyes with a challenge. "And I am come to assure you that I believe that to be the best thing for both you and your daughter. If you do not agree to this you are hampering your lord's ability to speak for you."

"It is good of you to trouble yourself with our affairs, Lord William," Anne said, returning his gaze. "But surely, if I pass over my rights to my lord he will not be speaking for me any longer, but for himself? I am afraid that this does not satisfy the case for me and I cannot agree to it." Anne was wearied by the endless debate and answered without fervour, but Richard burst out,

"You see, my Lord William, what I must grapple with! She is the most stubborn woman I have ever met, and it is my poor lot to be married to her!" He beat his fist against his chest as he spoke.

"Now, let us not be quarrelsome!" William said. "I believe Anne will listen to a reasoned argument and we should make the case to her calmly."

"I have spent years making reasoned cases to her and she refuses every argument without fail!" Richard sputtered. "I have lost patience and will have no further truck with it! I ask you once more, my lady, as does my Lord William; will you pass your rights in Westmorland to me and The Child, or no?"

"No," Anne said. "I wish you good night, my lords." She heard expletives uttered as she turned her back on them and left the room. The footman closed the door behind her.

❧

A few minutes later someone knocked at her chamber door. Faith opened it to Legge, who stood awkwardly on the threshold, looking as though he would prefer to be elsewhere.

"My lady," Legge began, and then cleared his throat. "Lord Dorset has bidden me inform you that you are to return to Knole immediately. The coach will be ready for you at eight o'clock and he wishes you to leave then. I regret being the bearer of such a message," he bowed.

"But it is half past seven now!" Anne protested. "How am I to be ready to leave again in thirty minutes? I have been here but a few hours; I came to town to order my mourning clothes and that is not yet done. The message must surely be a mistake, Mr Legge. Pray check with my lord as to its meaning."

Legge stepped into the chamber and continued quietly;

"My lady, those were his lordship's words and he is much chafed. There were other words as well, that I would not repeat to your ladyship, but I have no doubt he wants you to leave. Indeed he orders it."

"Very well, Legge. Thank you. I am sorry you have been put to this trouble but, be assured, I shall leave by eight o'clock and you shall not bear the brunt of my husband's temper on my account any more this night. I should be glad if you would come down to Knole tomorrow, for there is much I would discuss with you."

Legge inclined his head in assent, backed out and closed the door. Anne turned to Judith, who stood with her mouth agape.

"Judith, gather together my furs for the journey. Even a June night can be chill. Tell Kath Buxton she is to come with me and send Faith to inform my cousin Cecily Neville and Mistress Willoughby that I am leaving again. Tomorrow, pray pack my chest and bring all the rest of my goods back down to Knole as soon as you can."

Judith bobbed a curtsey and jerked into action and for a few minutes all was flurry and bustle. Marsh was there to hand his mistress into the coach and wish her a safe journey. There was still plenty of light in the evening sky, but darkness fell when they were barely half way there. By the time they reached Knole it was midnight and they had to awaken the keeper of the gatehouse to let them in. As she left the coach Anne could hear him grumbling with the coach-driver and footman about the late hour and the lack of warning. She hoped they didn't think it was her idea to return at this hour.

Anne spent the next morning working furiously at her needlework. She was making a cushion in cross-stitch with a Celtic cross worked in shades of blue, pink and brown. At least something must be achieved! But her stitches were too tight and some of the work was spoiled and would have to be undone.

Legge was as good as his nod and arrived on horseback just after noon.

"I am glad to see that you arrived here safely, my lady. You wished to speak with me?"

"Indeed, Mr Legge, you are welcome and there is much I would discuss with you," Anne said. "The last time I spoke with Mr Marsh of this business, he suggested the possibility that there might be a way of making an agreement with my Lord without losing my inheritance. I thought it an idea worth considering, but we failed to find a course of action that might bring it about. I have tussled with it since, without success, and wondered whether you have any notion of how it might be achieved? We are sore in need of it."

"I believe that is what you and Lord Dorset both truly desire, my lady," Legge said. "And I think it must be possible to come to some compromise which would be acceptable to you and also meet his lordship's needs."

"It is certainly my greatest wish," Anne said immediately. "But have you heard my Lord's latest demand of me? He wishes me to pass my rights in the lands of Westmorland to him and our Child. He had Lord William Howard come to persuade me yesterday almost as soon as I had arrived and then, when I would not be persuaded, he sent me away again, as you know."

"It was unfortunate and most upsetting."

"It was harsh dealing, was it not? I'm still angry to be treated thus," Anne said. "But I must take a calm look at my lord's proposal to see whether, with some amendment, it might perhaps lead to an accord. Can you see any way of this becoming a compromise which we could both accept?"

"His lordship wishes you to surrender your claim to Westmorland in favour of himself and little Lady Margaret?" Legge asked, for confirmation.

"Yes, and I have refused. I think he believes that bringing The Child into it will soften me. But it would still involve me giving up my rights, which I will not do." Anne's colour was high and she spoke with determination.

"Do you have any objection to Lady Margaret being part of an agreement?" Legge asked.

"No, none at all, Mr Legge," Anne said. "But I do not wish to surrender control of the matter to my husband. Lady Margaret's inheritance of Clifford lands must be secured and I fear my husband might not respect that."

"His lordship's greatest need is for money, is it not?" Legge pondered.

"Indeed, yes. He leads an extravagant life and will never have enough. I would not have him waste our Clifford inheritance, if it is ever to come to me," Anne said.

"That is something we can never know, my lady. But I think it is telling that your kinsmen, Lord Cumberland and his son, have offered a great fortune for your agreement and that the judges have endorsed the idea," Legge said.

"What is your meaning, Legge?"

"I mean that Lord Cumberland, Henry Clifford, and the judges all seem to have accepted that your claim is valid – to the extent that many thousand pounds is the price put on it," Legge said.

"Yes," Anne said, hesitating. "I had never quite thought of it in that way. Is there something in it that can help us get closer to an accord?"

"His Lordship's creditors are very pressing, I believe. They threaten him and demand repayment of his debts, do they not?" Legge said.

"That is how he has put it to me," Anne said. "I think he threatens me because they threaten him. If he has to flee the country, he says, it will be my fault." She fought back panicky tears and slumped hopelessly.

"Do you think there is any hope that the prospect of him gaining from your lands in the case of your death might be sufficient to satisfy these creditors?" Legge asked.

At this she sat up with more interest.

"I don't know, Mr Legge; I suppose that is possible. But it would not meet my need to secure my inheritance for my Child, as my lord would be taking from our daughter instead of from me," Anne said.

"Hmm . . . quite," Legge pondered, his expression becoming doubtful. "Then, if it were specified that you would pass the inheritance of Westmorland to your Lord, but only if you had no surviving direct heirs; would that meet the case?"

Anne was silent, thinking about Legge's last words. The implication of her having no surviving heirs was an unbearable idea. She shuddered, pushed it away and forced herself to look at it simply as a solution to the impasse; she would retain her claim to Westmorland and could continue to fight for it. The Child's inheritance would be preserved, provided she outlived her mother.

But Richard would have the prospect of inheriting the claim on her death, if The Child died before her. It might be enough to satisfy his creditors and save him from insolvency. Would he accept it? Could he afford not to accept it? Suddenly, for the first time, she realised that if he carried out his threat to leave her, he would still have no solution to his problem. He needed money, and he needed her! She looked up at the steward's serious face with a glimmer of hope. Perhaps things were not as bleak as she had believed.

"You may have found the answer that I have sought for so long, Mr Legge," Anne said slowly.

"I shall be exceeding glad if that is the case, my lady. But think about it until tomorrow and we shall examine it again then, before I take it to Lord Dorset. We may think of aspects we have not yet considered."

By the following morning it was clear to both Anne and Legge that a possible solution was in their hands. Legge set off early to London to put the amended idea to Richard; Anne would agree to the Clifford estates in Westmorland passing to Richard on her death, provided she had no surviving direct heirs.

Anne worked away at her cross-stitch in a tizzy of agitated anticipation, hardly daring to hope that Richard would be satisfied by this alteration to his plan. The pattern on the cushion was intricate and took a lot of concentration; she kept making mistakes and had to unpick her work. Eventually it was finished and she proudly displayed it to Judith, who had come to inform her that Basket and two other gentlemen had arrived to see her.

Anne was surprised and delighted to find that one of the gentlemen was Ralph Coniston, an attendant of her mother's, come from Westmorland. She welcomed him warmly, accepted his expressions of sympathy on her loss and enquired after his family. She then turned to Basket and the third visitor, an elderly gentleman with smiling grey eyes in a lined grey face.

"Why, Doctor Layfield! What immense pleasure it gives me to see you! It is a good number of years since I had the honour of attending your sermon at St. Clements Danes, when you spoke of your work on the King's revision of the Bible. But I remember it clearly and have often thought of it since," Anne said.

"I am honoured, Lady Anne," Dr Layfield bowed. "And may I offer my deepest condolence to you upon the loss of your mother, my dear friend, Lady Cumberland. This must be a very hard cross for you to bear. I confess myself, also, much grieved by her death for she was undoubtedly one of the finest and most remarkable women of the age."

"I thank you, Dr Layfield. The memory of my lady mother is one which many friends hold dear, but none perhaps so much as you," Anne said. "Have you yet received the great silver dishes that she left to you in her will?" As Dr Layfield nodded, she continued, "Ah, I see; Ralph Coniston brought them to you, as was her wish. It is well done. But pray, what business do you have at Knole at this time?"

"I have brought the conveyance document that has been drawn up at Lord Dorset's request. He wishes you to read it and then return to London with me, to set your hand to it in the presence of the lawyer," Dr Layfield said.

"I shall read it carefully, Dr Layfield, but as to signing it I am not so sure. There may be alterations I would wish to make," Anne said.

Sensing that she might have the upper hand for the first time, she then decided to tell the whole truth to this dear old friend of her mother's and took a deep breath.

"But principally," she said, "I am unwilling to return to London today at my Lord's bidding since it is but two days since he suddenly sent me back down here at short notice and at night, so that I did not reach Knole until midnight on the same day that I had left here."

"Very well, my dear lady," Dr Layfield said, unsuccessfully trying to hide a smile. "I shall return to Lord Dorset with your reply if that is your wish. But he was most insistent that you should come to him with all haste and I do believe that if you have reached an accord with him, after all your disagreements, it would be wise to seal it without further delay."

"I thank you for your advice, dear Dr Layfield, but I am not willing to rush back after the way I was treated this week. I will sign the papers, but first I require some indication that my lord repents of his behaviour towards me," Anne said.

"Very well, Lady Anne, I shall take your message to him." Old Dr Layfield's grey eyes twinkled as he spoke and Anne felt sure that her message would be delivered in a tactful and charming way that would not jeopardise the agreement.

Two days later Dr Layfield returned, and with him came Richard.

"Will you return to London with me tomorrow to sign the agreement before the judge, my lady?" Richard asked without preamble.

His tone was more conciliatory than she had heard in many months, and she glanced appreciatively at Dr Layfield for the magic he had wrought.

"I am minded to, my lord, if you are content that I should pass my Westmorland inheritance to you only in the case that I have no heirs of my own body."

"That seems to offer a way out of our impasse. If you will agree to that and sign the papers, you will find that I shall be the kindest and best husband to you that you could wish for," Richard said.

"At last I think we have reached a solution and I am very glad on it," Anne concluded.

Richard took both her hands in his. This time their smiles were of genuine pleasure, not simply relief.

CHAPTER TWENTY
July-August 1616

Dr Layfield travelled up with them the next day in the great Dorset carroch with its green and black silk lining and liveried grooms, drawn by six proud bay horses. They thundered through the lush Kentish countryside and villages, past churches, cottages, orchards and hop gardens. They reached the narrow streets of London in time to attend Judge Hubbard so that Anne could sign the conveyance. There was a feeling of celebration in the air, but they had work to do before they could take their ease.

Richard wrote letters to Lord William Howard, who was now back in Cumberland, asking him to ensure that the possession of Brougham Castle be very carefully secured. Lady Cumberland's body was still there and no-one wished it to be disturbed by any clashes between Richard's men and those of Francis and Henry Clifford, who might try to claim the castle. Marsh was sent to deliver the letters to Lord William and to Brougham Castle, instructing the servants.

Richard then went down to Horsley to see the Child and his sister, while Anne was measured for her mourning clothes by the tailor whom Lady St John had recommended and chose fabrics of different weights for the various garments. Once these were ready, she would plan her journey north to complete her sad task. Her resolve to undertake it was stronger since she and Richard were on good terms again, but it still preoccupied her unhappy thoughts.

On Richard's return from Horsley she begged him for news of The Child.

"She is well and very bonny," was his reply, "She never stopped talking all the while I was there!"

"Has she forgotten me entirely?"

"No, of course not," Richard said. "We spoke of you and she

hopes to see you soon. I explained to her that you must make a journey but will see her on your return. She asked if it would be a great journey, like the one from Knole to Horsley. I told her it would be a very great journey and that I too would make that journey to come and see you while you are in the North."

"Oh, Richard, that is good news indeed! And will The Child be returned to my care when I come back?"

"You shall have the care of her then and I'd like your opinion as to her care at present. My sisters believe that she no longer needs the nurse who accompanied her there and that she would prosper now in the care of a governess. What do you think?"

"I think that's a sound idea; I have been of a similar mind lately. Shall Nurse Bathurst go away, and I will send Willoughby down to have charge of her until I can appoint someone to that position?"

Anne felt joy for the first time in many weeks. There had been no sign, or even mention, of either Edward Sackville or Caldicott since her return to London and Richard was attentive and benevolent. Things were so good that she took the opportunity to raise the subject of her jointure and was given Richard's faithful word and promise that he would see to it in the autumn when the new legal term began. Death was an unpredictable and ever-present part of life.

The following Sunday, Richard and Anne went together to St Bride's Church to hear a sermon. Later they planned a visit to the court at Greenwich for the next day; the party, which included Cecily Neville, decided to travel down-river by barge as the weather was hot. They reached Greenwich Palace just in time to attend Chapel in the company of the King and Queen, though there was no opportunity to speak with them. After dining with relations and other old friends, they visited the Gallery at Greenwich Palace.

"My dear Countess, you are most welcome!" Queen Anne said. "We have not seen you here for far too long. We were most distressed to hear of the death of the dear Countess of Cumberland. Shall you travel to the north?"

"Your Majesty," Anne gave her 'best curtsy'. "I am exceedingly pleased to be here and am honoured indeed by your kind thoughts and words. Yes, I shall go to Westmorland very soon for my lady mother is not yet buried."

She was shown plans for a new palace, to be built at Greenwich. Anne was delighted to discover that her old acquaintance Inigo Jones had been commissioned to design the Queen's house, and she was impressed by the plans for a stylish classical building unlike anything she had ever seen before, except in drawings of ancient Greek ruins.

☙❧

Anne was happy to be with Richard, in society and among friends again, and felt herself to be emerging into the light from a dark and dreary place, like a butterfly from a chrysalis. Still sometimes she was pensive.

"Sweet Heart, don't look so downcast, for are we not fortunate indeed to be reconciled?" Richard looked at her and smiled as he spoke, his eyes reminding her of the night they had just spent together. It was so long since he had shown any interest in her that she blushed, with surprise and pleasure, like a virgin. He took her hand and kissed it.

"Of course," Anne said. "And I do now feel blessed by good fortune, my dear lord, with you at my side. But sometimes I cannot dismiss sad thoughts of my lady mother, however happy I am in every other regard."

"That is not surprising. We must attend to the question of your journey into the north to see her buried. I'm awaiting word from Kendall regarding your Clifford uncle and cousin and whether there is danger of trouble from them. I should hear from him soon." There was tenderness in his tone which she couldn't remember ever hearing before and it threatened to bring tears to her eyes.

"I thank you for your kindness, Richard," she said, with a catch in her voice. "My mourning clothes will be finished in a few days' time, then I wish to go there as soon as possible, for I would not be thought neglectful of my duty towards my dear mother. It has been so long; it distresses me and I would have it done." She pressed his hand and they looked into each other's eyes. We were never greater friends than this, she thought.

❧

When the coach was ready Richard led her down to it and embraced her lovingly, wishing her God-speed and renewing his promise to come north to her as soon as he could. She set off in good spirits with the company of Rivers, Judith, Faith and a good number of other attendants. The summer journey was much less hazardous than her winter travels had been, but her sadness and apprehension increased as they approached Brougham, knowing that this time there would be no warm welcome from her mother.

Three days of preparation for the funeral followed Anne's arrival at Brougham. During the morning of the fourth day a servant brought a message that the burghers of Appleby had refused permission for Lady Margaret's body to be buried there. Except for the castle, Appleby was not part of the Clifford estates but an ancient Royal Borough, answerable only to the King. Anne consulted Rivers, who proved to have a clear grasp of the local politics.

"The burghers are proudly independent, my lady, and are wont to stand on their dignity if they feel they have been disregarded or slighted. It is certainly within their powers to refuse permission for the burial to take place in their parish church, but I suspect that they may be amenable, even honoured, if consulted with the respect they see as their due."

"Then I shall write a respectful request for a favour, and you shall take it to them and ask their forgiveness for any previous unintended disrespect or discourtesy they may have felt from our people. Pray hasten there now and return immediately, that we may proceed. Word has come that cousin William Howard is on his way from Naworth and we must have the business in hand today."

Rivers rode post-haste the 12 miles to Appleby and secured the permission, returning by 5 o'clock, when William Howard and his party also arrived. Lady Margaret's body in its lead casing was carried from the keep by six men and loaded with difficulty into her black-draped coach. Four horses with black plumes were harnessed to pull it. Anne, weeping, followed with Judith in a small coach and pair, and then came the rest of the company, forty all-told, both men and women on horseback. They left Brougham at about eight o'clock.

The sorrowful procession moved slowly through the long summer twilight, watched in silence by many of the tenant farmers and their families along the way, and reached St Lawrence's Church in the dark at half past eleven. Lady Margaret was finally laid to rest in torchlight at about midnight on the eleventh of July, almost two months after her death.

Anne then began to imagine a magnificent memorial which she would commission from the best sculptor and poet of the day. There would be a beautiful life-like effigy of her mother, with devotional inscriptions and coloured heraldic devices. It would be worthy of Westminster Abbey – here, in the 'barren' north!

❧

Relieved now that her duty was done, Anne found little time for either mourning or relaxation. The King had given instructions that she was to be left unmolested at Brougham, but there was still no decision about the current ownership of Lady Margaret's jointure estates. Clifford's men were prowling the area like a pack of wolves, waiting for an opportunity to seize what they could. She needed to inform the tenants about the situation without compromising her position and warn her servants to be on their guard against the Cliffords' men. But she would take no rents from the tenants until her ownership was confirmed, so she instructed them to keep the money until it was certain who had the right to it.

❧

The working of the land had to continue and the next task was hay-time. Anne sent her servants into the park to make hay, but towards noon they were set upon by the Earl of Cumberland's men. The servants defended themselves with whatever implements they had to hand and two of Cumberland's men were injured by a pitchfork, one in the leg and one in the foot. A complaint was made to the judges at Carlisle, who issued a warrant for the arrest of all of Lady Anne's servants who were in the field at the time and they were bailed to appear at the next Assizes in Kendal.

A short while later, two of the judges, Lord Bromley and Judge Nichols, and a crowd of their clerks and servants, visited Anne at Brougham on their way from Carlisle to Kendal. They received a warm welcome and expressed their sorrow at the death of Lady Margaret, offering their condolences to Lady Anne at this time of grief. They both spoke effusively of the dowager countess's reputation for fair dealing and justice for all, her culture and refinement, and the loss to the whole area occasioned by her death. They expressed the hope that her daughter would continue in her footsteps, which seemed to Anne to indicate a preference for her as heir to the jointure lands, rather than her uncle.

"My lords, I thank you for your sympathies," Anne said. "It is indeed a great loss to me, as to many others. You do me great honour by your visit and I bid you all welcome. May I offer you some refreshment?

"I had not thought to be so favoured, especially after the complaint made against my folks by Lord Cumberland's men. But it is not my intention this morning to bend your lordships' ear on that subject; that would be quite improper."

"On the contrary, Lady Anne," said Lord Bromley, "We should be pleased to hear a statement from you about the events of that day and what transpired."

"Indeed, Lady Anne, pray give us your guidance on that unfortunate incident," Judge Nichols added.

Anne took a deep breath and, realising that she must not exaggerate any of the things she had been told by the protagonists, cautiously proceeded to tell the story as accurately as she could.

"Your lordships will understand that I was not present in the field at the time, did not witness the events myself, but have been informed since, by several of my retainers, as to what happened." The judges nodded for her to continue.

"It was a fine morning and I sent as many of my servants as could be spared from other duties to make hay in the park close to the castle," Anne said. "They were overseen by Mr Kidd, who is the Steward's man here at Brougham and was ever a faithful servant to my dear lady mother. They worked steadily until about eleven, with the sun beating down on their heads. Mr Kidd sent for some bread and ale to quench their thirst and allowed them to rest in the shade of the trees for a while.

"Just as they were about to take up their implements again there was a commotion at the entrance and Lord Cumberland's men came running towards them shouting threats and oaths and brandishing sticks. Mr Kidd faced up to them with a pitchfork and did his best to protect my folks, especially the women, from this onslaught. He did not threaten, but in defending he stretched out his arm with the pitchfork and the first man approaching fell over it, then the second fell over his comrade, both sustaining an injury. When they saw this, the others ran off and were followed by the leaders, limping pitifully and uttering impieties. None of my folks was hurt and this is the tale told to me by several of them."

"We thank you for your frank telling of the story, your ladyship. We shall release the bail monies and your people will not be bound to appear at the Assizes. The matter is ended," Judge Nichols said. Baron Bromley nodded in agreement. Their clerks murmured and scratched a note in their books. Anne sighed with relief and invited the judges to stay for dinner, which they were pleased to do; she was a generous host and the castle held a fine cellar.

❦

A week later Anne was joined by William Howard to ride to Appleby and meet Richard, who was coming north with a great company of men and horses; she saw him immediately at the head of the column. After anxiously searching the crowd with her eyes, Anne was delighted to conclude that Caldicott was not among them. They returned to Brougham before nightfall and were shortly followed by another group, including many of the women servants. But the household goods and furniture, which were supposed to come with them, had been held up by the loss of a wheel from one of the carts and they all spent the night lying three or four in a bed, much to everyone's amusement. Thomas Glenham, who had arrived with Richard, commented "I fear they will all be too tired to do anything but sleep abed this night!"

The castle was still hung with black mourning drapes, but as soon as the furniture arrived Anne and her ladies set about dressing the main bedchamber and setting up the green velvet four-poster bed which had come with Richard's chattels. To Anne this was symbolic of the restoration of her marriage, and she and Richard did indeed sleep there together for the two weeks' duration of his stay at Brougham. When the task of dressing the house was finished, their domestic joy was clear to the household as they sat quietly together near the window, Anne embroidering a new cushion and Richard reading at her side. None was more pleased than Judith to see her mistress so content.

Richard showed Anne his Will.

"I have decided that The Child shall have all my land and there will be an annuity from it for my brother, and an annual payment towards my debt. But most importantly, sweet heart, I have kept your jointure free of any encumbrance. You shall have your portion at Bolebroke Castle, whatsoever other calls there may be on my estate. It is a reflection of my esteem and love for you."

"I am more than satisfied with this news, my Lord, and I thank you most gratefully for myself and on behalf of The Child. I shall rest easier, knowing this, though I hope and pray that we shall spend many more happy years together.

"You do know that I am your loyal and loving wife and always have been, even when we have disagreed?"

He put his arm round her shoulders and kissed her forehead. "Yes, I do know that, and that is why I have made this provision."

CHAPTER TWENTY-ONE
August-December 1616

Serenity's reign was brief.

"My lord," a breathless and red-faced Basket rushed in the next day still wearing his spurs and a heavy leather jerkin, with three other panting servants at his heels, "My lord, Henry Clifford has arrived in Appleby with a troop, aiming to occupy the castle."

"How big a troop does he have?" Richard asked, cursing the impudent dog under his breath.

"Oh, much smaller than that which accompanied your lordship from the south, but useful nevertheless . . ."

"I thank you for this news, Basket." Richard said, "And for the speed with which you have conveyed it. Take these companions of yours and ask for ale to be served to you in the Great Chamber. You have done well. I shall send for you again when I have decided what course we shall pursue."

Anne had noted with satisfaction that her cousin Henry's train was smaller than her lord's.

"Will you challenge him, my lord?" she asked.

"No, I don't think so," Richard said. "We have the King's letter forbidding them to molest you at Brougham, but nothing has been decreed concerning Appleby. Let's wait and see what happens so that there is no danger of them accusing us of being in the wrong. When I return to London, I want to be assured that you will be safe remaining here; I don't wish to provoke any hostile acts from them."

Anne was aghast.

"You will leave me here, Richard?" Things had been going so well; she had been day-dreaming of surprising all at court with the joy of their mended marriage, of being reunited with The Child, of meeting old friends again and catching up on court gossip. Remaining at Brougham, alone, was not a possibility that had even crossed her mind, nor was it something she wished to contemplate.

"It is important that you remain here throughout the winter, Anne. If you abandon Brougham, what is there to stop Henry and his men from seizing this as well?" Richard said. She could think of no answer to this argument. There was a prolonged silence until she asked, in a small voice,

"When will you leave, my lord?"

"Don't look so crushed," Richard said. "We have been happy these two weeks. You could not have expected that I would stay and I'm certain you see that you must remain here, don't you? I'll leave in two days' time, for the court will reassemble very shortly."

 ❧

Anne saw him off as bravely as she could, but she was very dejected at the thought of the lonely, cold, dark winter ahead. The castle seemed to go into hibernation as soon as Richard and his large retinue had left and she immediately sat down to write a letter telling him how much she missed him and begging him to let her come up to London soon.

After that, her time was spent seeing to the household accounts, reading and embroidering. She watched the foxgloves' flowers slowly creep up their tall stems beside the lanes, signalling the end of summer when the topmost bud faded and fell. The trees in Whinfell forest began to turn from green to yellow and brown. Mr Dumbell, a clerk at Brougham, read a *History of the Low Countries* out loud to her, and she found his deep voice, slow manner and broad north-country accent soothing. But she was low in spirits and felt isolated and abandoned as time crept by and there was no response to her plea. Every day she wore a simple black taffeta gown with a yellow waistcoat. Here she was her own mistress; she could direct the servants, influence the running of the castle and had no need to observe Richard's stricture about her clothes. After sleepless nights, she would rise early and took to walking on the roof at dawn before hearing readings from the Bible.

Towards the end of September Rivers returned, with news of events at court and a message from Richard repeating that she must remain at Brougham all winter. Rivers stayed on and between them he and Marsh read most of Montaigne's Essays to her while she embroidered a cushion in Irish stitch, emptying her mind of everything but the intricacies of the work.

In the short grey days of mid-November letters arrived from London, including a personal one from Richard. She needed a candle to read the news; he had recently sent a challenge to her cousin Henry Clifford, he told her, but before the duel could take place the lords of the Privy Council got wind of it and he and Clifford had been summoned before the King and Council to explain themselves.

'The King was angry at first' Richard wrote, 'because he is intent on banning the practice of Duelling, but when he had heard the Substance of the Argument, he insisted that we must make Friends. He sees Himself as a Divinely inspired Judge and, thinking this a good Occasion on which to exercise his Judgement for the Benefit of all, he flattered me with marvellous good Words and ordered me to send for you, so that he can Himself settle the matter of the Clifford Inheritance. You must come up to London as soon as possible and present your Case to the King so that we can make an Agreement with Him. I shall send Basket with all the horses to bring you here within the fortnight. I know you will be pleased by this news.'

Anne, with the sparkle back in her eyes, immediately started making preparations. She sorted out her clothes and jewellery. She took pearls and diamonds which her mother had left her and strung them into a necklace. She visited friends at Blencow, with whom she played backgammon and shared the excitement of the forthcoming trip. She assured them that she had no fear of putting her case before the King, as he would be certain to see the virtue of her claim. She bought a heavy woollen cloak and a thick black rug edged with lace to keep her warm on her journey and she visited other friends to wish them goodbye.

She was troubled by rumours of quarrels in Appleby between some of her supporters and those of Henry Clifford and she wondered just how safe Brougham would be in her absence. She spoke with the servants, guiding them on how to behave. She assured them that she would return, having no doubt that the King would find in her favour when he had heard her arguments. They all swore their loyalty to her and wished her Godspeed.

❦

Faith rushed into Anne's chamber above the gatehouse on the fourth of December.

"My lady, Basket is here!"

"Why are you so flushed and out of breath?" Anne laughed, "He has been expected these ten days!"

"Yes my lady, but he was to bring the coach to fetch us and is come with only horses and some carts for the chattels!"

They were interrupted by a loud knock at the door and Faith opened it to admit Basket himself on a wave of cold air, his nose red and his eyes streaming from riding against the east wind. He bowed low to Anne, who said.

"Welcome back to Brougham, Basket. Faith tells me you have come to fetch us but without the coach?"

"Indeed, my lady, I thought it prudent to leave the coach at Roses in case this evil wind brings snow and the way becomes difficult before we reach the well-trodden road. It will mean your ladyship riding the first twenty-five miles on horseback with your ladies mounted behind the grooms, but I did not believe this would present any problem to you. I hope I was not mistaken, but if I am it is easily remedied by sending for the coach."

"I thank you for your careful planning, Basket," Anne smiled. "There will be no need to send for the coach, will there, Faith?"

Faith blushed. Anne knew which of the grooms would take Faith behind him for the first leg of their journey, and that Faith would have no objection at all. "No, my lady" she giggled, eyes downcast.

As Basket had predicted, the first day's journey brought flurries of snow on the east wind. The ride to Rose Castle near Carlisle took six hours. Anne and her ladies were grateful for the comforting warmth of their horses, but even more thankful to see the red sandstone towers and battlemented parapets of the ancient castle, seat of the Bishops of Carlisle. They passed through the gatehouse into the shelter of the enclosed courtyard, where they could dismount and hand over the horses to the grooms.

Bishop Snoden was not in residence, but they were given a warm welcome by his Steward and shown through the porch and screen passage into a long, vaulted hall with tree trunks burning in the grates at the side. A meal of pottage, hare and venison pie had been prepared and would be served when they were warm enough to remove their outer clothes. Anne and Basket were shown to seats at the table on the dais with the officers of the Bishop's household, while her ladies and the grooms ate at a long table in the lower part of the hall. Later, Faith and Judith showed Anne to her chamber and helped her out of her heavy travelling clothes and into the four-poster bed, which they covered with the cloak and furs they would use for travelling in the coach, then retired to their own pallets at the side of the room.

In the morning there was much to be done before their departure at dawn. The days were short and they had to make use of all the daylight hours, but a problem arose that threatened to delay them. Anne had mislaid the diamond ring given to her by Richard on the birth of The Child and she did not want to meet him again without it. Judith, Faith and Anne searched every room that she had entered, and when Basket insisted that they must leave without further delay Anne instructed one of the young grooms.

"William, you will remain here until you have found the ring. I had it when we arrived but I don't have it now. There is no other place it can be except here, so you will search until it is found and then bring it to me along the road."

For the rest of the long journey Anne and her ladies travelled together in the jolting coach, accompanied by the grooms and servants on horseback. They spent nights in inns or great houses along the route to the capital, leaving at dawn and arriving at dusk, or often after dark, making slow progress through the frozen landscape of eastern England. Anne was reminded of those contrasting summer journeys with the Queen's train twelve years ago, when the new monarchs had made their way from Scotland to Windsor. It felt as though she herself was now making a royal progress through the land; she would meet the King and Queen at her journey's end and put her case before them. As their rumbling course became more and more tedious she began to imagine a time in the future, when her inheritance would at last be secured and she would be able to return north to take possession of the other four castles, as well as Brougham, and be recognised as the rightful landowner of all the Clifford estates.

Anne had been silent for so long that Judith, who had been dozing, and Faith, who for once had been quietly gazing out at the icy scenery, both started when she spoke.

"When I have my inheritance, I shall make progresses between my castles with all my friends, tenants, and servants accompanying me from place to place. I shall go from Skipton to Pendragon, from Brough to Appleby and always to Brougham!"

Judith knew her mistress well enough to realise that this was what she had been contemplating for the last few hours.

"My lady, that time may come soon, now that the King is to hear your case."

"Indeed, Judith, that is the direction my thoughts have been following and I pray to God that it may be so. The King is just and with divine guidance will see the power of my arguments, I believe." And then, with a touch of impatience, "If only this endless journey would end!"

Her mood lifted that evening when William finally caught up with them, bringing her diamond ring, which he had found when a little maid asked him to help her shake out the blankets of Anne's bed in the chamber at Rose Castle and it had clinked to the floor.

After ten days they reached Islington where, this time, Richard and many friends met them and there was a joyful welcome. The final triumphant stage of the journey, with her lord at her side in a great convoy of ten or eleven coaches full of friends winding its way through the crowded streets of London, passed in an exultant flash. Their arrival at Great Dorset House aroused further excitement, but even that was surpassed when little Lady Margaret was brought to greet her. It was the first time they had been together in six months; they both wept tears of joy and clung to each other through hours of meeting friends again and exchanging news, until The Child fell asleep in Anne's arms with a contented smile on her lips and was carried to her bed.

CHAPTER TWENTY-TWO
New Year 1617

There were great preparations in hand at Dorset House. The London mansion was dressed in anticipation of its mistress's arrival, but now there was also Christmas to think of, less than a week away. And although still in mourning, Anne must be looking her best for the festivities; for the royal encounter, for being the focus of fashionable interest and gossip, but most of all for the husband with whom she was now reconciled (to everyone's surprise, not least her own).

"Judith, please arrange for Lady Manners to come on Saturday to dress my hair. And I need to see my Lady St John's tailor about the new black taffety gown she is making for me. She is a most kind and obliging woman.

"Faith, you and my little Lady Margaret's maid must hasten to arrange for the cooks to make all The Child's favourite sweetmeats for the feasting. And pray send William to me when you find him.

"Oh, and Judith, before you send to Lady Manners and Lady St John's tailor, pray buy some Spanish leather gloves for them both so that I have gifts to present to them when they come. And Faith, check with my Lady Margaret's maid that she has purchased gifts for The Child to give to my husband and me, for she will no doubt be upset if gifts are being exchanged but she has none to give.

"And tell the maid to prepare my Lady Margaret's best clothes for the many visits we shall make over the next two weeks and the many friends whom we shall receive. She must be looking her best now that her mother is returned! Soon I am minded to arrange for Master Sumner to paint her picture, for she is become truly bonny."

There was extra feasting to celebrate Anne's return, as well as for Christmas. She felt fortunate that she could spend this joyful season with her husband and child when she might have been alone at Brougham, but the ache of her mother's absence never left her.

Anne was both surprised and delighted that so many relations, friends and acquaintances rushed to fuss over her and her daughter. Being wrapped around by all this love was truly consoling. No-one could believe that what had looked like a disaster for her had worked out so well. Invitations were issued, compliments flew, gifts were bestowed, advice freely given. The fashionable world's curiosity was excited by her situation and no holds were barred in pressing her to leave matters to the King. The entire world assured her that her troubles would soon be over; she nevertheless took the precautionary measure of sending a very expensive gold-embroidered sweet bag to the Queen, as a New Year's gift.

Alethea was one of a very rare species who resisted speaking of the dispute. She contented herself with demonstrating her affection for Anne by showing her the latest additions to the pictures and statues which she and her husband had collected and displayed in the lower rooms of their great London house. Together again, they chuckled over the memory of their conversation in that place before Anne's marriage.

"Little did I know what a see-saw my marriage would prove to be!" Anne declared, but Alethea kept her counsel, assuring her friend that such an experience was not unusual.

"I valued your advice then, dear friend, and have never regretted my decision since, in spite of all the difficulties," Anne said.

"I am gladdened to hear it, my dear, for I have often wondered how you were bearing the ups and downs of fortune," Alethea replied, then pointed out a particularly delicious statue of a splendid Greek youth. They laughed again and Anne was grateful for the soothing effect of friendship and laughter.

On another day Anne played cards; an exciting game of Glecko resulted in her losing a considerable amount of money to her friend, Lady Gray. Afterwards she was remorseful and troubled by this, telling herself that it was hypocritical to be censorious about Richard's gambling debts if she behaved in the same way. She vowed to give up playing cards for money and stuck to the oath for many months, but really missed the fun of it. Richard didn't appear to notice – either that she had lost money gambling, or that she had given it up.

New Year's Day was a bustle of visits and greetings. It seemed the whole world was out and about. By the end of the day Anne could think of no-one whom she had not encountered, either at the Savoy or at Somerset House, where she had been greeted and kissed by both the King and the Queen, or at Essex House, or at her sister-in-law's. But she awoke with a start in the smothering blackness of the early hours, recalling that her husband's kinswoman, Frances Howard and her husband Robert Carr, had been imprisoned in the Tower for almost two years now, since being found guilty of the murder of Sir Thomas Overbury. She determined to visit them the next day, as she had not seen them since they were arrested.

She found Lord and Lady Somerset comfortably established in the Tower, where they were accommodated together in a certain degree of luxury and had some of their servants to attend them. Frances was pleased to show Anne their apartment and the messages of good will they had received from friends during the festive season. Anne noted that Frances remained as alluring as ever, with the plunging neckline for which she was (in)famous, and the simpering manner towards her husband which kept him enthralled. If they haven't tired of each other after two years of incarceration together, she thought, they probably never will. A stab of something like longing brought her up sharp; surely, she would rather have her freedom and quarrel with Richard sometimes, than be imprisoned in the Tower with a death sentence over them?

As she emerged from the gloom of the Tower into the weak January sunlight and climbed into her coach, Anne shook herself and felt the relief of freedom, dismissing the dark questions that had crept into her mind under cover of that dismal place. However difficult life sometimes was with Richard, she would not want it any other way.

❦

Towards Twelfth Night, the celebrations became ever more hectic and Anne and Richard attended court to see the King bestow an earldom on his favourite (many said his lover), George Villiers. Frequent comments were heard concerning the appearance of the new Earl of Buckingham.

"My dear Lady Anne, did you see the way he allowed his robes to flow behind so that his legs were exposed as he approached the King, with the Garter tied just below his left knee to draw attention also?" said Lady Gray when Anne met her afterwards. "He has exquisite legs, I grant you, so long and shapely, but he was really making the most of them today. And his face has the skin of a young girl, with his cherry-red lips and soft blue-grey eyes beneath that head of dark hair. No wonder they say the King adores him. He has been at court but a couple of years and is today become an earl – all through being the 'handsomest man in all of England'!"

"Indeed, his lordship cut a fine figure today," Anne said, hoping that her thoughts did not show in her face and voice, for she was thinking of Matthew Caldicott and the effect he had had on her husband and her marriage. A mistress, even Martha Penistone, was one thing, but someone who was constantly at his side and whispering in his ear was something altogether more disturbing, she brooded. She wondered how the Queen tolerated Buckingham's antics. She forced a bright smile, took Richard's arm and they went in to supper with Lord and Lady Arundel, her dear friend Alethea. There was another entertainment later, with the play *The Mad Lover* in the hall, and her mood lightened. She was smiling happily as cheerful good-nights were exchanged and Richard handed her into the coach.

❦

On Twelfth Night, the last of the celebrations, Anne and Richard went to court again and met with many friends.

"You must allow the King to decide your business," Lady Anne Beauchamp, her sister-in-law, said. "He will prove a wise judge in such matters."

"It is fortunate that the King wishes to involve himself in deciding amongst you all," Susan, Lady Pembroke said. "Put yourself in his hands and your troubles will soon be at an end."

"Trust the King," Lord Arundel said. "You are sure to receive justice at his hands."

"Give the matter over to the King," Lord William Howard said. "He is the highest power in the land; there must be an end to your quarrels, once he has spoken."

Thus it went on. Everyone was winding down from the festivities and therefore looking for the next event on the horizon that might provide a fertile source of gossip. Many believed that the King intended to make his judgement on the Clifford business before the end of January, so Anne felt she would be the subject of speculation and interest for at least a few weeks to come. She resolved to bear it without compromising her belief in the rightness of her cause, as much for her mother's memory as for her own sake.

The final masque of the Christmas season was held that night. Anne stood with friends in Lady Ruthven's box to watch the spectacle, remembering the times when she had been on stage with the Queen and had been admired and courted. It seemed a lifetime away and made her feel old, but she reminded herself that she had never regretted her choice of husband, and most of her friends from those times were still around her today and wished her well. Only the thorny presence of Matthew Caldicott and Edward Sackville sometimes dimmed her pleasure.

❧

The journey back to Knole was uneventful, but when they arrived, Anne commented on how much she had enjoyed the Christmas season. Richard's demeanour changed.

"You know that you would not have been there had I not been ordered by the King to bring you back," he said. "In my view you were needed at Brougham to protect it from any seizure of the land before a settlement is reached.

"We still have to appear before the King for his judgment," Richard continued. "I think it will be soon and we must prepare our case. We need to be united in persuading him that the most just outcome would be for your uncle and cousin Clifford to pay us a substantial amount in recompense before taking possession of Westmorland as well as Craven."

Anne turned slowly to face him, her spine tingling and her face draining to show all the exhaustion of the last twelve months. What had he just said? She could not believe that the bludgeoning quarrel was starting again.

"There is no question of any such 'recompense', Richard. You know that I shall never agree to sacrifice my inheritance."

"You must face the facts, Anne. If the King makes that judgement you will not be able to stand against it. The King will have the final word, and it will be the best thing for us both – for we shall then be friends again with no dispute between us."

"That I wish more than almost anything else, Richard," she looked up at him with tears of disappointment in her eyes. "I thought we were already reconciled and there was no longer any dispute between us. But I shall never agree to relinquish my lands."

"You are speaking very foolishly. We must settle this matter by agreeing to do as the King says. But we must also present him with a single united argument, for that will strengthen our case. Together we can argue for the fact of your inheritance, but the equal fact, that the Cliffords are in possession of the lands, must also be acknowledged. There must be adequate compensation to us for that situation."

"No. Nothing could compensate for the loss of my inheritance," Anne said. "Think, Richard; if we win back my rights and we have a son, he will become the Earl of Dorset *and* Cumberland."

Richard sighed.

"Go to bed now and think hard on what I have said. Tomorrow, tell me what your position is to be when we go to the King. Good night."

They spent the night apart and Anne passed the following day in her closet, where a secretary read to her from a book about the government of the Turks. Richard spent the day reading and talking to Matthew in his own closet.

By the following afternoon, Anne felt uncomfortable with this aloofness and asked Judith where his lordship might be. Judith asked William, but he had been out all day and didn't know, so he said he would ask one of the stable boys.

He returned a short while later, removed his cap, scratched his head and reported that the stable boy had seen Lord Dorset and Mr Caldicott departing for London before seven o'clock that morning. A look of horror flitted across Judith's features, but she thanked him and returned to Anne's chamber.

"My lady, William has it from a stable-boy that my lord went to London early this morning. He seems to believe it to be true, says he saw it with his own eyes."

Anne's look of astonishment confirmed to Judith that she had had no idea that her husband had gone away. "Did he leave any message?"

"None that I know of, my lady."

Anne dismissed Judith and sat perfectly still, running through their last conversation in her mind. He had said they must present a united front to the King and had asked her to tell him what her position would be. She had not spoken to him since. But he knew what her position would be, surely; surely, she had made it clear every time the subject came up during the months and years of argument? He had left without telling her because she had once again refused to give in to his wishes. How much of this treatment could she bear? How long could she hold out against him? Was she battling against one man, or three?

CHAPTER TWENTY-THREE
Mid-January 1617

Anne received a letter from Richard, informing her that she should come up to London the next day (Friday) because she was to go before the King on Monday. She didn't know whether to laugh, cry or stamp her foot; relief that something was happening at last was stirred in with anger that he had left her for days with no word, and anxiety about the possible outcomes of the King's intervention. She recalled the meeting at Dorset House almost a year ago, when she had faced a great company of men all trying to force her agreement. On that occasion she had managed to defy them and secure her visit to her mother. If only her mother was here to support her as she always had done; but this time she was truly alone, and it was hard not to see the King as one more of those powerful men, indeed the most powerful of the men, who were ranged against her.

When she arrived at Dorset House, Richard came out to welcome her and handed her down from the coach. He led her into the library, which revived an intense memory of her interview there with the Archbishop. She shook her head impatiently to rid herself of that image.

"I hope you're prepared for your audience with His Majesty on Monday," Richard said as they sat down. "It seems that he may also wish to speak to you tomorrow, but these things are never certain. It is best if you are ready to present your case at any time, so that there is no shock when you are called. Remain at court, that there may be no delay in finding you or in reaching the King when he sends for you."

"I thank you, my lord, for your counsel. I shall be ready, have no doubt," Anne said.

"I don't doubt it, for you're a brave woman and I'm proud of you, whatever opinion you take. For the first step, at least, we're united in wishing to persuade the King that you have a just claim to the Clifford lands in Westmorland."

"Your words bring me great comfort and strength. I hope to be worthy of your confidence in these coming days. And it's my dearest wish that our unity may continue to the second step and beyond, once my claim is established."

Richard glanced sideways at her with one eyebrow raised and a half-smile on his lips as he left the room without further comment.

During the short journey to court after dinner the next day, Anne suddenly felt weak and shaky; her hands were cold and clammy and her stomach seemed to turn over every few seconds. She couldn't remember what she wanted to say to the King and her head felt full of dough. She pressed on to the Queen's Drawing Chamber, with the climb up the great staircase calming her nerves as she breathed more deeply. There she found the Queen with Elizabeth, Countess of Derby, the most senior of the Ladies of the Queen's Chamber.

"Lady Dorset, pray come and sit with us!" the Queen called out, "What brings you to court today?"

Anne curtseyed low and took the seat the Queen had indicated. Before she could speak Lady Derby, full of importance, began to explain.

"Madam, Lady Dorset has business with His Majesty regarding her disputed inheritance. Her late mother's jointure lands in Westmorland are part of the Clifford inheritance, which Lady Dorset's uncle, Lord Cumberland, and Henry Clifford, his son, claim was bequeathed to them by Lady Dorset's father.

"Lady Dorset claims that her father's will was illegal because there was an entail in place from Edward II guaranteeing the inheritance of the estates to direct Clifford descendants, whether male or female. Therefore, Lady Anne believes, the lands should be hers. Lord Dorset challenged Henry Clifford to a duel over the dispute and His Majesty, displeased by this, has declared that he will judge the matter."

Queen Anne nodded and looked at Anne, who held her gaze. The Queen seemed to be recalling something and eventually in her strong Danish accent she said,

"The first time I saw you, I remember remarking that you were my namesake. There is no point in having a namesake if you do not look after her, so I will do all the good for you with the King that I am able. I wish you well in the business." Then the Queen beckoned Anne to come closer and as she stood and bent her head towards the Queen's long, pale face she heard her whisper,

"But don't trust your matters absolutely to the King, lest he deceive you."

Anne, astonished by these words, heard them echo in her head as she rose and backed away from the Queen to curtsy low again and thank her ". . . with all my heart . . ." for her support.

A footman came to take Anne to the King's apartments, where she would join her husband and be escorted to the King's presence. Lord Buckingham met them in his own room adjacent to the King's and they followed him into the King's drawing chamber, which was hot, dark and stuffy, crowded with courtiers all vying for the monarch's attention. When they entered, Anne noticed that the King was engaged with Lord Burleigh. He glanced round and saw them, immediately breaking off the conversation with a dismissive gesture, whereupon Lord Burleigh told everyone to leave and followed them out, a footman closing the door quietly behind them. A thick silence blanketed the emptied room and Anne could hardly breathe as King James beckoned them forward.

"Dorset, Lady Dorset, come here and kneel beside me!" he commanded, his Scottish accent undiminished despite all his years in England. As they approached him they bowed and curtsied deeply, but the King gestured impatiently to the side of his chair where large red cushions were arranged. They knelt.

"I have asked you to attend me today because I wish to avoid argument at the great audience on Monday. This dispute between you and Cumberland and his son must be resolved and I intend to make peace between you all, so that matters can be agreed without further rancour." He glared at Dorset and continued, "I will not countenance duelling between members of my court; this must be stamped out."

Dorset bowed his head in contrition and apologised. Anne did not look at her lord or her King, but kept her eyes fixed on the carved and upholstered arm of the King's chair in front of her. The furnishings were all in a dark claret-coloured velvet, which added to the suffocating atmosphere of the chamber.

"I wish there to be peace between you and Cumberland," the King continued, "But first there must be peace between the two of you, which I believe has not always been the case.

"Perhaps we can agree today on just one thing; I ask you each to put the matter wholly into my hands and swear to abide by whatever decision I shall make when I have heard all the arguments. Am I not known as a wise and learned man, a just and fair judge, the representative of God's will on earth? If you will make this vow, then we can proceed from a place of accord and there need be no more hostility." He paused, allowing his words to muffle in the quiet chamber.

"Dorset," the King said finally, "Do you agree to put the matter into my hands and abide by whatever ruling I shall make?"

Dorset cleared his throat and spoke confidently,

"Yes, Sir."

"And Lady Dorset, are you minded to accept my judgment?"

The moment had come. This was the test of her resolve. Could she hold to her truth? Anne clenched her fists, took a deep breath and looked up into the King's serious face.

"Your Majesty, I beseech you to pardon me for that I will never part with Westmorland while I live, upon any condition whatsoever," she said.

There was the sound of a sharp intake of air from Dorset and then silence. As the King's eyes hardened she looked down at the edge of the cushion on which she knelt and felt afraid. The King snorted.

"So, you will only accept my judgment if it goes in your favour!" She remained silent, head bowed.

"Have you understood me correctly?" the King said, more loudly. "I am offering to judge this matter and put an end to the disputes that have plagued your family for years. Are you refusing me?" The silence that followed became so uncomfortable that she had to give some sort of answer.

"I have understood, Your Grace."

"Will you reconsider, then?" The King was almost pleading. "Your husband has agreed to accept my conclusion, whether it answers his cause or no. Can you not do the same, take the same chance?"

"I cannot, Your Majesty," Anne said.

"This is preposterous! Do you deny the right of your King, the highest authority in the land, to judge the legality of competing claims to parts of this land?"

"I do not dispute your authority, Sir, but I cannot wager on so serious a matter, nor agree to anything which may deny me and my descendants our rightful inheritance."

"Who are you to judge what is your 'rightful inheritance', Lady Dorset? It is I, your sovereign lord, who must decide that question, is it not?"

"Sire, my lady mother spent many years researching the Clifford papers and proved the case beyond doubt. I cannot go against her work in this, God rest her soul."

"God rest the good Countess's soul indeed, but we are not discussing the case today! All I require is your word that you will put the matter wholly into my hands and agree to accept whatever judgment I make when I have considered all sides of the question. I ask for your trust. Is that clear to you?"

"It is, Your Grace."

"Good, then we are making progress. And will you agree to my request?"

"I beseech you to forgive me, Your Majesty, but I cannot."

At this the King smacked his hand down on the arm of his chair and colour began to flood his sallow features. Anne's knees were aching and her thighs began to tremble. It was all she could do to stop herself sitting back onto her heels. Suddenly the Queen's whispered words echoed in her mind once more and gave her strength.

"So, you will defy your King! I could accuse you of *treason*, Lady Dorset. Many have gone to the Tower for less. It seems you put your loyalty to your late mother above your loyalty to me."

"No, Sir. Please pardon me. I put my faith in the facts which my mother has laid out, and in my Lord God who has always held me in His safe keeping."

"I must persuade you then? I am God's representative in Scotland, England and Wales, am I not?"

"Yes Sir. And I am your Majesty's loyal subject."

"Then you will accept my authority?"

"Not without Westmorland, Your Majesty, because I believe that that would be against God's will."

"And you think you have better knowledge of God's will than I do? Are there no bounds to your pride, Lady? You defied Archbishop Abbot last year, did you not? You would put yourself above the Archbishop of Canterbury *and* the King?"

Anne noticed some grey hairs mingling with the brown in his beard, and lines of pain or worry between his brows. She struggled to reply. Bringing the Archbishop into the discussion threw her thoughts away from the present and back once more to that awful day at Dorset House. She was silent.

"I hope your silence signifies that you are willing to ponder your stubbornness and revise your loyalties," the King said. "I am displeased. Go now and return on Monday, when I shall ask you the same question again – and shall hope for a more dutiful reply."
The last sentence was spoken as a command.

Richard leapt to his feet and offered her his hand to help her rise and prevent her tripping on her heavy skirts. They stepped backwards away from the King and Richard took her elbow as they left the Chamber.

As they crossed Buckingham's crowded room, Richard guided Anne through the throng while all eyes turned to stare at them.

"Well! That was quite the lion's den, was it not, Daniel?" he said, squeezing her arm as they made their way over to the Queen's apartments. "You certainly didn't waver in your resolve, even against his worst roaring and snarling. I didn't like his threatening tone, especially his mention of treason, and I'm very concerned lest he bring any public disgrace on you, for that would be very damaging to us both. I would have you agree to his demand, but I admired your strength today."

"I thank you for your understanding, my lord. It is more than I had expected and I'm most grateful to you. The King employed every fair and foul means he could to break me down, but I was firmly resolved not to concede and your presence was of great comfort and aid to me." She also thought with gratitude about the Queen's secret support, but she didn't mention that.

"I shall always try to protect you from any public disgrace," Dorset repeated.

☙◦❧

Sunday was spent listening to a long and rather tedious sermon in a crowded chapel, then Anne dined with Lady Ruthven and together they went up to the Queen's court, although the Queen was not present. Elizabeth, Countess of Derby again approached Anne in a cloud of importance, bustling to her side and exclaiming,

"My dear Lady Anne, it is a great thing to see you here again! How are you, and how goes your business? Did the King see you on Saturday?"

Anne gave a polite smile and greeted her in the same vein. The Countess's loud voice had attracted attention and they were joined by her sister Susan Countess Montgomery, Lady Ruthven and

Lady Burleigh. All were anxious to hear how the private audience had gone.

"Yes, my ladies, my lord and I spent many minutes with the King, who wanted assurance that we would put our business over to him and accept his judgment in the matter."

"And did you agree to that?" Lady Derby asked.

"My lord did readily agree, but I said, begging his Majesty's pardon, that I would never part with Westmorland upon any condition."

"Oh! Surely that was unwise? What response did the King give?" Lady Burleigh said.

"The King tried all means of persuasion," Anne said. "But I had made up my mind before we entered the chamber, so nothing he said could move me."

"And what said your lord to this?" asked Susan.

"Nothing in the King's presence, but when we had come out, he said he disliked the King's attitude and admired the way I had stood up to him."

"But surely it would be better for you if you agreed to accept the King's judgment?" Barbara Ruthven asked.

"No, I can't, for if he was to find against me, I would have denied my inheritance, which I truly believe to be mine by right. I shall continue to fight for it, whatever the judgment."

"The King is known to be a wise and just ruler," Lady Burleigh said. "And a divinely inspired judge, Anne. What could go wrong if you put your matters into his hands?"

"I think many things could go wrong, Lady Burleigh. There are many powerful men working against me and they all have great influence here at court. I may be a mere woman, but on this one thing I have determined that I shall not yield."

"Your Lord is right that you are to be admired for the way you have tenaciously pursued the business," Elizabeth Derby said. "But I cannot think that you will gain anything from it and fear you may lose much. You are risking a charge of treason by going against the King! For your own sake, I beseech you; agree to let the matter be judged by the King."

"Yes, let the King be the judge, otherwise it cannot go well with you. Elizabeth is right; you risk everything if you defy him – even your life, God forbid!" Susan Montgomery agreed with her sister.

"I agree with the other ladies," Lady Burleigh nodded, turning to Anne. "I think you are brave and strong but you cannot win this dispute by defying all those who stand against you and it would be much wiser for you to leave matters in the King's hands. You may find his judgment to your liking after all!"

By this time Anne had had enough. It was tiring, standing against the whole world, but she clung to the memory of her mother and the recent secret advice of the Queen. She refused the invitation to accompany the Ladies to a masque which was to be danced at court, with the excuse that she had already seen it, and went home with Richard.

Monday, which Anne thought of as the day of reckoning, dawned misty and mild but without any of the portents, such as thunder or snow, that she might have seen as a bad omen. She spent a long time at her prayers, asking God to forgive her trespasses and hold her safe this day. After dinner she and Richard travelled to the Palace together but parted when they arrived there. Richard turned towards the King's apartments and Anne climbed the stairs to Lady Ruthven's chamber, where she remained until about eight o'clock, when she was sent for to go over to the King's Court.

She was the last to arrive and the door was locked after her. The room was dimly lit by candles, tapestries hung on the walls and red velvet glowed from furnishings; the atmosphere was heavy. Her glance around the chamber found it full of men, as she had expected, all quietly anticipating her arrival. Her Uncle Cumberland and cousin Henry Clifford were there; also Lord Arundel, husband of her friend Alethea (and therefore hopefully an ally); William Herbert Lord Pembroke and his brother, Philip Herbert Lord Montgomery, Susan's husband and for many years one of the King's favourites; and Sir John Digby, Ambassador to Spain, and in high favour with the King in spite of his reputation for a violent temper. In addition to these noblemen, she noted a handful of lawyers, including the Lord Chief Justice and the King's solicitor, Sir Randal Crewe, who was to speak for her and Richard.

The Lord Chief Justice requested silence and the King began to speak.

"My purpose today is to establish ownership and disposal of the lands which are disputed between Cumberland and his son on the one hand, and Dorset and his Lady on the other. First, I need to ask you all whether you will submit to my judgment in this case. Cumberland, how say ye?"

"Aye, Sir, I will respect your judgment."

"Henry Clifford?"

"Yes, Your Majesty, I will abide by your ruling."

"Dorset?"

"Yes, Sir, I am content."

"Lady Dorset?" The King looked intently at her and anxiety twitched his lip.

"I beseech you to forgive me, Your Grace, for that I will never agree to any judgment that denies me Westmorland," Anne said.

There was a hiss and murmuring around the room.

The King grew red in the face and began to shout.

"What is this? You seek to defy me again? You will not acknowledge my right to pass judgment in this matter? Crewe, Pembroke, how are we to proceed? What is to be done?"

"Lady Dorset, this will not do," said Crewe with agitation. "We are all come to find a solution to the question of the Westmorland estates of your mother's jointure, which I believe you wish resolved. But without your agreement to accept the judgment of the King we cannot proceed and . . ."

"Preposterous!" interrupted Pembroke loudly. "It is preposterous that this woman is denying the King's right to govern in the name of God! It cannot be borne, it is beyond belief. Lady Dorset," he wagged a finger at her, "You must accept the King's judgment now, so that we may proceed."

The King spluttered as if he was about to speak but seemed unable to form any words. Anne stared at the floor in silence. She had no more to say. She stood, a tiny figure at bay in the centre of this hostile and angry pack. There seemed no escape. She caught Richard's eye as her panic rose. He touched Digby's shoulder and motioned to him to unlock the door and take her out.

Once they were outside, Digby continued the tirade,

"Lady Dorset, you must accept the King's judgment," he insisted. "It is unreasonable to baulk at this. The King has the power to make the decision and the more you stand against him the less likely he is to make it in your favour. Don't you see that you must accept?"

"I cannot yield, Sir John," Anne replied. "I am resolved to hold to my rights and remain loyal to my mother's blessed memory."

"Come, come, lady. It does you no credit to be obstinate; your lady mother was never so stubborn."

At this, Anne felt hot tears run down her cheeks. She turned away from Sir John and dashed them away with her fingers, to see Lord James Hay approaching. His look showed great concern and he led her away to sit down and explain to him how things stood. Sir John, relieved of responsibility for her, scuttled back to the King.

Anne was calmer once she had spoken with Lord Hay about what had transpired in the King's chamber. She began to realise that, as long as she never agreed to any award, they could decide whatever they liked but she would not be party to it. They would need her signature before any judgment could be finalised, and they were not going to get that. So, when Richard finally emerged and told her that it was decided that if she would not come to an agreement, then an agreement would be made without her, it was perfectly acceptable to her. They returned to Knole together.

⁂

Ruminating later on the events of the day, she praised God for his providence, Richard for his worthy and noble disposition, and the Queen for taking her part. She realised that neither she nor anyone else could have thought that she would come through it so well. It felt miraculous.

CHAPTER TWENTY-FOUR
February-March 1617

Anne's return to Knole was accompanied by a feeling of relief which occasionally bordered on elation. She received visits from friends, including Lady Selby of Ightham Mote.

"Lady Anne, I had to come and pay my respects as soon as I heard you were returned."

"Thank you, Lady Dorothy, and welcome. It is a great pleasure to see you again. Was the way mired after the rains?"

"It was a little muddy and slippery, but our grooms and horses handled it without mishap," Dorothea said. "But pray, tell me how your business progresses, for I am most anxious for your news."

"Patience, Dottie, patience!" Anne laughed, "I shall send Judith for some sack and marchpanes, then we shall sit comfortably and I'll tell you how things went with the King." She led Dorothea into a small sitting room with a view of the deer park.

"I see from your demeanour that it did not go badly for you!" Dorothea said.

"No, it went better than anyone had expected. I could easily have been overwhelmed by the King and all the nobles and lawyers, but I survived – through the protection of my lord! He risked his position with the King for me, when, as you know, we have not always seen eye-to-eye over this matter. He is determined that the King shall not publicly disgrace me and for that I shall be forever grateful to him. I was also most fortunate in having the support of Her Majesty, which was more than I could have supposed and it gave me strength and hope."

"I am gladdened to hear that your lord supported you and the Queen was kind to you. So, is your inheritance secured?" Dorothea asked.

"Oh no, that decision is yet to be taken, by the King," Anne said. "I have no great hope for it, but whatever is decided I shall have had no part in it. I have not agreed to anything and shall sign nothing. No-one can ever say that I approved, agreed or accepted the judgment. My claim stands, and if my uncle's line reaches an end of male heirs, as my father believed it would, then the estates revert to me and my descendants under the terms of my father's will. They cannot have it both ways: if my father's will is legal, this is what it decrees. If my father's will is illegal, then the entail makes the inheritance indisputably mine!"

"Congratulations, dear lady, I am delighted that you are so calm about it now. You must be very relieved." The two friends embraced and continued chatting about the latest fashions at court, especially the complexities of folded and pinned ruffs.

The relief and pleasure were short-lived. The next morning Anne was called to The Child's side to find her alternately flushed and hot, then cold and shaking. She placed a hand on her forehead, which was burning and dry, but The Child pushed her hand away and turned to the wall, whimpering. The servants said this was the sixth time the ague had taken her like this. Anne was angry that she had not been told and immediately wrote a letter to Richard, to tell him of The Child's state and to thank him again for the way he had treated her in London. She sent the letter with a servant in the coach and, as she had hoped, Richard returned in the coach that same day to see The Child. He stayed only one night and returned to London the next day, seeing that The Child appeared to have recovered and after watching her put on her new red coat.

The last few days of January were spent worrying about The Child, who had a further attack of fever and shaking lasting about six hours. Anne ordered that her curtains be kept closed and spent the days going up and down to her and doing all she could to soothe her, but the illness continued to recur every few days for several weeks and The Child became very weak.

Anne tried to distract herself with needlework, reading and

being read to, but could hardly concentrate on anything. She wore the same comfortable green flannel gown and yellow taffeta waistcoat every day. Half way through February she feared for little Lady Margaret's life and the doctor sat by The Child throughout an afternoon after giving her a salt powder in her beer.

Time dragged tediously and there were few visitors, apart from Dr Amherst, the Rector of a nearby parish, who told her that people in London were now beginning to think that she had done well in not referring her business to the King. Everybody, he said, believed that God had had a hand in it. She agreed without hesitation. From him she also gathered that there was still a great deal of activity at court about the legal complexities of her case, with many meetings between the protagonists, the Chief Justice and the King. He could not tell her how things stood, however, so she tried to put it out of mind.

Anne well understood that Richard had to remain at court, not only to attend the meetings about the case, but also to repair his reputation with the King since the audience, when his behaviour could have been seen as disloyal. There were those at court who would have no hesitation in murmuring against him to the King if they saw advantage in it. Richard's way of currying favour, she knew, was to join in the gaming at court and make sure that he lost a great deal of money to the King. Cock-fighting was the favourite sport, bringing him into frequent contact with the King, who was delighted with him and often spoke of him in admiring terms. The money he lost was well-spent and she had no argument with that.

A letter came from Richard during the first week of February, which she opened eagerly, hoping for words of affection or at least interesting news of the activities at Court.

'Madam,' she read, 'It has come to my notice that your recent Behaviour regarding the King's Judgment has done our Cause no good whatsoever, indeed it has damaged our Reputation in Society and set many faces against us. I have no more Patience. The Matter must be resolved as soon as possible and I insist that you make no further attempt to delay a Settlement. If you do so

I shall understand from it that you no longer wish to remain my Wife. Richard Sackville, Earl of Dorset.'

It hit her like a blow to the head and she reeled. What had she done to make him write to her like this? He had been kind to her, they had been friends; why had he now turned against her so suddenly? She sat down and her thoughts slowly cleared; others had been involved and those who wished her ill had been feeding their poison to him while he was at court. It didn't help that, in gambling with the King, he had lost a great deal and was now desperate for money again. She sighed deeply, reflecting bitterly on those whom she perceived as her enemies. They were increasing in number; to be added to Edward Sackville and Matthew Caldicott were her uncle Cumberland and his son, her cousin Henry; perhaps even the King was criticising her in Richard's presence. Martha Penistone, she knew, still featured in Richard's life; there was no doubt whose side she would take. And who knew how many more had her husband's ear and were whispering against her for their own private purposes. Anne had no idea what other company he kept at court; unspecified enemies seemed even more threatening than those she could identify.

She received a visit from a friend who had recently been at court and she was diverted for a while by his gossip about a French Baron who was amusing everyone, including the King and Queen. But when he talked of the opinions of the world on her business and the censure of her that he had heard, she knew that there would be no remedy until the case was concluded.

That evening she went into the chapel and knelt before the altar to pray, entrusting herself wholly to God who had always helped her and asking that He would send a good end to her troubles. She prayed, as she always did, for her mother's soul and for her husband and tonight particularly for The Child, whose fever was raging again. She took down from the windowsill one of the carvings of Christ's passion that had belonged to Mary, the Scottish Queen, tracing the rough surface of the wooden figures with her fingers and remembering the trials faced by both Jesus Christ and that unfortunate Queen. Her own troubles seemed less dreadful – at least she was not under sentence of death as they both were; she must not despair. But still she could not sleep for all the thoughts whirling round in her head and she rose before dawn to pray again. Above all, dear God, I pray you, please spare the life of my Child.

Rivers brought news from London: the business had been discussed many times with the King, the Chief Justice, Richard, the Earl of Cumberland, Cousin Henry and both counsels. It had also been talked of endlessly by members of both the King's Court and the Queen's. The general opinion was that the outcome would be similar to that reached previously by the judges. Rivers said he had seen Lord William Howard, Richard's uncle, who was now against the agreement, despite having been a supporter of Richard all through. Rivers could not explain this change of heart but commented that the relationship between Richard and Lord William had certainly cooled, with Richard beginning to harbour some ill opinion of his uncle. Anne was grateful for his news, and that she was away from all the conflict.

After supper, Mrs Willoughby rushed to Anne with news of The Child.

"My lady, Lady Margaret's nose is bleeding and she is distressed at the sight of all the blood!"

"I shall come to her now, Willoughby. Please bring water and a cloth."

Anne entered The Child's chamber to find her crying amid her blood-stained linen. She held up her arms to her mother, who put the wet cloth to her face and scooped her up into her arms. In a while the bleeding stopped, Margaret was soothed and Anne hummed a little tune to her as she rocked her on her lap.

"There, dearest, there, there. You will feel better now; your humours will be balanced and your ague will be over. Penny will change your linen and put fresh covers on your bed, and then you can sleep sweetly. When you wake you will be cured of everything." Anne laid her down on the bed she shared with Penelope; Margaret was already asleep.

Anne's prediction of an end of the fever was premature, however. Ten days later The Child had an extreme fit of the ague and the doctor had to be summoned again. It was a month before the cause of all the troubles was revealed, when they found she had cut two new big teeth; following that, there were no more agues.

❧

Life was unbearably dull and the occasional snippets of news from London were far from cheering. Richard visited Knole to see The Child at Anne's request and complained again, in front of the triumphant Caldicott, that Anne was not suitably dressed for one in her position. He was cool and distant, stayed only one night and told Anne that the King was bitterly opposed to her and she would lose her claim. There was also news from court that the Earl of Buckingham, the King's new favourite with whom he seemed to be besotted – he had kissed him passionately on the lips in public – was sworn into the Privy Council. Anne's faith in humanity faltered, but never her trust in God.

Days and weeks passed slowly. She took to going to bed early and rising late, wearing the same clothes every day, reading the bible with the rector, walking in the garden, saying her prayers, embroidering cushions and playing cards with the Steward in the evening. Her ladies remonstrated with her for wearing such ill clothes, reminding her of her Lord's words, but she had no will for adornment when she felt herself exiled from the world.

❧

After the King's departure to Scotland, Richard left London feeling ill. On the way to Knole he had to keep stopping so he decided to stay at Buckhurst, sending to Knole for a cook and a page to come and look after him. Anne sent a letter with them, begging him to let her come and join him there, but received no reply. As the year since her mother's death was not yet ended, she decided to wear her mourning clothes and spent a day walking in the park with Judith and her Bible, brooding on her troubles but thankful that The Child had recovered.

After ten days of illness Richard came to Knole for three days. He was still coughing and chose to sleep in another chamber. They walked together in the Wilderness and the garden. He was not in a good humour but told Anne that there was still time for her to be involved in the settlement of matters with her uncle.

"The agreement is more in our favour than I had thought it might be," Richard said. "It would be an advantage to you if you were a party to it. Many are saying that you should agree and no longer stand opposed. It is seen as a mark against you that you still stand against the King's wisdom in this, but it is not too late for you to repair your good name."

"I can imagine who may have besmirched my good name, my Lord, and how they have done it," Anne said. "I would that you did not listen to them for they were ever my enemies. You were kind when I was with you in London, but since you have remained at court you have gained a very low opinion of me, which I have done nothing to deserve. The poet says that absence makes the heart grow fonder, but with you I perceive it to be the other way around." There were tears in her eyes.

"You have brought these troubles on yourself, there is no-one else to blame," Richard said coldly. "I have worked for years for the best outcome for us and you have been naught but an obstacle all along the way. I don't need anyone else to tell me that you are the most stubborn woman in the world, I know it. How can you be surprised that my patience with you is at an end?"

Anne remembered what she had heard about Lord William Howard's position and asked,

"Have you spoken with your uncle about it?"

"No," Richard frowned. "Why should I consult with Lord William? He has been no help either, and his opinion changes like the weather. He cannot be trusted. Your uncle Cumberland has agreed that he will pay the award but remember that the papers are not yet signed and sealed; that is left until next term now that the King has gone to Scotland, so it is not completed. There is yet time for you to sign."

Anne was surprised to hear this; she had believed that it was finished. She did all she could to put on a brave face and a chatelaine's gown and make his stay as comfortable and pleasant as possible, but the next day he returned to London. After she had seen him down into the coach, she contemplated what he had said. Walking in the garden again, she realised that he was more satisfied with the agreement than she had expected. Although he had encouraged her to agree to it, it could still go ahead without her involvement and he would be satisfied with that. There was no need for her to do any more.

At the Standing in the early spring sunshine she felt more at peace than she had done before Richard came from Buckhurst; he had assured her that he would return in a few days' time and The Child was well again. God had answered her prayers with blessings.

CHAPTER TWENTY-FIVE
April-August 1617

When Richard returned to Knole, he brought more news of the award. They sat in the spring sunshine on the south side of the house, sheltered behind the marble pillars of the Colonnade. Richard told Anne the King had judged that the entail should be ignored and her mother's jointure lands in Westmorland be passed to Lord Cumberland as part of his inheritance from her father. To Richard's delight, Lord Cumberland was to pay him seventeen thousand pounds in instalments over the next two years. A final instalment, of three thousand pounds, was only to be paid if Anne agreed to it and Parliament ratified it. In addition to these arrangements, the King had specified that, should she survive Richard and then start any further law suits concerning the inheritance, she would lose all her rights under her father's will.

"So you see," Richard concluded, "The King's judgment is fair to everyone and gives you far more than you have deserved by your stubborn behaviour."

Anne frowned at him.

"I don't think I deserve to lose my lands," she said, "And I do not think I gain anything from this award. I will never give up Westmorland, and nothing will persuade me otherwise, whatever judgment anybody makes."

"Can you not see the result as benefitting you, when it is far more generous than you could ever have hoped?" Richard said.

"I hoped nothing of it. You know I shall never agree to this, yet you listen to others and lose patience with me," Anne said. "Sometimes you are kind and I think you understand, yet at other times, when you have been influenced to think ill of me, you forget that I made up my mind long ago and am not to be dissuaded."

"I admire your determination, my lady! You are like a great

rock in the road, blocking the way and immovable. Who would think that so tiny a woman could prove such an obstacle to so many powerful men?" Richard's eyes twinkled; he was proud, almost laughing.

Anne was relieved by his change of mood, but wary, nevertheless. Then the picture of herself as a large rock in the road came into her mind and she laughed. But relaxation brought tears of relief to her eyes.

"Don't weep, sweet heart, we shall be friends. Let's play Barley Break after supper and then I shall lie in your chamber tonight, eh?"

She smiled up at him through her tears and his arm went around her waist. There was such comfort in his touch.

Anne felt herself reconciled, not only to her husband, but also to the King's award as far as the effects of it would bear on the tenants in Westmorland. She decided to obtain their addresses and send letters to them explaining the situation in order to keep herself in their minds. She signed thirty-three letters with a characteristic flourish and sent Marsh north to deliver them; they told the tenants that the outcome of the King's judgment meant that their landlord was now Lord Cumberland, and they must pay their rents loyally to him. But, she added, although she accepted the ruling in practice, she still did not agree with it in principle and had not endorsed it.

Richard returned to London to assist in Francis Bacon's celebrations on becoming Lord Keeper. Bacon was renting Dorset House until his permanent quarters were ready, and his procession would set out from there. Anne received no letters or news from Richard, nor did she write to him. She busied herself with The Child and, as the weather grew hot, they took to going outside only during the evening, after supper. Lady Margaret began riding on a piebald pony from Westmorland, and Anne, as the anniversary of her mother's death approached, became more and more aware of the presence of those lands in her thoughts. Mr Woolrich, her mother's chief servant, came to tell her that all the estates in Westmorland had surrendered to Lord Cumberland. She talked with him for hours about her mother and they shared many memories, which, though they made her sad, also brought comfort.

Legge came from London and told her that Richard was annoyed with her again for not accepting and signing the agreement. He explained that the discontent arose from some need to buy land, but this made little sense to her and she privately believed that the change of heart drew its sustenance from the constant diet of malice about her with which Richard was fed by his closest companions. She missed him and time was tediously slow in passing.

Legge's view was proved right when she heard from her cousin, Francis Russell, that the King's award was to be finalised the following week as all those involved, bar her, were now in agreement on it, and Richard had cancelled the jointure he had promised her the previous year.

She was hurt, angry and frightened. She felt isolated and powerless. There was nothing she could do to change this; at the age of twenty-seven, after a twelve-year battle, her inheritance had been taken from her and there was nothing to fight against any longer, even if she had had any fight left in her. Her jointure, too, was now in doubt. She brooded about it for days and eventually concluded that The Child, the love she bore Richard and his love for her, were the only parts of her life that were still important to her. She resolved to hold fast to those with a stubborn love, to replace the stubborn opposition with which, for years, she had stood against the world.

She wrote a resigned letter to Richard telling him that she was very unhappy about the jointure but assuring him of her love and determination to endure patiently whatever he thought fit. After that, she wrote friendly letters to both her sisters-in-law and to Richard's aunt, sending them locks of The Child's hair. She wanted to win the love and good opinion of his relations as best she could. She felt better when these letters were despatched, but the bitter thought of Matthew Caldicott and Edward Sackville and the part they were playing in her troubles remained in her mind like a speck of grit in the eye.

᳇

Richard, Matthew and Edward came down to Knole together. Pleased as she was to see Richard, she felt oppressed by the constant presence of the other two men. She tried to put a brave face on it and express merriness she did not feel, especially when they played Barley Break on the green in the evenings. But when she came into a room where the three of them were already ensconced, she felt her heart beat harder in her chest as a wave of hostility rose towards her. Having them all there was hard to bear and she protested to Richard, but his only response was,

"If you don't like the company you needn't join us!"

"But, my dear lord, I long for your company. I find it very galling that I cannot spend time with you, as Matthew does, without others being present."

"We do spend time alone together – when I come to your chamber!"

"That is not my meaning. Of course I am very happy when you spend nights in my chamber; that is as it should be for husband and wife. But at other times I often long to be with you, to talk and discuss things as we used to, for there are many times when you are absent altogether and my own company becomes very dull."

"I don't see how Matthew being here prevents you from enjoying my company. Is it not more diverting to have more of a crowd? Let yourself enjoy the times when we are all together!"

"I wish you could see my point of view, Richard, but I find that you are determined to cling to your favourite and allow him to come between us."

Anne left the room on the verge of tears. The anniversary of her mother's death had just passed, bringing waves of sadness. Where could she turn? During the night she was unable to sleep;

Richard had not come to her chamber and she was tortured by images of him with Matthew. Before dawn she decided to write to the Bishop of London about Matthew's actions and influence against her. She would plead for his intervention for the sake of her marriage. Then she cried herself to sleep.

The following day Anne was walking quietly along the Brown Gallery, admiring the Howard portraits which had been hung there by Richard's mother, representing members of her family. She could hear voices coming from the Spangle chamber at the far end of the gallery and as she drew nearer she could distinguish those of Richard, Edward and Matthew. They were discussing the arrangements Richard had put in place and she heard Edward's voice raised against Richard.

"Of course I am angry!" Edward boomed. "You have made a will leaving me with nothing but responsibilities and debts, while you leave her with all the comforts and income at your disposal, when she has been nothing but trouble to you for all the years of your marriage. If you want me to pay off your creditors and look after the estates after you have gone to meet your Maker, you need to provide me with the means to do so! Don't restore the jointure! No! Change its terms, for God's sake – so that I can have some hope of an income. That is the least you can do!" Matthew murmured in agreement.

Anne had heard enough and she hurried quietly away. Her suspicions had been proved; Edward was the influence which made Richard surge to and fro like the tide, taking her fortunes with it. Edward wanted to prevent her and The Child from inheriting anything from Richard. And Matthew was backing him up.

When the men left Knole she wondered whether her complaints had driven Richard away. She busied herself with correspondence. Her letter against Matthew was dispatched to the Bishop. An exchange with her cousin Russell assured her of his great care of all her affairs, and in gratitude she sent him half a roe buck which had just arrived with a letter of lukewarm good wishes from Richard. She also wrote to the Queen, thanking her for all the favours she had received from her.

The new dresses she had ordered at the end of her mourning period arrived from the tailor in London and provided one bright moment in a miserable week. She tried them on with the help of Judith and Faith, who were both overjoyed to see her smile.

"My lady, this sea-green satin gown is perfectly suited to your complexion!" Judith declared.

Faith giggled and said, "I don't think Judith means that your complexion is sea-green, my lady!" Judith frowned at the younger woman, which made Anne laugh.

"No, Faith, I don't think that was Judith's meaning," she said. "Come, help me take this off and I shall try the damask embroidered with green and gold – perhaps that one will be a better match for my complexion!"

The maids admired the way the tailor had made the necklines suitable for the open French ruffs that were newly fashionable, but Anne wondered when she would be able to show them off at court. She stood in front of the mirror and gave thanks for her still-slim waist and her creamy breast. Judith nodded and Faith burst out,

"Oh, my lady, your lord will delight to see you in these new gowns!"

She learned from both servants and visitors that the Clifford inheritance was still the talk of the court and that many still condemned her for holding out, while some commended her for being just and honourable. She also heard with satisfaction that the tenants in Westmorland were discontented with their new landlords and looked favourably on her. Josiah, the Page, cheered her while they were picking cherries by telling her that all the men in the household loved her exceedingly, except Matthew and two or three of his close associates.

These lighter remarks, however, were outweighed many times over by the news she heard from several quarters that Richard and his brother Edward were very thick together at court and were both in the good books of the King. She shuddered at this news, knowing that Edward was behind the decision to cancel her jointure and would be working on her husband, and possibly even the King, to sway their opinions against her. In her darkest times she also believed he was pushing Richard towards Martha Penistone. She wondered what he would pursue next; would it be The Child's inheritance? She was certain that, whatever it was, it would be intended to hurt both her and her daughter.

A reply came from the Bishop to her complaints against Matthew, but she was disappointed by its noncommittal tone and bland emollient words, which were like thick ointment to smother her anger and hurt. She threw it into the fire.

Soon after, she received a letter from one of the lawyers informing her that Richard was indeed willing his estate to his brother. It was a repeat of her father's will, but this time there was no entail to protect her and The Child. A cloud descended on her, and no matter how she tried to distract herself she wept for hours almost every day. Melancholy and sadness pervaded her being. She felt very tired but couldn't sleep. She began to feel ill with headaches, pains in her side, and a constant feeling of anxiety. She could not identify the exact source of this unease; each time she tried to pin it down her head seemed to spin with the many troubles she faced and tears flowed again.

She wrote to Richard asking him to come to her because she was so ill, but more than a week passed before he arrived. In the meantime, she had received a copy of the King's Award which she could hardly read but perceived to be as bad for her as possible. Richard was shocked to find her in such a state and tried to reassure and console her but stayed only a night or two before leaving again to go hunting.

She wrote further letters to friends in Westmorland to inform them of the terms of the Award and sent gifts to some of them. She heard Dr John Donne preach in the parish church near the gates of Knole and invited him and many other people to dine with her in the Great Hall. This did prove to be a distraction and she enjoyed her conversations with the great man, who admired her ability to discourse on any subject under the sun, *'from slea-silk to predestination'* as he put it.

Richard re-appeared and was loving and attentive, but the next day demanded that she go to London to set to rights Dorset House, which Bacon, the Lord Keeper, had now vacated.

"No, my lord, I am certainly not well enough to undertake either the journey or the task; I am but lately very ill and troubled. Pray ask the servants to see to it, for I am not willing to risk my health again."

"I take it badly that you refuse this request," Richard complained. "I rarely ask you to undertake any such work for our common good. You say you are finding life tedious here, yet you are unwilling to do this small thing for me which you would surely find diverting."

"I do not need diversion, my lord, but rest. I do not wish to be treated like a servant, to be at your beck and call and answer to your every whim and it is not meet that you should demand it of me."

Richard turned on his heel and left the room, but he did spend the night with her – to her surprise. Next morning he was going to Penshurst to visit Lord and Lady Lisle, but forbade her to accompany him, even when they sent a servant specifically to ask her to come.

"You have told me you need rest. I do not think it would be wise of you to make this journey, short as it is, when you are still so unwell."

"I think I would find the company of friends restorative, but will bow to your wishes, my lord."

She didn't feel as meek as she sounded, seeing this altercation as a continuation of yesterday's bad-tempered exchange, but when he left he gave her a token of his affection – the ring he often wore, which had been his grandmother's wedding ring. She allowed this gesture to soothe her, convincing herself that he believed that the journey would be too much for her and had no other motive for preventing her from going.

~

While he was away, she received a visit from Mr Rann, the vicar.

Rann cleared his throat.

"My lady, I have it in mind to speak with you about a subject which has been troubling me for some time."

"And what may that be, Mr Rann? Does it concern me?"

"It does, my lady." He cleared his throat again. "I hardly know how to begin..."

"Well, I think we shall not get far with this question unless you make a start, my dear Mr Rann. Pray tell me what has been troubling you."

"We have been friends for a long time, Lady Anne, and we have spent many instructive hours reading Holy Scripture together and discussing matters of religion."

Anne nodded and made as if to speak, but he waved a hand and continued,

"This matter of which I would speak does not come directly from those previous discussions, but indirectly, I believe. We have often spoken of love and forgiveness and it is that which I wish to mention, particularly in relation to the young man whom your husband has selected as his companion."

"Matthew? You would speak to me of Matthew Caldicott, Mr Rann?"

"Yes, my lady. It has come to my notice that there is little in the way of cordiality between you and him. Sometimes, you know, the carrying of hard feelings towards another human being can prove a very heavy load and I have seen that, of late, you have been struggling with many burdens. Will you not consider relieving yourself of one of those – the burden that is Matthew?"

Anne laughed. "How I wish that were possible, Mr Rann! If Matthew were to disappear from our lives I would certainly feel a lightness of heart that has been absent from me for a long, long time."

"Then I urge you, make friends with him and take him into your heart so that you are no longer troubled in this way!"

"I am afraid that is not possible, dear friend. Caldicott has done me so many injuries that I would be very hard pressed to forget them. He has worked against me with my Lord ever since he was first in his service."

The next time she saw Mr Rann, he brought a message from Matthew, telling her that he would be very pleased to have her look favourably on him. This led to another lengthy discussion during which Mr Rann brought up the subject of Christian forgiveness. Anne eventually told him,

"I cannot be his friend, Mr Rann, but you may tell him that, as a Christian, I forgive him the wrongs he has done me."

After Mr Rann left, Anne puzzled for a time about his visits and his knowledge of her household and family matters. She wondered why he was concerning himself with Matthew, then the memory of her letter to the Bishop came to her mind and she wondered whether Mr. Rann was acting on directions from the Bishop.

Part of the reason she had mellowed was that by now she knew that she was pregnant with a child who would be born in February. And Richard was delighted. This was not only a reason to be happy and an explanation of some of the illness she had been suffering, but an event with implications for everything in the future; if this child is a boy, she told herself, there will be no question of Richard leaving his estates to his brother. And she had a very strong notion that it was a boy.

CHAPTER TWENTY-SIX
August-December 1617

Richard was planning a progress throughout Sussex and beyond, in the company of over thirty horsemen who would tour many gentlemen's houses and hunt in their parks. On the eleventh of August they drank a stirrup-cup in the stable yard at Knole. Anne handed the silver goblet up to Richard, who drained it in one gulp, stooped from his saddle to kiss her hand as he returned it to her, then clattered off in high spirits. He led the way with his Master Huntsman, Thomas Leonard beside him, sounding great blasts on the horn; the rest of the company responded merrily, the horses became skittish and the dogs bayed in excitement.

As silence fell in the yard, Anne felt the stab of loneliness again and turned back to the house wondering how she would fill the empty hours for the weeks of her lord's absence. Fortunately, the knowledge that there would be another child next year gave her hope for the future and she didn't feel the utter despair that had been her companion not long ago. She was further cheered a few days later by a very kind and loving letter from Richard in Lewes. He was pleased and excited about her pregnancy and said he longed to be with her.

Anne rode over to visit friends and received many visitors at Knole. From these conversations she learned that opinion seemed to have swung in her favour; her opposition to the King's Award was now seen as a cleverly calculated gambit – so clever, in fact, that some were inclined to credit it to Richard rather than his wife.

She tried to fill the time, but there was still emptiness and tedium and sadness; her situation contrasted starkly with the news she received of Richard's merry progress through Sussex. Then she heard that he had gone to Woodstock to meet the King, and then that he was in Bath. He returned to London towards the end of

September and on the 29th he finally came down to Knole with the news that he had received four thousand pounds from Lord Cumberland. He was in an expansive mood and they entertained friends and relations. Richard showed off his stables and all his great horses; Anne and her ladies made quince marmalade and she bestowed it as gifts on their visitors and strolled with them in the Wilderness as they chatted about this person and that and expressed their admiration of The Child.

At the beginning of November Anne felt well enough to go up to London to make some plans for Christmas and take part in court activities. Richard did not accompany her, but she made the most of the opportunity to see many old friends and acquaintances and show off her new gold-embroidered green damask gown, wearing it without the farthingale because of her expanding belly. She spent a large amount of money on a gift for the Queen – white satin skirts which she had had embroidered with pearls and many colours. The following day she went to Whitehall and sought out Lady Ruthven, who was with Alethea (now also an important member of the Queen's inner circle) and they gave her the news that she would see the King.

Alethea took her aside for a brief private chat.

"How goes life with you, dear friend?"

"I thank God every day for my blessings, Alethea," Anne replied. "I could never have imagined that things would work out so well for me. My lord is content and has received the first instalment of money from Lord Cumberland, so we are loving friends again, yet I have not signed away my inheritance. And I am hopeful that the child I am bearing is a son who will, by his very existence, prevent the Sackville estates from falling into the hands of my brother-in-law, my greatest enemy.

"I thought by now to be at least an outcast from society, if not divorced or accused of treason and thrown in the Tower, but here I am, at court, with many friends around me and my dear lord still wedded to me! I marvel – God is truly merciful to me, dear Alethea."

They embraced warmly.

The Queen sent for Anne. When she entered the Bedchamber, she found the King also there and he greeted her with a kiss. She was surprised, but there was comfort and satisfaction in knowing that she was not ostracised, despite her refusal to sign the agreement. The King was kindly and spoke graciously to her, telling her to speak to his lawyer, who would give her more information about the award and answer her questions. She sensed that he truly believed he had made a decision which was not only just, but favourable to her.

As she left the chamber, the Queen also kissed her, putting a hand on her elbow and moving with her towards the door. She bent down to speak quietly, out of earshot of the crowd around the King.

"I wish you well of your delivery and hope for a boy for you, then some of your troubles will be solved, will they not?" the Queen said.

Anne gave a deep curtsy and thanked her majesty for all her kindness. She was astonished at the depth of the Queen's understanding of her situation and anxieties; she wondered if it was possible that Alethea had spoken of her woes to the Queen.

Anne followed the King's suggestion and took her lawyer, John Davis, to see the King's attorney in his grand chambers at Gray's Inn. Discussion with them settled her mind about the award, which was very similar to the one that the Judges had given before the King became involved. She decided not to fight against it any longer, although she would never agree to it. She would work quietly to support the Westmorland tenants in their battles with Lord Cumberland, who now needed to raise their rents in order to pay the compensation which the King had ordered for her and Richard. When she mentioned this idea to Richard he chuckled, saying he was in favour of it, and pointing out to her that it was no different from the way the Cliffords had incited the tenants when she was in possession of Brougham Castle.

It came as a surprise, one morning later in the month, when Richard opened the door of her chamber and declared in a loud voice,

"Here we are, my lady, see who has come to pay his respects to you!" He was waving his arms as a signal to someone on the other side of the door to come forward. There was a pause, as if the other person was reluctant to appear; Richard vanished for a moment and came back dragging Henry Clifford by the arm. Clifford bowed and stammered,

"Lady Anne, forgive me, Coz, I . . . I do not wish to disturb you. Your lord was . . . was . . . most, most . . . er . . . insistent. That I should pay my respects. Which I do," and he bowed again.

Anne rose from her chair with a frosty glance in Richard's direction. She inclined her head slightly.

"Cousin Henry, I trust you are in good health? And my Lady Frances?"

"I thank you, we are well," Henry said. "I bring the next instalment of the King's award."

Anne had no intention of discussing the award with him and ignored the last remark.

"And your lord father, my uncle. Is he well?" she said.

"Thank you, cousin, he has been somewhat below par these two months past but is recovering now." Then as an afterthought he added, "... and greets you."

Anne observed that the weather had turned quite cold and Clifford attempted a smile as he replied that it was much colder in Skipton. Anne did not respond and Clifford looked to her husband for help, but Richard avoided his glance and suggested that he should sit down. Neither Anne nor Henry wanted this, so after exchanging a few more stiff courtesies he withdrew.

Anne returned to Knole, feeling neither well nor content. She resented Richard's clumsy attempt to bring her and her cousin together, putting it down to his delight that money had started to flow in and his usual assumption that what pleased him must also please her. He was prepared to build friendship, or at least reduce enmity with Henry, and had no idea that this was anathema to her.

Anne's pregnancy was becoming burdensome and her anxiety about it was increasing. She spoke to Richard.

"My lord, if the child I bear is a son, will you remain determined to leave Knole and the Sackville estates to your brother as you have planned?"

"I have not yet given the matter consideration," Richard said, "The event is still some time off and such a decision would be premature at present."

"I ask because it troubles me to think that I and my children might find ourselves in the same difficulty as my mother and I after my father's death," Anne said. "Your will might repeat the troubles that his will brought on me and I would seek to know whether this is what you intend."

"You are mistaken," Richard said, "There is no entail on the Sackville estates, so nothing to prevent me from leaving them to whomever I please. Therefore, it's not the same situation at all."

"You are right. There wouldn't be the same wrangle to be had over the legality of your wishes," she conceded. "But I still feel that your wife and children deserve better treatment from you."

"Be assured that I will provide for you and The Child as best I can," Richard said. "I've told you that your jointure will be free of encumbrances, but you must also remember that I am so heavily in debt that there will be little gain from the estates for many years to come and I do not wish you, or our children, to be responsible for the repayment of those debts. My brother is unhappy about the apportionment already. If, when, I have a healthy son I may be able to consider the matter again, but I make no promises."

Anne felt wronged and blamed her enemies; Edward Sackville, for scheming to deny her and her children their rights, and

Matthew Caldicott for encouraging Richard into extravagance and debt and backing up Edward. She clung to the hope that the child in her womb was a boy and that there would therefore be no more dispute about the inheritance.

Richard went to Buckhurst with many companions to hunt and feast for three days and remained there afterwards for a further week, alone with Matthew. It took all her strength to put this out of her mind, but there were few distractions. She received only one visitor, Richard's aunt, Mary Neville, to whom she gave a pair of Spanish leather gloves. The rest of the time she tried to quell misery by preparing for Christmas in London.

Richard returned on the 20th December and two days later the whole household moved up to Dorset House for the festive season. The Child and her governess went ahead in a litter carried by the most docile pair of horses, one in front and one behind, each ridden by a groom. Richard and Anne followed in the great coach, then came Richard's senior servants, grooms, footmen and cooks on horseback, Anne's gentlewomen in a lesser coach, and a long train of wagons and carts carrying all the household goods and servants required for their busy stay in the capital. They were to celebrate the twelve days of Christmas in extravagant style, with feasting and music and many friends and neighbours visiting to enjoy the fruits of the hunting season.

Lady Penelope Rich, the Queen's principal Lady of the Bedchamber, was delivered of her sixth child and first son, which seemed to Anne a good omen for her own confinement, but when both mother and child contracted smallpox and the baby died a few days later, she wished she had not entertained that thought. She prayed constantly that her own baby would be a healthy boy. Richard's company and his good cheer and optimism about the New Year buoyed her along as her confinement approached and, thankfully, she saw little of Edward or Matthew.

CHAPTER TWENTY-SEVEN
1618

Anne and her retinue travelled down to Knole after Twelfth Night and well before her twenty-eighth birthday, which fell on the 30th January. The birth of her baby was now so imminent that she hardly noticed it, although in previous years she had usually marked it in some pleasant way.

Judith, Willoughby and Faith prepared everything for the confinement as soon as they arrived. The subsequent days of waiting grew increasingly wearisome for all of them; Anne was tired and irritable, trying to hide her apprehension and discomfort, but fooling nobody. They kept her as busy as they could with card games, chatter, reading and embroidery and the hours ground by. There was little daylight on these mid-winter days; the weather was overcast with heavy rain most days and the nights were longer than ever because she slept badly; they took it in turns to keep watch with her round the clock. Despite the gloom, Anne was content to trust in God, as ever, seeing birth as a natural event and being less terrified this time than she had been at The Child's birth four years ago.

They often retired early and Willoughby had just fallen asleep on the pallet in Anne's chamber when she was woken by a sharp cry from behind the curtains of her mistress's bed. She spoke briefly to Anne, found that her waters had broken and labour had begun, and then ran to wake Judith and Faith, sending the younger girl to fetch the midwife. On returning to the chamber, Willoughby fussed around, checking that the windows were closed and the curtains drawn, then she moved the birthing-chair from the corner, placed it near the fire and lit six more large candles which she distributed around the room. Judith came in with a pot of caudle; she placed it near the fire to keep warm and called a footman to bring enough logs to last the night. Another groan from the bed alerted them to their mistress's immediate needs and they discussed when would be the best time for her to move to the chair.

Several hours later Anne's back was aching severely, so they took her by each arm and helped her over to the chair, where she sat with her back to the fire and Judith rubbed her lower back and shoulders between contractions. Faith came in with the midwife, who now took charge and persuaded Anne to sip some of the warm spiced wine from the caudle pot. Faith threw handfuls of sweet-smelling herbs on the fire and the hearth and was sent out again to alert the wet-nurse that she would be needed later. The scents of rosemary, thyme and lavender filled the stuffy chamber and Anne, relaxing a little with the warmth of the fire and the soothing effect of the wine, felt safe and well-supported by her ladies and the midwife.

A particularly sharp pain made her cry out from time to time, but the regular rhythm of the gradually increasing contractions left her unable to notice anything else. She was in a cocoon of pain, clinging to the rock that was her mind within the turbulent storm of her body. When Judith attempted to wipe her face with a damp cloth, Anne pushed her away and snapped "No! Don't!" because she needed to concentrate all her resources on this physical and mental battle. She accepted a piece of wood on which to bite, recalling with a grimace that Judith's hand had been black and blue for days after the birth of The Child.

Many hours passed. After the late dawn had broken and following a scare when labour stopped for a few minutes but then started again more strongly than ever, the midwife's careful examination showed that the baby was presenting some dark matted hair to the world and was ready to be helped. Anne was nearing exhaustion and the baby needed to be born. Willoughby put her solid weight behind the chair and held Anne firmly under the armpits, while the midwife prepared to ease the baby's head out at the next push so that she could grasp it by its shoulders and heave with all her strength. Anne screamed and blood spurted on to the floor. Two more pushes and pulls and the midwife held up the baby for Anne to see,

"A son, my lady!"

She tied and cut the umbilical cord and delivered the afterbirth. The baby was swaddled, to protect him from chills and evil spirits, and placed in the crib. Then Willoughby, Judith and Faith carried Anne back to the bed, made her comfortable and left her to sleep.

When she awoke hours later, she found herself almost unable to move or to remember what had happened. She called for Judith, to ask her whether the baby had been born.

"Yes, my lady, you have a son!" Judith replied.

"And is my son healthy?" Anne asked.

"He seems healthy, my lady. He is not very big, but your ladyship being small, perhaps that was a blessing."

"It did not feel as though he was small, Judith; he was big enough to tear my body apart! What was the date of his birth?"

"He was born at noon today, my lady," Judith said. "The second day of February."

John Coniston rode to Dorset House to bring the news to Richard, who came down from London two days later to see his son and visit his wife. He kissed her twice and declared his delight and Anne began to comprehend that an event, for which she had hardly dared to hope, had occurred. They had a son, an heir, a Sackville male who would continue the line and be the saviour of his sister and his mother. There would be no question of her enemy usurping her children's inheritance and she... Richard looked down indulgently at his wife, who had fallen asleep again with a slight smile on her pale lips. There would be time later to decide on the baby's name and have him christened; Richard's grandfather's name, Thomas, was his favourite.

Although forewarned by Judith, Anne was alarmed when she saw how tiny her baby was. He fitted easily along her forearm, small as that was, with his dark head in the palm of her hand and his tiny purple-mottled heels barely reaching to the crook of her arm. His fingers were like pink segmented maggots and the skin of his arms was blotchy and dark. He looked so fragile that Richard was afraid to touch him and refused to pick him up. When he cried it was the pitiful mew of a small animal in distress.

The wet-nurse came to feed him.

"Don't worry, my lady," she said, "We'll soon have him filled out. He'll be a bouncing boy in no time, won't you, my little scrap?"

Anne couldn't free herself from doom-laden thoughts of the dangers that threatened and she remembered her two brothers who had both died at the age of five. She thanked God for the gift of a son and prayed that He would protect him, and she longed to see him grow fit and strong, but she felt a nagging doubt every time she looked at him and she couldn't shake it off. She cried a lot during her lying-in weeks and had little appetite for food or rejoicing; sleep often evaded her and the fitful nights were long and disturbing.

When Anne was able to stand and walk again, her son was christened Thomas in the chapel at Great Dorset House and there was much rejoicing, but she found it difficult to join in and remained anxious about this precious son. Richard, loving and attentive, tried to raise her spirits. He brought her touching gifts and keepsakes, as well as trinkets for the baby, and tried to cajole her into a merrier frame of mind.

"Sweet heart are you not delighted that our young Lord Thomas Buckhurst has arrived at last?" he said as they stood together in the nursery, looking down into the crib where Thomas slept.

"Lord Thomas Buckhurst?" she queried, not recognising the name.

"I wish our son to have the title I held as a boy," Richard said. "Are you not pleased?"

"Well, yes, of course, but I would wish that he were stronger."

"He is but a few weeks old; you must be patient and give him time to grow! I am so proud that you have borne him and I would have you rejoice with me and be happy that the event that we have so long awaited and desired has come to pass, by God's mercy."

"God is indeed merciful, I thank Him each hour of every day. What more would you have me do?" Anne heard her own voice, flat and expressionless, hardly above a whisper, and found she was unable to meet Richard's eyes. She felt ashamed that she could not rejoice with him.

"Can you not at least give me some sign that you welcome his birth? And that together we have reason to celebrate it?" Richard said.

Anne sighed.

"I welcome his birth, of course I do," she said, "But as for celebrating, I do not feel well enough to join in any feasting or dancing. Pray do not let that keep you from enjoying the occasion." She turned away from him to hide her stinging eyes.

"Why are you so gloomy?" He placed his hand on her shoulder. "It seems to me that you have no gladness at this time, when surely the birth of a child, especially a son, is one of life's most joyous events."

She shook her head silently and he left her to her gloom.

The weather was dreadful throughout the spring and Anne kept to her chamber. She received few visitors and rarely saw anyone but her gentlewomen, who grew increasingly concerned about her state of mind. They brought her frothy pots of Sack Posset to aid her recovery, but she found it difficult to swallow the thick creamy liquid which smelled of eggs, mace and alcohol.

She showed no interest in her new-born son and even The Child's presence failed to cheer her and became too much for her after a few minutes. Richard's birthday on March 18th was a date she had always marked, but this year she didn't mention it and seemed unmoved when they reminded her. When Easter approached, they felt sure she would buck up, but things only got worse. Willoughby sought advice from the wet-nurse and the midwife and tried all the remedies they suggested, but nothing made any difference.

Anne was by turns restless and agitated, then withdrawn and tearful. She was sometimes more talkative than usual, but would suddenly become irritable and suspicious, accusing them of speaking ill of her or wishing to harm her with bad food or drink. Her wild behaviour turned their world upside down and they became afraid for her and for themselves. She sensed their fear and that made hers worse. On Easter Day, April 15th, she declared in Judith's hearing that she wasn't certain that Thomas was her child; Judith and Willoughby decided to speak to Lord Dorset as soon as they could. A physician was called, to Anne's annoyance.

"Why would I need a physician when I am in the best of health? Our son is now over two months old; he is christened, I am churched and all that business is behind us. I have no complaint that a physician can cure!"

Richard tried to convince her that it would be a good idea to have the doctor check that all was well, but Anne became angry and Richard feared that the book she was holding might soon be hurtling in his direction. The physician was sent away.

Gradually after Easter Anne seemed to settle down and the household breathed more easily. By the middle of May Richard's loving attention was welcomed in Anne's chamber once more. Thomas was beginning to grow a little, but Anne still had moments of dread when she saw his frail form. The Child, now in her fourth year, liked to hold his tiny hand in hers and this, for Anne, just served to emphasise the differences of size and strength between them. She counted the weeks since his birth and it seemed miraculous that he reached twenty weeks, then twenty-one, twenty-two. At twenty-three weeks he sickened and on the day exactly twenty-five weeks after his birth, he died, as quietly as he had lived, in the arms of the wet-nurse.

The whole household now shared Anne's gloom and despair,

though for her there was no change. This event was what she had been expecting and it came as no surprise to her; it was almost a relief that the dread was over and she found the reality more easily dealt with. Thomas's tiny body was buried close to his grandfather and great grandfather, in the family vault at Withyam church on the outskirts of Ashdown Forest. Life began to return to normal, except for Anne, who discovered, with a mixture of joy and dread, that she was already pregnant again.

❦

The summer was lush and fruitful after all the rains of the spring and Anne felt in tune with the fertility of the land as her belly grew large once more. She was content to be at Knole, to receive friends and to help with harvesting in the orchards, filling baskets with ripe plums, cherries, quinces, apples and pears and making cordials and preserves. She thanked God for her good fortune and His blessing. She told herself that everything was well in her world and tried hard not to brood on the knowledge that Richard was more deeply involved than ever with Martha Penistone. There were rumours that a child had been born of this coupling, which made it especially painful and hard for Anne to ignore at this time.

Richard knew that she was hurt by this relationship but seemed unable to end it; he kept it away from her as far as he could, by conducting his liaison mainly at the lady's mother's house in London. Anne supposed that Martha's husband, Sir Thomas Penistone, turned a blind eye to it, either because he felt there was advancement to be had if he showed himself willing to allow his lord this *droit de seigneur*, or because he was too afraid to challenge Richard. She sighed deeply. At least Richard was still affectionate towards her when they were together; that was some small comfort.

❦

Richard announced that he had engaged the services of William Larkin, a very fashionable portraitist, who would come to Knole for several weeks during the summer while the light was good in order to paint their likenesses. Anne protested.

"I am worn out from grief and illness, and I am carrying another child. I look at my reflection and wonder who this stranger is. You can't be in earnest in desiring a drawing of your wife in such a condition!"

But Richard was reassuring and insistent.

"You are my beautiful Countess and I do indeed wish for a portrait that will remind us of these important times. Pray indulge me?"

"I have a better idea; The Child is like a fresh opening blossom, why do you not have her beauty recorded instead of my drabness?"

"That is well thought, my lady, except that I still wish for your portrait! But I shall certainly arrange for The Child to be drawn as well."

She gave him a wan smile of agreement and, once she had consented, made a serious effort to do it properly, as with everything she did. She sat for Larkin through the summer days, wearing a pearl on a fashionable black ear-string in her left ear and dressing in her richest apparel, as for a court occasion, despite the warmth of the weather. She was not displeased with the finished painting, and asked Larkin to make a second copy of the picture which she would give to her cousin. She could see a new maturity in her face which pleased her, although she knew that it was a product of the troubles she had endured.

As autumn progressed and the leaves fell from the trees, Anne recalled the Christmas celebrations she had taken part in the previous year and began to think about returning to Great Dorset House for the festive season. Although she was not feeling well, she had been too long away from society and decided she would go up to London early. Surely the bustle of town and the court at Christmas would set her to rights; she instructed Judith to plan for the journey.

They arrived in London in November and Anne began the social round of visits and receptions and ordered a cushion to be made as a gift for the Queen and a new crimson velvet coat with silver lace for The Child. But she found she had little energy for it and her health worsened. She expected the child in her womb to have quickened by now, but she had felt nothing and within two days she went into labour again. This delivery was mercifully quick and the tiny body of another dead son was whisked away before she caught sight of him. She felt too ill to protest. Richard was sympathetic but rather remote and she saw little of him; she supposed that he was spending time at the house in the Strand belonging to Martha's mother. Even that thought was insufficient to stir her and for weeks she lay in bed in the dark with her bed curtains closed, refusing food or company. Judith tried to involve her in the preparation of the house for Christmas but was shouted at and sent away. The cooks asked what she wished them to prepare for the feasting but were barred from her chamber. Visitors were turned away until word went round that she was not receiving anyone, and thereafter no-one called. No greetings or gifts were exchanged.

Christmas passed by in a feverish haze; Anne hardly knew what day it was and took no interest in the season. Richard, finding her company very unrewarding, guiltily kept away, preferring the amusements of the court and the company of his mistress. Judith brought daily offerings of food and drink to try to tempt her mistress' appetite and eventually, a few days before New Year, Anne sat up and took a small cup of specially prepared broth. She was very pale and weak and could hardly stand, but at last she was responding to her ladies' care and, they hoped, had found the will to recover.

CHAPTER TWENTY-EIGHT
January–March 1619

On New Year's Day Anne asked for her curtains to be drawn back and sent for the Child to come and put on her new velvet coat. She directed that the richly embroidered cushion she had ordered six weeks ago be sent to the Queen and declared that she would be ready to receive visitors the following day. She seemed, like Zellandine, to have woken from a long and troubled sleep.

Friends came to see her and shared court gossip. She was distressed to hear that the Queen was very ill and had not been able to move from Hampton Court during the Christmas season; it was rumoured that she might be dying. Richard, she heard, had been enjoying the company of the King and had lost a huge sum – four hundred pounds – gambling with him. Prince Charles had staged an elaborate Twelfth Night masque at the Banqueting House, which the King had attended, but six days later the Banqueting House had burned to the ground.

Richard went to Knole, but Anne, still too weak to make the journey, spent two more weeks enjoying the company of her many visitors at Dorset House. The subjects of their discussions ranged from Greek and Roman statues with Alethea and her husband, to the ins and outs of her inheritance disputes and the Matthew Caldicott business with Lady Wootton, and to religious topics with Lady Dormer and her daughter-in-law. Relatives on both sides of the family came to dine with her and Lady Warwick brought her a great deal of news. She was sad to hear that her sister-in-law, Cecily, had separated from her husband. She planned a family supper including Cicely and her estranged husband, Sir Henry Compton and hoped to bring them together again, feeling some satisfaction when they appeared to be reconciled.

*

Finally well enough to travel, she ordered the old-fashioned horse litter for the journey to Knole. As she was still weak it would enable her to lie down, wrapped in furs. The small cabin was fixed to two long poles slung between two horses, one leading and one following. Progress was slow, with a groom leading the front horse and a footman mounted behind, keeping the horses to a steady walk. Willoughby rode beside the litter to help Anne should she need it. They set off through the city and over the bridge, through the narrow, crowded, dark passageways between the buildings, leaving the bridge at the southern gateway where tall poles bore the heads of traitors aloft as if in triumph.

The Child rode to Knole in a coach with her ladies and took a different route, crossing the river by ferry. On reaching Knole at dusk Anne was delighted to find that Richard was still there. He was pleased that she had been able to make the journey, although he could plainly see from her pallor that she was still far from well. He lifted her tenderly from the litter and carried her into the house.

"You weigh no more than The Child, my lady! And you are as pale as parchment. We must hope that country air and country food will soon bring you back to health!"

"I am tired now and would go to my chamber. Tomorrow, God willing, I shall be recovered enough to enjoy those delights of which you speak."

It took longer than that, and Anne stayed in her chamber for the week leading up to her twenty-ninth birthday, feeling ill and weak. The 2nd of February was the anniversary of Thomas's birth; grief and sadness overwhelmed her again, yet she found solace in prayer. Shortly after that, Richard decided to go to Buckhurst for two weeks with Matthew and a small band of servants and Anne felt her jealousy spike again. She reminded herself of her husband's tenderness towards her and was then distracted by several pieces of news from the north. Both Mr Davis and Ralph Coniston wrote that there was trouble between her cousins, Henry Clifford and the Howards of Naworth, creating factions in Westmorland. This left her entirely untroubled; indeed, it could only be a good thing for her own fortunes in that country, she thought. Let them squabble!

෨‿ඏ

On Shrove Tuesday, with a surfeit of eggs in the house, Anne proposed to her gentlewomen that they should make pancakes in the Great Hall. Faith ran to find a bell and danced in and out of the two doors under the elaborately carved screen, ringing it and singing of the pancake bell, which signifies a holiday for all. A groom lit the fire under the decorated wooden over mantle. Kitchen staff brought flour, eggs, salt, spices and lard. John Morockoe, his dark face grinning with glee, brought pitchers of water, bowls, spoons and frying pans from the scullery and placed them on the long table in front of the fire. Everyone laughed as he and Faith capered round the hall. Great bowls of mixture were prepared and ladled into the hot lard in the frying pans, and then there was the competition to see who could toss their pancake the highest without it landing on the floor. Anne proved deft at this and the consensus was that she was the champion. She couldn't remember when she had last had such fun or laughed as much, but she was very tired when it was over.

෨‿ඏ

Anne intended to fast for Lent and began taking only a piece of bread and a cup of ale for breakfast and foregoing all meat at dinner and supper. When Richard returned from Buckhurst he was horrified.

"Why are you fasting?"

"In recognition of Our Lord's penance and sacrifice, and to examine my sins and seek reconciliation with my maker," Anne told him. "Lent is the time set aside for this by the Church since ancient times and I wish to be cleansed in preparation for the Easter Communion."

"Your sins cannot be so great as to require mortification of your flesh!" Richard said. "God will certainly forgive you and grant you dispensation this Lenten-tide and I beseech you not to keep this strict fast. You are still weak and unwell from your great misfortunes of the last year. You need sustenance; promise me that you will allow yourself proper nourishment until you are fully recovered."

"I thank you for your concern, Richard. You are a loving husband and I will do as you ask."

☙

A week later Anne found herself in turn trying to extract a promise from Richard, who had decided to go up to London the following day. They had just come in from a visit to the stable yard with The Child to look at the puppies that had been born to her beagle. They were relaxed and happy. Anne turned to Richard,

"My lord, I entreat you to stay here for another day! One day is all I ask!"

"Why this urgency for me to stay one more day? I shall certainly return after two or three days," Richard said.

"Do you not remember? The 25th of February? Is that not a date with a very special meaning for you and me?"

Richard looked puzzled: "I am not able to recall its significance, unless it is to do with the ill-starred birth of Thomas a year ago?"

"No, my lord!" Anne smiled. "It will be the tenth anniversary of the day we were wed, in my mother's chamber at Austin Friars. It is therefore – for me at least – a day of jubilation!"

Richard covered his face with his hands and bowed his head, but when he looked up she could see a twinkle of amusement in his eyes. They laughed.

"Very well, my lady, you have your wish. I shall stay here with you for another *three* merry nights! Will that satisfy you?" Anne nodded and took a deep breath, laughing as she tried to prevent a flush of pleasure rising to her face.

☙

Richard's delayed departure meant a further change of plan,

because when they awoke on the 27th they found there had been a heavy snowstorm and this prevented him from taking the coach. He had to ride instead and, once arrived in London, fell ill, which necessitated extending his brief stay there to ten days. Anne, believing that he had gone there to visit Lady Penistone, wondered whether the longer stay was the penalty his mistress had extracted for his delayed arrival, but when he returned he was still unwell, taking physic and specially prepared food, and she regretted her suspicions. She recalled that Richard had recently had several bouts of illness and she worried that his way of life, with its constant demands on his mental and physical energies, was undermining his health and wearing him out. She must try once more to persuade him that a quieter life, with her and The Child, would be better for him.

At the beginning of March, Legge brought news of the death of the Queen at Hampton Court. Although she had been ill for some time, this news was shocking and Anne could not believe that she would never again see her namesake, ally, protector and liege. She remembered the advice the Queen had given her concerning her inheritance during the hardest days of the hearings and the many other kindnesses she had received at her hands. The event was also a reminder of her mother's death and of the abandonment and aloneness she had felt then, and it seemed that she must face again.

The Queen was only forty-two years old at her death and had borne the loss of several children in infancy and the tragic death seven years ago of her beloved and much-admired first-born son, Prince Henry of Wales, at the age of only eighteen. Anne knew how strong the bond between the Queen and this son had been and how hard she had fought during his younger years for the right to remain closely involved in his upbringing and education. She prayed for both their souls and that they would be reunited for eternity.

She heard also that her own relation, Lord Warwick, had died and that the King, who was staying at his hunting lodge at

Royston to avoid the plague in London, was sick. Ill news was piling up, one thing after another.

Thoughts of all these misfortunes preoccupied her for much of the last three weeks of Lent leading up to Easter and when she thought of the crucifixion of the innocent Son of God, she began to re-experience some of the disturbing ideas that had been in her mind during her illness of a year ago. Was Thomas really her son? Surely, if he was, he was meant to protect her from her enemies, especially Edward Sackville who was plotting to steal The Child's inheritance. Why did Thomas die? She must have done something very sinful to have received that punishment from God. And she had been so easily persuaded to give up her fast this Lent – she would not be forgiven. Her sinfulness must be punished and if God did not see fit to do it, she must do it herself. She should die; she did not deserve to live and she was not worthy to remain on this earth. She had been well-trained by her mother to recognise many herbal plants, among them Belladonna, Lily of the Valley, Hemlock and Aconite, and she knew where to find them close by. Her mother must have known how much she would need this knowledge.

Some days these thoughts were loud and clear, voices telling her to go and find the poisons. On other days she knew that killing herself would be the greatest sin of all and she had the strength to withstand the disturbing ideas. She attended Mr Rann's sermon on Good Friday and after supper retired to her chamber, trying to read her Bible. She could not concentrate and began to cry, throwing herself face-down on the bed. When Richard came in, he found her distraught and dishevelled, weeping as he had never seen her before.

"My lady! What ails you? Are you ill? Anne, Anne, answer me!" He ran to her, put his arm around her shoulder and tried to raise her head to see her face. She resisted him and keened all the louder. He sat beside her and stroked her arm until she calmed.

"Now, pray, tell me what is wrong," Richard said. "What has upset you so much? I've never seen you like this, Nan. It is not your nature to be so given over to weeping." The name her father had used for her as a child was enough to set her crying again and he waited until this bout subsided. He kissed her hand and was silent until she took a deep shuddering breath and shook her head.

"I have been overcome by the sadness of everything. A year ago Thomas was on this earth but since he was taken from us my mind is so troubled, my thoughts are so strange; I have examined my soul and although I had intended all through Lent to take the Communion this Easter Sunday, now I find myself unfit to receive it."

"You are tired, Anne. You are still weak and you have been doing too much. You must not blame yourself for events in which you had no part. Sleep now. Tomorrow, when you are rested, you will see things in a better light."

The next morning Anne sent for Mr Rann.

"You sent for me, Lady Anne. What would you have me do?"

"Mr Rann, I find my mind so troubled with dark thoughts and sinful intentions that I do not believe I am fit to receive the Easter Communion tomorrow. I pray you will understand my absence."

"My lady, you do not need to excuse yourself. I am certain there is no reason why you should not take Communion, for you are one of the most Christian people I have ever known."

"I wish it were so, Mr Rann, but sadly it is not. You do not see the darkness in my soul nor hear the voices of evil that beset me."

"Would it relieve your mind to speak of these things, my lady?"

"I am troubled by many things, Mr Rann," Anne said. "And I am ashamed of the thoughts of my own mind. God must be very angry with me." Tears came again. He watched her in helpless silence and waited for her to speak. She took a great breath.

"God will never forgive me, Mr Rann, if I allow these thoughts to make me take that which is only His to take. If He wished my life to end, He would bring that about, I tell myself. But He bestows only greater suffering upon me, which He wishes me to endure. I believe He tests me, but I am weak and rebellious and am tempted to take things into my own hands. Pray for me, Mr Rann;

and please understand that I am unable to receive Communion tomorrow. Ask God to look kindly upon me."

"Let us pray together, Lady Anne," Mr Rann said. They knelt and recited the Lord's Prayer, and then Rann blessed her in the name of the Trilogy and left her. She sat for a long time, her mind blank. She felt calmer but knew that the troubling thoughts would return; indeed, in trying not to think about them she was opening her mind to them again and bringing about that which she most feared. She must banish them altogether.

When Richard heard how she had spoken to Mr Rann, he asked him simply to preach in the Chapel on Easter Day and cancel the Communion service for the Household, giving permission for anyone who wished to take it to attend the Parish Church.

Anne had recovered by the evening and regretted that she had not taken the Easter Communion. There was a dream-like, unreal quality now to the thoughts that had plagued her.

Chapter Twenty-nine
May 1619 – January 1620

Richard went to Lewes for the muster commemorating the thirteenth century battle between Henry III and Simon de Montfort. There was gaming and entertainment and he lost a lot of money, but Anne was proud of him when she learned that he was held in such esteem and affection there that the town had honoured him with a fireworks entertainment.

The King was still at his favourite hunting lodge at Royston, recovering from his illness and grieving for his Queen. On Richard's return to Knole he received a letter advising him to go to the King, because most of his peers had already been at his majesty's side during his sickness and Dorset's absence had been noticed. He went immediately to Royston and spent a few nights with the King, who welcomed him and treated him well, to Richard's relief.

Richard then returned to London, where Anne joined him a few days later for the court's period of mourning for the Queen and for the funeral, which had been postponed for a month because of the King's illness. They heard that Edward Sackville was ill and Richard hurried to his brother's lodgings, returning with the news that he was indeed very sick. Anne received this information with mixed feelings, but tried to show loving sympathy to Richard.

Anne was now well enough to spend several periods watching by the Queen's body at Somerset House. She was satisfied that she had honoured her friend by staying there throughout one night, not leaving until 5 o'clock in the morning, whereas most of the other mourners left before midnight. As all the noblemen and their ladies gathered in London, the funeral became a huge social occasion for visiting, gossiping and showing off fashionable mourning clothes.

Anne ordered a black mourning dress and Richard spent time cock-fighting and gaming, attending the King, seeing Lady Penistone and visiting his brother Edward, who was still sick – sometimes even rumoured to be dead. Anne felt both anger and guilt when she heard these stories and often chastised herself, begging forgiveness from God. Occasionally Richard accompanied her for a walk in Hyde Park or a visit to their kinswoman, Frances Somerset and her baby, still imprisoned in The Tower.

❧

A new scandal had now replaced the Somersets in fashionable interest and everyone was talking of the problems besetting two prominent families; Anne heard the story from her friends.

"Have you heard about the separation of Lord Roos and his bride?" Alethea said.

"Separation?" Anne said. "Do you mean the Lord Roos who is grandson to the Earl of Exeter? Whose bride was Anne Lake, daughter of the King's Secretary? Surely they are only recently married?"

"Yes indeed, barely a couple of years since! It seems they have had a most bitter quarrel," Barbara Ruthven said.

"What was the argument about?" Anne asked.

"I don't know but wait!" Alethea said. "There is more to come! It is very complicated."

"What do you mean?"

"It is said that Sir Thomas Lake, the bride's father, wished to claim some land at Walthamstow from Roos as a settlement for his daughter, but Lord Exeter refused."

"And has there been some argy-bargy about that?" Anne said.

"No, nothing of that sort," Barbara said. "But then came accusations from the Lakes that Roos had had an incestuous affair with his grandfather's much younger wife! She is 38 years junior to her husband, you know, and only ten years older than Roos."

"Well, there is no blood relationship between them is there?" Anne said.

279

"That's true," Barbara said. "But letters were produced accusing the Countess of Exeter of plotting to poison both Lady Roos and her mother, Lady Lake. Arthur Lake, Lady Roos's brother, attacked Lord Roos and there was to be a duel, but the King intervened and has sent Roos to Italy on state business. The case is passed to Star Chamber for judgment. Now we hear that Roos has died in Naples."

"No doubt all will become clear when the case is heard!" Alethea said.

❦

Interspersed with such gossip, Anne received news of various problems in the North. She was pleased and flattered to hear that the tenants preferred her to the Cliffords. Mr Davis told her that her Uncle Cumberland and Cousin Clifford were bringing a case against their tenants in Kings Meaburn. Some of the tenants came to London and asked for her support. She instructed Mr Davis to speak to the Lord Chancellor on their behalf, but the Lord Chancellor took the Cumberlands' part and admonished Davis for meddling in a case which was nothing to do with Lady Anne. She tried to comfort and encourage the tenants, who were perplexed and troubled and she discussed the problem with her cousin, Lord William Howard, who promised to do all he could, when he returned home, to help them in their difficulties.

Richard managed to maintain reasonably friendly relations with Henry Clifford through all of this, doing jousting practice with him, tilting at the ring and hunting together in Hyde Park. Anne supposed he was doing it to ensure that the flow of money kept coming, but the news that Henry Clifford's wife was expecting a child was a great worry; a son born to them would destroy Anne's hopes of inheriting her father's lands.

❦

Anne and Richard both walked in the Queen's funeral procession from Somerset House to Westminster Abbey. Anne's black gown, which she showed off to her friends and family, was made from many yards of heavy material; it was tiring to wear, but she felt strong now and reassuringly well.

Richard arranged a supper at Dorset House for some of the Frenchmen who had accompanied their Ambassador to London for the funeral. He followed it with a play and a banquet which was attended by a great number of their friends, including, to Anne's annoyance, Lady Penistone, whom she managed to avoid for the entire evening.

After a final meeting with the Westmorland tenants to give them a generous gift of gold and silver, Anne went down to Knole with Richard and their whole household. They were joined there by Edward Sackville, still recovering from his illness, whose presence was usually like a nettle against skin to Anne. This time, he seemed to be trying to be friendly towards her.

"I have a fancy to ride in the Park tomorrow morning early, sister," he said. "Will you do me the honour of joining me? It would be a pleasure to have your company."

Surprised, Anne responded in like vein to this overture,

"I am often abroad early, brother Sackville. It will be a pleasure to me," Anne said.

They found a mutual interest in the herd of fallow deer in the Park and rode quietly, sending the dogs away so that they could approach the herd and count the speckled young fawns. The following day, after supper, Edward suggested a walk in the Wilderness so that they could admire the early pink foxglove flowers coming out in the glades. Anne resisted the comment that rose to her lips about the foxglove's poisonous properties and agreed to take the air.

As they wandered along paths between the trees and saw many butterflies among the flowers, Sackville spoke of his recent illness.

"My experience of the closeness of death made me think about mortality, sister," he said. "I became aware, during those dark hours, of the importance of making peace with those close to me. We must all live each day to the full."

Anne had some cynical thoughts about the influence of this man on Richard's fluctuating resolve concerning her jointure, but she did not challenge the truce, which continued for four or five days until Edward took his leave to return to London. She would never put her trust in Edward or believe in his sincerity towards her, she told herself.

Subsequently, Anne complained to Richard that he was using her jointure as a weapon against her and that he was good to everyone else but unkind to her. His response was a half-hearted promise of a jointure of four thousand pounds. When he returned to London, Anne felt sad and lonely again; she spent sleepless and melancholy nights and dull working days writing, reading and doing needlework. Sometimes she went riding or played with The Child and occasionally she visited a neighbour or friend.

Richard received with delight the penultimate payment from the Cliffords, bringing the total to seventeen thousand pounds. The final portion, of three thousand, was only to be paid with Anne's agreement and Parliament's ratification.

Summer arrived, but with it no brightening of Anne's mood. Lady Penistone came to spend the season taking the waters at the Wells near Tunbridge, a mere dozen miles away from Knole. Her presence sparked gossip among the local gentry and nobility and Richard was condemned for it, Anne knew. She felt angry, humiliated and irritable.

She had a series of fallings out; with her cousin Mary, who had been reading to her, and with Kate Burton, one of her servants, whose father was sent for from Sussex to take her away. A broken tooth did nothing to improve Anne's mood. Then Richard insisted that Sir Thomas and Lady Penistone be invited to stay at Knole for a night or two, along with another couple for whom he was preparing great entertainment and feasting. In the end it seemed she had no choice but to agree and she tried to be as gracious as she could, but it was a difficult time.

A small nugget of relief came to Anne with the news that the son born to Henry Clifford's wife had survived for less than seven hours, leaving her Uncle's line without male heirs beyond Henry himself. At the same time, she felt sympathy for Frances Clifford, for she well knew a mother's despair at the loss of a longed-for son. She thought of the Shepherd Lord's prophesy. Then came both apprehension and rejoicing when she found that she herself was pregnant once more.

Richard returned to London as the law term started in September and Anne received an unkind letter from him, demanding her agreement to the payment of the final £3,000 from the Cliffords. She refused, but she missed her husband and longed for a return to the days when they had been the best of friends; even her pregnancy did not seem to move him this time. She took solace in the company of her sisters-in-law, but there was little comfort for her when she thought about her situation.

"You must be very careful of this child, sister," Cicely Compton advised. "I feel certain that Frances Clifford will be desirous of getting with child again. If she bears a son your inheritance will be another generation away!"

Anne did not need reminding. She decided to do as most of her friends suggested and stay in her chamber for the remaining five months of the pregnancy, to avoid another miscarriage. The only exception she made was to dine with Richard in the drawing room one afternoon at the end of October, but the question of the final payment hung like a thunder cloud over what could have been a pleasant interlude.

She passed some of the time by playing cards with Legge and Basket but lost so much money to them that she vowed again to renounce cards for six months. She had concerns about The Child, who kept taking colds and chills with the result that she was very out of sorts and her speech was difficult to understand.

Two reports provided Anne with cheer in this dull wait: Mr Davis recounted how things were not going well for the Cliffords in Westmorland, and she had further reason to rejoice when she heard that Richard's affair with Martha Penistone was finally over.

❧

Lady Selby visited, bursting with news from town.

"I'm so pleased to see you, dear Dorothea," Anne said, rising to greet her. "I've been having such a dreary time! And I can't wait to hear the latest turn in the story of the Lakes and the Exeters!"

They wandered into the garden and admired the turning colours of the Wilderness, bathed in autumn sunshine, before resuming discussion of this topic.

"Well, my dear Anne, it is certainly an interesting tale and a surprising one when you consider the people involved – surely some of the highest in the land," Dorothea said. "It was revealed in court that Lady Roos and her mother, Lady Lake, had produced letters accusing the Countess of Exeter of plotting to poison them. The Countess responded by bringing a charge of defamation of character against them. But the letters were shown to be forged and it was found that Sir Thomas Lake, the King's secretary (Lady Roos's father), had aided and abetted his daughter and his wife in this wrong-doing. The judgment went against them; they were all heavily fined and sent to the Tower, where Anne Roos admitted her guilt."

"What a scandalous business this has been, from start to finish," Anne said. "The ending seems to be a case of 'just deserts'."

Dorothea agreed and they laughed over the many libellous ballads and obscene poems which had been heard around town celebrating the notorious affair.

"I am unable to remember all the lines," Dorothea said, "but I do recall the ending of one of these scurrilous verses."

"You must repeat it for me!" Anne said.

"Very well, but you must promise not to think ill of me for it!" Dorothea said.

"Of course," Anne said, "You tell it at my request!"

Dorothea took a deep breath, giggled and recited:

> *"A bitch of Court, a common stinking snake*
> *Worse than all these, here lies the Lady Lake."*

Anne commented that the admission of guilt showed that the verses were not undeserved, but she couldn't help laughing.

Richard returned to Knole before Christmas and they took legal advice about an amount of money still owing to Anne's mother from the Westmorland tenants. They signed a letter of attorney and sent Ralph Coniston to the north to collect the dues. They fell out again about the land because Richard wanted a promise from her that if she ever did inherit it, she would use it as he wished – to pay off some of his debts – but Anne was not prepared to make this promise. They made up again a few days later and he supped with her in her chamber for the first time since his return. Christmas passed very quietly in the anticipation of the birth of the baby.

The new year began with the news of the death of Lady Penistone from smallpox. Then came the desolate still-birth of their third infant son.

CHAPTER THIRTY
1620–24

With the loss of this son, Anne despaired. She could see no way through a stark and uncertain future. Her thoughts constantly roamed through the maze of problems that beset her. At thirty years old, she had borne four children but only her beloved daughter survived. She had failed to provide an heir to her husband. Her detested brother-in-law, Edward-the-Scheming, stood to inherit the Sackville estates if Richard died. And Richard kept changing his provision for her and The Child, using her jointure as a weapon against her if she opposed his wishes or demands.

The terms of her father's will, which she and her mother had fought so hard to overturn, had been endorsed by the highest authority in the land. Her spendthrift husband had received a fortune in return for this settlement, to which she had never agreed, and had lost it in gambling and made himself ill by the pursuit of an extravagant life at court in which she had had little part. Her two champions, her mother and Queen Anne, were both dead. She was barred from raising any further court hearings concerning her inheritance and, in the eyes of the rest of the world, the issue was concluded and closed, finished and settled. Her only hope, over which she had no control, was that she would outlive her cousin Henry and that he would die without a male heir.

Richard, unaffected by these troubles, was constantly seeking sources of money. He rejoiced when he won a gamble, but his debts were far outstripping his income and, as he often reminded her, many of his creditors were losing patience with him. He had no hope of any further bounty from the Cliffords as long as Anne refused to agree to the settlement, but there was still the final three thousand pounds outstanding if only he could get her assent. By letters and on his infrequent visits to Knole he continued to put pressure on her to sign, and tried to force her to promise that, if she did eventually inherit her father's estates, she would use them to pay off his debts and salvage his reputation. She steadfastly refused all his entreaties but held resolutely to her stubborn love for him.

"I bring you good cheer, my lady!" was his declaration when he arrived, having won a game of cards or a bet on the cock-fights. She knew they would be friends for a short time and welcomed him affectionately, hoping to avoid any discussion that might turn his mind to their quarrels. She had to bite her tongue when he spent the money he had won on trinkets for The Child or fashionable ornaments for his own or Matthew's shoes, and she resented his comments on her dress when she tried to reduce her own expenditure and continued wearing clothes which had long gone out of fashion.

"Why don't you order some more attractive gowns and have your hair done in the latest style?" was a question to which she could find no satisfactory answer. To do as he suggested would increase his debts, but to give this as her answer would provoke his fury about her refusal to hand over her rights. And she loved fashionable clothes! She was caught in the dilemma of her own long-favoured motto: 'Preserve your loyalties, defend your rights'. It was very difficult to walk that tight-rope year after year, but that didn't dent her belief in the virtue of both strictures; she was loyal to Richard *and* she would not give up her rightful inheritance.

The new Spanish ambassador would soon arrive by ship at Gravesend and Richard was honoured by the King with the task of escorting him to London.

"I must perform this task in the most imposing way possible," he told Anne before he set off. "It is essential to give a lavish welcome to the Ambassador, such as the King himself would give.

Anything less than majestic might be perceived as an insult by both the Ambassador and the King."

"Richard, this is a great honour, but how are you to bear the cost of such an undertaking?" Anne asked. "You always complain of a lack of funds, even for the household's usual expenses, and this sounds like a much greater extravagance!"

"Of course it is! I need more funds," Richard said. "As you will not co-operate, I am forced to sell some of the land from which our income is derived. England's cornucopia must be spread out before the representative of the King of Spain!"

Anne bit her tongue, regretting her words as Richard glared at her.

"I shall not argue with you about your intransigence now," Richard said. "I have far more important things to do in planning the Ambassador's welcome. You know my thoughts. I cannot raise any more loans, so selling the land is the only way I can fulfil the King's commission."

The Ambassador's progress to court was achieved to the satisfaction of all and the King was full of praise for the Earl of Dorset's arrangements. But subsequently Richard turned increasingly to this means of supporting his spending which Anne knew was, in the long run, very unwise. Gradually his fortunes dipped and his influence at court began to wane; to her chagrin this was happening at the same time as Edward Sackville was greatly improving his own position at court, winning the favour of both Buckingham and the King.

❦

Richard and Anne both suffered from recurrent bouts of illness as the strain of their worries began to take a toll on their health. Anne caught her husband on a better day in November and made a suggestion which she hoped would ease some of the burden:

"Richard, shall we not celebrate the twelve days of Christmas here at Knole this year? Court events are less attractive to me now, without the Queen's presence. We could gather friends and family in the country and have a very festive celebration, without all the trouble and expense of removing the whole household up to Great Dorset House and attending court."

Richard was pleased with this idea, which would give him some respite, as Anne had intended, from the loss of face that he was experiencing at court. He was not as pleased as Anne was that Edward decided to remain at court for the Christmas season, seeing him as currying favour with the King, but he felt too unwell to put up much of a battle about it. Edward was rewarded by the King with a commission in Italy.

The Dorsets pleaded ill-health and excused themselves from the court celebrations, and both benefitted from the repose they found together and away from the throng. Richard went hunting with Matthew, who stayed mainly in the background as he had done since the cessation of hostilities when Anne had agreed to forgive him. Anne went riding, she and Richard played with The Child, they walked in the gardens and the Wilderness. They discussed literature, recapturing their youthful enthusiasm for books and each other's company as friends. They heard Christmas sermons in their own Chapel and at Sevenoaks Church outside the gates of the deer park and entertained the preacher and many local gentlefolk to feasting and celebrations. It brought them closer, as Anne had hoped, and, to her joy, Richard spent most of the nights in her chamber.

It was no great surprise then that by Easter Anne was able to declare herself pregnant again. She wrote to Richard, who was in London, and received a reply full of his love, delight and generosity:

Sweet Love, The News you sent me was the best that you could send, or I could have. I send you the half-year's Allowance for my Lady Margaret, your hundred Pounds, and Mr Marsh, as soon as he can be found, shall be sent, and it is twenty to one I will not foreswear coming to you ere it shall be long. God bless you and my Lady Margaret. Farewell. Your very loving husband, Richard Dorset.

She sighed and smiled.

❦

Once again, Anne took extreme precautions to protect this unborn child, remaining in her chamber for many weeks at a time, hoping and constantly praying that it would prove to be a healthy boy. Richard was pleased and affectionate the next time he came to Knole and they sat together in her chamber one morning discussing names.

"My preference," Anne said, "Would be for our son to be named Richard after his noble father."

Richard grinned at her and said, "I can't argue against that, can I? But what would you suggest as the name for a daughter?"

Anne had not wished to think about girls' names while she was concentrating all her energy on making a boy, but after much thought she said,

"I would be pleased to honour my ancient ancestor, Isabella, if that name is agreeable to you."

In May he wrote to her from Great Dorset House:

Sweet Life, God bless you and my Lady Margaret, and the little sweet thing in thy belly be it a Richard or an Isabella. Farewell. Your very loving husband R. Dorset.

It was easy to be loyal to him when he wrote like that and she kept the letter for the rest of her life.

❦

Isabella was born the following October, a strong and healthy baby who thrived. She was named after the thirteenth century heiress, Isabella de Vipont, from whom the Westmorland titles and lands had descended to Anne's father. She was doted on by both her parents and her elder sister. Anne had no recurrence of the problems that had beset her after her previous confinements; she admitted to herself that she welcomed this rare period of contentment.

Unwell, and mindful of his wife and two children, Richard finally settled the deeds for Anne's jointure the following summer. To her relief she learned that she would be well provided for if he were to die, even though she had still not furnished an heir to the Sackville estates. There was satisfaction in knowing that she would be considerably better off than her brother-in-law, who would inherit the title, the estates and a sackful of debts, but not the wealth needed to maintain them.

The following Ash Wednesday, early in February, Richard kissed his wife and daughters and they waved him off to London for a meeting of Parliament. As the coach disappeared from view, the Child looked up into Anne's face with tears in her eyes and said, in her lisping voice,

"I miss my lord father while he is away from us. Why does he always go away, lady mother?"

Anne swallowed hard and looked down at the baby Isabella in her arms, wondering why she found The Child's words so moving. She handed her small bundle to the nurse and bent down to kiss the top of Margaret's head, murmuring

"We shall see him again soon, sweet heart. Don't be sad. Let's go and play with the puppies." As she'd hoped, this brought a smile back to her daughter's face as they made their way into the stable where the Beagle had pupped.

Less than four weeks later, illness struck them all. Anne, unwell herself, was nursing The Child, who had smallpox, and she was

unable to go to Richard in London when she heard how ill he was. He complained of fever, cramping pains, terrible thirst, sickness and a bloody flux. She wrote lovingly to him, offering to come to him when The Child was sufficiently recovered. On the morning of Easter Sunday, 26th March, she received a welcome reply:

Sweet Heart, he wrote,

I thank you for your Letter. I had resolved to come down to Knole, and to have received the Blessed Sacrament, but God hath prevented it with Sickness, for on Wednesday night I fell into a fit of Casting which held me long, then last night I had a fit of a Fever. I have two Physicians and would not have you trouble yourself till I have Occasion to send for you. You shall in the meantime hear daily from me. I thank God I am now at good Ease, having rested well this morning. So, with my love to you, and God's blessing and mine to both my Children, I commend you to God's protection. Your assured loving husband, Richard Dorset.

Anne, clutching this letter to her breast, hardly had time to feel the relief it brought before a breathless and distraught Legge arrived, having ridden hard from London with the news that Richard was dead. Anne could hardly take this in, but asked Mr Legge what had happened.

"My lord was sick for several weeks, as you know my lady," Legge said with a deep sigh, propping himself against the fireplace. "He suffered from vomiting, pain and flux, which got worse and the flux became bloody in recent days. This morning he felt better and wrote you the letter that you still hold in your hand, but then he suddenly fell back, gasping for air. His skin went grey. He was sweating and clammy and unable to breathe, then his fists shuddered in the air and there was a strange sound in his throat as the life went out of him. His physician was there but nothing could be done. I am very, very sorry, my lady." Legge broke down in tears.

Anne could not speak. She glanced down in bewilderment at

the letter in her hand. Legge helped her to the nearest chair, where she sat staring sightlessly into a void.

Richard's funeral was held at Withyam, where he was interred in the family vault alongside ancestors and his infant sons, on a damp, grey day with a bitingly cold wind sweeping across the Sussex Weald from the east. Anne was unwell and needed support from William Howard and Francis Russell throughout the day. Bereft, she was also sickening with smallpox, caught from The Child while devotedly nursing her for weeks.

Anne had never been so ill and was convinced for many days that she would die, but she welcomed the prospect of being reunited with Richard and gave herself and her daughters into God's hands. She drifted in and out of feverish dreams full of haunting fear, tossing on a turbulent sea of anxiety whose cause was beyond her grasp. When she recovered enough to ask Willoughby to pass her a mirror, she wondered whether death would perhaps have been preferable to these ruined looks.

"Dear Willoughby," she said, "I thank you and Judith from the depths of my heart for all the devoted service you have given me and my children. I thank God that you have been spared this disease; He is merciful. But I hardly recognise myself in the mirror and know for certain now that I will not marry again, for this martyred face would put off any man."

"Dear lady, I am only pleased to see that you are recovering and that your two sweet little daughters are not to be completely orphaned within one month, as we had feared. They need you and I know that you will delight in them again when you are fully well. Lie back and rest a while until I fetch you a jug of broth."

The full impact of her husband's death took some time to strike Anne as she slowly recovered her health and strength. She had not only lost a loving and beloved husband who had been the hub of her existence for fifteen years, but her entire life had been re-arranged into a bewildering disorder where nothing remained the same. The turmoil in her grief-filled mind combined to make the world a distant and unreal place; somewhere she did not belong and could not comprehend. She responded to the kind words of many visitors, friends and family, in a mechanical manner most unlike her usual warm engagement. Without Richard she felt she was floating out of her own life into an empty chasm. Although well used to spending seemingly endless time alone, nothing had prepared her for this.

A widow at 34 years old, Anne was now styled Dowager Countess of Dorset. A bitter realisation came when she had to recognise that Edward Sackville had become the fourth Earl of Dorset and his wife, her friend and 'sister' Mary, had taken Anne's title as the new Countess. They would reside at Knole and Great Dorset House when Edward returned from Florence in May; Anne and her daughters would leave their main homes of the past fourteen years. The single positive outcome of her widowhood that Anne could identify was that she would never again be at the mercy of Matthew Caldicott; after witnessing Richard's will he had disappeared from the household and she made no attempt to discover his whereabouts.

Her jointure house was Bolebroke in Sussex, but there were other properties belonging to members of her family where she could stay. Spending time at Chenies, her mother's family home in Buckinghamshire and Cousin Francis Russell's main residence, was some comfort; it brought memories of childhood and of her mother and she was close there to her nearest male relative. It was important to her to retain her social position, as much for her daughters' sake as her own but it was difficult to do this as a widow without influential supporters at court and it would take time to discover on whom she could depend; she knew it would never be her brother-in-law.

Part Four

CHAPTER THIRTY-ONE
1625–30

A year after Richard's death, news reached Anne at Chenies that King James had died and the Prince of Wales had succeeded him as King Charles the First. It was hard to comprehend that the King, who had been such a dominant figure in her life, had vanished from the world. She remembered the times when she had refused to accept his judgment, his anger and his subsequent kindness to her, and wondered at her own courage. She prayed for his soul and that of his Queen, who had surely protected her from his fury and possibly his punishment.

This event also turned her thoughts back to the death of Henry Prince of Wales, Charles' older brother, who had carried the greatest hopes of his parents and of the whole of England. He had been cut down by illness before he reached the age of twenty and she recalled Richard's grief for the Prince who had been his close companion. She wondered how Charles, as King, would carry the responsibilities that had fallen to his lot; she had never been well-acquainted with him. It all seemed very far away, dreamlike, another life, even someone else's life, unreal.

Recollections of the battles she had fought over her inheritance reminded her that she had believed then that life could not be any crueller, yet her present situation seemed even more difficult. In those days she had, at various times, drawn strength from the support of her mother, her husband, her friends and the Queen. Now, although financially secure, she was alone, a widow without power, influence, protection or support and responsible for the welfare of her two little girls. And she constantly longed for Richard's presence. The friends she had been surrounded by in Kent were far away and were probably, she thought bitterly, bestowing their attention on the new Countess at Knole. Had she become nobody? She felt lost and anxious and nothing soothed her. Her faithful gentlewomen remained at her side, but she was responsible for them, too, and there was no-one with whom she could share her burdens.

Anne knew she could not stay at Chenies indefinitely, however comforting its warm red brick and its many memories of her mother and her childhood; a few months later she made the decision to move to Bolebroke, her jointure house in Sussex. Here, on Lady Day near the end of March, she collected the rents from her tenants, carefully counting in and recording the income that would keep her household running for the coming months.

Several days after the rents had been received, she was in the garden helping four-year-old Isabella to make a daisy chain. Isabella loved those rare daisies that had pink tips to their petals and she was running about in the spring sunshine, searching for them in the short grass. Each one she found made her squeal with delight and she would drop it into Anne's lap to make the next link. When the chain was long enough, its ends would be joined and the pink, white and green coronet would be gently placed on her fair curls. For the rest of the day she would require everyone to bow to her as to a crowned queen.

Running footsteps made Anne look up from her task and Jack, a groom, rounded the corner of the house waving a stick. He stopped before her, panting heavily.

"My lady," he gasped, "My lady, 'tis sure they were after the rents!"

"Jack, get your wind, then tell me what has happened," Anne spoke calmly and Jack took a moment to recover his breath.

"My lady," he began again, "I was jus' walkin' down the passage from the stable yard and when I got through to the road and turned towards the 'ouse, I saw three men at one of the windows. They 'ad the casement prised open and two were pushin' the other up to get through. I shouted and ran towards 'em and at that they let go the man at the window and all ran off towards the village."

"Did you know any of these men, Jack?"

"No, my lady, I never seen any of 'em before. They're strangers, not from these parts, for I do know all who live 'ereabouts."

"Well done, Jack, you acted bravely and have surely prevented a robbery," Anne said. "Take a jug of ale in the kitchen before you return to your work."

When Jack had gone, Anne found she was shaking. Unable to make any more slits in the stalks of the daisies, she walked unsteadily towards the house, ignoring Isabella's protests. She sent for her Steward and went with him to inspect the window on the front of the house, close to the lane from the village. They found it still open and gave orders for it, and all others on that side of the house, to be securely nailed up. The incident had given her an unpleasant fright, but she gave thanks to God that the outcome was no worse. Still shaken, she spoke to Judith about the robbers.

"Who would have set up such a thing, Judith? Jack said he had never before seen any of these men, so they must have come from some distance away. Local people know that the rents were lately received here, but those from further away would not have been privy to that knowledge without knowing that this is my house."

"It is a mystery, my lady," Judith said. "The house is a little distance from the village and I cannot think that three men would have come this way without intention. What business could they have had that would bring them here?"

"I find it very strange and troubling," Anne said. "Someone, not from these parts, knew that the rents were here and deliberately made my house their target. If one of my children had been in that room when they broke in, I cannot bear to think what harm might have come to them."

"Don't let such thoughts disturb you anymore," Judith said. "Give thanks that no greater harm was done than a damaged window frame, and that the robbers were driven off." But Anne could not let it go.

"I can think of more than one enemy who might have plotted

such mischief against me, but chief amongst them is my brother Sackville, who was always full of anger and spite towards me. He is one who well knows that this is my house. He thinks his venom justified now, I suppose, because I have the means to live comfortably on Dorset lands, while he has inherited only my lord's gigantic debts but no money. I hear he's been driven to selling land again and has disposed of many acres.

"Another is my cousin Clifford, who is angry that my late lord took a fortune from him but never did persuade me to sign away my lands to him. Perhaps he thought to reclaim some of that money. I doubt, though, whether he would trouble himself to set such a plot in these parts. No, I think it is the former, Judith: Edward's ill-will never ends, even as he would persuade me otherwise."

There was no repeat of the burglary and gradually, after adding it to her growing list of the disadvantages of being a woman alone, Anne's mind turned to other things. She was barred, by King James's judgment, from bringing any further claims against the Cliffords, on pain of losing the rights granted her by her father's will. But she wanted to maintain her claim under the entail to the lands which she believed were legitimately hers. She must protect the interests of Margaret and Isabella, just as her mother had done for her, and the fact that they were potential heiresses would improve their marriage prospects immeasurably. In 1628 she took counsel's advice and registered her legal claim to clarify the entail upon her and her successors.

Anne had settled half of her jointure income on Margaret and Isabella as their dowries and in 1629 she found a husband for The Child and secured Margaret's enthusiastic approval of the match. At the age of barely fifteen, Lady Margaret Sackville was married to Lord John Tufton at the ancient Church of Saint Bartholomew in Smithfield. Attending the ceremony, along with Anne and

Isabella, were John's parents the Earl and Countess of Thanet, and many other noble courtiers from the two families. Margaret was given away by Anne's cousin, Francis Russell, heir to the Earl of Bedford, whose help Anne had requisitioned in securing the match. It was a grand occasion and a joyful triumph for Anne after the years of worry.

∞

In spite of the ravages of smallpox on her face and her vow that she would not marry again, Anne, chafing at her powerlessness, began to think that a second marriage might be the solution to many of her problems. But it must be the right marriage, one which would restore her to her accustomed position in society. She kept these thoughts to herself but then there was news that prompted her to an urgent discussion of the idea with Cousin Francis Russell.

"My dear Francis," Anne said. "How good it is to see you, coz, and how kind of you to come so far at my behest. It is not the easiest of journeys from Chenies to Bolebroke, as I well know. First let's take supper together and share news of the family and King Charles's court, then there are things I wish to talk over with you."

After supper they retired to the privacy of Anne's chamber and sat by the fire, for the March night was cold. Anne wrapped a shawl around her shoulders and an owl hooted outside before either of them spoke. Francis looked at her expectantly, his head on one side.

"Francis, I must tell you first how difficult I have found the five years and more that have passed since the death of my dear lord. It has been a time of fear and worry for me such as I have never known. Many times at Knole I was lonely and sad, but I never felt threats such as I have been under since I have been a widow and I can tell you that I have feared for the future of myself and my children.

"I must thank you for your part in securing Margaret's marriage to Lord Tufton; it is a good match from every point of view and they seem well content with each other. That has given me great satisfaction and reduced my burden somewhat, but my situation remains precarious. I also have undying gratitude for your support in establishing our claim to the entailed lands of Westmorland. You have done all you could to help me; for that I thank you, and God for his mercy."

Francis cleared his throat.

"Have you brought me here to thank me, for the third time, for doing what any cousin would have done?" he asked. "I think not! I am your closest male relative, Anne, but being a cousin gives me little power to aid you in the way that a brother or a husband could, so I know that my support may be somewhat lacking in authority. Is this what you're saying? You needn't beat about the bush with me, pray speak plainly."

"How well you read my purpose, Francis! Don't think of my gratitude as anything less than completely sincere, but you are right; a brother's or husband's power would be a greater support than you can provide. Yes, that is why I wished to speak with you."

"You have no living brother, so I must needs ask whether you are looking for a husband, coz?"

"Don't you agree that it might be a solution, both to my loneliness and to my powerlessness?" Anne said.

"Go on, continue," Francis said. "Have you someone in mind for this honour?"

"Yes. I am no virginal maid to dissemble. My Lord Montgomery is lately widowed. He is in a position of great power at court; he was the old King's first favourite twenty-five years ago and has continued to gather offices and rewards ever since. He and I have known each other for twenty years and more and I knew his lady, Susan. I would have you speak to him on my behalf before some other match-maker gains his ear. What do you say?"

Francis's grey eyes were wide and his mouth slightly open; he said nothing for several minutes. Anne looked at him curiously. She had never seen this resourceful man lost for words. He was struggling to untangle and express his responses. He stood up, shaking his head, and walked up and down the room with his hands clasped in front of him like a supplicant. Eventually he sat down again, still agitated.

"Forgive me, Anne, you have taken me by surprise. I had not anticipated this notion of re-marriage. And I had even less idea that you were holding someone in mind. I need to take in this news before I can say anything about it. First, pray confirm for me that what you are suggesting is marriage to Philip Herbert, the Earl of Montgomery."

"That is my intention, Coz," Anne said. "I see that you are taken aback by the notion. Steady yourself before answering me. I'll send the page for some refreshment."

Pleased to have some reason to remove herself from his astonished and questioning gaze, she went to the door. The page returned with oatcakes and sack and put another log on the fire, making it flare. Francis was roused by this and paced the room again. Anne felt impatient and not a little anxious; she picked fluff from her skirts and looked up at Francis as he sat down.

"Well?" she said.

"Well! I have my thoughts in some sort of order now and can say that I see that the idea of you entering into a second marriage has certain clear advantages for you. I think of you as a strong woman, but the strongest of women is weak, I suppose, in comparison to a man. A protector would make you feel safer and might accomplish things for you that you can't do yourself. Nor can I fill that place."

Anne began to speak, but Francis had not finished and held up his hand.

"But I wonder at the speed and wisdom of your choice," he said. "My Lady Montgomery is barely a month dead and you would replace her? And tie yourself to a man of Montgomery's character?"

"I think speed is vital to ensure my success in this venture. The marriage need not take place until the mourning period is ended, but securing it is paramount, is it not? And my Lord Montgomery is one on whom I believe I could depend for my purposes. He remains one of the highest in the land, has been so ever since King James first honoured him and has lately, I hear, also found favour with King Charles."

"You are right that he was Knight of the Garter and Privy Counsellor for the whole of the old King's reign and is now Lord Chamberlain of King Charles's Household. But those qualities that have so endeared him to our Princes may not be the ones to be esteemed by a wife. Not to put too fine a point on it, Coz, he has a well-earned reputation for intemperate argument and infidelity."

"Argument and infidelity?" Anne said. "Pah! Don't you think that I have experienced those ugly twins many times in the past? They were the stuff of my first marriage; by now I am well acquainted with them, so do not fear them. Lord Montgomery is known by all as an honest man. Don't forget that I have the advantage over you in that I have had longer to think it over and get used to this idea, so I have already answered for myself any doubts that you may raise, and more."

"All the same," Francis said, "I urge you to consider very carefully before committing yourself to that man. Honesty is one thing, but coarseness, bluntness to the point of rudeness, and even blasphemy is another. And I find much fault with him besides. I will bid you goodnight, dear lady, and wait for your further instructions when you have had time to consider." He walked towards the door and Anne rose from her chair, bidding him wait.

"I'm firmly decided on this course, Francis, and am not to be swayed," she said firmly. "Please speak of me to Lord Montgomery. That is my final word. Good night."

There was no further mention of the plan before Francis Russell left Bolebroke the next morning. He wrestled with his better judgment about this unwanted task for a few days, until a sharp reminder from Anne sent him scurrying to Montgomery to press her suit. Anne read with satisfaction a message from him; her suggestion had received a cautious welcome until further details could be discussed.

Anne had been aware for some time that Edward Sackville's rise had been swift since he had inherited Richard's title. In 1625 King Charles had made him Knight of the Garter; in 1626 he became a member of the Privy Council and in 1628 he was appointed Lord Chamberlain of Queen Henrietta Maria's household. This degree of power in the hands of her oldest and greatest enemy was, for Anne, most alarming and the worst imaginable situation. It had to be countered by whatever means she could command. Montgomery was the only man in the land whose power was equal to, possibly greater than, that of Edward Sackville and the timing of his wife's demise might almost suggest divine intervention. Anne's answer was Philip Herbert, First Earl of Montgomery, whose power would keep her and Isabella safe.

Montgomery's elder brother, William, had inherited the title Third Earl of Pembroke from their father. Barely three weeks before her marriage to Montgomery Anne received a message bearing his seal; William, she learned, had died of apoplexy in London after a sumptuous meal. He had no sons; Philip had become the Fourth Earl of Pembroke.

Anne chose the chapel at Chenies for the marriage. Here, in the house which was the seat of her mother's family, she was close to the tombs of many of her ancestors, including those of her beloved Aunt Warwick and her dear cousin, Frances Bourchier. The ceremony, in June 1630, was attended by a handful of her living relatives, including Isabella. Anne, Dowager Countess of Dorset, at the age of forty also became Countess of Pembroke and Montgomery and celebrated her deliverance, by the providence of God, from *'the envie, malice and sinister practices of my Enemyes'*.

CHAPTER THIRTY-TWO
1630–41

The reasons for Anne's second marriage and, in particular, her choice of husband, were a mystery to most of her friends and family. To her it all made complete sense: Pembroke was, as she said, '*one of the greatest subjects in the Kingdom*' and therefore perfectly placed to protect her and her daughter and to give her the social standing that she had always enjoyed until her widowhood. Pembroke's position as Lord Chamberlain gave him intimate access to King Charles and Queen Henrietta Maria, who were frequent visitors to the Pembroke seat, Wilton House in Wiltshire.

"This is one of our favourite houses in all the land, Lady Pembroke," Charles remarked over dinner during the first royal visit following Anne's marriage. "We have long admired it and have suggested to your husband some ways for making it even more magnificent. We have discussed appointing Inigo Jones to design a new front and entrance."

"That is a most interesting idea, your Majesty," Anne said, with a glance towards Pembroke. "The Palladian style of Inigo Jones would lend great dignity to the house. I know him from long ago when he designed my costume for a masque at the behest of your Majesty's mother, the late Queen. I shall look forward to seeing what plans he will make for us."

"You may be assured, Lady Pembroke, that there is none better to undertake such a renovation," Queen Henrietta Maria said. "I have engaged him to complete the Queen's House at Greenwich and I am pleased with his work. I believe you will find Wilton, beautiful as it is, much improved by his designs."

❦

Pembroke's duties at court meant that he and his new Countess spent a lot of time at Whitehall, where he had a large apartment close to the royal household and busy with the constant comings and goings of servants and courtiers. Anne was close to the seat of power and once again at the centre of interest for fashionable society. A few of her close companions ventured to question the wisdom of her decision, but she would tolerate no criticism and continued to insist that the marriage was the result of God's providence towards her. She was confident that she had protected herself and Isabella from the machinations of her enemies and she was delighted by her return to court in such an elevated social position.

Her spirits were further buoyed early the following year by the news that Margaret was expecting a child in the summer, and she rejoiced at the birth in August of her first grandson, Nicholas Tufton.

She took pleasure in her involvement with the plans for the renovation of Wilton, even though her old friend Inigo Jones was now too fashionable, and therefore too busy, to give it much attention and had delegated his assistant, John Webb, to the task. Anne was fascinated by the design process and the practicalities of building work, storing up knowledge for the responsibilities that she believed would be hers in the future.

Anne and ten-year-old Isabella found themselves, for the first time in their lives, part of a large and vigorous family; Philip had five living children from his first marriage, ranging in age from six to eighteen. Anne enjoyed the family atmosphere and got on well with the young Herberts, particularly Anna Sophia, the eldest, who was already married to Lord Caernarvon. There were times when only Anna Sophia could calm her irascible father and Anne was grateful for that.

One morning, when they had been at Wilton for a few months, Anne encountered Isabella's governess in the library one morning.

"My lady, I would not seek to alarm you, but may I speak of a matter which is concerning me?" she said.

"Of course, pray tell me what worries you, Mrs Petley," Anne said.

"I have noticed in recent weeks that Lady Isabella has become quieter, less interested in her studies and more listless in her general demeanour. She is neither as cheerful nor as studious as she was."

"Then I shall speak to her today," Anne said. "I thank you for bringing this to my notice, Mrs Petley."

Anne sent for Isabella and they wandered into the gardens and sat on a carved stone seat near the lake. They commented on the antics of the ducks and then Anne asked,

"Is anything troubling you, my dear?"

"No, my lady mother," Isabella said, her eyes wandering back to the ducks. "I am content." Her voice was flat.

Anne thought about Mrs Petley's words and then about her own experience of moving to Wilton and joining the Pembroke family. She had found the four boys, ranging in age from eight to sixteen, by turns interesting and irritating; they gave her a taste of what life might have been like had her own brothers or sons survived. She observed that they were tolerant of Isabella, but she now began to look at them from Isabella's point of view.

"The boys are quite lively, aren't they?" she said. "Like that noisy family of young ducks!"

Isabella nodded and looked down at her hands.

"Do they overwhelm you sometimes?" Anne asked.

Isabella's lower lip trembled and she looked away. Anne took one of her cold, clammy hands and warmed it in both of her own. Isabella turned towards her mutely, with tears in her eyes.

"Bella, tell me what troubles you. Do they tease you, are they cruel to you?" Anne said.

"No, they don't mean me any harm lady mother," Isabella said, rubbing away her tears, "But they like to chase each other all over the house and gardens, or race each other on horseback. I can't keep up with them! They play Nine Pins and Quoits very roughly and compete in archery and throwing rotten fruit and vegetables as far as possible with a stick in the orchard. They are so energetic and noisy and … and … I'm just not used to it!" Her shoulders shook and she pressed her lips together.

"My dear, I didn't realise you felt so overpowered and I am sad to hear it. Why didn't you tell me sooner?" Anne said.

"I don't know. I thought it was my millstone to endure," Isabella said. "You were so pleased with all the new arrangements and I didn't want to spoil it for you by being miserable."

Anne put her arms round her daughter's slender shoulders and swallowed hard to suppress tears of her own. Isabella sobbed.

"Well now that you have told me, Bella, perhaps we can do something to make things better. Shall we read together sometimes? And I believe there may be some girls in the locality with whom you could enjoy pastimes more suited to our sex. Shall I arrange a visit?"

Isabella looked up at her mother and gave her a wobbly smile through her tears,

"Thank you, lady mother. I feel better already," she said.

❧

Isabella settled and Anne was more content than she had been for a long time. For a period of two or three years she and Pembroke managed life together well enough. Two pregnancies occurred, both ending prematurely with the birth of stillborn sons. This was not the tragedy that the loss of the Sackville sons had been, though Anne would have liked to have at least one living son.

But Pembroke's habit of boasting publicly about his multiple infidelities made Richard look like the most chaste and faithful of husbands and Anne felt more and more shocked and humiliated. They were alone in the grand drawing room at Wilton, where they had been looking at plans and imagining how the remodelled front might look, when she had an opportunity to broach the subject.

"We are of one mind over these plans, are we not, as in other things?" Pembroke said.

"I am satisfied that we are well-suited, my lord, and at ease with the blending of our two families. I would crave but one favour from you to complete my contentment," Anne said.

"And in what way am I found scant, my lady?"

"I am at times embarrassed by your talk abroad concerning your conquests, Philip," Anne said. "I expect, at the least, more discretion from my wedded lord."

"Damn your impudence, Madam!" Pembroke thundered. "I will fuck who I like, when I like, where I like – and you will endure it if you cannot reconcile yourself to a man's needs."

"I would ask you to respect my views," Anne said quietly, "And be less blatant in your dissolute behaviour, my Lord. It is not the satisfaction of your needs that I find troubling, but your public bellowing and trumpeting about it." She looked levelly into his blood-shot eyes.

He stepped forward, towering over her. For a moment Anne thought he would strike her, but she held her ground without flinching and reminded herself that she was the woman who had stood up to King James. Pembroke stopped, grunted and crashed out of the room, leaving her trembling with anger and fear.

Pembroke took to going up to London without her, leaving Anne at Wilton, where loneliness began to remind her of all those sad times she had spent alone at Knole. She tried to please him, as she had done with Dorset, but this time the strategy was not successful. Increasingly she gave herself over to keeping records and reading good books, as she had done in the past. Later she wrote: '*the marble pillars of Knole and Wilton were to me oftentimes but the gay Arbours of Anguish.*' But she was unwilling to be banished from the life of the court as she largely had been when The Child was young, and she determined to spend as much time there as she could.

She went up to Whitehall for a court occasion when she knew that Alethea, Anne Warwick and other friends would be there. Her coach drew up outside Pembroke's apartment in Whitehall at the end of an unpleasant journey and her footman ran up the steps to knock on the door. The hour was late and the heavy door was slow to be unlocked, but eventually she and her gentlewomen were admitted by Pembroke's chief footman. Halfway up the stone staircase she encountered her husband, descending in a fury, waving his arms.

"What is this? What are you doing here at this time of night?"

"We were held up on the road, my lord; we couldn't get here any earlier," Anne said.

"I don't want to hear about your journey! I had no idea you were coming. Who let you in?" Pembroke shouted.

"I didn't tell you I was coming because I thought I would be here as quickly as the messenger could come to you. I had not anticipated the difficulties we encountered with highwaymen near Putney."

"Don't make pathetic excuses! You arrive unexpectedly and hope for a welcome – well you're not going to get one! Tell me who let you in and I'll deal with him later. In the meantime, if you ever present yourself in London again without my permission, I'll give you a beating. Leave immediately, confound you! Get out!" He made a dismissive gesture.

"But my lord, the hour . . ." Anne said.

"Be gone now! Remove your poxy face from my sight! I won't have you turning up like this!"

He came towards her as if to push her backwards down the stairs, eyes bulging and spittle forming in the corners of his mouth. She clutched at the stone balustrade then turned and fled with her women, back into the night and the coach.

"Take me to the Earl of Caernarvon's house," she said breathlessly to her puzzled coachman as the door slammed behind her.

Anna Sophia Caernarvon, Pembroke's daughter, was dismayed to see her in such distress and made her welcome. In the past Anna Sophia had been sympathetic and helpful in restraining her father's wild behaviour; on this occasion she was horrified by the story and full of compassion and solicitude. She suggested that if her father was to be at Wilton, Anne could go to Ramsbury, his smaller country house forty miles to the north, which increasingly she did.

❧

In 1634 Anne attended a masque at Whitehall with her husband; Pembroke was carrying the slim white staff of office in his official capacity as Lord Chamberlain of the King's Household and his duty was to keep order. The King and Queen were present, with a multitude of courtiers, and in the crush the King's private secretary, Thomas May, stumbled against Pembroke. Pembroke's temper flared and he struck May so hard over the shoulders with his staff that it broke in pieces. Violence erupted in the crowd, with strong feelings against Pembroke who was clearly the aggressor. The King reprimanded him and he had to apologise abjectly to May. Anne was publicly embarrassed by her husband's actions and began to realise that her position could be compromised in many ways by his uncontrolled and boorish behaviour. She was reminded of Cousin Francis's words regarding Pembroke before she married him.

❧

Anne was anxious to re-establish her claim to the Clifford inheritance in the event of the ending of her uncle's male line, although she was barred by King James's award from challenging his right to it. She chose her moment to broach the subject with Pembroke when they were together, for once, at Wilton. He was preparing to go hunting, which always improved his mood, and she spoke whilst his man-servant was helping him pull on his boots.

"Will you favour me, my lord, with your support for my claim to the lands in Westmorland and Craven should my uncle's line fail? My Cousin Henry's marriage has not yet been blessed with a male heir; should this remain the case at Henry Clifford's death, my father's will provides for the estates to revert to me."

"I'll thank you not to bother me with this nonsense," Pembroke said. "It is of no interest to me whether you inherit the land or no;

if you insist on pursuing it you must do it yourself."

"But it is impossible for me to pursue it without your support," Anne said. "A married woman is dependent upon her lord for the legal advancement of her affairs and I simply ask for your support."

"Get your cousin of Bedford to back you then," Pembroke said. "That is what you did before, is it not? He has more interest in it than I. Now cease your abominable provocation."

"Your own support would be far more welcome, my lord," Anne pushed on, "And certainly more efficacious. But if that is not forthcoming and if I do succeed in procuring claims through my cousin, may I then count on your signature?"

"Anything to stop my being forced to hear about it every time I see you!" Pembroke barked as he rose to his feet and turned away.

"My most grateful thanks, my lord," Anne said and curtseyed to his back as she crept from the room.

Francis Russell, as she expected, was reluctant to be pulled back into her affairs, fearing Pembroke's unpredictability, but he spoke to the lawyers for her and her claims were twice registered during Pembroke's lifetime and eventually gained his signature.

Her cousin Francis did, however, work hard on Anne's behalf to negotiate her jointure from Pembroke, securing the latter's agreement that she should have the lands in Kent which had been promised as the jointure of Susan, his first wife. More importantly, Pembroke agreed to give up any claim he might have had to the lands in Westmorland and that £5000 from the lands in Craven should form part of Isabella's dowry, should Anne inherit them.

Despite her difficulties with their father, Anne was getting on well with the Pembroke children and grew increasingly fond of them. But another issue arose to alienate the Earl and Countess of Pembroke further from each other.

"Your daughter's marriage should be considered soon," Pembroke said one bright spring morning as he came into her chamber while Anne was preparing to write a congratulatory letter to Lady Margaret, who had informed her that another grandchild would be born in the autumn.

"I have spoken with her about that but recently," Anne replied.

"Then what are your plans for her?"

"I have none, my Lord."

"You have spoken with her concerning her marriage, and yet you have no plans for her? You speak in riddles, Madam!" Pembroke said.

"I have told her that it is her right to choose her husband, as indeed my mother told me. She shall not be forced into a marriage that is not to her liking."

Pembroke's handsome face darkened and his moustache twitched. There was a pause before he spoke again. Anne gazed out of the window at the shiny buds on the branches of a stately sycamore, avoiding his eyes.

"Has she expressed a preference for anyone she knows?" he asked.

"No, she has not," Anne said. "At fourteen she has had little need to consider matrimony as yet."

"You have made a foolish decision!" Pembroke said. "The question of marriage is not one to be left to children. Parents with experience of the world are far better placed to assess the advantages and disadvantages of matches than are silly young girls!"

"I disagree," Anne said. "Parents cannot truly know the hearts of their children and the best marriage is one where the hearts beat together. Isabella is no 'silly young girl' as you call her. My choice of Dorset was supported by my dear and blessed mother. He was of a just mind, a sweet disposition and very valiant in his own person and I never regretted my marriage to him, through all our troubles."

"Your mother saw that his breeding and fortune were of great advantage to you and therefore approved your choice," Pembroke argued. "But what would her response have been if you had chosen unwisely?"

"My mother had raised me to think clearly and judge wisely

and she trusted me to do so concerning marriage, as in everything else," Anne said. "I have raised my daughters in the same way and Isabella will choose wisely when the time comes." Anne looked at him defiantly and held his eyes.

"Ah! Your guidance will be available to her then! That's more like it!" Pembroke said, more calmly. "We shall put my younger sons before her and guide her towards them so that she may choose one from them for her husband. Thus we shall have a good match, shall we not?"

"No, that is not what I shall do," Anne said. "The choice is Isabella's, without interference, and when she shows interest in a young man, I shall support her choice. Neither she nor I shall be driven by you!"

Anne had been expecting and dreading this proposal from Pembroke ever since he had agreed to the settlement of five thousand pounds for Isabella along with Anne's jointure. She had discussed it with Cousin Francis and they had agreed that it was to be resisted, at least for the time being. Isabella was young, had shown no interest in the younger Pembroke boys other than as occasional companions, and Anne's suspicion was that Pembroke's interest had more to do with her dowry than any other consideration.

Pembroke did not let the matter rest there. He mentioned it to Anne at every opportunity and raged at her when she continued to reject it. He even mentioned it to Isabella and to his sons. They all laughed at the idea and teased one another, but Anne grew increasingly angry and her relationship with Pembroke took another turn for the worse.

As was her habit at times of difficulty, she withdrew into literature and religion, neither of which was of the slightest interest to Pembroke, who could barely read. They felt uncomfortable in each other's company; both were discontented and it became impossible for them to live together. They agreed to spend most of their time apart, Anne at Ramsbury or Wilton and, in London, at Baynard's Castle, while Pembroke would live in his Whitehall apartment and at Wilton. They agreed that they would still attend official functions together when the occasion demanded, but Anne extracted a promise of acceptable behaviour from Pembroke.

Pembroke engaged Anthony Van Dyck to paint a huge family portrait to celebrate the marriage of his eldest son, Charles, to Mary Villiers, daughter of the Duke of Buckingham. These were possibly the two richest families in England and were both close companions of the King, but they had been at loggerheads for many years until King Charles conceived of this marriage of their children as a kind of treaty between them.

The Pembroke family, including Mary Villiers, was to gather at Wilton for the sittings. Anne was not minded either to celebrate or to join them there and remained stubbornly at Baynard's Castle. She ignored Pembroke's demands and threats. Eventually, Van Dyck came to Baynard's and drew sketches of her, for which she sat rather unwillingly. He translated these into a portrait of her, which he inserted into the space he had left for her on the vast canvass. When she saw the finished work, she thought she looked strangely detached from the scene and all the people in it, with her arms folded across her body in a gesture of self-protection. It seemed to her to be an illustration of Francis Russell's remark that she *'lived in those my Lords' great families as the River Rhone runs through the Lake of Geneva, without mingling any part of its streams with that Lake.'*

Baynard's Castle was a vast palace on the banks of the Thames below Saint Paul's. It had belonged to Henry VII, Henry VIII and Catherine of Aragon and was said to be big enough to garrison five hundred soldiers. Anne described it as the most luxurious place in which she ever lived. She was there when she received the news of the death of her uncle, Francis Clifford, Earl of Cumberland, which brought her one step closer to her inheritance. Cousin

Henry, now the fifth Earl of Cumberland, still had no son and heir. Far more grievous to Anne, later in the same year, was the death of her cousin Francis Russell, Earl of Bedford, who had played such an important role in helping and protecting her during her widowhood. He was her trusted kinsman, a link to her mother, and she mourned his loss for many years.

Having withdrawn into her own world, it took some time for her to become aware that much around her was changing. Pembroke sometimes mentioned difficulties between the King and Parliament, but she barely registered this. It didn't impinge upon her life. She was a lifelong supporter of the monarchy; to her, the King was the divinely appointed ruler whom God would certainly protect. But she was startled into taking notice in 1641, when another incident involving Pembroke turned her world upside down.

This time, Pembroke's violence turned on Henry Howard, Lord Maltravers, second son of her old friend Alethea. During a committee meeting in the House of Lords, Pembroke accused Maltravers of lying and struck his opponent's head with his staff. Maltravers retaliated by throwing a pen and ink case at him, creating so much outrage that the committee had to rise and a complaint was made to the King. Both men were sent to the Tower and it proved to be the last straw for King Charles, who, incensed by the uncontrolled, indiscreet and increasingly insolent behaviour of Pembroke, took advantage of the situation to relieve him of his office as Lord Chancellor and appoint the Earl of Essex in his place. With Pembroke disgraced, Anne's cherished position, as the wife of the 'greatest servant in the land' and one exceptionally close to the monarchy, was destroyed.

CHAPTER THIRTY-THREE
1642-46

When Pembroke was released from the Tower a few days later, he sent urgent messages of his continuing loyalty to King Charles, but his resentment at the loss of his position and the flattery he received from some Parliamentarians led him to waver in his fidelity to the monarch. With the outbreak of civil war in the autumn of 1642 Pembroke, Anne and Isabella left Wilton for London, two days' journey away.

"I desire you, Ladies, to take up residence at Baynards," said Pembroke as they slowly made their way towards the capital. "You are seen as lifelong and committed supporters of the King, therefore your presence there will be some sort of warranty that the castle will not be attacked by the Royalist forces."

"Why would the Royalist forces wish to attack Baynards?" Anne asked, "Is it not universally known to be your property, my lord?"

"Yes, and that is exactly the reason for them to try to take it. From now on I shall support the Parliamentarians; I have taken lodgings in the Cockpit in Saint James's Park, near Whitehall, to be close to the Parliament," Pembroke said.

There was silence inside the jolting coach as Anne took in this perturbing statement. She was aware of the eyes of her husband and her daughter on her, seeking to interpret her expression, as she digested his announcement. He had always been unpredictable, unstable even, but treason such as this was beyond anything she had ever imagined him capable of. She must deal calmly with him, in this confined space and with Isabella at her side. It was not worth arguing; she knew beyond doubt that his mind was fixed. She was nevertheless extremely shocked to find her husband willing to take up arms against the King and knew she could never be reconciled to this position.

Pembroke suddenly leaned out of the door.

"Crack your whip, Biggs!" he shouted. "We must make more speed to reach London before nightfall. Don't spare those idle horses!"

Anne eventually said,

"So . . . we shall be on opposite sides in this war of the English against the English. Is it not an irony that the war you and I have fought with each other for nigh on five years is now become the war of the whole country?"

Pembroke snorted.

"Aye, Madam, and perchance it would be amusing to look at it like that, were it not so dangerous," he said. "This will be no mere skirmish, but I trust you and Isabella will be safe at Baynards. I would counsel you to remain there until the fighting is over, for your own safety as well as the protection of my property. I am told the King may move to Oxford to be away from the Parliament; the fighting is up-country and not like to come to town, but you must not attempt to travel while turmoil is still rife in the land."

"We shall be comfortable as well as safe at Baynards," Anne said, squeezing Isabella's hand to reassure her, "For it is full of treasures and luxury. I am grateful, my Lord, that you have thought of our safety as well as your interests, and for that I thank you."

Shortly after they had settled into life at Baynards, Anne and Isabella received a visit from 'The Child', Lady Margaret Tufton.

"Lady mother and dear sister, I come to tell you that I am leaving to join my lord in France while this dreadful war rages. He sees no likelihood that he will be able to return until the King's fortunes improve. His actions in leading a regiment in support of the revolt against Parliament in Kent and Sussex, and his surrender when this collapsed, mean that much of his land has been seized by Parliament and he believes that our children and I cannot be safe in any property of his. I hope it will not be long before peace is restored and we can all return to this blessed kingdom but, for now, we must go."

"I am distressed that you must leave," Anne said, "I echo your hope that peace will soon be restored but I believe it is best that you assure your own safety, and that of my grandchildren, in the meantime. Go with my blessing, my dear ones, and that of the Lord God; may He protect us and our King."

Isabella clutched her sister to her breast and wept.

"How has it come to this? How has the Parliament's disagreement with the King caused the destruction of our family and brought about our separation from each other? When shall I see you again, sweet sister?"

"May you both be safe in God's keeping until I return," Margaret managed to say as she turned away from them, holding back her sobs until the door of the coach had closed behind her.

News of the war reached Anne sporadically in her cloistered incarceration at Baynards. Her steward, Christopher Marsh, sometimes managed to send a message to her and occasionally came himself, but most of the time he stayed in the North so that he could gather news for her. As Pembroke had said, the journey was difficult and dangerous because of the unpredictable clashes taking place up and down the country between the armies of the various factions. Anne forbade Marsh to attempt it unnecessarily, but he declared it his duty to keep her informed – and he always enjoyed her company and hospitality.

In 1642 he arrived without warning.

"My lady, I come to bring you word of events in the North. I did not want you to hear it from anyone else, or even receive a different version of what I come to tell you. The matter concerns Skipton Castle."

"It is a comfort to me that you have such concern for my affairs and that you are so protective of my welfare, Mr Marsh. I am grateful and would have it no other way, yet I worry for your safety when you undertake that endless journey from the North in these dangerous times. I ask God to keep you safe. Pray be cautious," Anne said. "And now, tell me, what is happening at Skipton that has brought you here?"

"I would assure your Ladyship that I take no risks that can be avoided," Marsh said. "The news from Skipton is that your cousin, Lord Cumberland, has garrisoned the castle for the King and is holding it in the King's cause. He has many soldiers there to defend it and, as you know, it is also well-protected by its natural position high above the river. Your forebears built it solidly and designed it to withstand attack also from the town-side, away from the river."

"I remember the great drum-towers at the gatehouse, from the night when my dear mother and I were turned away by my uncle's insolent guards," Anne said. "But I have not entered that castle since I was ten days old, so I have not seen the side where the river runs below the castle walls. I hear it would be nigh on impossible for any enemy to scale that cliff. Is the castle then safe from the King's enemies, Marsh?"

"Of that we cannot be certain, my lady. The Parliament's forces have besieged it and are demanding its surrender, but so far the garrison is holding out. Their water supply is safe and they have good stores of food for both men and beasts. I am told that the townsfolk are loyal to my Lord Cumberland and the King and will do all they can to supplement the stores, perhaps secretly venturing down the river to fill lowered baskets; but the river is swift, rocky and dangerous and I fear there may be loss of life by that route, especially if they are forced to attempt it during the hours of darkness."

Anne shuddered.

"The situation sounds desperate, Marsh. Is my cousin Henry there with the soldiers? What do you believe the outcome will be?"

"I cannot guess, my lady. I believe Lord Cumberland is in Yorkshire, trying to negotiate peace for that county, but I hear that he may be planning to try to raise and lead another force to attack the besiegers from the rear. I personally believe that would be a dangerous tactic, and he is not renowned for military prowess, but the story may not be true. There are many people with their own motives for spreading false information in this chaos; one cannot tell where to give credence and what to discard. It is a sad time for right-thinking folk.

"The garrison could be capable of holding the Castle against the Roundheads for a long time, so if the war were concluded early in the King's favour all may be safe at Skipton. But who can say?" Marsh shook his head.

"My noble father's grave is in Skipton church, hard by the castle," Anne said. "I hope there is no vandalism of it by the Parliamentarians. When all this dreadful fighting is over, I shall build a fine decorated tomb over his grave showing his coats of arms and describing his honourable life. It shall be no less magnificent than the one that I erected at Appleby in 1617 for my blessed mother."

"I have no doubt that the good folk of Skipton would be most grateful to you for such a monument, my lady."

With the business done, Anne and Marsh settled down to a serious game of cribbage in front of the fire, whilst sharing memories and tales of the Clifford family in times gone by. Anne was impressed that Marsh had almost as much interest in the history of the Cliffords as she did. She knew that he understood her situation and at one point in their long conversation he said, "I think we can rest assured that fathering a son is the last thing on Lord Cumberland's mind at the moment."

Anne laughed and patted his arm, saying "It is delightful to spend time with such a faithful old friend!"

They declared the cribbage match a draw in the end.

These were turbulent times, news was sporadic and, as Marsh had observed, unreliable. Throughout the following year stories flew of battles and skirmishes, heroism and ignominy, defeats and gains and defeats again. Apart from Marsh's occasional visits and eye-witness accounts, Anne never knew what truth there might be in the stories she heard.

When a messenger arrived post-haste with news that her cousin, Henry, Earl of Cumberland, was dead, Anne did not know whether to believe it or not. It was unclear how, where or of what cause he had died. If true, it was of such moment that it would completely change her life; the message excited her and yet she dared not believe it.

For three more days she was on tenterhooks until Marsh was able to reach her through the winter mires of the battle-torn country and could finally confirm that the story was true; Henry had died of a fever in York and would be borne to Skipton with a military escort, to be buried there on the last day of 1643.

Anne was now the undisputed heir to the Clifford estates in Westmorland and Craven. The great castle of Skipton in Craven, where she had been born fifty-four years ago and later so ignominiously turned away from with her mother, was hers. She inherited also the ancient castles of Pendragon, Brough, Appleby and Brougham in Westmorland.

She had spent a lifetime preparing for this moment and she longed to hurry north to take possession of her property. But there were many obstacles in her way: Pembroke required her to remain at Baynards for its protection; it would not be safe for her to travel, with hostilities breaking out all over the country; she was a Royalist supporter and the Parliamentary forces were winning the war, so she could be arrested and impeached. There was also the question of Isabella's marriage to consider. She knew that their best interests were to be served by quietly remaining close to Pembroke and residing in his property and she had to accept this, however frustrating it was. Sometimes she dreamed of the northern hills, other sleepless nights she spent burning with frustration at not being able to take up her inheritance.

While she waited for the opportunity to go north, she had to deal by letter with matters relating to her tenants, who were dismayed and, in some instances rebellious, at having to pay another round of taxes to their second new landlord in two years. She was unknown to the populace, even in Westmorland; she had not been seen there for almost thirty years. Skipton was her birthplace, but none there had ever met her and who knew what poison might have been spread about her by her hostile relatives. She relied heavily on her cousin in the area, Sir John Lowther, to act as intermediary with her tenants and to convey her wishes for their happiness and blessing, whilst passing on her instructions. She stressed that she wished to be a fair and good landlord, but there were inevitable difficulties; she and her tenants were not only on opposite sides of the tenancy barrier, but some of them were also on the other side of the Royalist-Parliamentarian divide, which could continue to be a major problem for years to come.

Pembroke renewed his interest in Isabella as a bride for one of his younger sons, since she was now heir to the Clifford wealth along with her sister Margaret, Countess of Thanet. Isabella remained implacably opposed to such a match. Until her marriage to an acceptable nobleman could be secured this was another important reason for her and her mother to remain in London, but it flared into a bitter argument between Anne and Pembroke, making their relationship more difficult than ever.

"Now that your inheritance is finally settled, perhaps you will give time and thought to other matters," was Pembroke's opening remark when he came to Baynards to inspect some minor damage inflicted by a roving mob in Bear Alley during the peace riots.

"I do not grasp your meaning, Philip," Anne responded, maintaining an air of cool politeness and wondering fearfully what other matters he had in mind.

"Matters such as your daughter Isabella, Anne. She is now twenty-one years old. If you don't get her married off soon, she will be an old maid and no man will have any interest in her. You can't rely solely on the older girl to keep your line supplied with heirs, even if she is breeding like a doe-rabbit."

Anne bit her tongue, not wanting to provoke his temper. It was true that the Tuftons already had five children, but to her that was cause for rejoicing. His rudeness and crude language were insufferable. She looked away, trying to suppress anger and muster a reply that would be diplomatic and non-committal, but she knew she could neither pacify him nor meet his next demand.

"Come, madam, what do you say?" Pembroke said. "Our two great houses are already conjoined by our own marriage, what objection can there be to sealing the connection by a marriage treaty between our children? Would that not be in everyone's interests? She can take her choice of my three younger sons – I cannot be more accommodating than that!"

"Much as I would desire to fulfil your wishes, my lord, I am not able to do so in this matter," Anne said. "The choosing of a husband is my Lady Isabella's decision and no-one else's, as I have always said. She has never given any sign of considering one of your sons as a possible match; I will speak to her again if you wish, but I do not anticipate any change in her view."

"You are both impossible!" Pembroke spluttered. "It is well within your gift if you would just reason with her. You could order her to accept – it is hardly a dire prospect! But you are both as stubborn as the locked doors of heaven!" and he left. She could still hear him shouting as he strode down the long corridor and the echoing stone staircase at its end. At least he had not assaulted her this time.

Isabella would never accept him as her father-in-law and she could not blame her for that, but his words had stung her and she wished her daughter would find a suitable husband. Everything was made difficult by the civil war; many noble families, like The Child's, had fled abroad, especially since the King's cause had been weakened by defeats. And with no court life or official events, the opportunities for meeting and speaking to potential suitors were almost non-existent. At first she had thought the fighting would be over quickly, but it seemed to be getting worse and there was no lessening of the enmity between King and Parliament.

It was impossible to know what was going on in the country, with armies springing up and battles being fought all over the north, the midlands, and the south-west. The King was in Oxford with a ring of defences around it; the Queen was rumoured to be bringing convoys to support him and to be joining him there. There was swirling talk of truces between some of the many factions; it was chaotic and, Anne found, very frightening.

Anne decided to allow herself some distraction from all this desolation, and relief from the boredom and frustration of her confinement at Baynards, with a big, complex new project. Inspired in part by her conversations with Christopher Marsh, she decided to commission a painting illustrating the history of the Cliffords and celebrating the means by which her inheritance had come down to her through the centuries. It would be a rival to the great Pembroke family portrait by Van Dyck, she decided, but hers would be bigger and altogether grander. She commissioned a copyist, Jan van Belkamp, who had worked extensively on copies of portraits in the royal collection, to undertake the picture at Baynards Castle.

"How do you see this picture in your mind's eye, Lady Anne?" Belkamp asked in his slightly accented English when they met to discuss it.

"I see it as a record tracing the inheritance of the Clifford lands and titles from my ancient ancestor, Isabella di Viteripont, to myself," Anne said.

Belkamp gazed out of the window at the River Thames flowing past Baynards. The tide was falling, revealing the river's muddy flanks like thick shining brush loads of paint on a palette. The traffic of barges, ferries and merchant ships had thinned. He turned back to Anne with a smile.

"I shall be honoured to paint this great history of the Clifford

Family. There are portraits of your ancestors in the royal collection, including your father and mother and both your husbands, which I can copy to portray them as they were in life. Your Ladyship's vision shall become a reality for future generations." He bowed.

At Baynard's she kept a close eye on the painting's progress and, in many discussions with the artist, provided information about her family's history which would be incorporated into the work. She believed that Belkamp would do as she demanded and the work would be as much hers as his.

CHAPTER THIRTY-FOUR
1646-49

When they next met, Belkamp had sketched an idea.

"Would you give me your opinion on this suggestion, Lady Anne?" Belkamp said, spreading a large sheet of paper on the table near the window overlooking the River Thames in the room that had been designated as his studio.

"I like the idea of the triple composition," Anne said, after gazing for a long time at the sketches. "It tells of the three stages of my life, does it not? It begins before my birth, with the central part showing my noble parents, and those two sweet brothers of mine who were doomed to die in childhood. Then there is myself, as sole heir to my father at the time of his death, when I was but fifteen years old and was denied my inheritance. And finally I think you are proposing a portrait of me as I am now, the acknowledged successor to the Clifford lands and titles. If those are your intentions, I am well satisfied."

"Thank you, my lady. You have completely understood my thinking. My vision is that the three stages will be on three separate panels, their frames hinged together as a triptych," Belkamp said.

"Yes, that will show them to advantage, I agree," Anne said. "I wish it to show also the forty coats of arms and names of all the forebears and marriages through which the inheritance has passed. Perhaps they could be shown down each side of the central panel?"

Belkamp agreed and was about to roll up his sketches when another idea seized Anne.

"In the background there could be small vignettes of other important figures in my life – my aunts, my governess and tutor, my two husbands!"

"I fear the paintings would have to be enormous to accommodate all these figures as well as the coats of arms," Belkamp said, looking alarmed.

"Yes, yes, they must be enormous!" Anne said. "Giant even! I wish them also to contain inscriptions telling the history and accomplishments of my ancestors and myself so that the whole Clifford story is clearly shown. Each panel will be many times bigger than the Pembroke Family portrait by Van Dyck!"

"Very well, my lady, I shall order yards of canvas and gallons of oil and pigments, if it please you," Belkamp said.

As Belkamp had said, many portraits of Anne and her family already existed and he used his copying skills to create accurate representations of the faces of all the important people in her life. It proved more difficult for him to compose the figures and dress of the time and Anne tried to help him in any way she could. There was no full-length portrait of her at fifteen, so she rummaged in her old chests for a dress that he could use for that panel and found the sea-green satin which she had ordered after coming out of mourning for her mother. With its open ruff it was a style that had been fashionable about a dozen years later than they needed, but it was all that could be unearthed so they would use it. A young maid from the kitchen was pressed into service to model it for the artist.

"Oh, no, my lady! I couldn't do that! My Ma would chase me round the kitchen with the broom 'andle an' I should be so shamed!" was Jane's response to Anne's request. "Dressin' up like a lady an' showing myself off! Please, my lady, please don't make me do it."

"Peace, Jane, peace! We mean you no harm at all, we simply ask for your help for a few hours, for which I will pay you royally. Come, let us see whether the dress fits you, for if it doesn't you will be of no use to us and can return to your kitchen duties. Come with me into the little chamber across the passage."

Anne managed to persuade Jane into the heavy dress, which fitted the child's small frame perfectly. She continued to protest that she would be shamed and that her mother would never allow it, whilst beaming with excitement at the adventure and the luxurious feeling of the fine silk.

"Your face will not be shown in the painting, child," Anne said. "It is only the dress that is to be copied into the picture. No-one will ever know that it was you in the dress! Look, here I have the miniature from which my face will be copied instead of yours."

There was silence while Jane examined the tiny portrait, then she said,

"Oh . . . but this picture doesn't look like me."

"No, it is not you, Jane, it is me when I was just three years older than you are now. Because I was always very small, I chose you to wear my dress for the portrait thinking that it would fit you. I was right in that, but Master Belkamp will not paint a picture of you, do you see? It will be a portrait of me!"

Anne watched the girl as she thought about what she had been told. Her head came up slowly and her blue eyes narrowed as they met Anne's.

"How much will you pay me?" she asked.

"When the painter has finished with you, however long that will take, I will pay you one shilling."

Jane nodded. "Ma would be pleased with that. I'll do it," she said quickly.

"I will send a servant to speak to your mother, so that she will know how you came by the money," Anne said.

After that the picture, which would take more than two years to complete, proceeded slowly but without disruption. The most difficult part was the figure of the third Earl of Cumberland; his dress and his right arm were not quite resolved to Anne's satisfaction, but she let it go for fear that further alterations might upset another part of the picture. The blank spaces were filled with lengthy inscriptions by a calligraphist's distinct but tiny writing, using all the results of Lady Margaret and Mr Kniveton's researches. They told the story of the Clifford ancestors from the time of Isabella di Viteripont all the way down to Anne. Over eight feet high and in three panels totalling about eighteen feet wide, the triptych was a splendid statement of the importance of the House of Clifford and the indisputability of Anne's inheritance. Christopher Marsh declared himself thrilled by it and congratulated Anne on the conception and completion of such a magnificent project. She was immensely proud of it and ordered a copy to be made so that it could be displayed in both Appleby and Skipton Castles.

◎〜◎

News of the north from Marsh was disturbing. Skipton Castle had surrendered to Cromwell after holding out against his forces for three and a half years. The tenants around Kirkby Stephen and Stainmore, some of whom were supporters of the Parliament's cause, were still refusing to pay rent to another new landlord whom they had never seen. Anne had to write and beg them to wait until she could come north and consider their claims.

News was received that a large part of the new south front of Wilton House had been destroyed by fire only a short time after its completion. Pembroke was no longer employed by the King, and the country remained in the throes of civil war, but nevertheless he set about putting it to rights. Anne reflected that she was lucky to be protected in the luxurious surroundings of Baynards Castle, largely untroubled by either the war or her unpredictable husband.

◎〜◎

It was difficult to move around in the city whilst the hostilities were continuing, but on the second anniversary of the death of the Earl of Northampton at the battle of Hopton Heath, Anne ventured out to visit his widow, Lady Mary Compton. When Lady Compton paid a return visit to Baynards, Anne ensured that Isabella was available to be presented to her. This manoeuvre had the desired outcome and led to a discussion between Mary and Anne about the unmarried state of their children, James, now the third Earl of Northampton, and Isabella. Isabella accompanied Anne on her next visit to the Compton's grand residence on The

330

Strand, and Isabella and James were reintroduced. They were both now twenty-four and the meeting amused them because they had not met for seven or eight years and had become adults in the meantime. They were delighted to find that they each held equally strong royalist opinions.

Isabella came to speak to Anne after Lady Mary's second visit to Baynard's Castle. Anne put down her embroidery when Isabella announced,

"Lady mother, I need your advice! Before you joined us, I was sitting in the drawing chamber with my Lady Northampton and she made an extraordinary suggestion."

"I should like to hear what she proposed," Anne said, without giving away her own thoughts.

"Well, proposed is exactly the right word! She suggested that I might like to consider marrying her son! I tried to be calm, but I was taken aback by her directness."

"And what reply did you give her Ladyship?"

"I told her I would beg to have time to think about it and discuss it with you."

"Have you had time? What are your thoughts?" Anne asked with a smile.

"My thoughts are . . . that I have rarely met anyone who would suit me better as a husband!" Isabella said.

"Then you have my blessing to accept the proposal. His Lordship is as staunch a supporter of the King as we are and has distinguished himself in battle at Newbury. I believe he would please you as a husband."

"And I like his wide-apart eyes!" Isabella laughed, her reserve at last overcome by excitement.

"Then we must lose no time in conveying your acceptance to Lady Northampton!"

❦

The wedding was arranged to take place at the beginning of July and Anne noted that Isabella was never happier. It was a great relief to her that her younger daughter was to be settled at last. That topic of argument with Pembroke would, thankfully, be closed for ever. Only a few weeks before the wedding she told Pembroke of the plans on one of his rare visits to Baynard's.

"No! I shall not give permission for this marriage to take place," Pembroke stamped, the sound of his leather boot echoing round the stone walls. "I will never agree to it. You must cancel this arrangement immediately. The marriage cannot take place, I will not permit it!"

"There is no question of breaking the agreement. Isabella is happy with it and so is James Compton; they are well matched and will be wed in July."

"I told you, I will not give my permission. It cannot go ahead. I have waited years for you to come to a decision; you will arrange the marriage of your daughter, but it will be to my son, not some other upstart! You will order your daughter to do as I say!" His red eyes were bulging and spittle flew from his mouth and lodged in his beard as he spluttered.

"No, Philip; your permission is not required for my daughter to wed. She is of age, she has my agreement, her marriage is arranged and the banns are to be read. There is nothing you can do to prevent it and Isabella has many times refused to consider marrying any of your sons."

"Damn you, Madam," he exploded. "It is intolerable to be told what I can and cannot do by you! I am the head of this household and any decisions to be made will be made by me. I... I... refuse your refusal!" He was shouting as he grabbed a heavy silver candlestick from the table in the centre of the room.

Anne tried to remain calm as he turned towards her and raised his arm.

"We shall never agree on this, my lord. I think it would be advisable for you to leave..." and she ducked sideways as he hurled the candlestick towards her, missing her shoulder by inches and making a gash in the wall behind her. She was shaking for a long time after he stormed out; it was the first time he had physically

332

assaulted her and she was lucky to be unhurt.

On the day of Isabella's wedding at Clerkenwell Church, where Anne and her mother had often worshipped during her childhood, Anne was unwell and assailed by fears. She had been at Baynards for five years, as its protector but also as a near-fugitive being protected by it and she had rarely left its shielding bulk. The war was going against the King and there was unrest on the streets of London; it would be unsafe for her to venture out, particularly in a carriage which would bring her to the attention of the throng that was always milling around the streets near Parliament. After the last incident she was also fearful that Pembroke might turn up at the church and make a scene. She thought her presence might provoke him. She reluctantly decided not to attend. She kissed her daughter fondly as she left Baynards for the church with her brother-in-law. It was enough for Anne to know that Isabella was being married; she didn't need to see it.

The following year was ill-starred for the King and his supporters; several Royalist uprisings in different parts of the country were put down, but a decisive victory of Cromwell's Parliamentarians over the Royalists and the Scots at Preston resulted in the capture of the King and the beheading, to Anne's dismay, of three prominent royalist peers at Westminster. Pembroke was active still in the Parliamentarian cause and Anne heard rumours that he was involved in negotiations to take the King from the Scots and bring him to trial. She refused to believe that the King could be arrested and tried by his subjects, but, in these days of turmoil and war, especially when Pembroke was involved, who could predict anything?

By the end of the year Parliament had been purged of supporters of the King and the remaining members had set up a High Court to try Charles for treason. They found him guilty and he was beheaded on a scaffold in front of the Banqueting House in Whitehall on Anne's fifty-ninth birthday. The Commonwealth of England was declared.

Isabella was married, the war was over, the Tuftons had returned to England, Baynards needed her protection no longer, and finally, six months later, Marsh declared it safe for Anne to travel. She gave instructions to her servants to prepare for the journey and went to Pembroke's unwelcoming lodgings in the Cockpit.

"I have come to take my leave of you," Anne said with crisp finality. "Unfortunately you and I were never the best of friends," she continued. "Your part in the death of the anointed King is unforgivable. I am leaving, to take up my rightful place in the lands of mine inheritance. We shall not see each other again."

Her words reverberated round the cold, bare room.

Pembroke said nothing; he slumped and his eyes, when they met hers, registered defeat and surrender. He had chosen the winning side in the civil war and he had kept his head. But his wife had conquered him in matrimonial hostilities.

On the day of Anne's triumphant departure her grandchildren came to wish her goodbye and God speed, along with Margaret and John, Isabella and James. The hugs and kisses took a very long time. Many promises of visits were made, tears were shed and good wishes reverberated as she left London for Skipton Castle, for the first and last time.

THE FINAL CHAPTER
1676

I left the capital with a great sigh of relief. I had had more than enough of battles, my own and other people's, and the last straw had been the deplorable beheading of the King. Regrettably, my second lord was involved in this and I never wanted to see him or the city again – and I never did. Now I could put all my thoughts and deeds into the lands of mine inheritance in Westmorland and Craven.

Less than a year after I left London, I learned of the death of my said second lord. To my inheritance and my jointure from my first lord was thus added my jointure from Pembroke and it was said then that I was one of the richest women in the whole of England. I determined to use my wealth wisely and ensure that my name would live on.

By the time I reached my lands, I was an old woman with little time left and there was much to be done. Of my five castles, only Brougham was immediately habitable; Skipton had been under siege for three years and had then been slighted by the Parliament's forces after surrendering to them near the end of the Civil War. Appleby had suffered a similar fate, though it had not been besieged for so long a time; Brough and little Pendragon (said to have been built by Uther Pendragon, father of King Arthur) were both in ruins.

I set about restoring the castles to ensure that I could live in them all and be close by my tenants. I made progresses between them regularly, often using my horselitter, accompanied by a great train of servants and tenants on each journey. Whilst I was repairing my castle at Skipton the local officers complained of it to Oliver Cromwell, but he said I was to be left alone to set it to rights so long as the roof was made too weak to bear cannon. In my castles at Appleby and Skipton I installed the Great Pictures that I had had made by Belkamp in London, telling the story of my inheritance. Near my castle of Brougham, I caused a decorated pillar to be erected to commemorate the spot where my last sad parting with my beloved mother took place and I made a bequest of bread and money, to be laid out each year on a block of stone nearby, for the poor of that parish. I also raised a great column outside the castle gates at Appleby and had my motto written there for all to see: 'Preserve your loyalty, Retain your Rights'.

To begin with there was trouble with some of my tenants to the south of Brough, who had been supporters of the Parliament. They had objected to paying their taxes to me only two years after they had had to pay the same to my cousin, Francis Clifford, but judgments were made in my favour in the courts in London and the opposition gradually faded away. And that reminds me of the tenant at Skipton who was obliged to pay me an annual tax of one chicken. To begin with he delayed and then refused, so I insisted on his dues. When I received the chicken, I invited him to dine with me and together we ate the chicken, well-roasted.

At Beamsley, near Skipton, I completed the almshouses begun by my blessed mother forty years earlier and at Appleby I built and endowed Saint Anne's Hospital – almshouses for a dozen elderly widows who couldn't work any longer. I often visited the widows in their homes and sometimes brought them to dine with me at the castle, so that we became firm friends. They were entertaining company once they had overcome their shyness and I enjoyed their way of speaking.

I restored many of the churches, chapels and bridges on my lands. In Holy Trinity Church close to Skipton Castle I erected a fitting monument above the tomb of my noble father, decorated with his coats of arms. In St Lawrence's church at Appleby I built a monument for myself above the vault in which I intend to be buried. I shall lie close to my beloved mother and to the memorial to her blessed memory, with its beautiful marble effigy, that I commissioned for her many years ago. The works were all decorated with my initials.

I have never travelled out of Westmorland and Craven again, but I often correspond with old friends in the south of England and am always delighted to receive news and visitors. My elder daughter

Margaret, Countess of Thanet, has been blessed with ten children who survived beyond infancy and many of them frequently come north to visit me. To my great grief, my younger daughter, Isabella, Countess of Northampton, died in 1661 at the age of 39, but her young daughter Alethea later visited me. I always kiss all my grandchildren and great grandchildren with much joy and contentment. I appointed my grandson, Thomas Tufton, to be Member of Parliament, or Burgess, for Appleby and sit in the House of Commons – against some opposition, it has to be said, but I prevailed. When he comes to see me, I ensure that he visits as many of his constituents as possible in the time he has here. They are satisfied, and I am very proud of him. The Tuftons will inherit these lands from me in accordance with the ancient entail that my mother and I proved.

God has blessed me with a long life to enjoy this country I love, so that I have had a great many years of satisfaction here. I have written that I do more and more fall in love with the contentments and innocent pleasures of a Country Life and I often quote Psalm 16: "The lot is fallen unto me in a pleasant place. I have a fair Heritage".

I believe I have fulfilled God's purpose for me on this Earth and have done good works. I am well-beloved now in the lands of mine inheritance and I know that my name will live on; I have had it carved in stone on all the buildings I have restored. But I am 86 years old and I tire. In this chamber at Brougham my father was born and my mother died. I went not out of the house nor out of my chamber all this day. I suppose the world will continue without me, as it always has, by God's mercy.

Fin

Postscript

Anne Clifford left London at the age of fifty-nine to take up the inheritance in Craven and Westmorland that she had been fighting for since the age of fifteen. She continued to keep detailed records of all her transactions and works and wrote memoranda about her life. She always remembered and commemorated the dates of significant events and even minor ones.

Lady Anne's reputation in the Eden Valley lives on to this day. When my family moved there in the 1950s, we heard local people speak of Lady Anne as though she had dropped in a couple of weeks ago and assumed they were referring to one of the existing 'great and good' of the county. We were somewhat surprised to discover that she had been dead for nearly three hundred years.

She is buried close to her mother's tomb in St Lawrence's Church at Appleby, beneath the memorial which she built during her lifetime and her beautiful almshouses in Appleby are still occupied by elderly widows. The inscription on the plate that was attached to her shroud is typical of the styling of herself that she left on many buildings in Craven and Westmorland:

'The body of the most noble virtuous and religious Lady Anne Countess Dowager of Pembroke Dorset and Montgomery, Daughter and sole Heir to the late Right Honourable George Clifford Earl of Cumberland, Baroness Clifford, Westmorland and Vescy, Lady of the Honour of Skipton in Craven and High Sheriffess by inheritance of the county of Westmorland, who departed this life in her Castle of Brougham in the County the 22nd March 1676 having attained the age of 86 years the 30th of January before.'

The ancient counties of Cumberland and Westmorland, together with small parts of Lancashire and Yorkshire, were merged to form the single county of Cumbria in 1974.

Of her castles, Skipton and Appleby are still inhabited but can be visited, while Brougham (pronounced Broom) and Brough (pronounced Bruff) (both English Heritage) and Pendragon are now in ruins. Her triptych, attributed to Jan van Belkamp and known as The Great Picture, is on permanent display at Abbot Hall Art Gallery in Kendal, Cumbria, together with smaller portraits of her in later life. Other contemporary portraits of her are in the National Portrait Gallery in London, at Knole House (National Trust) in Sevenoaks, and in the private collections of Lord Hothfield and Lord Sackville. Lady Anne's Great Books of Record and many of her autobiographical writings are in the Cumbria County Archives at the County Offices in Kendal and Carlisle. Sackville records, from Knole House, are in the Kent County Archives in Maidstone.

Glossary

Ague: Malarial fever with cold, hot and sweating stages. A fit of shivering.

Apoplexy: Stroke. Sudden inability to feel and move, caused by blockage or rupture of brain artery. Cerebral haemorrhage.

Assizes: Periodical session of County Court for civil and criminal justice.

Barley Break: An outdoor game in which a minimum of three couples took part, the object being for one couple to try and catch another before they could claim a base.

Caudle: A warm drink consisting of thin gruel mixed with wine or ale, sweetened and spiced, given to sick people, especially women in childbed. (O.E.D.)

Closet: A small private room adjacent to the bedroom, where people could go to read or enjoy works of art in private.

Entail: To settle (land, an estate, etc) on a number of persons in succession, so that it cannot be bequeathed at pleasure by any one possessor. (O.E.D.)

Flux: Diarrhoea.

Glecko: A card game for two or three players using 44 cards, popular C16th – C18th.

Jointure: An estate settled on a wife for the period during which she survives her husband. (Pocket O.D.)

Muniments: Documents kept as evidence of rights or privileges. (Pocket O.D.)

Posset: A popular seventeenth century British drink made of hot milk curdled with wine or ale, often spiced. Used as a pick-me-up.

Privy Council: Body of advisers chosen by the sovereign. (Pocket O.D.)

Shallop: A small open boat fitted with oars or sails, or both, and used primarily in shallow waters.

Steward: A person employed to manage another's property and/ or be responsible for supplies. (Pocket O.D.) In the C17th, a senior officer in a large household.

Wilderness: A woodland area planted with shrubs and trees divided into 'quarters' by regular avenues, giving long vistas. Popular on large private estates from Elizabethan times onwards. The Wilderness at Knole has a 'Patte d'Oie' (goose-foot) formation.

Zellandine: The medieval version of the Sleeping Beauty theme, from Princess Zellandine in the long medieval romance 'Perceforest'.

ACKNOWLEDGEMENTS

My first acknowledgement must be to Lady Anne Clifford herself for all her incredible writing and record-keeping and her determination to be remembered. I am grateful to all the distinguished authors and scholars who have edited and annotated her works, including, D. J. H. Clifford, Professor Jessica Malay and Professor Katherine O. Acheson. The most comprehensive biography is by George C. Williamson (original edition 1922, second edition 1967), to whom I am greatly indebted. Richard T. Spence's more recent (1997) biography provides a more complex picture which has been enlightening, and Martin Holmes's (1975) biography is brief but very much to the point.

My own efforts to weave all this material into a novel, in the hope that Lady Anne's story might reach a wider audience, have been supported by so many people that it is hard to know where to start. Inspiration began with brilliant tutoring, organised for many years by Ways with Words at Villa Pia, from Helena Drysdale, Blake Morrison, Mark McCrum, Julia Blackburn and Wendy Holden. To them all I offer much gratitude. I have also received invaluable help and encouragement from Robert Sackville-West, Chris Donnelly, Kay Dunbar and Stephen Bristow (Ways With Words), Charles Mitchell, Deborah Swift, Lord Hothfield (Lady Anne's 8xGreat grandson) and Margaret Thomas. They all offered assistance, advice, unfailing patience and stimulating conversations, for which I sincerely thank them. Mark McCrum also sensitively edited at least two drafts and mercilessly urged me on; I am grateful now!

My thanks also go to Lord Strathcarron, Chair of Unicorn Publishing Group; we happened to meet (thanks again to Ways With Words) at just the right moment and he has been a rock of dependability and efficiency through the publishing process, as has Publishing Director, Ryan Gearing and Publicity and Marketing Manager, Louise Campbell.

Meeting Pam Grant was another serendipitous event which resulted in the delightful cover design.

A special thank you goes to Mary Robinson who contribüted the lovely poem, *Not Without Westmorland*. I have also appreciated friends who have found just the right balance between support and criticism: Janet Denny, Jill Treseder, Ann Underwood and Hilary Thompson. Many friends have kept me going with encouragement and have tolerated my absence from social gatherings for the past few years (they know who they are); I thank you all.

My twins, Omar and Zena Raafat and my daughter-in-law Natalie and my granddaughter Leila, are unfailingly loving and supportive and I send them big hugs.

My most particular thanks go to Tony Firth, to whom this book is dedicated, who has supported, enabled and accompanied me on the Lady Anne trail and has suffered years of neglect with a good grace in the interests of my work.

❧

Mary Robinson has published poetry for many years. In 2013 she won the Mirehouse Poetry Prize and in 2017 the Second Light Poetry Prize. Recently she published *Alphabet Poems* (Mariscat Press, 2019). She lives in North Wales.